Caught between

Marz was playing with fire.

He damn well knew he was. But that didn't make him want to pull away.

He just wanted more of the heat.

Marz nuzzled the side of her face with his nose, his lips. "Emilie," he whispered.

She turned her face toward him and offered her lips.

He couldn't refuse.

Capturing her mouth on a tortured groan, Marz poured every ounce of his longing and confusion and desire into the kiss. They grasped at each other and Emilie turned in his arms. He pinned her against the railing and planted his hands in her hair. She opened to him and accepted his tongue, sucking him in until Marz's blood ran hot and his hard-on ached. He ground himself against her and devoured every little moan and whimper and gasp she spilled.

Trailing kisses from her mouth to her jaw to her ear, Marz dragged a hand down her body and grasped her breast in his palm. She cried out and her head dropped back, drawing his mouth to her neck, where he licked and sucked and nipped as he kneaded her soft flesh.

"You are so damn sexy."

Her hand flew to his hair and grasped the back of his head. "Touch me," she said. "Don't stop touching me."

By Laura Kaye

HARD TO COME BY
HARD TO HOLD ON TO (novella)
HARD AS YOU CAN
HARD AS IT GETS

Coming Soon

HARD TO BE GOOD (novella)
HARD TO LET GO

LAURA KAYE

HARD TO COME BY

A Hard Ink Novel

AVON

An Imprint of HarperCollinsPublishers

AVON BOOKS
An Imprint of HarperCollins*Publishers*
195 Broadway
New York, New York 10007

Copyright © 2014 by Laura Kaye
ISBN 978-0-06-226792-4
www.avonromance.com

First Avon Books mass market printing: December 2014

Printed in the U.S.A.

10 9 8 7 6 5 4 3 2 1

To Christi, for always marching with me.
And to my family, for their heroic support.
Thank you.

HARD TO

COME BY

Chapter 1

$\mathcal{D}$erek DiMarzio was going bat-shit crazy. Between days of forced inactivity, being cooped up in an old warehouse with a bunch of equally edgy meatheads, and the riskiness of the hack they were attempting, he was the personification of nervous, restless energy.

Eyes glued to the computer screen, Marz paced back and forth behind the chair occupied by Charlie Merritt, who'd been quiet as a stone as he'd typed strings of complicated code into the keyboard. Charlie was the civilian son of Marz's deceased—and dirty—Army Special Forces team commander. More important for their purposes right now, he was also a computer genius and a hacker by trade. In his real life, Charlie used those hacking skills for good, testing out companies' computer security systems by trying to hack into them. Lucky for

Marz, the guy was willing to go off-roading a bit, too.

Their current target: Army Human Resources Command records—essentially, the database of all Army personnel records. Hopefully, their first and last stop for the information they needed on a SF veteran named Manny Garza, who Marz and his team had recently learned worked with the enemies connected to the conspiracy that had ruined their lives and reputations and killed seven of their teammates.

Pausing behind Charlie's chair, Marz leaned in over his shoulder and willed this to work. He sighed.

Charlie shoved long strands of dark blond hair from in front of his eyes and peered over his shoulder, one eyebrow arched.

"Now I'm driving you bat-shit, too, aren't I?" Marz asked, backing off a good step.

Throwing a small smile at him, Charlie shook his head. "Don't worry. I got this."

Crossing his arms, Marz nodded. "Of course you do." Charlie had done something similar once before, when his crook of a father died and dropped a series of mysteries on his doorstep. If anyone could manage it, Charlie could.

Problem was, when Marz wasn't the one perched at the keyboard, he was antsy as all hell. He wasn't used to being second string when it came to computers, not that he resented Charlie for a minute—not when the guy represented a second pair of desperately needed hands on the mountain of computer research their investigation required.

They'd been searching for Garza for days, but though they'd seen him with their own eyes, online the guy was a ghost.

Minutes passed. Marz stretched his neck and tried

to shake some of the tension he'd been carrying about the clusterfuck of a situation he found himself in. Not just him. Him and the other four surviving members of his Army Special Forces unit—Nick Rixey, Beckett Murda, Shane McCallan, and Easy Cantrell—as well as a whole host of new friends and allies. Over a year ago, the five of them had barely made it out of a checkpoint ambush in Afghanistan alive—an ambush they quickly realized had occurred because their commander, Colonel Frank Merritt, was on the take.

And that wasn't the worst of it. As if the critical injuries three of the five survivors had sustained weren't bad enough, they'd been blamed for the deaths of their teammates, discharged from the Army, and sent packing back to the States without their friends, their careers, or their honor. Figuring out how and why the shit had landed on their team—and who was behind it— were the questions that had brought them all together again about ten days ago.

And Marz was ready for some damn answers. A thought came to mind, and Marz leaned in again. "Hey, what if you—"

"Marz, get over here and leave Charlie alone for five minutes," came a gruff voice from across the cavernous unfinished space that was part gym, part mess hall, and part war room. In the far corner from the computer setup, Nick Rixey and Beckett Murda, two of Marz's other SF teammates, had been sparring for the past half hour. The pair circled one another, getting in hits wherever they could. Whereas Nick had speed and agility on his side, Beckett was like a Mack truck on legs, all stubborn bullheaded strength.

Clapping Charlie on the back, Marz said, "Shout as soon as you—"

"I will," the guy said without looking away from the screen.

Scrubbing his hands over his face, Marz crossed the room. Nick's hair was so damp it almost appeared black, and as he turned his back toward Marz, a massive tattoo came into view of a fierce dragon curled around a long sword. Then it was gone again. The guy delivered a roundhouse kick that nearly caught Beckett in the chin. Beckett grinned and charged, his lethal intensity nearly a physical presence in the room. Apparently, Marz didn't have the market cornered on going stir crazy, if the energy these two were expending for the hell of it was any indication.

"Why is it I want to watch you two beat each other bloody?" Marz asked as he stood at the edge of the unofficial ring. He eyeballed Nick, their former second-in-command, whose request for help had reunited the five former teammates, as the guy dodged one of Beckett's rib-breaking punches.

"Time out," Nick said, crossing one gloved fist over the other to form a T. He tugged off the thick black fingerless gloves and flung them at Marz. "You're not watching. You're working off some of that damn restlessness before you end up going postal. Or making one of us go that particular route."

Marz caught the first padded missile against his chest, but bobbled the second one, dropping it to the floor. "Asshole," he muttered with a grin as he awkwardly bent to retrieve it. Things like waist and knee bends—not to mention more routine movements like climbing stairs or walking over uneven outdoor surfaces—didn't come as easy when one of your legs wasn't flesh and bone. The day of that fateful ambush, Marz had left a good forty percent of his righty lying on a dusty road in the middle of Bum Fuck Afghanistan after a grenade literally blew him to pieces. Turned out that in a grenade-versus-leg scenario, the grenade won. Go figure.

Not that Marz would undo how it'd all gone down. Because him losing his leg meant that Beckett, Marz's best friend in the world and the closest thing he'd ever had to a brother, got to remain a biped. Marz hadn't hesitated for a moment to knock Beckett clear of the explosion. Better to take the hit himself than let a buddy get hurt. And seeing the guy get around with little more than a limp made Marz's sacrifice more than worth it. One thing Marz had always admired about the SpecOps community wasn't just that you could count on someone having your back, it was knowing you had theirs. No matter what.

"I'm not being *that* annoying," Marz said, knowing full well that, yeah, right now, he probably was.

"Dude, you've gone total hovercraft," Beckett said as he wiped sweat off his forehead with the back of his arm.

Eyebrow arched, Nick pointed at Beckett and nodded. Marz groaned and jammed a hand into one of the gloves. "Fine. *Maybe* you have a point," he muttered. "Besides, kicking Beckett's ass always makes me feel better, so at least there's that." He threw a smirk toward his friend.

And didn't like what he found at all.

Beckett had the bluest eyes you ever saw on another human being, and right now they were fixed on the lower half of Marz's right leg, where his black track pants shielded his prosthetic limb from view. Beckett's guilt over Marz's amputation was pretty much always clear in the lines on his face. No matter what

Marz said or did, Beckett didn't seem to be able to shake the feeling. Ten-to-one odds that Beckett was going to—

"Nah, that's all right," Beckett said, tugging off his own gloves. "You two have at it. I've got some calls to return."

Sonofabitch. Sometimes Marz hated being right. Not often. But times like now, when his gut had screamed that Beckett wasn't going to spar with him? Yeah, definitely then.

"Dude. Don't wuss out on me," Marz said, pretending like he didn't know the potential universe of *why* Beckett was bowing out of fighting him. Because he didn't want to hurt Marz. Because he thought Marz was too . . . what? Vulnerable? Defenseless? Weak?

Beckett threw a droll stare his way as he scooped his cell off a vinyl bench. "Another time maybe."

"What's with the *maybe* crap?" Marz said, finding it harder to keep up the happy-happy/joy-joy. Growing up the way he had—abandoned into the foster care system by parents he didn't well remember—humor had always been his go-to defense mechanism. But that shit took work. Sometimes more than he wanted to put in. He stepped in front of Beckett.

The big guy stared down at him, the shrapnel scars around his right eye making his gaze look more severe. "Figure of speech. That's all," Beckett said. Marz inhaled to call bullshit on the declaration when Beckett's cell buzzed in his hand. He thumbed a button, placed the cell to his ear, and said, "Murda, here."

Marz backed down. For now. At some point, they were going to have to have a damn come-to-Jesus meeting about Beckett always treating Marz with kid gloves. That sure as hell wouldn't work for Marz in the long term, not if they were ever going to get past what had happened.

"I'll be happy to kick your ass," Nick said from behind him. "Let's do this."

Turning, Marz watched Nick grab another pair of gloves off a metal shelf and pace to the center of the ring. The guy's oddly pale green eyes silently asked if Marz was in or out. Marz knocked his gloved fists together and joined him in the middle of the open space.

Nick had him on speed and agility, but Marz was a scrappy fighter. Always had been. You grew up half on the streets, you learned to fight dirty. And, in a real-world situation, he carried the equivalent of a titanium baseball bat on his leg, so there was always that hidden advantage.

They circled for a minute and Marz settled into the rhythm and movement of his body. He didn't move exactly as he used to, but he'd come a helluva long way in the last fourteen months. Marz feinted with his right and delivered an uppercut to the jaw with his left. "Don't take it easy on me, Rixey. You hear—"

Wham!

Punch to the gut. Marz muscled through the ache and looked for his next in.

"Wouldn't dream of it." Nick smirked and winked.

Then it was on. Five minutes. Ten minutes. Twenty. The only thing Marz couldn't do as well as Nick was make use of the kickboxing moves he'd once mastered. On the one side, he wouldn't chance hurting his friend with the inanimate object on the end of his leg. On the other, he no longer had the same strength in his right thigh, and he didn't want to chance hurting himself by pushing harder than his leg was ready to handle. For all the distance he'd covered, he still had more to go.

A split second of inattention, and Nick had grabbed his upper body, swept a leg behind Marz's knees, and knocked him to the ground.

"Aw, shit, man. Are you okay?" Nick asked. "I wasn't thinking."

Marz rolled onto his back and smirked. "What was there to think about?" As if he had to ask. "It was a clean takedown. Fair and square. And I'm fine."

"But, I, uh . . ." Nick tugged a hand through his damp hair.

The guy was dancing all around the elephant in the room. Marz's amputation. And that sucked some major ass, especially as Marz lay there, knocked on his own gluteus maximus. Maybe they were right. Maybe he was the weak link now. At the thought, ice slid into his gut and he shook his head.

"Just didn't want to knock your limb off or damage it. That's all," Nick said, planting his hands on his hips.

Pulling himself out of his mental funk, Marz decided to give Nick the benefit of the doubt and believe him. Besides, since some prosthetic limbs *could* be knocked or moved out of position, Marz couldn't deny it was a legitimate concern. One he could put to rest.

"No can do," Marz said, unzipping the track pants at the ankle and hauling the material up over his knee. "I am vacuum sealed into this mother. You couldn't remove it if you tried." He chanced a glance at Beckett, and, sure enough, the guy's gaze was glued to them. Which probably meant he'd seen Marz get his feet knocked out from under him. *Peachy.*

Nick crouched down and took a closer look. Marz reached into his pocket and removed a small black remote control. He held it up between his fingers. "I am literally a machine." The remote operated the limb's vacuum, the part that ensured that the socket and outer sleeve held an airtight, immovable grip on his stump.

"You're the Six Million Dollar Man," Nick said with a grin as his gaze scanned over his limb.

"No, no. I am the Terminator," Marz said, affecting *Ahnold*'s accent. Having grown up on the *Terminator* movies and reruns of the bionic man, he did rather enjoy both references. "Here, I'll show you." He lifted his leg toward Nick. "Grab the shank and try to pull my leg off."

Nick's eyes went wide before his brow cranked down. "Uh . . ."

"It's not like pulling my finger. I promise." He grinned.

"Well, that's good to know. I guess." Humor slid into Nick's gaze, but it didn't replace any of the skepticism.

"I'm serious. You won't be able to do it. Bet you a twenty."

Rising, Nick took ahold of the black metal shaft that extended up from the foot. "You sure about this?"

Marz laughed. "Dude, pull my leg already."

With an uncertain smile, Nick pulled. Marz's body followed, his shirt riding up against the cold floor. Nick's smile broadened and he pulled harder, dragging Marz across the floor. Soon, Marz was fighting against him, trying to find purchase against the smooth concrete or by grabbing at a weight bench. No luck. When Nick twisted his ankle, Marz did the same thing he would've done if he'd had his real leg—his body flipped in the direction Nick twisted.

The longer it went on and the more they laughed and cursed at each other, the more Nick's reservations appeared to melt away until they seemed to be gone entirely.

Wonder if it's working on Beckett, too.

"See? I told you," Marz said as he slid across the concrete.

"This is the most fun I've had in days," Nick said.

"Yeah, yeah. You can let me go now."

The devil in his expression, Nick went faster.

"All right, asshole. Hands off the hardware."

"You're at my mercy now," Nick said, waggling his eyebrows. When Nick peered over his shoulder to check his path, Marz used the moment of distraction to his advantage.

"Says who?" he called as he hooked his free foot behind the back of Nick's knee and tugged the guy down.

"Shit!" Nick said as he lost his balance and fell, laughing.

For a long minute, they lay on their backs side by side chuckling and breathing heavy. "That's some cool-ass technology." Nick rolled his head in Marz's direction. "Proud of you, man. Not everyone would deal with an amputation as positively as you have. Just want to say that."

The words hit Marz right in the chest. He gave a jerky nod. "Thanks."

"Whoa," came Charlie's voice from across the room. "I'm in! Marz, I'm in!"

He and Nick scrabbled off the floor and jogged across the room, Marz's heart pounding now for an entirely different reason than moments before. He came to a stop behind Charlie's chair and watched as code scrolled against a black background. After a moment, the screen went gray and the AHRC's internal intraweb interface loaded.

"Holy shit," Marz said, staring at the screen. His

pulse tripped into a sprint. Nothing like the thrill of a clean hack.

"Gotta get in and out fast," Charlie said, navigating through the pages to conduct a personnel search. He entered, "Garza, Emanuel." Some of Marz's own team had crossed paths with Garza back in Afghanistan. More recently, though, they'd discovered him providing muscle at a major drug deal for the Church Gang, whose kidnapping of Charlie—resulting in the amputation of two of his fingers—almost two weeks ago, provided the initial incident that necessitated the team's reunion. An overheard conversation at the deal revealed that Garza knew and probably also worked for the party on the other side of that exchange—and finding out who those players were had comprised a lot of Marz's research the past few days. Someone somewhere would provide the link between the Churchmen who had been after any information Charlie might have on his father's illegal activities and what had gone down in Afghanistan. And Marz's gut was on Manny Garza.

One by one, three records returned. Fuckin' A. One of those three was their guy. Charlie clicked on the first listing.

Marz leaned in closer, barely resisting the urge to crawl into the screen and grab the information with his hands. "Just open and print. We'll read the details after you're out."

The printer came to life. "Already ahead of you."

Filled with anticipation, Marz could barely stand still. He paced behind Charlie, exchanging looks with Nick and Beckett, both appearing to be every bit as eager, and then leaned over Charlie's chair again.

File one, file two, file three. Done.

"I gotta get out so we don't get traced," Charlie said.

His fingers snapped over a series of keys and the screen went black. The lines of code returned. He typed in a few more lines and the machine powered down. Charlie stood up, turned around, and looked at Marz with wide blue eyes.

"Holy hell, Charlie. Holy fucking hell. You did it," Marz said, grinning and staring between Charlie's amazed and excited expression and the stack of paper on the printer's tray.

The guy pressed his hand to his chest. "My damn heart is pounding."

Everyone laughed. Elation almost made Marz's head spin. "That was a rush just watching it, my man. For real."

Charlie shook his head. The high of success was half the reason hackers did what they did. "Let's hope we got what you need."

Marz grabbed the papers from the printer, heart in his throat. *Please don't let this be another dead end.*

For days, he'd had a Web crawler looking for any mention of Garza. But nothing had turned up, which was ten kinds of fishy. Even if someone steered clear of social media, most people would turn up in a newspaper mention, a professional newsletter, a staff listing, a public record, or even a basic people-search database. The fact they'd come up totally fucking empty on both Garza or any possible relatives seemed improbable in the extreme. Nobody lived that far off the grid.

Marz's eyes raced so fast over the words he barely absorbed what the first file said. But his shoulders fell as the data sank in. The information detailed a man too old to be their Manny Garza. He chucked those sheets to the desk.

He couldn't have made himself disappear from these records, too. Could he?

Problem was, it wouldn't be the first time in their investigation that they'd come up against erased evidence. Charlie's sister, Becca, had made 9-1-1 calls to report break-ins at both her and Charlie's houses, and the records of both had disappeared, leading the team to question the integrity of the Baltimore City Police. Fact that someone had taken the trouble to hide Garza's presence from the world was just more proof it was no coincidence they'd encountered another SF guy hanging with the drug-dealing scum who'd kidnapped Charlie and tortured him for information about his father's dealings. Namely, that Colonel Merritt had been running a black op, cashing in on the heroin the team had confiscated in their counternarcotics missions back in Afghanistan. It'd been a lucrative side business, if their commander's twelve-million-dollar Singapore bank account was any indication.

The second file was more of the same—the guy had served in Vietnam. "Fuck me running," Marz said as he tossed more papers to the messy piles on the desk. If they didn't find Garza here, that left a hack into the Veterans Affairs records, or a potentially lengthy and equally dangerous dive into the Deep Web—the dark, hidden, and much larger part of the internet not indexed by standard search engines, which provided a haven for all kinds of criminal activity.

"Tell me he didn't manage to have his service records erased, too," Nick said, crossing his arms.

Marz's gaze scanned over the beginning of the third file. And then a slow smile crept up his face.

This Manny Garza was the right age and had served in the SF in Afghanistan as recently as two years ago, which fit their guy's profile to a T. Even better? The file didn't list a current address for Garza but did list two next of kin—a mother in Northern Virginia and a sister who lived in Annapolis, Maryland.

"How the hell far away is Annapolis?" Marz asked. Being from Atlanta and having had no time to see anything here unrelated to their mission, he had no idea.

"Forty minutes, maybe. Depending on traffic," Nick said, stepping closer and peering over the top of the page. "Why?"

"Got you, Garza," Marz said, smacking the papers against his hand and grinning at Nick, Beckett, and Charlie in turn. "Who wants to take a ride to Annapolis?"

Chapter 2

$\mathcal{E}$milie Garza eased her car up to her bright red mailbox and rolled down the window. Recently, her daily stop here had delivered more and more evidence of how her life had changed. Each new bill, solicitation, or letter brought with it a dose of healing and a twinge of hurt in equal measure. What would today bring?

Reaching out of her window, she lowered the mailbox's door and retrieved the thick stack of envelopes and advertisements. One by one, she flipped through them. More than half read, "Emilie Garza," but a fair number were still addressed to "Mr. and Mrs. Jack Saunders" or "Emilie Saunders." But she wasn't Mrs. Saunders anymore. Legally, not for the past five months. Emotionally, not for the past two years.

Not since she'd learned that her ex-husband had been playing house with another family, lying about frequent travel for work to facilitate the time away from their home . . . and their bed. And Emilie had believed every last lie until the day the other woman had shown up at her door.

Now Emilie didn't know who Jack Saunders actually was. Maybe she'd never known. Worse, his betrayal left her wondering who *she* was, too. And how she could've missed all the signs.

Enough, Em. It's over. And you're figuring it all out one day at a time.

"Yeah," she whispered to herself as she tossed the mail on the passenger seat and pulled up the long drive surrounded by leafy green woods on both sides. As she came around the bend that led up to her small cottage, her gaze settled on a squat black Hummer parked right in front of her porch. "Shit," she said. Manny had a key to her house that she'd given him once when he'd offered to help with a repair, and he'd been using it a lot lately, showing up at odd times. With the string of emotionally difficult cases she'd had today, her brother was the last thing she wanted to deal with. Guilt curled through her gut.

Once, the knowledge that her older brother had come to visit would've brightened every dark corner of her day. But since he'd come back from Afghanistan, he'd changed. And Emilie never knew which version of Manny she'd find. She parked, grabbed her purse, the mail, and the three bags of groceries, and made for the porch.

As her foot landed on the first step, she slowed, then froze. Her gaze drew across the little white house from right to left. All the plantation shutters were closed—and they hadn't been when she'd left for work this morning. Her shoulders sagged and her stomach flipped.

So it was going to be *the other* Manny, then.

The paranoid one. The nervous one. The angry one.

In her mind's eye, she saw herself hightailing it back to her car and getting the hell out of there. Problem was, no doubt he already knew she was home, and she didn't want to deal with whatever drama leaving without seeing him might cause. Not to mention, this was the big brother she'd idolized her entire life. The one who'd protected her from playground bullies and taught her how to drive and had walked her down the aisle because their father was no longer around to do it. Emilie didn't want to do anything to hurt *that* Manny, not after everything he'd always done for her.

Besides, maybe you're wrong. He could be fine. There could be a rational explanation for why he closed the shutters.

Sure.

She climbed the stairs, held the screen door open with her foot, and inserted the key into the lock.

Just as she turned the knob, the door wrenched open, a hand closed around her wrist, and she was hauled into the dimness.

She crashed into the wall behind the door—or was pushed into it—and was so surprised by the whole thing that she dropped the stack of mail and one of the bags she'd been carrying. Something shattered against the slate floor.

Manny secured the door with a series of clicks, then whirled on her. "Did they follow you?"

Emilie swallowed around her heart where it hammered in her throat. "Did who follow me?" she asked, ice trickling down her spine. Definitely not her Manny.

He stepped closer until he towered over her, his

longer-than-usual dark waves hanging messily over his forehead and casting shadows over dark, disturbed eyes. His whole face frowned and he shook his head. "Anyone. Did *anyone* follow you?"

The pain in her chest was her heart breaking. "No one followed me, Manny. Why would they?" Needing a break from the intensity of his gaze, she looked down to where his hand remained manacled to her wrist. "Please let me go. You're hurting me."

His fingers were off her skin in an instant, proof that her protective brother was still in there somewhere. He retreated from her, shifting his feet and raking at his hair, agitation rolling off him in waves.

"I'm gonna put these in the kitchen," Emilie said, gesturing to the bags. Stepping over the mess covering the foyer floor, she made her way through the normally light and airy den to the kitchen. Except for the big windows over the corner sink, Manny had darkened, one way or another, every window she passed. Emilie settled the bags on the tile counter, then grabbed the roll of paper towels.

She turned and found Manny hovering in the darkness just outside of the kitchen, as if he was hiding from the light cast by the corner window. Long-sleeved black shirt. Black jeans. Black boots. He nearly blended into the shadows. As she passed him, Emilie gently rubbed his arm and mentally willed her brother to come back to her.

As a sister, wishing and hoping and yearning were all she could do.

As a clinical psychologist, she knew it to be completely futile. You couldn't help someone who refused to be helped. Or, more aptly, someone who refused to recognize there was a problem in the first place.

Manny followed her to the foyer and hovered over her while she collected the mail, wiped up the spilled salsa, and carried the dripping bag to the sink. With her back to him, she removed and wiped down all the other items in the bag one by one. "Who do you expect might be following me?" she asked quietly.

Long pause. And then, "It's me they're after."

It wasn't the first time he'd given voice to his paranoia. Worst part was, as the months had passed and Manny's mental health deteriorated, Emilie wasn't sure what part of what he said was in his head and likely caused by some untreated PTSD from his years in Iraq and Afghanistan, and what part might be fed by reality. Once at a holiday get-together, she'd overheard the tail end of a phone conversation that made her wonder exactly what Manny *did* for Seneka Worldwide Security, the defense contractor that he'd worked for the past few years. Maybe some of his paranoia was justified—and that didn't make Emilie feel even a little bit better.

When the last of the cans and jars sat clean next to the sink, Emilie turned and rested her back against the counter. "Why would someone be after you?"

Manny's dark brown eyes, so like her own, stopped the incessant scanning from the front door, along each of the windows, and then over her shoulder out the big window to the water beyond, and focused on her. "You wouldn't understand."

"I'd like to, if you'd let me." She smoothed her hands over her skirt, then laced her fingers together in front of herself to keep from fidgeting.

His gaze narrowed. "Don't psychoanalyze me, Em."

"That's not what I'm doing, Manny. I just want to know what's going on with you. That's all. Like old times."

He appeared to consider her for a moment, and then he shook his head. "Old times are gone."

The declaration propelled her across the kitchen to him until she came to rest against the arch that led into the den. "But why? Are you in some kind of trouble?"

The skin around his left eye ticked. "Nothing I can't handle. Anyway, I just needed a place to lay low for a few hours. As soon as I get the signal, I'll be gone."

"You don't have to leave, you know," she said. Relief and guilt flooded through her in equal measure. "Stay. I'll make dinner."

The distrust in his gaze made the back of her eyes prick.

The rumble of an engine sounded from out front. The UPS truck, by the sound of it. No one else ever came this time of day.

Manny moved so fast that Emilie could barely track what was happening. He forced her to the ground and hissed at her to stay there. In a low crouch, he raced across the room and, gun drawn, took up a shielded position at one of the front windows, where he opened the plantation shutter just the smallest bit.

In that moment, odd things registered in Emilie's brain. The throbbing in her knees from how Manny had pushed her down. Momentary, out-of-place pleasure at the thought that it was probably the maxi dresses she'd ordered last week being delivered. Fear that Manny was going to shoot Burt, assuming she was right about it being UPS, who was almost so good-looking he could be the driver from those funny UPS commercials about the women who wait to see the sexy delivery man every day.

More sounds filtered in from outside. The truck's

brake. Burt's footsteps on the wooden deck out front. Two knocks against the door.

All the while, Emilie lay there, afraid to get up and risk startling Manny, whose finger was poised to wrap around the gun's trigger.

The footsteps receded, and then the truck itself. Emilie finally felt like she could breathe again. Slowly, she eased up onto her knees. "It was just UPS," she whispered. "Right?"

Manny ignored her, his gaze glued to the view out the front window until the sound of the truck disappeared altogether. Finally, he looked at her. "Get the package," he said.

Emilie blinked, too dumbstruck by the command to move.

"Em," he said, impatience and irritation filling his tone. He waved at the door with the hand still holding the gun.

She hauled herself off the floor, across the room, and onto the porch, where the package marked with the logo of one of her favorite clothing brands sat. Harmless, of course. She brought it inside only to have Manny swipe it out of her hands as soon as she crossed the threshold. He placed it onto the coffee table and leaned over to press his ear against it.

"Manny, it's dresses—"

He glared and waved a hand at her. Emilie stared at him in confusion, a rock sliding into her gut.

Apparently satisfied, he sat up, holstered his gun, and retrieved a knife from his boot. God, he was still totally in soldier mode, wasn't he? Even two years out of the Army. Before she could stop him, he stabbed the knife into the top of the box and drew it back toward him.

My dresses!

Emilie pressed her hands to her mouth to keep from crying out in anger or fear. It was like she'd stepped into an episode of *Law and Order* or *The Sopranos* or . . . God only knew! All *she* knew was there was absolutely nothing normal about her brother's behavior. What the hell had brought this on? She'd *never* seen him this bad before.

He ripped open the top of the box and unceremoniously pulled out the contents—which, she could tell from the huge holes in the packaging, he'd damaged.

Angry heat pooled in her belly, overcoming whatever fear she'd felt moments before. She inhaled to speak as Manny's cell phone buzzed and he placed it to his ear. "Yes?" he said, going totally still. "Yes, got it." He slipped the cell back into his pocket as he rose to his feet. "Gotta go."

Emilie scoffed. "That's it? That's what you're going to say? You just pulled your gun in my home, scared me half to death, and destroyed two-hundred-dollars' worth of dresses. Now you're just gonna go?"

Manny was in her face in an instant. Brow arched. Eyes cold. Mouth in a sneer. "Don't push me, Emilie. Understand?" He stared at her a long moment, during which all she could manage to do was swallow and nod. Finally, he holstered the blade. He opened his wallet, grabbed some cash, and shoved it into her hands. "Keep an eye out. And keep your mouth shut."

With that, he slipped out the door, jogged around to the driver's side of the Hummer, and drove away.

Emilie looked down to the wad of hundred dollar bills in her hand and silently counted. *Fourteen of them!*

"Holy shit!" she rasped. She counted again just to

prove to herself she wasn't imagining it. Why the hell was Manny carrying that kind of money on him? Who did that? And who gave it away like it was pocket change? They hadn't been poor growing up, but they hadn't been rich, either. They'd grown up in the kind of family that scrimped and saved for everything they got. Where you were expected to get part-time jobs and contribute, and scholarships made the difference between attending college or not. She'd landed them where Manny hadn't, which was why he'd gone the route of the Army.

And now he was throwing money at her like . . . like . . . like it made up for any of the bullshit that had happened during the last half hour.

Manny's voice echoed in Emilie's ears. *Don't push me.*

Or what? What might he have done if she'd gone off on him?

Releasing a shaky breath, Emilie closed and locked the door, throwing the dead bolt for good measure. Although she was completely aware that she couldn't keep Manny out if he really wanted in. Not just because he had a key, but because even if she had the locks changed, he knew how to pick them. It was beyond reassuring to know you had someone with his training and skills on your side. Knowing that person might use those skills against you? That was something else entirely. She shuddered and dropped the wad of bills to the coffee table.

Red-hot anger surged through her until she nearly shook. She stomped through the house, threw out the destroyed dresses and box, marched into her bedroom to change, and wrenched open all the shutters and curtains Manny had closed. She was a damned adult and a highly educated professional. No one had the right to scare her in her own home. Family or not.

And the truth of that just made her angrier, because she'd been scared of Manny. There at the end, when he'd nearly trapped her against the wall, knife in hand? She'd been scared, and she *knew* she wouldn't pick a fight over his behavior if he did it again.

Emilie hated that reality. She hated that feeling. And a part of her hated Manny for all of it.

It's not his fault. He's sick. Probably. Definitely.

But that didn't make the way he'd acted okay. The hardest thing about knowing someone grappling with mental illness—besides standing witness to their pain—was that sometimes it was so damn hard to blame the illness and not the person.

Emilie sat heavily on the edge of her bed. Right now she was having a hard time making the distinction.

Chapter 3

As the SUV came to a stop, Marz scanned the woods around where Beckett parked. The narrow dirt road would give them a place to ditch the truck while they scoped out Garza's sister's house.

"Let's do it," Marz said, needing to fill the silence. The forty-minute trip from Baltimore to Annapolis was probably the first time he'd been alone with Beckett for more than a few minutes since they'd been sent stateside a year ago. And the whole ride had been quiet as a tomb. In the Army, despite being an odd pairing— Beckett the strong, silent, scary type, and Marz an outgoing chatterbox—the two of them had been tight. More than just friends, they'd been like brothers. Marz had always considered it a major victory when he got the big guy to crack a smile or, God forbid, laugh out loud.

But the moment the insurgents had thrown that grenade during the ambush, everything had changed. Marz had seen the incoming projectile first, and he'd shoved Beckett out of the way. The explosion had taken them both down, injuring Beckett's left leg and blowing Marz's righty clean off below the knee. Since then, it had become clear that act had formed a wall between them, one Beckett wouldn't let Marz get over or around.

Beckett turned his head toward Marz. Though dark sunglasses shielded the other man's gaze, some sort of struggle was clear on Beckett's face. No doubt he was debating whether or not to ask if Marz was up to this. Granted, walking over uneven surfaces proved a challenge, but that was why Marz had donned the prosthesis with the more responsive—and stable—foot and ankle system. Some men had a suit for every occasion. Marz had a leg for every occasion.

"We got a problem?" Marz asked as he gripped the handle on the door.

"Nope," Beckett said after a long moment.

"Good," Marz said.

They got out of the SUV and met at the rear. From the back, they retrieved packs with surveillance equipment, tracking devices, and other supplies. Silently, they double-checked their equipment and weapons, a habit ingrained from their years of service, and shouldered their packs.

"Lead the way, hoss," Marz said.

With a last glance at his GPS, Beckett guided them down the overgrown dirt road and into the woods.

Marz chose his path carefully and made out fine. The ground was mostly level and solid, the lack of rain the past few weeks working to his advantage. On alert for any signs of company, they quietly made their way through spots of dense undergrowth interspersed be-tween more open forest.

Half an hour earlier, they'd driven by Emilie Garza's property to get a feel for her location. Turned out luck was on their side, because her house was isolated on a narrow point of land that fronted the Chesapeake Bay. They hadn't been able to see the house from the road, which was why they'd decided to overland it so they could get a good look on their own terms.

They were close to nailing down Manny Garza. Marz could feel it.

Ahead through the trees, the house came into view. Beckett signaled with his hand and guided them through the woods to a position where the trees closed in on the far edge of a circular drive. Crouching behind neighboring oaks, they scanned the house and yard.

Whereas big houses with soaring windows domi-nated most of the surrounding properties, Emilie Gar-za's house was small enough you might've called it a bungalow. The yard was almost triangular in shape, narrower where the drive wound down to the road and wider where the grass sloped off toward the water. A white Toyota Camry sat near the front of the house. What the place lacked in grandeur, it made up for in hominess. The blue shutters against the white siding, ferns hanging in pots along the whole expanse of the front porch, and American and Maryland flags flapping gently off poles affixed to the porch columns made it appear the kind of house you called a home. Something he never had.

Everything was quiet, and it wasn't yet dark enough to discern lights or movement within.

Marz slipped the pack off his shoulders and removed a few pieces of equipment as Beckett did the same. One thing they'd always bonded over: gadgets. They both loved to use them, and Beckett had always been particularly good at modifying them. As Beckett powered up an X-ray camera with see-through-the-wall technology, Marz slipped on a pair of headphones that connected to a bionic ear, a handheld listening device that amplified sound from up to a hundred yards away.

The moment Marz turned on the supersensitive microphone, he picked up the soft strains of music from inside. No voices, but there were other noises. A soft clinking, a low hiss or sizzle—sounds that made him think of cooking. He looked to Beckett, who tilted the screen of the tablet camera toward him. The cutting-edge technology was essentially a radar system that measured changes in WiFi wave frequency through walls as thick as one foot. The screen revealed one disturbance to those waves.

One person inside.

Marz nodded to Beckett.

"Oh, my God, that's good," came a woman's voice through Marz's headphones. His gaze returned to the house and scanned from window to window as he imagined what Emilie Garza was doing. Sounds like doors or cabinets opening and closing. The clinks of plates and glasses. The scrape of a chair against the floor. "Oh, forgot the jalapeños," she murmured.

She apparently had a habit of talking to herself, as it continued throughout the whole meal until the rushing sound of water suggested she was doing the dishes. And then it got quiet again.

A cool darkness had fallen over the peaceful yard. Lights illuminated the front porch and glowed from the water side of the house.

Marz's thighs were pitching a fit about kneeling, so

he carefully readjusted onto his hip. He didn't even have to look at Beckett to know the guy's eyes tracked his movement.

"Okay, stop putting it off," Emilie said in a soft voice.

And then music to Marz's ears—the tones of a phone dialing. Finally, something he could work with. He closed his eyes as they sounded out and immediately translated them to numbers. He pulled out his cell and texted Charlie: *Look up 703-555-2496*. When he was done, he put his hand up to his own ear to signal to Beckett that Emilie was making a call.

A moment later, he received back: *Will do*.

From inside, one ring, then another, and another. "Hi, you've reached—" *Click*.

Damnit. No conversation and not even a name from the message. At least Charlie could trace the number. Marz made a cut signal across his neck, and Beckett nodded his understanding.

More time passed. Nothing glamorous about surveillance. Most of the time it was a whole lotta sitting around hoping something informative would happen while you fought to keep your mind focused and your eyes and ears sharp.

Numbness radiated from his right hip and crawled down his thigh, and Marz shifted again. Having lost a leg wasn't all bad. His leg might be weaker, but at least it no longer mattered when one half of a pair of socks went AWOL in the dryer.

Silver linings, man. He'd always looked for them. Because, really, what choice was there? To wallow in life's hard knocks and give up? He'd have been down and out at the age of five if that'd been his approach. Fuck that.

It wasn't that Marz didn't think losing a leg sucked

ass. It totally did. For a time, it had shredded his psyche, his soul, his sense of self. And it definitely changed his life—like right now, when the squeeze of the sleeve, pressure on the stump, and weaker muscle tone of his thigh made it harder to hold his position. But at least he still *had* a life. Seven of his best friends—his brothers—no longer had that privilege. In his thoughts and the ink on his body, he included the Colonel in that number, because once Frank Merritt had almost been like the father Marz had never known. That counted for something, even if Merritt had thrown it all away.

Anger and disappointment weighed on Marz's chest as it always did when he thought about what Merritt had done. Marz couldn't understand how their commander could've cared so little for his team when each of them would've laid their lives down for the man in a heartbeat. Sometimes, Merritt's betrayal felt a whole lot like being discarded by his parents all over again.

He blew out a long breath.

Still, any way Marz sliced and diced it, he'd been one of the lucky SOBs. So he'd found a way to screwing his head on straight about his leg. He hadn't yet achieved the same level of Zen about his fallen friends. Probably never would.

But some justice would go a long way toward helping. And his gut told him Garza was key to a shot at that.

Finally, timers shut out the front lights around eleven, and the inside went dark just before midnight. Beckett's camera confirmed that Emilie was asleep by showing her in one nonmoving position.

"Ready?" Beckett asked, rising to his feet.

"Let's do it," Marz said, using the tree to steady himself as he got up, a helluva lot less gracefully than his friend. And damn if he didn't feel the impact of every single minute of sitting on the ground in the joints and muscles of his lower half. Pins and needles were like fire in his right leg. It was entirely possible that an eighty-five-year-old had temporarily inhabited his thirty-four-year-old body.

"Okay?" Beckett asked, half looking like he wanted to help but not sure if he should.

"Good as gold," Marz said, gritting his teeth as he put his weight on his stump. "Let's go."

They took off at a low run across the yard, Beckett toward the side of the house and Marz toward the Toyota. Well, Marz sorta hobbled. But under the cover of darkness, it hardly mattered. He'd still get the job done. While Beckett hard wired a listening device onto the exterior landline to the telephone, Marz planted a tracking device connected to an app on his phone under the rear bumper of the car.

If this wasn't enough to get what they needed, Marz might have to find a way to get hold of Emilie's cell phone. Do a quick install of some spyware and *bam!* One-stop shopping for pretty much any kind of surveillance he could want as long as the phone remained on. Hopefully, they could get what they needed without having to go that route. They were already dancing pretty far on the wrong side of the law.

Marz met Beckett back in the shadows of the tree line within two minutes, where they settled in for the night. They kept watch together for another hour, and then they took turns sleeping and standing watch until day broke five hours later.

When morning came, Marz was almost disappointed. Not that he'd expected Garza to drive up to his sister's house, hold his arms out, and say, "Here I am!" But they needed intel on the guy, and Emilie Garza was the most direct route to it. And they didn't have time to be patient.

Beckett shifted and his eyes opened, immediately alert and awake. "Hey," he said to Marz.

"Hey. She's up but otherwise it's quiet," Marz said, nodding toward the house. "Also, Charlie texted. That phone number was Garza's mother's house over in Northern Virginia."

"Which we already had," Beckett said gruffly.

The guy sounded as frustrated as Marz had felt when the message came through. "Yep."

"My gut's telling me waiting for a call or visit from Garza is gonna take too long," Beckett said.

Marz sighed. "I was thinking the same thing."

Beckett took a long pull from a water bottle, then wiped his mouth with the back of his hand. "One thing's certain. With the attack on the Church Gang the other night, he and his remaining henchmen have to be looking for the culprits."

"Meaning us," Marz said.

His friend nodded. "Meaning us. No way they don't want revenge. So the question is, are we gonna let them find us first, or are we going to do whatever it takes to find them first?"

Marz frowned. "Not even a question."

"No, it isn't," Beckett said, piercing blue eyes nailing Marz with a stare.

Looking at Emilie's house again, Marz's brain churned on the best way to get what they needed. "Which means we need to step things up." Beckett nodded, and Marz rubbed his hands over his face. "Let's follow her this morning. If we're still not getting anything, then one of us will talk to her. See what we can learn that way. Failing that, we break into her house and hope there's something useful there, or I find a way to grab her cell so I can upload some spyware."

"Works for me," Beckett said, standing and stretching. "Let's hump back to the truck so we're ready to go when she leaves."

"Roger that." Marz packed his gear and looked up to find Beckett offering him a hand. Glancing between the guy's big paw and the hard blue of his eyes, Marz swallowed his pride, clasped Beckett's hand, and accepted the offer of help. "Thanks," he said, shaking out the cramp in his thigh and shouldering his pack.

"Yeah," Beckett said in a low voice.

Fifteen minutes later, they were back at the SUV. They loaded their gear into the rear and Beckett grabbed a banana from their supplies as Marz pulled a fresh shirt out of the overnight bag he'd brought. He tugged his shirt over his head, tossed it onto the floor of the open hatch, and grabbed the clean tee.

"I like the phoenix," Beckett said.

Marz looked from Beckett down to his own right shoulder, where a black-and-orange tribal phoenix stretched over the joint, across the top of his chest, and down his right biceps. "Yeah? Thanks. Seemed fitting."

Brow furrowed, Beckett gave a nod as he busied himself with something from his bag.

The phoenix was a newer tattoo among his twenty-four pieces, a fair number of which he'd had done since his amputation. Ink had always been a way of claiming a sense of self and creating identity for him. When you grow up without a family, you don't have the usual ways of defining who you are. Marz had never been someone's son or someone's brother—not by blood, anyway. Bouncing between foster families and group homes, he hadn't grown up with particular familial values or traditions the way other people had.

Underage, he'd used a fake ID to get his very first tattoo, a tribal on the outside of his right calf. Gone now, of course. Ink had taken on renewed significance after being accused of wrongdoing and discharged from the only career—calling, really—Marz had ever known, all on top of losing a part of his body. He'd returned stateside with a pretty badly rattled sense of self. Tattoos had helped Marz nail that back down again and reminded him what was most important.

His brothers. His honor. And justice.

Marz tugged the clean shirt over his head and raked his fingers through his hair.

His cell buzzed and he retrieved it from his pocket. A notification from the tracking app connected to the device he'd planted on her car. "She's on the move," he said.

"Good. Let's go," Beckett said, closing the rear hatch. They hopped in the SUV and Beckett backed it up until they found a place to turn around, then they waited for Emilie to pass their location. The tracking device meant they didn't have to follow her too closely. Then they were back on the narrow roads leading off the peninsula on which she lived.

With one eye on Beckett's GPS and the other on Emilie's car, they followed her along country roads heading toward downtown Annapolis until crossing a wide bridge dumped them into the old colonial town. Minutes later, she turned into a lot on what looked like a small college campus. Marz hopped out so they wouldn't lose track of her while Beckett found a place to park.

A low brick wall ran around the campus. On his phone's map app, the buildings appeared to fill several city blocks. Marz followed a sidewalk into the quad just in time to see a brown-haired woman in a flowing yellow dress leave the white Camry and make her way across the parking lot toward a big red-brick mansion.

So that's Emilie Garza, he thought as she jogged up onto the wide porch and disappeared inside.

He got close enough to read the sign in front of the house, which identified it as a student health and counseling center. Made sense. The research they'd done on Emilie Garza before traveling here yesterday identified her as a psychologist.

Footsteps sounded, and Marz turned to see Beckett coming up behind him. The pack over his shoulder might've almost allowed him to blend in as a student, if he wasn't so fucking big. And scary.

"Where'd she go?" Beckett asked, those blue eyes making a sweep of the area.

"Student health center over there." He pointed to the mansion. "Let's find a spot to set up."

Big, sprawling magnolia trees surrounded the other three sides of her building, providing them some cover to get closer. Their part of the campus was relatively quiet, so they had that working for them, too. Marz pulled up the college's website to find Emilie's office location. "Bingo," he said. "She's on the first floor."

"Use the ear to identify which office?" Beckett said.

"Yup." Marz slipped the headphones on and directed the microphone toward the building. A mix of voices, ambient noises, and other sounds filled his ears, but nothing sounded like the voice he'd listened to the night before. Maybe too many voices to discern hers from the cacophony?

Finally, on the far side of the building, he heard a woman's voice say, "Emilie, your nine o'clock is here," along with Emilie's answering instruction to send him in.

"I got her," Marz said. "Right through the trees there." They didn't have a view, but the bionic ear confirmed that she spent her morning counseling a string of patients. In the parts Marz listened to, Emilie Garza proved herself kind and thoughtful and smart, challenging people to push through their fears, backing off when she'd gone as far as she could take them, and building her patients up in a way that sparked a kernel of admiration in Marz's chest. An odd feeling for someone he'd never met.

Especially someone who could be actively involved with her brother's illegal activities.

Sixteen hours of surveillance had his gut disagreeing with the notion, but the thing that made good criminals so hard to catch was that they often didn't look or seem like criminals.

As the morning passed, what they didn't get were any personal calls made by or to her that might've given them anything useful.

"Assuming she works an eight-to-five," Beckett said, "maybe we should go see what we can find at her house."

Marz inhaled to speak when he heard Emilie's voice through the headphones. "I'm going to walk down to the coffee shop for lunch. Want anything?"

An idea came to mind, and Marz rushed to pack up his equipment. "I agree. You go case the house and I'll find a way to talk to her. She just said she's going to a coffee shop. Maybe I can strike up a conversation." Beckett frowned and shook his head as if he planned to argue. "We'll cover twice as much ground. When you're done, come back. Easy as."

After a moment, Beckett sighed. "Okay. But don't take any damn chances."

Marz smirked. "Who me?"

"Stay in touch," Beckett said with a scowl. "It shouldn't take long."

Handing off the pack to Beckett, Marz nodded. For a moment, it felt just like the old days: the two of them working together and having each other's backs; Beckett's gruffness that was really concern in disguise. Marz cleared his throat and nodded. "You got it. Now, let's go get what we need."

Chapter 4

$\mathcal{B}$eckett took off just as Emilie rounded the front of the building and started along a diagonal sidewalk that cut across the quad. Marz ducked behind a magnolia tree and waited for her to pass. When the sound of her footsteps receded, he leaned out to see her, letting her get far enough ahead that she wouldn't have any reason to notice him.

Keeping the better part of a block between them, Marz fixed his gaze on the sway and billow of Emilie's pale yellow dress until she disappeared inside a shop. When he got there a few minutes later, he followed her in and saw her getting settled at a table.

The smell of food and coffee made Marz's stomach grumble, so when he reached the counter to order, he chose a turkey sandwich and a bottle of Gatorade. Maybe he'd grab one for Beckett on the way out. Drink in hand, he sat down at the table next to Emilie's to wait for his food.

It was the first time he'd gotten a good look at her . . . and, man, if she wasn't absofreakinglutely beautiful. Curves hugged perfectly by the pretty dress, a sweet, warm face, and long, wavy brown hair that made his fingers itch to be buried in it. There was no question Emilie Garza was a mission asset, but talking to her wouldn't be any kinda hardship, either. That was for damn sure.

He cracked open his drink and took a long pull. From the corner of his eye, he watched as Emilie retrieved her laptop from a bag and opened it. Hours of studying her brother's picture in the surveillance images they took the night they first saw him made the familial resemblance clear. Which reminded Marz that this woman was the sister of his enemy.

Right. Don't forget it.

The waitress placed a plate with a sandwich and chips on Emilie's table. "Here you go," she said. "Enjoy."

"Thank you," Emilie said, offering up a big, open smile to the girl.

Pretending to read something on his phone, Marz debated the best way to initiate a conversation.

Emilie frowned at her monitor and held up her hands like she was asking a silent question. She rose from her table and went to the counter. "Excuse me?"

Marz eyeballed her cell phone, tucked between the keyboard and the wall. So close.

From behind him, Emilie said, "I can't log onto the WiFi. Can you help me?"

"Oh, no. I don't know. I'm sorry," one of the workers replied. Marz smiled to himself. Could there have been a better in for him?

"Okay, thanks," Emilie said, frustration plain in her tone. She returned to her table, looking a little lost.

"Hey, uh, I might be able to help," Marz said.

As the waitress brought his sandwich, Emilie turned to look at him and glanced at his plate. "Oh, well, I don't want to interrupt your lunch."

"No worries," he said, smiling at her. "I work in IT so it shouldn't be a problem."

"Really?" She glanced to her computer and then nodded. "Okay. I appreciate it. I wanted to get some paperwork done while I'm away from the office because I can never get it done while I'm there."

Marz pushed his plate out of the way and reached out a hand. "Let's get you fixed up, then. Here. I'll take a look."

Emilie handed him the thin notebook computer and pulled a chair from her table toward his. "Thank you," she said as she sat.

Marz inhaled, about to respond, and caught a hint of her scent, something warm and fruity. His mouth watered. "You're welcome," he managed as he navigated to the control panel to troubleshoot the network connection. A few clicks later, the machine connected. "See? All set."

"Aw, my hero," she said with a beautiful, genuine smile that reached inside him and made him want for more. "Seriously, thank you. I think I have a bad-day hangover from yesterday, so I can't tell you how much your kindness means to me."

Marz had three reactions. First, no way this woman was involved in criminal activity. That one was an instinctive gut-check. Second, what the hell had happened yesterday? Nothing had occurred after their surveillance began last evening that offered any explanation. And third, what else could he do to make her look at him like that again?

"Not even a thing, but I'm glad I could help." He handed her the computer, regretting that doing so sent her sliding back over to her own table. "I'm Derek, by the way."

"Emilie," she said, holding out her hand. Pretty brown eyes stared at him across the narrow space.

Marz returned the shake, liking the way her soft, slender hand fit inside his own. Touching her made his brain imagine doing more. Dragging his fingertips up her arm, caressing along the V-neck of her dress, tucking a dark brown curl behind her ear. "Well, I hope you manage to get through your paperwork, Emilie," he said, swallowing down a knot of desire.

"Thanks. Uh, me too," she said, turning toward her work and lunch. She peeked at him from behind the drape of her curls, and it made Marz grin as he picked up his sandwich.

Eating in silence, Marz's mind wandered. He'd had sex since his amputation. He'd met a female vet at PT with an above-the-knee amputation. They'd become friends, went out for drinks one night, and she'd been brave enough to ask him if he was nervous about being with someone for the first time, post-amputation. An hour later, they tumbled into her bed. It had been an amazing affirmation that he was still a man, leg or no leg—and he certainly hadn't seen her as any less of a woman for missing a limb. But they'd just been friends, and she moved away to live closer to her parents.

Taking a long drink of his orange Gatorade, he tried to shake the thoughts away.

How Marz had gone from a handshake to sex, he wasn't exactly sure. Without question, Emilie was beautiful and smart and kind—the type of woman any man would be lucky to have. And Marz *was* a man, a man who'd had sex only once in almost two years. But Marz was also someone who had gone through life without feeling particularly well connected—except for his years in the Army. Truth be told, he *craved* belonging somewhere and with someone. He hadn't had it as a child. Maybe he wouldn't have it as an adult, either. Maybe he was meant to walk through this life alone.

The thought drew his hand over his heart, where his shirt covered a tattoo of seven blackbirds and the letters YNWA. *You never walk alone.* Marz might not have had a family by blood, but he'd damn sure had a family created by the bonds of honor, shared purpose, and brotherhood—one that Merritt had shattered with his deception and betrayal. Now, his four remaining team-mates were all that was left of that family, which was why getting together with them meant so damn much. After returning stateside, they'd all retreated to their own corners of the world to lick their wounds, so Marz thought he'd lost them, too. But now they were back together. And damn it all to hell but Marz didn't want that to end.

He shoved the woe-is-me bullshit away.

Thinking of his dead teammates was another good reminder that the woman beside him was an operational asset. Nothing more. Certainly not someone to look at for . . . anything beyond her ties to Manny Garza.

Right.

Movement from the corner of his eye just as Emilie's fingers gently landed on his forearm. His gaze swung toward her.

"I'm sorry. I said your name, but you didn't hear me," she said. "You okay?"

"Yeah. Just, uh, work stuff," he said, kicking himself for not staying present in the moment. He clued in enough to see that she had most of her belongings in her arms.

"In case the waitress tries to clear the table, would you tell her I haven't left. Just need to use the restroom." She gestured toward the back.

"You got it. Your sandwich is safe with me. Unless you take too long, and then I might polish it off myself."

Emilie grinned and chuckled as she rose. "Try to resist."

As if the words had lured him in, Marz's gaze swept over her body. "Resistance is futile," he said with a wink.

She licked her lips and swallowed, her gaze all tangled with his and humor still bright in her eyes.

He let her off the hook and reached for his drink. "Leave your stuff if you want. I'll watch it for you. And I won't eat any of it. Promise."

She looked hesitant for a moment, then clutched her laptop tighter to her chest. "That's okay. Thanks, though. Be right back."

Marz nodded. Smart woman for not leaving her electronics behind. Bad luck for him, though.

He shot off a text to Beckett. *Find anything?* When staring at the screen didn't bring a response, Marz finished his sandwich.

Emilie returned a few moments later. "Look at that. You resisted."

Humor and challenge slid into his gaze as he looked at her. "Some things are easier to resist than others."

Her laughter was nervous and embarrassed and lit

him up inside, too. "You're too much, Derek," she said. "So, do you live around here?"

Now they might be getting somewhere. "I've got a consulting gig in Baltimore. Down here for a few days on business. You?"

"I work at the counseling center at King's College, but I just live a few minutes from downtown."

Marz nodded, hoping he could keep her talking. "Nice. Would love a piece of land right on the water out here."

Emilie turned toward him in her chair. "We're on the water—I mean, I am. And, uh . . ." She shook her head and it was almost like she deflated a bit. Concern slid into Marz's gut as he watched her demeanor change. What had caused it? "Well, anyway, I've always loved it."

"Yeah?" he said, feeling like he wanted to bolster her up again. "What's your favorite thing about the water?"

She tilted her head and considered him. "Besides how beautiful it is? I'd say that my favorite thing is how peaceful it is. I love the sound of it. When I'm going to sleep, I can hear the waves against the beach. During storms, there are foghorns that go off in the distance and it's such a . . . I don't know, reassuring sound to me. I could sit on my porch and watch the water for hours. The movement of it, the seagulls and ospreys and eagles, the big ships going up to port." Emilie shook her head. "Sorry, didn't mean to go on and on."

Smiling, Marz turned toward her in his seat. "No, I liked it." He really had, too. The sound of her voice, the thoughtfulness behind her words. This was a woman who valued the small things in life, and who understood that sometimes the small things meant a lot. His gut was once again rejecting the idea that she was in on anything with her brother.

"What do you like about the water?" she asked.

He leaned his elbows on his knees. "This probably sounds weird, but I really like to float. To just lay back, close my eyes, and give myself over to the buoyancy and motion of the water." Derek enjoyed that feeling even more since the amputation. The water took all the stress off his limb. He shrugged.

Emilie smiled. "That *is* a nice feeling, isn't it? Except growing up with a brother it was never particularly safe to do it without risking getting dunked." She laughed, the memory clearly a fond one.

Marz chuckled. "Oh, you have a brother? Does he live around here, too?"

Something flickered in Emilie's eyes. "He's in Baltimore, actually. But he visits sometimes." Marz's phone buzzed an incoming message, attracting Emilie's gaze. It buzzed again. What fucking timing. "Well, I don't want to keep you."

Scooping the phone into his hands, Marz shook his head. "You're not keeping me. This is my free day. I'm just sightseeing and relaxing today." More buzzes, more messages. What the hell was going on?

"Oh, sounds heavenly." She set up her laptop again, and in his peripheral vision, Marz could just make out the forms she'd been working on. Looked like case files. "It was very nice talking to you," she said. "I feel like I should buy you a cup of coffee or something in thanks. Or a cookie. They're great here."

Another buzz. Chuckling, Marz slipped the phone into his pocket as he collected his trash and plate and rose. "Nah, I'm good. Thanks, though. And nice meeting you, too." Even though he hadn't managed to nab her phone or obtain any new information, he really meant it. He'd enjoyed the conversation, enjoyed talking to someone outside all the bullshit whirling around him. He'd enjoyed *her*.

"Are you sure? You can't grow up in a big Latino family without wanting to feed people," she said, looking up at him with that sweet smile.

"I'm good," he said with a grin. "But I appreciate it, Emilie." Something inside him hesitated. He didn't want to walk away. But all those messages had his gut clenched in fear and anticipation. Beckett was the one most likely to be contacting him right now, which didn't bode well. The guy was about as reserved a conversationalist as you'd ever find, and he hated talking on the phone. Hated texting even more. If the guy could get away without communicating in any form—ever—he'd be perfectly happy. No way all these messages didn't mean some shit was going down. "Well, take care," he said, offering a wave.

"You, too," she said.

When he stepped out onto the brick sidewalk and the glass door closed behind him, he noticed Emilie was still watching him.

Marz double-timed it up to the next intersection, turned the corner, and ducked into the first doorway he found. He pulled up the texts.

Jesus, seven of them. What the hell?

The first was from Beckett and listed two phone numbers that were somehow related to Garza. *Bingo*. If one of them was a landline, that gave them a direct connection to an address. The second read, *Half basement under the sister's house*.

And then there were pictures. Marz enlarged the first one, trying to figure out what he was seeing.

"Holy shit."

He looked at the next one. And then the next.

"Holy fucking shit."

Sweet, kind Emilie Garza had a basement full of drugs and guns. She had a fucking *stash*.

So much for his gut instinct. Anger crawled up his spine and had him thunking his head against the doorframe behind him.

The sixth one read, *Where the hell are you?*

And the last one: *Calling the team on this.*

Marz couldn't have agreed more. He needed to get to Beckett. He went to dial him when the phone rang. *Beckett.* "Holy shit," Marz said by way of answering.

"Yup. Talked to Nick, who talked to Shane, Easy, and Charlie. Charlie's running the phone numbers. The stash wasn't obvious. It was tucked into a totally dark room with a dirty floor that might've been a coal cellar or something. The sister might not even know, because the place doesn't look used. The guys are coming and we're taking it."

Digging his hand through his hair, Marz processed all this information. "We need the assets," he said.

"Yeah," Beckett said.

"Well, shit. You wanna come get me? Or have them pick me up?" he asked.

"Negative," Beckett said. "Your job is to keep Emilie Garza out of the house as long as you can."

Chapter 5

Last patient gone for the day, Emilie shut down her computer, packed up her belongings, and worried—as she had all day—about her brother. Why had he been in such bad shape yesterday? What had happened to set him off? Who had called? And where had he gone after "laying low" at her house?

She'd been so worried that, as the afternoon wore on, she began to fear she was too distracted to do right by her clients. But sometimes you just had to muscle through the bad until it got better—the last two years had taught her that. And she hated to let her patients down when they needed her.

Speaking of being needed . . .

Emilie pulled out her laptop and booted it up. The screen came alive to a form that her gut told her she might have to submit. The state's petition form for emergency psychiatric evaluation. For her brother.

She knew *exactly* what submitting this form would unleash.

Procedurally, it would enable the police to pick up Manny and escort him to an emergency room for a forced evaluation. After the incident yesterday, it was the only remaining recourse Emilie saw. The one time she'd suggested he be evaluated and seek treatment for PTSD, he'd nearly taken her head off. After yesterday, she was afraid rational discussion was off the table. Way off.

Emotionally, it would set off a firestorm on *so* many levels. As much as Emilie believed Manny required some sort of intervention, guilt ate at her for even thinking of doing this. Her mother, who thought Emilie's concerns were way out of proportion, would probably never forgive her. And Manny. Oh, my God, who even knew what Manny would do? But it wouldn't be good.

It might sever the relationship with her brother forever. And that made her heart hurt. Because somewhere inside him was the boy who'd helped her build blanket forts in her bedroom when they'd been kids. Somewhere inside him was the young man who'd been so proud of her for graduating college that he'd surprised her with a car for her gift. Somewhere inside him was the gallant soldier who'd looked so dashing in his dress uniform as he'd walked her down the aisle on her wedding day.

But wouldn't losing him be better than letting him hurt someone else or himself?

Thing was, if what she knew about Manny she knew about one of her patients, she wouldn't hesitate for a minute.

Emilie sighed. She couldn't do this before talking to her mother. She at least owed the woman the respect of letting her know what was going on before taking this step, even though she had no illusions that her mom would agree. Closing her laptop, she heaved a deep breath and wished for the millionth time she wasn't going home to an empty house.

On her way through the center, she said a few good-nights to the other staff. The place cleared out pretty quickly after five o'clock, particularly with the semester winding down. She stepped out onto the front porch and froze.

The man from lunch—Derek—stood leaning against the column by the steps. The way his arms crossed his chest made his biceps and shoulders appear huge, which made her notice that he'd changed clothes since lunch. The minute his playful gaze landed on her, he pushed off the column.

"Hi," he said, looking sheepish and way sexier than any man had a right to look. From the way his blue jeans hung on his lean hips to the way his navy button-down hugged the muscles of his shoulders and chest to how tall he was, this guy was sex on legs.

But what the hell was he doing here? And had he been waiting for her?

"Uh, hi," Emilie said, coming to a stop and brushing a strand of wavy hair out of her face.

He took a step closer, making her notice once more that he had a slight limp. "So, I know this might be a little forward," he said, dragging a hand over his hair like he might be nervous—and that actually made Emilie feel a little better. "But, uh, I've been kicking myself all afternoon."

"Kicking yourself about what?" she managed.

Derek smiled and stuck his hands in his pockets. "About not getting your phone number or asking you out."

Emilie blinked. Did he just say . . . "Really," she said, hearing the skepticism in her own voice. It wasn't that she didn't recognize the chemistry when they'd chatted, but the whole thing with her ex had given her a new sense of skepticism about men. She hated that, and didn't want it.

He nodded and shrugged. "Really."

She drank in his handsome face. Square jaw covered in a thin layer of brown scruff as if he hadn't shaved in a day or two. Full mouth that always looked seconds from breaking into a smile, just as it did now. Intense brown eyes with corners that crinkled when he smiled or laughed. Add all that to how helpful and friendly he'd been at lunch—not to mention what a good listener—and any woman would be lucky to have him show up on her doorstep.

"Well, uh, okay," she finally said, her head whirling from the surprise and the headiness of having a man like Derek show such interest.

"Okay?" he asked, stepping closer. "As in, you'll go out with me?"

Emilie laughed. The guy was kinda adorable in a totally masculine way.

When she didn't answer fast enough, he said, "I told you some things were harder to resist than others. Turns out you're one of them. I haven't been able to stop thinking about you, and about how much I wanted to keep talking to you."

Her heart raced and her stomach flipped. When was the last time a man had talked to her like this? One of the signs of Jack's infidelity that she'd missed or explained away had been the disappearance of the flirtatiousness they'd had earlier in their relationship. *Damn, it feels good to experience that again.*

And, truth be told, she'd been a little sad to see Derek leave the coffee shop.

Grasping the strap of her computer case with both hands, she tilted her head and looked at him. "I enjoyed talking to you, too," she said, her stomach giving a little flutter.

He grinned. "Well, then, we're agreed. We are damn fine conversationalists."

Emilie burst out laughing and nodded. "That we are."

Derek held out his hands. "So have dinner with me. Tonight. It's a beautiful Tuesday evening. Save me from wandering the streets of Annapolis all alone." His eyes sparkled with mischief, and his humor was infectious.

"Oh, well, I wouldn't want that," she said. Was she seriously considering this? The attention was totally flattering, but the whole thing with Jack had left her heart feeling more than a little beaten up. But Jack was the past. Was she going to let him rule her future, too?

"So, is that a yes?" he asked, stepping closer again, close enough that she could reach out and press her hand against the hard plane of his chest if she wanted. And truthfully, she wouldn't have minded touching Derek. Or him touching her. God, but she missed the warm, strong hold of a man's arms.

"Come on. We can walk downtown. I'll take you to your favorite place. Wherever you want. And then I'll walk you back to your car."

Butterflies whipped through her belly, but what did she have to lose? Except for a disastrous blind date one of her cousins had arranged, she really hadn't dated since she'd gotten divorced. What better opportunity would she have than with a man who was as gorgeous and fun as Derek? "You know what? I'd love to have dinner with you."

He clasped a big hand over his heart. "You've made me a happy man."

Smiling, she nodded. "Just let me throw some things in my car first?"

"Of course," he said. "May I?" Before she realized what he was doing, he gently removed the bags from her shoulder.

"Oh, you don't have to do that," she said as he was already putting the straps over his own shoulder.

"No," he said, looking down at her. "But I want to."

Emilie swallowed, sure she must be imagining the way his gaze seemed to flicker to her lips and away again. "Well, thanks."

"After you," he said. His fingertips lightly touched the small of her back as he guided her across the porch and down the steps.

I can't believe this is happening! I can't believe this is happening!

And, God, did he smell good. Clean and soapy and a little spicy. As they crossed to the parking lot, she took a deep breath and tried to hold it together. But on the inside, she was almost giddy.

"Mine's the white one," she said. At the car, she stowed her laptop in the trunk and double-checked that everything was locked up. "Ready."

"Great," he said. "Where would you like to go? What's your favorite place? Or a place you've been dying to try?"

"Well, you're the guest here. I feel like we should go somewhere you'd—"

"Nope. This is all about you."

Emilie hugged herself, loving what he'd said but also

feeling a little bit like she wanted to squirm. She wasn't used to putting herself first. "But . . . why?"

"Because when you said yes, you gave me what I wanted. So I'll be happy anywhere." He shrugged as if it were just fact.

Heat crawled up her face, and she wasn't usually a blusher. She'd never met a man who just put what he was feeling out there as directly as Derek. It was freaking refreshing. "Well, uh, okay," she said, unable to resist him. He'd been right—resistance *was* futile. At least where Derek was concerned. "There's a great seafood restaurant right across the water. A water taxi runs from City Dock to the restaurant every couple of minutes. How does that sound?"

"The girl, a great dinner, *and* a boat ride all in one night? Sounds fantastic." He winked and offered his arm.

Emilie laughed, realizing she did that a lot around him. It was almost like she couldn't be in his presence and not feel good. He just had a great energy about him. She looped her arm around his, bringing them closer and making it even more clear that he had a good six inches on her. Nothing like a big man to make a woman feel feminine.

"Lead the way," he said.

They walked across campus and into town, and all the while Emilie couldn't wrap her head around how her evening had gone from lonely dinner for one to fairy tale in ten minutes flat. Well, as close as she was getting to a fairy tale, anyway.

"Have you lived in Annapolis all your life?" Derek asked. "Seems like a cool place to live."

"Oh, it definitely is. I couldn't have been more ex-cited when I got the job here. But I grew up in Northern

Virginia, over in Fairfax. Still have family over there," she said. "How 'bout you?"

"Oh," he said, looking down the street. She would've sworn something uncomfortable flashed across his face, but then it was gone again and she wasn't sure. "I grew up in Ohio, but I haven't been back in years."

"No family left there?" she said, looking up at him.

He shook his head. "Never had a family."

Emilie's sandal snagged on an uneven brick and she stumbled, but Derek caught her against his chest.

She peered up at him, her heart quickening. "Thanks," she said.

"You okay?"

She nodded. "No family?"

Still holding her against him, Derek shook his head again. "Nope. Mother abandoned me when I was five. We'd been living with one of her friends and one night she didn't come home. Left a note saying she couldn't deal. Sure my mother would change her mind, her friend kept me around for a few weeks, but when my mother never returned, she turned me over to the cops who dumped me into the system. Mostly group homes after that."

"Oh," she said, the word so insignificant compared to what she felt and what he'd been through. The man was a stranger, but her heart still broke for him. Who did that to a child? And what must it have been like to grow up without . . . anyone? Emilie's mother was one of six siblings, so between her brother and all her aunts and uncles and cousins, her family was huge and loud and in each other's business all the freaking time. But she wouldn't want it any other way. Because the alternative—what Derek had experienced—must've been lonely and quiet and so, so solitary.

His dark eyes searched hers and scanned her face. "Yeah, so, it's just me," he said, his gaze landing on her lips.

Emilie swallowed and suddenly became aware of just how close they were. Her breast pressed against his chest. Her hand gripped his arm. Her hips were tight against his. Suddenly, the warmth of the early May evening flashed red hot.

God, she wanted . . . she wasn't even sure. Something. From him. With him. For him.

A car tore down the narrow street, throwing Emilie out of the moment. She pulled back and righted herself, but she didn't look away from his gaze. "Well, not tonight. Tonight it's the two of us," she said. "Remember? I'm saving you from wandering the streets of Annapolis all alone."

His lips slowly quirked up into a playful smile. "You sure are. Come on," he said, offering his arm again.

Silently now, they made their way to State Circle, where the big colonial statehouse towered over everything. On the far side of the circle, she led him down a hill toward Main Street, which was bustling with diners and window shoppers. This was the touristy part of Annapolis, and the streets, shops, and restaurants were always busy.

"The water taxi's just down at City Dock," she said, pointing toward the water.

Fifteen minutes later, they were on the squat red-and-white boat cruising across the harbor. The warm breeze tousled Emilie's hair until she turned her face into the wind, which forced her to look at her handsome and somewhat mysterious seatmate. Where in the world had Derek come from? It was like he'd dropped into her life out of the sky or something.

Maybe she was overthinking it.

He turned and smiled at her. "It's beautiful."

Her gaze scanned over the harbor, from the bustle of City Dock, to the stately buildings of the Naval Academy, to the three soaring radio towers that stood as sentinels over the open Chesapeake Bay. "Yes," she said. "It is." When she turned back to him, he was still staring at her.

"Yeah." He tucked a strand of hair behind her ear.

Before she even realized it, they were docking on the restaurant's pier.

"Chart House stop," the captain said.

"This is us," she said.

Derek held her hand while she stepped to the pier. Inside, they got a table with a wonderful view of the marina and harbor. Almost as if on cue, the lights in the room dimmed, highlighting the flickering of the votive candle on the table. Emilie looked across the table and smiled, still finding it a little hard to believe this was actually happening.

Nothing's really happening, Em. It's just dinner.
Right.

They ordered and the waitress brought their drinks and a big basket of fresh, warm rolls.

"You have to try these," Emilie said as she broke one apart, steam rising from within.

Derek took one and followed suit, slathering it with butter. "So tell me about this big family of yours. What's that like?"

Emilie debated where to begin. "Well, I have five pairs of aunts and uncles, one living pair of grandparents, and fifteen cousins, plus my brother and mom. Family get-togethers are big, loud, and involve lots and lots of food. And some occasional arguing. But it's mostly pretty awesome."

"Do you see them often?" he asked.

She nodded. "Pretty often. Growing up, our whole social life was our family, so we still get together for holidays and major birthdays or anniversaries. In fact, this Saturday I'm hosting about thirty of them at my place for an early Mother's Day celebration." Emilie chuckled. "Some of the cousins can't make it, so that number is smaller than usual." Smaller, but still big enough to mean she had quite a bit of prep work yet to do this week.

"Smaller?" he said, eyes going wide. "Damn. That's something."

"Yeah. And that's just my mom's side. We don't see my Dad's side much since my parents split when we were kids." Mostly because Dad was out of the picture. One day he'd been there, the next day he wasn't. No good-byes, no nothing. Her mom's family had stepped in and made sure they were taken care of, though. Just another reason Emilie cherished them so much.

Derek nodded. "How the heck do you do Christmas with all those people?" he asked, taking a drink of his water.

"Secret Santa. For as long as I can remember, we picked names. No one in my family had enough money to buy something for everyone." Except for Manny, apparently. She thought of the hundred-dollar bills still lying on her coffee table. She'd felt too weird about them this morning to put them in her wallet.

"Damn, your family is huge," he said. "Is it hard to manage all those people at get-togethers?"

"Oh, my God, sometimes it is. Aunt Sofia isn't getting along with Aunt Lucia, so they can't be seated together. Cousin Danna felt slighted because the last get-together wasn't at her house, but there aren't enough seats, so everyone needs to bring folding chairs with them. Or you need two platters of enchiladas when the Espinoza cousins are coming because those boys can *eat*."

"Wow," he said, smiling. "I can't imagine all that. But it sounds cool."

"It really is, in a totally neurotic kinda way." She laughed, thinking about all the crazy stories she had about her family. Like the picnic when the boys had all held a disgusting hotdog-eating contest and Manny had lost to Robbie Espinoza. A twelve-year-old Manny had accused Robbie of have an unfair advantage because the older boy could fit half a hot dog in his mouth at one time. The story was on the tip of her tongue to share, but the thought of sharing information about Manny brought his words slamming back into her mind. *Keep an eye out. And your mouth shut.*

Okay, see?

Now Manny's paranoia was wearing off on her. She sighed.

"Hey, you okay?" he asked.

"Yes," she said, forcing the BS with her brother out of her head. Just for tonight. "I'm great. Thanks again for inviting me to dinner."

"My pleasure, Emilie," he said as the waiter brought their food.

They ate and talked and laughed, and it was one of the nicest nights Emilie had had in a long, long time. She didn't feel like a divorcee or a woman who'd been cheated on or a woman who'd somehow deluded herself into thinking she had a happy marriage.

For once, she just felt like Emilie. Like a woman. Carefree and happy and enjoying the company of a man.

Looking across the table, she smiled at a story Derek

was telling about a three-legged puppy his friends had. And his obvious affection for the pup made her fall just that much more in like with the man.

And that made Emilie wonder. What did she want with this man? What was she even ready for?

She didn't know the answers to those questions. She only knew she didn't want this to be their only night.

Chapter 6

$\mathcal{M}$arz felt great.

And he also felt like the world's biggest asshole.

Great because he was having a fantastic time with Emilie. She was funny, warm, and genuine, the kind of woman you could talk to for hours about everything and anything and never once notice the passing time.

An asshole because the date was a pretense to keep her out of her house so the guys could clear out the stash Beckett had found.

Thing was, Marz had been *psyched* for the opportunity to spend more time with her. And he'd meant what he'd said—that he hadn't been able to stop thinking about her, and that her agreeing to go out with him made him happy. Not because it made his job easier, but because he was a man wanting to spend more time with a beautiful woman.

And, to be fair, he was a man wanting to know whether he'd really misjudged this woman. His brain knew Emilie had a pile of semiautomatics and heroin in her basement, but that *so* did not jive with how his gut read her. Elite operatives were trained to hone and trust their instincts. And right now, it was a freaking burr in his britches that he couldn't square what he knew with what he felt.

The waiter came and they ordered coffee and dessert.

"Would you excuse me for a moment?" she asked as she rose from her chair.

"Of course. But you better get back before that chocolate cake or I won't be held accountable for my actions." He winked.

She scooted around the table, rested a hand on his arm, and leaned down to whisper in his ear. "Never get between a woman and her chocolate, Derek."

He grinned and twisted in his seat to watch her walk away. Damn, if that dress didn't tease him with hints of her sweet curves. He sighed and pulled out his cell phone, which he'd put on silent before Emilie had walked out of her office. Three messages.

The first was from Beckett about fifteen minutes ago and gave him the all-clear to let Emilie return home whenever he was ready, then they'd rendezvous. The second one was from Charlie and reported an address on one of Garza's phone numbers, which was freaking fantastic news. And the third, also from Charlie, read, *Thought this might be important* and included a link. Marz clicked through to a news story.

"Aw, hell," he said to himself as his scalp prickled. Two execution-style murders in Baltimore City today, both of known members of the Church Gang. The media was speculating about a connection to the bombing of Confessions, one of the gang's known hangouts, and a shootout and car chase that had occurred that same night. His team had been involved in both of those ops, so Marz *knew* those two were connected. Question was, what were these executions about? And did they represent an opportunity or a threat to his guys and their mission? "No way that's not important," he murmured.

"Everything okay?" Emilie slipped back into her chair.

Marz looked up and smiled. *Damn, she's gorgeous.* She'd applied something glossy to her lips, and they were now a deep, shiny red that reminded him of a candy apple. *Bet she'd taste just as sweet.* "Yeah, just some bad stuff from the nightly news."

"Is there any other kind?" Emilie asked. "I almost hate to read the news anymore." She gestured toward his phone, which he slipped back into his pocket. "What happened?"

"Oh, uh, some murders in downtown Baltimore."

Just then, the waiter delivered their coffee and desserts—the chocolate cake for her, and key lime pie for him.

"Look at that," Marz said, "your chocolate cake is safe after all."

Emilie reached across the table and snatched his fork, then she sliced it into her dessert. "Never let it be said I'm not a giving person," she said, returning the fork to him with a big scoop of cake.

Marz shook his head and grinned. "Those words will never slip past my lips." He enjoyed the taste of her dessert, which was rich and creamy and delicious. He held his plate out to her. "Try mine?"

"Nope. I appreciate it, but I'm all about this cake."

She scooped up a piece and ate it. "Mmm," she moaned, her eyelids fluttering shut. Her face was a mask of pleasure, making Derek wonder what else might cause her to convey those sounds and that expression.

He shifted in his seat, heat spearing through him. "So, uh, I take it you like chocolate."

Her eyes flipped open. " 'Like' would be an understatement. Did you ever see the movie *Forrest Gump*? There's that scene where the guy is reciting, like, a hundred things you can make out of shrimp?" Marz nodded. "Well, that's me, except switch out the shrimp for chocolate. If it's chocolate, I will eat it or make it."

"Is that so?" he asked, loving learning all these little facets of her personality.

"Mmhmm," she said around another bite. "Ever had enchiladas with chocolate sauce?" Marz wrinkled his nose, and Emilie laughed. "It's called mole and you'd never know it has chocolate in it, but the Mexican chocolate gives it this deep and delicious flavor that is to *die* for." She licked chocolate icing off her fork, and Marz tried like hell not to stare. But, damn.

"If you say it's good, I would definitely try it," he said.

She tilted her head. "So, no one you know was hurt today, were they? In that news story, I mean."

"Thankfully, no," he said, his gut clenching at the thought. His team had experienced enough loss. He refused to lose even one more of the guys. Not if he could help it. Shoving the thoughts away, he took a bite of his pie and focused on enjoying the sweet-and-sour key lime. Fantastic graham cracker crust, too.

"There's a lot I love about Baltimore, but it's also such a troubled city," Emilie said. "I do pro bono counseling at a clinic up there once a week, and there's just some rough stuff."

Why wasn't he surprised to learn that about her? But how did pro bono counseling at an inner-city clinic square with being involved with drugs and guns? "Oh, yeah? That's really great of you, Emilie. Is it safe?" he asked.

"Yeah. I mean, it's certainly a change of pace from working with college students. And it's definitely different walking into a facility that keeps an armed guard on staff in the waiting room, but they're good people without sufficient access to care of all kinds. I'd do more if I could."

Their meal ended and Marz took care of the check over Emilie's protests, and then they went out to the pier to wait for the taxi. Darkness had brought a chill to the air, and Emilie hugged herself and rubbed her arms.

Marz found himself torn in two. On the one hand, he wanted to pull her in against his chest and warm her with his hands and heat. On the other, he hated to initiate anything physical with her, given the circumstances that had brought them together. He already felt like a big enough asshole, especially since he genuinely liked Emilie. She might've been a mission asset—no, she *was* a mission asset—but she was also someone Marz enjoyed immensely and at any other time would've wanted to pursue.

Maybe he could, down the road, assuming there was a good explanation for her stash *and* she could forgive the way and reason they'd met. But he couldn't get involved with anyone with so much shit on his plate, even if she didn't come with a dangerous brother who might or might not be gunning for them. Marz and the guys had to clear their names and settle the score with Church. And Marz also had to find a way to clear the air with Beckett, even if it meant tying him to a chair until the stubborn ass talked. Damn it all to hell.

"Do you want to wait inside?" he asked.

She smiled, and it almost looked like her teeth were chattering. "No, I'm fine. It'll be here soon."

As if her words conjured the water taxi, the boat's navigation lights came into view. Minutes later, it drew up along the pier and they went aboard.

The chill was worse when they got under way. Marz couldn't resist the urge to make her more comfortable. "Here," he said, projecting over the wind and the motor, "lean against me. I'll keep you warm."

Emilie curled into him, tucking her face against his neck and folding her hands against his chest.

And *damn* if that didn't feel good. There was just something about sheltering a woman's body with your own that Marz really dug. He wrapped his arms around her and pulled her in tighter.

This trip was longer than their earlier one as it stopped at several other piers. Emilie's arms below the short dress-sleeves were freezing. He rubbed her skin with his hands and just barely held back from pulling her into his lap so he could hold her even closer.

"You okay?" he asked with his lips against her ear.

Emilie tilted her head back. "Yes, thanks to you," she said, a small smile playing around her lips. She was so close . . .

Heat sparked in the air between them until Marz could no longer feel the breeze. All he knew was the thunder of his heart, the rush of his blood, and the fucking urgent desire to taste her, kiss her, claim her.

The little voice in the back of his head reciting the long list of reasons why any of that would be a bad freaking idea? He kicked that mother into a dark, distant corner.

Marz felt her answering desire in the way her pulse ticked up under his hands and against his chest, and saw it in the way her gaze flickered to his lips and away again. She wanted him, too.

Sonofabitch. He leaned down, bringing their lips closer. Her breath caught and her fingers curled into his shirt between two of the buttons as if she was pulling him down, too. Everything else died away—the boat, the wind, the other people. Until it was just them and the closeness of his mouth to hers.

"Derek," she whispered.

It was the pleading sound of his name on her lips that did it.

Whatever had held him back in the seconds before she'd spoken disappeared in that instant. His lips brushed hers. Just a soft dragging of skin on skin that was somehow sexier for how tentative and incomplete it was, especially when she gasped and pressed herself closer, like she was hungry for it.

Jesus. Marz certainly was.

He captured her top lip between his and tugged, just the littlest bit. Continuing to tease her—and himself—he dragged his lips over her cheek, her eye, her nose, before he came back to her lips again.

And then he stopped teasing. Marz kissed her, softly but thoroughly, not waiting long at all before he gave in to the urge to taste and swept his tongue into her mouth. She tasted of chocolate and woman and a sweetness he couldn't get enough of. He'd already been hard before their lips ever met, but now he was like steel. Emilie was right there with him, surrendering to the kiss but giving back everything he gave her.

Damn, it was a good thing they were in public, because Marz didn't want to stop.

As if on cue, they pulled up to their mooring at City Dock, and the boat bumped against the pilings. They broke apart, breathing hard and looking at one another as if neither quite knew what had just happened, or what would happen next.

Marz guided her off the boat and pulled her in against his side with an arm around her shoulders. They didn't talk, but it wasn't uncomfortable. The tension roiling between them was purely sexual in nature, and Marz didn't know where the hell to go with that. Not with the falsehoods between them, not when he wasn't sure where she stood or what she was involved in, not when she didn't know their meeting hadn't been an accident.

She shivered and tucked herself closer to him. Marz needed to fix that problem now. He pulled her into the first souvenir shop they came to. "What's your favorite color?"

"What?" she asked with a suspicious smile. "Why?"

"Just tell me," he said.

"Okay, it's turquoise. Now can I know why?" she asked, laughing.

If he told her his plan, she would protest. So Marz kept quiet as he scanned the racks and zeroed in on a target—a turquoise blue hoodie that spelled out Annapolis in both letters and nautical flags. Perfect. He grabbed one that looked about the right size. "Come on," he said, grasping her hand in his.

"What are you doing?" she said, following him.

"You'll see," he said. "Oh, wait." He stopped over a table of T-shirts. If *that* wasn't freaking Jeremy . . .

"I have a friend who collects dirty and funny T-shirts. Whatd'ya think?" He held one up to her that had a picture of a black lab with a crab in its mouth.

She smiled and read aloud: "Our dog has crabs. Dirty Dog Crab Shack. Cold beer and hot legs. Annapolis, 1649."

"Very cute," she said, "but who's the other one for?"

He threw Jer's T-shirt over his arm, grabbed her hand again, and pulled her in so he could whisper into her ear. "You, babe." Then he kissed her cheek and led her to the register.

"But . . . we'll be back to the car in a few minutes," she said as the teenager checked him out.

"And by then you'll be freezing. Besides, how can you deny me my God-given American right to spend money on souvenirs?" He handed the guy the money and accepted his change. Ripping the tag off her jacket, he held it open for her. "Madam," he said with a bow.

Looking like she still wanted to argue, she slipped it on, and the way she snuggled into it filled him with all kinds of satisfaction.

"Thanks," he said to the guy as he grabbed the bag with Jeremy's shirt. They made their way back out to the street. "See, now you can enjoy the walk."

"Well, that might've been the sweetest thing anybody's ever done for me," she said, squeezing his hand.

Marz narrowed his gaze and hoped that wasn't true, because that had been some basic decency right there. What kind of guys was she seeing, anyway? His gut clenched, both because his kneejerk reaction to the thought had been to dislike the idea of her seeing *anyone* else. Strongly. Followed closely by the interjection of cold-hard reality that it wasn't any of his business. It *couldn't be* any of his business.

They returned to her car far too quickly for Marz's taste, because he wasn't sure where this left them. This *should be* good-bye, but a part of Marz sure as shit didn't want it to be.

Emilie leaned back against the driver's door and looked up at him. The turquoise really was pretty on her. "I can't thank you enough for tonight. It was a wonderful, unexpected surprise and I really enjoyed myself."

Marz stepped closer until he was just shy of touching her. He leaned a hand against the top of the car. "Me too." He swallowed hard and looked down, trying to restrain himself from taking anymore. But that was really freaking hard when the invitation was so plain in her eyes. He looked back up again and met her waiting gaze. "When do you do your pro bono work this week?" he asked against his better judgment.

"Thursday," she said.

He leaned his other hand against the car and boxed her in. The tension and desire were so thick between them, he could've cut it with a knife. "Thursday," he said. "Maybe we could"—*What the hell are you doing?*—"get together after you're done."

She smiled and licked her lips. "I'd like that." Tentatively, she brought her hand up to his chest. He nearly groaned as her heat seeped through the cotton.

"Should we trade numbers?" he managed. In his mind's eye, he saw Beckett's gaze narrowing at him, silently asking him what the fuck he was doing.

Emilie nodded, and they broke apart a little as they grabbed their cells and took turns reciting numbers. And then he leaned in to kiss her cheek. He meant to be good, he really did. But her scent and her softness and her warmth drew him in. Her arms came around him and his body trapped hers against the car.

There was nothing teasing or tentative about this kiss. Marz kissed her like a starving man at a feast—devouring, claiming, commanding. She moaned into his mouth and drove her fingers into his hair. When she tilted her hips into his erection, he grabbed her ass in one hand and held her tighter to him.

He had to stop this. Now. Before things went any further. Because, God forbid, if she invited him to leave with her, he was going to get in that fucking car.

And wouldn't that be a damned mess.

He broke away from her lips and they were both breathing hard, chests heaving. Kissing her forehead, he whispered. "Be safe going home." And then he forced himself to step away.

Emilie stood there for a second like she couldn't move, and then she finally said good-bye and got in. She gave a little wave before she backed out, and then Marz was staring at her taillights as they crossed the lot and turned out onto the street.

Marz scrubbed his hands over his face and hair. "Fuck," he bit out. This thing with Emilie already *was* a mess. *Fuckfuckityfuck.*

He retrieved his cell and texted Beckett. *What's the extraction plan?*

Just waiting for your ass to text me, dickhead, came Beckett's reply.

On top of everything else tonight, Marz couldn't help but laugh.

Aw, you love me so hard, he texted back.

No response. Marz could almost hear Beckett cussing him out.

My ass and dickhead are in the college parking lot, waiting just for you. Marz sniggered.

Rot in hell, was the sum total of his response.

Chuckling, Marz walked out to the street and found a spot in the shadows to wait. Leave it to fucking Beckett Murda to kill his erection and make him laugh in one fell swoop.

Now the question was how much did he share about what'd happened with Emilie? Or the fact that he'd made plans to see her again?

Chapter 7

"Gimme the rundown," Marz said once he and Beckett were on the highway back to Baltimore.

Beckett's icy blue eyes flashed toward him, then away again. "Thirty bricks of heroin. Eighteen semiautomatics. And twenty grand in cash. We replaced it all with fake stand-ins to make it look undisturbed."

"Jesus," Marz bit out as he scrubbed his hands over his face. Once again, that did *not* square with the woman he'd spent a big chunk of the day and night with. "What does it mean?" he asked. "For argument's sake, let's say Manny Garza stashed it there for safekeeping. That amount of product is the kind of thing a big-time distributor would have."

"Like Church," Beckett said.

"Exactly. So is Garza freelancing or hiding assets until the shit stops hitting the fan in Churchland?" Marz didn't too closely examine his motivation for wanting Manny to have been the Garza sibling responsible for the stash. Not that he really had to. Damn it all to hell.

"Million-dollar question," Beckett said.

Marz crossed his arms. "Yeah."

Beckett stared straight out the windshield. "Well, as soon as we get back and briefed, the team's raiding Garza's address tonight. So maybe we'll be able to just ask him."

"Fuckin' A," Marz said, although the little bit of conflict slinking through his brain revealed that he'd gone and gotten all *involved*. And wasn't that a smack in the ass. Even if Garza was a dangerous, corrupt, drug-dealing mercenary, he was still Emilie's big brother. The way she talked about the importance and meaning of her family, Marz had no doubt that taking Manny down would tear Emilie up. And he hated that for her.

"How 'bout you? Learn anything?" Beckett asked after a while.

Oh, that could be answered so many different ways. Marz sighed. "I *thought* I'd learned that Emilie Garza was squeaky clean. Not a thing about her read suspicious all day. I didn't get access to her cell, but I did learn she's having a big family get-together at her house on Saturday," Marz said, his thoughts churning.

"Built in chance to grab Garza if we don't manage it sooner."

"Let's hope we do." For lots of reasons. Not only didn't they have all week to nab him, not with Church looking for them, too, but no way did Marz want to bring a shit storm down on the heads of a bunch of innocent civilians. No way did he want to do that to Emilie.

The rest of the trip back to the Rixeys' Hard Ink

building was quiet, and Marz was glad for it. Glad to have the time and space to put his house in order before they were back in the thick of it again.

When they returned to the sprawling red-brick warehouse that had been their temporary home for the past week and a half, most of the group was hanging around mission HQ—also known as Marz's computer station—and waiting for them in the gym. Nick and Becca, former teammate Shane McCallan and his girl, Sara Dean; and Easy and Sara's younger sister, Jenna, all stood in a circle talking.

Marz's gaze scanned the group. Blond-haired Becca was Charlie's older sister, Nick Rixey's new girlfriend and, mostly important, an ER nurse. Between her and Shane, who'd been trained as their intelligence officer and a backup medic for their A-team, their ragtag group had enough medical expertise in-house to deal with all but the most critical cases. Damn reassuring on a night like tonight, when they might encounter just about anything.

Next to Shane stood Easy, being his usual reserved self but also looking a bit more relaxed than he'd been in days. Marz's stomach twisted as his memory replayed the pain in Easy's voice from just a few nights ago, as he'd confessed to having suicidal thoughts. Scared the shit out of Marz, because he couldn't afford to lose one more of these guys. Not after he'd just gotten them back. None of them could—and now that they knew the beast he'd been battling all on his own, they'd damn sure get him the help he needed.

"Hey," Marz said, shaking hands with each of the men in turn. Becca gave him a hug that made him smile. He'd liked her from the beginning, but the minute she'd apologized to the team for her father's actions and promised to help them right the wrong done against them, they'd become loyal friends forever.

As someone who hadn't really had a family until he unexpectedly found it in the Army, he knew exactly what that kind of loyalty meant. And Becca had put her actions where her words were every single day since. Not to mention her money, since she'd funded a lot of their operation with her lying father's life insurance money. Talk about your ironies. So, she was the real deal.

Like Emilie.

Aw, hell no. Not doing this right now.

Right.

"Good work down there, man," Nick said. "You two found some damn fine intel."

"Not to mention the mother lode of assets," Easy said, rubbing a hand over his dark head.

Nick nodded. "It'll allow us to get totally squared away with the Raven Riders and pull the Hard Ink building off the table as collateral. We've set up a meet with the club's leaders for tomorrow."

"That's good," Marz said. The Raven Riders were a local outlaw motorcycle club that had helped them with two ops against the Church Gang last Friday night. With the club's assistance, they'd been able to rescue Jenna Dean from Church's number two, take out the gang's main headquarters at the Confessions strip club, and intercept a guns deal such that his team had walked away with both the guns and the cash. It had been a triple whammy of awesomesauce for them, and the trifecta of bad luck for Church. And none of it would've been possible without the Ravens. But they didn't ride for free.

The door to the cavernous gym opened and closed

on the other side of the room, and Marz turned to find Charlie and Nick's younger brother, Jeremy, crossing the room, the little German shepherd puppy named Eileen dancing at their feet. The pup was an amputee just like himself, and a sweet little thing, too, even when she was being a monster.

In typical Jeremy fashion, he wore a raunchy T-shirt. This one was white with black writing and a hand pointing downward. It read, "May I suggest the sausage?" Marz sniggered as the two guys joined the group.

"Welcome home," Jeremy said, clasping Marz's hand and then Beckett's. Over the course of the previous almost two weeks, Marz and Jeremy had grown fairly tight. Jeremy didn't have the arms training to assist with their missions in the field, but he'd been a quick study where their computer and communication needs had been concerned, so the two of them had spent a lot of time together as Marz brought Jer up to speed.

Marz handed Jeremy a plastic bag. "Got you something," he said.

Jeremy tugged the gray shirt out of the bag and held it up. He chuckled and his pale green eyes flashed between the shirt and Marz. "Nice pick, my friend. Very nice." He turned the shirt around so everyone else could read it, showing off the N-O-R-E-G-R-E-T tattoo inked onto the backs of his fingers at the same time. Everyone chuckled.

"I still can't get over the sausage shirt," Jenna said, tucking a strand of long red hair behind her ear. Her other hand held Easy's.

Fact that three of Marz's teammates had found people they cared about in the midst of this clusterfuck had Marz thinking about his evening with Emilie. Damn it all to hell.

"Where do you even find a shirt like that?" Jenna asked to more laughter.

"Tip of the iceberg, Jenna. Trust me," Becca said as she threw a smile at Jeremy.

Marz nodded at Jenna, truly admiring how she was coming out of her shell. After being kidnapped, drugged, beaten, and bruised, he could hardly blame her for holding back and keeping to herself at first. But as the bruises around her eye and mouth faded from purple and red to that odd yellow that signified healing, so did her shyness. In fact, she seemed even more outgoing than Sara, her big sister.

"Becca's right," Jeremy said with a wink. Always the flirt.

"Charlie," Becca said. "What the hell are *you* wearing?" All eyes turned to the quiet blond standing beside Jer.

Charlie glared at Jeremy. "I told you I should've put this on inside out."

"No, man. That's a classic." Jer crossed his arms. "Ignore them."

Sighing, Charlie looked at his sister. "I got tired of wearing scrubs and sweats everyday so Jeremy lent me some clothes." His dark red T-shirt had a drawing of a smiling fire extinguisher that said, "I put out." More laughter went around the circle. Since both of the Merritt siblings had been attacked and their houses had been ransacked, they'd been forced to flee without any belongings, and Charlie hadn't been well enough after his rescue to go buy anything new.

"If this means we get twice as many dirty tees a day," Jenna said, "I totally approve."

Laughing, Nick rubbed his hands together. "All right, everyone. As entertaining as my brother's T-shirt collection is, let's get down to business. We have an op to plan and it's getting late."

THREE HOURS LATER, the team—with a little help from some allies—had taken up positions around a three-story, red-brick row house in the Franklin Square neighborhood of Baltimore. Shane, Marz, and Beckett were set up in the narrow street out back, while Nick, Ike Young, and Miguel Olivero were set up in the shadows along the side. All six would enter and clear the building. Ike was Jeremy's employee at Hard Ink and a leader of the Raven Riders. Miguel was Nick's police-officer-turned-PI friend. Both men had helped the team before. Easy had taken up a sniper position somewhere on the other side of the street to make sure no one escaped out the front, and Jeremy was waiting with a van two blocks away for the signal to haul their asses out of there.

Their objective: capture Manny Garza.

The quiet street hosted a mix of dilapidated and renovated houses, the kind of place where suspicious noises outside had neighbors drawing curtains closed and shutting off lights. Perfect for their needs. Garza's row house fell somewhere in the middle. Not boarded up but not well taken care of, either.

"Let's get some readings, gentlemen," came Nick's voice through Marz's earpiece.

"Roger that," Beckett said.

Crouching in the shadows of an overflowing Dumpster, Marz and Beckett used the cover of darkness to scan the building for occupants. Better than going in blind. Earphones on, Marz scanned for voices while Beckett used his camera to scan for the interruptions to WiFi waves that would represent bodies and movement.

"Basement and first floor appear clear," Beckett said in a low voice, tucking the device back into his bag. "But I can't get a good read on the top floor from here."

"All's quiet," Marz said, repacking his equipment.

"Prepare for breach and CQC," came Nick's voice. CQC. Close-quarters combat. Something they'd trained for and used extensively in Afghanistan. But Marz sure as shit never thought he'd be using it here at home.

"Got ya covered," Marz said to Beckett as he made his way to the back door. An expert at all things mechanical, Beckett made lock picking look like he was swiping a hot knife through soft butter.

"I'm in," Beckett said a moment later.

"Go on my count," Nick said.

Marz readied his weapon. Beside him, Shane did the same. Marz's body was a coil ready to spring.

"Three, two, one, go."

Because they had more experience, Beckett, Marz, and Shane entered the breach first and quickly cleared the first hallways, doorways, and rooms. Speed, thoroughness, and decisiveness characterized their movements. They stood ready to use gunfire or other aggressive means to control the space and subdue any defenders, but as long as things remained quiet, so would they. No sense alerting the neighbors who might either alert the authorities or, worse yet, the local thugs—which might just include the Churchmen. And wouldn't that be a pain in the ass.

While Ike and Miguel stood sentry over the first floor and covered their sixes, the other four cleared the basement. They repeated the procedure on the upper level, too, all the while Marz's heart thundered in anticipation of capturing Garza. Problem was his instincts jangled that their efforts were a bust because this house, in fucking typical Garza fashion, was a ghost town.

When Marz and Beckett had secured the top floor, they turned to look at each other. Beckett's scowl appeared as pissed as Marz felt.

"Goddamnit," Beckett bit out, starting down the steps.

"Zero unfriendlies," Nick said, frustration clear in his voice. "Split up and let's find something to make this worth our while, gentlemen."

"Might as well stay up here with me," Marz said to Beckett's back. The guy turned around and came back up.

Finding something useful to them was either going to be really easy or really hard, depending on how you looked at it. Because the place didn't appear well inhabited even though there were signs of life. A *very few* signs of life. So searching wouldn't take long, but they weren't likely to find much, either.

Downstairs, Marz had noticed relatively new cable jacks in the living room that proved the place had been used and improved recently, but there were no electronics. In fact, the room boiled down to a ratty old couch, two crates for a coffee table, and an ancient standing lamp. The dining room was empty, and the kitchen had a microwave and little else.

Upstairs, all of the rooms were empty except one— the rear bedroom contained a cot. Not a bed, but a standard barracks cot like the kind they'd had during training. One square and one oblong disturbance to the dust on the bedroom floor proved something had recently sat there, but no more. And the closet was empty, too.

Marz flashed a light in the heating vent, felt around

the inside of the closet for any hidden panels, and got down on hands and knees to look at the bottom of the cot. No goodies anywhere.

As he stood, he stared at the cot for a long minute, and got the gut feeling that Manny Garza was one of those guys who couldn't assimilate back to civilian life. The sparseness of the house, the very presence of the cot, the square corners and taut pull of the Army-issue blanket, all spoke of a man who hadn't let go. Who maybe even *couldn't* let go.

It wasn't uncommon. After years of living within the regimentation and command structure of the military, and after a long time of enduring high-stress, crisis situations, the loosey-goosey relaxation of normal life just grated on some men, leaving them unable to train themselves out of warrior mode and into civilian mode. Add to that the fact that images of wartime experiences often played like a nonstop horror movie on the inside of your eyelids—no matter how well adjusted you were—and some soldiers found themselves wishing to go back or unable to return despite the fact that their boots were firmly planted on American soil.

These kinds of adjustment issues were often tied up with undiagnosed PTSD or other disorders. Marz had seen it again and again among the men and women he met in the hospital, at PT, and even at his prosthetist's office.

And thinking that Manny Garza might not only be neck-deep in drug, gun, and human trafficking on behalf of one or more criminal organizations but also not quite right in the head? That didn't bode well for them.

Emilie.

Oh, shit.

How much did she know about her brother's mental health? She was a psychologist after all. Surely, she'd recognize the signs? But would she help him? Protect him? Turn him away? And what would she do if she both knew he wasn't well *and* knew what he was involved in.

Damn, it would be nice if every time they learned something it didn't raise a half-dozen new questions.

Marz peeked into the bathroom—the shower, the linen closet, and the medicine cabinet were all empty. One long-dry towel hung on the back of the door. Just for shits and giggles, he lifted the lid on the toilet tank to make sure nothing had been hidden inside. And that was a big fat no.

One thing was clear. Garza had gone ghost. Recently, if Marz had to guess. Maybe after Friday night when Church's empire went down in flames? No one left here who could say for sure.

"Got something," Shane said through his earpiece. "Kitchen."

Marz and Beckett double-timed it downstairs and joined the group congregated in the small space.

"Gun-cleaning kit," Shane said, waving to the tools and bottles he'd spread out on the counter. He tapped his finger against a dirty black cloth. "But this is what interested me," Shane said, and he unfolded the fabric.

It wasn't a cloth, but a T-shirt. Something that became more apparent as Shane stretched out the chest part of the fabric to reveal a logo.

A medieval helmet in profile with the words *Seneka Worldwide Security* stacked beside the image.

"Sonofabitch," said Nick. "Garza *is* SWS."

Seneka Worldwide Security was a defense contractor and security services provider known for recruiting SpecOps guys upon retirement or discharge. And a corporation that ran some sorta business through Pier 13 at Baltimore's marine terminal, where the Church Gang, including Garza, had conducted a major drug deal—not to mention some downright sickening human trafficking—not even a week ago.

"Or he was," Marz said. They'd suspected Church's use of that pier wasn't coincidental and might've been evidence of a tie between the gang and the contractor, but now they had proof. Not definitive, but as close as they were going to get. Garza either was or had been an SWS operative.

And that gave them a direct connection between the Church Gang, the heroin trade, Afghanistan, and Army Special Forces personnel. Moreover, Seneka was one of only four providers the Defense Department contracted for equipment, materiel, and services in support of counternarcotics activities in Afghanistan. In country, Seneka mentored Afghan officials in drug interdiction and counternarcotics, and trained the police in counternarcotics. Some of the same kind of work their SF team had done. Which meant they had access to product. Lots of access.

Damnit. Seneka was right in the middle of it all.

"Garza being SWS makes him doubly useful," Beckett said. "First, because he'd be able to identify the players on the other side of that drug deal. Second, because he'd be able to provide proof that Seneka formed the definitive connection between the Churchmen's heroin trade and Afghanistan."

"Was just thinking the same damn thing," Marz said, his brain reeling. They'd just significantly narrowed the degrees of separation between the Church Gang's activities and the ambush and frame job that had killed their friends, ended their careers, and tarnished their honor.

It was crystal fucking clear that people involved in counternarcotics—like their own commander—had been and likely still were taking the Afghani drugs that were supposed to be destroyed and selling them abroad, including back in the States. Given the charges of corruption that Congress, the media, and foreign governments often leveled against SWS, it wasn't a stretch to imagine them engaging in a little extracurricular activity. Especially of the incredibly lucrative kind.

Seneka operatives weren't called mercenaries for nothing.

Nick leaned back against the counter. "The operatives who work for Seneka make the Churchmen look like kids playing cowboys and Indians. Shit."

"Out of the frying pan and into the fire," Shane said. "You know, every time we peel back a layer of this onion, the sting is going to get worse and worse, right?"

Blowing out a long breath, Nick nodded. "Bring the shirt. Let's clear out of here and take this conversation back to Hard Ink. We've got some strategizing to do."

Chapter 8

Emilie sat at her kitchen table in a shaft of early morning sunlight and stared at her cell phone. Time to call her mother about Manny. She didn't want to put it off any longer, not with the party looming and Manny's behavior on the decline.

She'd meant to do it last night, but the unexpectedly wonderful surprise of her date with Derek had taken up the whole evening, and it had been way too late to catch her mother by the time Emilie had gotten home.

So worth it. Her night with Derek had been—she smiled and sipped her coffee—so amazing. The conversation had been great, the food had been fantastic, and the kissing—*Oh*—the kissing had been bone-meltingly good. The kind of kissing that made the world spin around you until it entirely faded away. The kind of kissing that left you hot and breathless and dying for more. The kind of kissing that made you wet just from the shifting press of lips and tongue and teeth.

The kind of kissing that had almost convinced Emilie to throw caution to the wind and invite Derek home.

A tingle ran over Emilie's skin just thinking about it.

Because, man, it had been *so long*. Too long. Even before Emilie had learned about Jack's infidelity, things had slowed down between them. A lot. Turns out that was because he was getting it elsewhere.

No, don't ruin your Derek buzz by thinking of Jack. Right.

Because Emilie was totally buzzing. She might just float through her whole day.

And there were so many other things about the date that had made it great, too. That he'd cared what she wanted to do. How he'd asked about her and really listened to what she had to say. That he'd held her and bought her a jacket when she'd been cold.

That he'd asked her out again.

Well, at least they'd talked about meeting after she finished at the Baltimore clinic tomorrow night. But they hadn't actually made any specific plans.

If he didn't call or text her, would she call him? Emilie's shoulders fell at the thought.

No, don't second-guess it. Derek hasn't given you any reason not to believe what he'd said. He'll call.

Looking at her phone again, Emilie sighed. If she put off this call with her mother any longer, she'd be late for her first patient. On the screen of her cell, she pressed her mother's number and placed the phone to her ear.

When her mother answered, Emilie's stomach went for a loop-the-loop. Ridiculous to be thirty years old and afraid to tell your mother something, but it was only because of how much Mama adored Manny. Years ago when their father split, Manny had stepped up to fill as much of the man's shoes as was possible for a sixteen-year-old. Emilie adored him for that, too. And always would.

She and her mother made the usual small talk and discussed Saturday's party plans, and then Emilie couldn't put it off another minute. "So, Mama, I need to talk to you about Manny."

"Oh, Emmy, not this again," her mother said. "I'm not sure why you—"

"He pulled a gun in my house," Emilie said, going the direct route to get her mother's attention.

"He . . . what? Well . . . there had to be . . . a good reason?" Sometimes people wanted something to be true so badly that they'd find a way to read any situation to make it that way.

"Mama, it was because the UPS truck had pulled up in front of my house. Manny thinks someone is after him—"

"Has he called the police? Who is after him?"

Emilie dropped her head into her hand and braced her elbow on the table. "*No one* is after him. That's the point. He only thinks there is. It's pretty classic paranoia."

Long pause. "He's under a lot of stress, Emilie. That's all." Her mother sniffed.

Choosing her words carefully, Emilie said, "I'm sure that's true, but I don't think that's all that's going on. Mama, he was in the Army for twelve years. He fought multiple tours of combat and must've seen so many horrible things. The Army has a huge incidence of depression and PTSD, and he's showing the signs. He needs help."

"Emilie," she said, and she could almost see her mother shaking her head. "I will talk to him."

No. Not this time. Her mother had said this before to get Emilie to back off. And though she'd never go as far as to call her mother a liar, she couldn't help but doubt that those conversations had ever taken place. "That's not enough. Not this time."

"Em—"

Emilie closed her eyes and rubbed her forehead. "He grabbed me, Mama. He shoved me up against a wall. He destroyed my property. And when I got mad about it, he got in my face and yelled while holding a knife. Does that sound like our Manny?" When her mother didn't answer, Emilie pressed. "Does it?"

A troubled sigh came down the line. "No, *mija*. No, it doesn't. What is it you want to do?"

It was a bittersweet victory at best, because Emilie did not relish the thought of having Manny picked up and hauled into an ER against his will. She explained the emergency evaluation petition and what it would unleash, and she didn't miss for a second the way her mother's breath caught when she'd explained that Manny could be held involuntarily for several days, longer if the medical staff agreed he was a danger to himself or others.

"Please, wait, Emilie. Let me see him. Let me talk to him," her mother pleaded.

"Mama—"

"Saturday. I'll see him at your house on Saturday. Let me see him with my own eyes before you do anything. It will kill him, Emilie." The strain in her mother's voice made the backs of her own eyes prick.

Blowing out a long breath, Emilie nodded. "Okay,

Saturday. But I'm filing the paperwork after that. If he hurts himself or someone else—"

"He won't. Okay, but he won't," she said.

Their good-bye was a tense, awkward affair. The phone sagged in Emilie's hand. Well, it had gone better than it could've but not as good as she'd wanted. Waiting made her uneasy, but Saturday was only a few days away, so Emilie could live with the compromise. She hoped. Boy, this was sure gonna make the party lots of fun, wasn't it?

She just barely resisted banging her head against the table. Instead, she got up, placed her mug in the sink, and grabbed her things for the day.

The morning sped by with a string of appointments. When lunch came, Emilie was almost tempted to walk down to the coffee shop again, but she didn't have the time today. She unpacked the lunch she'd made and ate at her desk while she surfed the internet. On Facebook, a news story one of her clinic colleagues had posted caught her eye: "Two Killed in Suspected Rival Gang Shooting."

Emilie recognized the story as the one Derek had mentioned last night, and she clicked through to read.

Two men were gunned down in separate incidents yesterday in what Baltimore City Police suspect were rival gang shootings. Police are still identifying the victims, whose bodies were found on East Preston Street in the Berea neighborhood and near Brehms Lane in Belair, both on the eastern side of Baltimore City.

A suspect is wanted for questioning in connection with the Belair murder, and is described as a Hispanic male, aged 28 to 35, with black hair

pulled back in a ponytail. Anyone with informa-
tion should call BCP.

A source at the police department said authori-
ties are speculating that yesterday's execution-
style murders are related to last Friday night's
explosion at the Confessions strip club on Weston
Avenue, a known hangout of the Church Gang.
Louis Jackson, director of the city's task force on
gang violence, said, "It's not uncommon to see a
series of high-profile gang-related incidents occur
when the power of the dominant gang wanes or ap-
pears poised to do so. This could be other groups
making their move."

Investigations into the city's gang violence es-
timate that the Church Gang is responsible for
nearly one-half of all gang-related murders in the
city and 23 percent of its overall murder rate. . .

And *this* was why Emilie hated reading the news. She
still did it, of course, but it was more than a little unset-
tling to hear that the city she worked in once a week
might be in the middle of escalating gang warfare. Not
that she was really surprised. She worked with patients
at the clinic who dealt with or were victims of the city's
gangs all the time. If not as victims of violence, then as
victims of the heroin addiction these gangs made possible. It wasn't for nothing that Baltimore was known
as the heroin capital of the United States. Government
agencies estimated that as many as ten per cent of the
city's residents were addicts.

Heartbreaking, really. Which was why Emilie gave
her time at the clinic up there once a week. She'd do
more if she could.

Knock, knock.

Emilie looked up from her computer to find Carol, the office receptionist, standing in the doorway. "Your one o'clock is here," Carol said.

Quickly cleaning off her desk, Emilie nodded. "Give me two minutes and send her in?"

"You got it."

The afternoon went by in a blur, a blessing when she had things she didn't want to think about. And then at five o'clock on the dot, her cell buzzed an incoming text message. Emilie retrieved her phone from her top desk drawer.

Derek.

Her smile was instantaneous.

This time last night I was on your front porch so I thought it would be a good time to text. ;)

She laughed, and was it any coincidence that the last time she'd done so, she'd been with him? Emilie debated how to reply and finally decided to just go for it: *Perfect timing, though I preferred you on my front porch . . .* Stomach flipping, she pressed Send and grinned like an idiot while she waited for his response.

Her cell buzzed again. *Me too, which is why I'm texting. Would either Little Italy or Inner Harbor work for you tomorrow night?*

They made their plans for a quiet little place with absolutely divine food in Little Italy. He'd offered to pick her up, and, though her instincts told her that was probably fine, she decided to meet him there instead.

She packed up her belongings to leave. And even though she was going home to an empty house, she was happy. Because Derek had given her something to look forward to, and Emilie hadn't had that with a man in a long, long time.

MARZ RECLINED IN his chair, laced his hands behind his head, and basked in the news that he was definitely going to see Emilie tomorrow night. Because that was one of the few things that had gone right about his day.

This morning, they'd debriefed last night's op and brainstormed scenarios for dealing with Seneka. The possibility existed, of course, that Garza was working on his own, but they had to plan as if they might be up against the whole corporate beast. Plus, something Garza had said that first night they'd seen him at the drug deal argued in favor of him not working solo. When the leader of the other side of the deal asked if Garza was staying with the Churchmen, Garza had replied that he had to because someone wanted him to keep an eye on business with Church.

At the time, their team had no idea who that someone might be. Now that they knew that Garza was SWS, that organization was a prime possibility.

And that was some bad frickin' news, because Seneka operatives were highly trained, well-funded, and not too concerned about scruples, morals, or ethics. When it came to getting a job done, the ends justified the means every damn time.

Marz and the guys knew that firsthand, since they'd been caught up in someone's "means" a year ago. If Seneka was mixed up in the ambush that killed half their team, like they believed, they already knew exactly what the organization was willing to do.

And now everyone was counting on Marz.

Because the last thing Nick had said as this morning's meeting ended was, "We can't consider going after Seneka until we know what's on that chip. We need all the available intel in hand and we need it yesterday. Can you do it, Marz?"

Of course, he'd said yes. What other answer was there when their lives, their reputations, and their honor were on the line?

Nick was talking about a tiny microchip they'd found a few days before, hidden inside a teddy bear that belonged to Becca. Her father—their commander—had sent her the bear months before his death, and the chip was just one in a string of mysteries they had yet to solve.

Correction: that *Marz* had yet to solve.

Which meant it was time to get back to work. Marz sat up in his chair just as Charlie and Becca walked into the gym.

"Yo," Marz said, giving a wave.

"I come bearing gifts," Charlie called. "Or, actually, *we* come bearing gifts, since—" He lifted the hand wrapped in gauze. The bandages hid the fact that he'd lost two of his fingers when the Church Gang had taken him hostage two weeks before. The gang had done such a butcher job on the digits that Becca had been forced to call in a few of her EMT friends to perform essentially a field operation to prevent infection.

"Prezzies are my favorite. Whatcha got for me?" Marz asked as they crossed the room.

Charlie and Becca walked up to the desk and each settled a drink and a plate with a giant sandwich and chips on the plywood surface. "Food," Charlie said. "I was starving, so I figured you might like a break, too."

"Aw, dude, you are my favorite person right now," Marz said, his stomach growling at the sight of the food.

"You realize you say that to everyone who makes you food, right?" Becca said with her hands on her hips.

Marz chuckled and winked. "I'm easy like that.

But, thank you, too, Becca. You're my other favorite person."

Shaking her head, she turned away and started back across the room. "Be good, boys."

"What fun is that?" Marz called, brushing crumbs off his jeans. Becca just waved. Smiling, Marz looked at Charlie. "You know, wearing your shirt inside out just makes me want to know *even more* what the shirt says." Today's shirt was gray-blue and the outline of a picture was visible through the cotton.

Across the room, Becca opened the door just as Nick walked in. Her laughter echoed through the gym as he tugged her into the hallway. He came back a minute later wearing a big grin.

Charlie sighed as he pulled up a folding chair and sat down. "Jeremy *literally* has no regular T-shirts."

"And?" Marz said, gesturing for the other man to keep talking.

"I'm wearing it inside out for a reason," Charlie said, eyebrow arched.

"Yeah, but I'm going to pester you until you tell me so take the route of least resistance." Marz grinned.

Charlie rolled his eyes. "Fine. This one has a Schnauzer wearing a saddle that says, 'Weiner rides; 25¢'." The guy threw him a droll stare, challenging Marz to laugh.

Marz worked at a straight face. "That's a good price."

Charlie threw a potato chip at Marz. He caught it and popped it in his mouth. "Don't worry. Your weiner rides are our little secret."

"Oh, my God," Charlie said, rubbing his good hand over his face. "So, how's the key search running?" He took a bite of his sandwich.

"Slow as fucking molasses," Marz said, grabbing a handful of chips.

"Faster now since we networked the machines, though, right?" Charlie shoved the long strands of his dark blond hair out of his eyes and scanned his gaze over the computers.

Marz nodded at Charlie. "Yeah. But it's not fast enough." He took a bite of his sandwich—turkey and Swiss on rye—and gave Charlie a thumbs-up. Chained to the computer station all day, Marz hadn't eaten much else.

"Hey." Wearing a gray t-shirt and jeans, Nick eyeballed them as he walked up to the desk, and his expression said he'd overheard some of their conversation. He grabbed a folding chair and sat backward on it, his arms resting on the backrest, then he glanced at the closest monitor. "So, can you explain this to me in layman's terms? What needs to happen and what do you need to make it happen?"

Marz glanced to Charlie, who waved a hand as if to say, *It's all yours.*

"Okay," Marz said. "Let's say you have data you need to send over the internet or on a disk, but you don't want anyone to be able to read it if they intercept it. To protect the data, you encrypt it. There are various ways of doing this, but no matter which you choose, encryption is largely accomplished by putting a big-ass math problem between potential snoops and your data. The answer to that math problem is the password or key that deciphers the encryption. The bigger the math problem, the longer the answer and therefore the password, and therefore the more possible number sequences there are in the password. Make sense?" He munched a few chips.

A look of concentration on his face, Nick nodded. "Following so far."

Charlie scooted his chair closer. "There are pretty much three ways to break a cryptograph," he said. He held up his uninjured hand and counted off with his fingers. "First, you can attack the cryptography itself. That's the code Marz is talking about."

"Essentially, solve the math problem," Nick said.

Nodding, Charlie continued. "Yes. Second, you can attack the software or hardware if you have a specific target in mind. And third, you can access relevant humans."

"Meaning someone gives you the key," Marz said.

"Okay," Nick said. "So . . . I take it we only have that first option at hand."

"Well, mostly," Marz said. "We'd been thinking that the bracelet Becca's father gave her might provide the passcode for the chip. That would've fallen under that human option. But no matter what we do, it's not working."

The bracelet was made up of a series of silver circles and bars. Charlie had recognized that those charms actually meant something—they translated to binary code. The string of circles and bars could also be read as zeroes and ones, but so far no joy.

Between the chip and the bear, at least they knew why the Churchmen had ransacked Becca's house and tried to nab her. She *had* in fact had information from her father, she just hadn't realized it. And they still hadn't figured out how to access it.

Marz took a drink of water and set his cup back down. "So, yeah, mostly, we're looking at solving the math problem. There are two main ways to do that. A brute-force attack, which simply means entering every possible key sequence until you hit the correct one. And a side-channel attack, which means finding some extra source of information that can be exploited to break the system."

"Like what? Gimme a concrete example," Nick said.

"Okay," Marz said. "Like the greasy smudges your fingers leave on the screen of your smartphone when you enter the passcode. Or the fingerprints you leave on an ATM's keypad after you enter your pin. In both of those instances, the extra information of those fingerprints significantly narrows your search from a key involving ten possible digits with nearly four million permutations, zero through nine, to a key involving just four digits, which only has twenty-four possible permutations."

"Do we have access to anything like that?" Nick said.

"I've tried," Charlie said. "I've tried different combinations of numbers that might've been personally significant to the Colonel, like family birth dates, but none of that's working yet, either."

From what Marz understood, Charlie's relationship with his father—who he always called the Colonel—hadn't been good, and Merritt apparently hadn't accepted his son's homosexuality. That made Marz wonder what was worse—having a parent in your life who rejected who you were to your face, or being abandoned by your parents for reasons you never got to know.

Damn, if they all didn't have a fuck-ton of baggage.

Marz sighed. "So that brings us back to brute force. And it *will* work. Eventually. With enough time and sufficient computing power."

"We don't have lots of time," Nick said, understanding slipping into his pale green gaze. "And I'm assuming we don't have sufficient computing power, either?"

"We spent the afternoon networking all these machines together, so it's going faster now," Marz said. "It's just gonna take time."

Nick tugged a hand through his dark hair. "And if it takes more time than we have?"

"I'm working on it," Marz said, a rock settling into his gut. The team was counting on him. No way he'd let them down.

Charlie clapped Marz on the shoulder. "We'll figure it out. Push comes to shove, I might be able to make some contacts."

Nick nailed Charlie with a stare. "You're a missing person, remember?" After they'd rescued Charlie, they'd decided it would be safer for him to remain "missing" rather than risk recapture.

The blond shrugged. "Well, at some point we might have to decide whether it's more important that I stay missing or chance being seen and get us stronger hardware."

Admiration washed through Marz at Charlie's offer. It wasn't the guy's fight, and he'd already lost so much.

Long pause, then Nick gave a sharp nod. "Fair point." Rising, he stepped toward the desk and stole a chip off Marz's plate.

"Dude," Marz said, holding out his hands, "get your own crunchy goodness."

Nick rolled his eyes as he munched on the chip, then he rubbed his stomach. "I just might. So, is there anything I can do to help you with this? I don't want you to feel like you're out flapping in the wind."

"Nothing for now, but thanks. Besides, I'm not alone." Marz gestured toward Charlie. "We got the brains *and* the beauty over here."

Nick leaned in quick and snagged another chip.

"Dude! Goddamnit," Marz said, laughing and taking a swing at his friend. "You're stealing food from a one-legged man."

Nick just laughed.

"Glad that's funny," Marz groused and ate a chip, then he kept his hand cupped protectively around them. One thing you learned in the Army—never let your food sit unprotected. Some hungry fucker would come snarf it down in the blink of an eye. Guess that still held even though they weren't in the Army anymore. "Oh, hey. Everything go okay with the Ravens this afternoon?" Marz asked.

"We're even-steven, and we have a standing offer of assistance," Nick said.

"That's good to hear, especially with Seneka in the picture." Marz took another bite of his sandwich.

"Exactly," Nick said. "We gave them the lowdown, so they knew exactly what they might be agreeing to get involved with. They were cool."

Agreeing to get involved with. Nick's words pinballed around Marz's skull and made him think of Emilie. "Oh, uh," Marz started, hoping Nick didn't shit a brick. "Speaking of getting involved."

Nick's eyebrow arched before Marz had even finished speaking. "Has anything good *ever* followed a segue like that?"

Probably not. But here went nothing. "Well, I kinda sorta made another date with Emilie Garza."

Chapter 9

*E*milie was ready to explode with excitement over Derek, so she called her best friend, Kelly Baxter, and begged her to go to dinner and do some shopping after work.

A true friend, Kelly hadn't really needed begging. She never did.

An hour later, they sat across from each other at a Thai restaurant near the mall. As soon as they ordered, Kelly leaned forward and nailed Emilie with a stare.

"Something's up with you," she said, interlacing her pretty manicured hands on the table. With her jet black hair, her black silk blouse was striking. "Spill."

Emilie couldn't hold back a smile. Where Emilie was average height and curvy, Kelly was tall and thin. And where Emilie had long, wavy dark brown hair, Kelly wore her dark hair in a supershort pixie style that suited her to a tee, and showed off her long neck and high cheekbones to perfection. But in all the ways that counted, they had tons in common. They'd met in a book club and had bonded over always loving and hating the same books. Long after the club petered out, they were still getting together to talk books, see movies, or go shopping.

When everything had fallen to pieces with Jack, Kelly was Emilie's main support system, next to her own family. So, yeah, she would be the one to notice something was up.

"Well," Emilie said. "I went on a date last night." She took a long drink of her ice water.

Kelly's hazel eyes went wide. "Oh, my God. Who . . . what . . . details!" she sputtered.

Emilie laughed, her friend's reaction being pretty much what she expected, especially since Emilie resisted everyone's repeated advice to get back out there again. "This perfect, beautiful man fell out of the sky and asked me out." When Kelly scowled, Emilie laughed again. "Okay, okay. Well, it *felt* that way, anyway. This guy—"

"Name?" Kelly said.

"Derek."

"Ooh, good name."

"Right? Anyway—"

The waiter interrupted their conversation, delivering their soups and a steaming porcelain teapot.

"Thank you," Emilie said. She fixed her tea as she spoke. "So, I went to lunch at the coffee shop and he helped me with a computer issue, and then we struck up a conversation. Tons of chemistry and everything felt great, but then he left. I didn't think anything of it. Except, when I left the office last night, he was waiting on the porch of the center." She took a sip of her tea.

Kelly's eyes narrowed and she lowered her spoon to her bowl. "Wait. How'd he know where you worked?"

Emilie waved her hand. "I mentioned it. Like I said, we probably talked for a good ten or fifteen minutes. So, I was totally surprised, and kinda freaking out because Hottie McHotterson is waiting there for me and asking me out. So I said yes." She wrapped both hands around the little porcelain teacup, letting the warmth seep into her skin.

Holding up her hands, Kelly said, "I have, like, a million questions."

Emilie laughed and dug into her soup. "Hit me."

"Well, first of all, why this guy? Don't get me wrong, I'm *glad* you went out. You know I've been telling you for months to start dating again. But what made you say yes?" She sprinkled some crunchy wontons into her bowl.

"I don't know, exactly. I mean, he is *really* hot, Kelly. Like, it's crazy. And he's funny and sweet and attentive. And it just felt easy being around him. So, I took a chance." Emilie ate another spoonful of soup.

"Aw, Em, I'm so glad, for real. It was time. I know it's only been a few months since the decree came in finalizing everything, but it was really over years ago. You're too awesome to be alone." Kelly reached a hand across the table and squeezed Emilie's. The words lodged a small knot in her throat, so she just nodded. "So, you said yes. Then what happened?"

Their meals arrived and Emilie gave her the play-by-play of the rest of the evening while they ate. She tried to skim over the juicy parts, but Kelly had none of it. Though she and her longtime boyfriend were totally and completely in love, Kelly said she wanted to relive every last detail of the first-kiss experience. Who was Emilie to deny her?

"I'm going out with him again tomorrow night," Emilie said after they'd finished eating. "He lives up in Baltimore, so we're going to meet after I'm done at the clinic."

"What are you wearing?" Kelly asked, wiping her mouth with her napkin.

"Just . . ." She shrugged and looked down at the white cardigan she wore over a pair of basic black slacks. "Work clothes."

Kelly's eyes went wide. "Oh, no. No, no. Hottie McHotterson deserves more than work clothes. Hottie deserves a little black dress or a pair of fuck-hot jeans and a slinky little top. And heels—sexy, tall heels." She arched an eyebrow.

"Uh. Well, I guess." Emilie nodded and mentally sorted through her closet. She didn't have a lot that fit Kelly's description. Working on a college campus, the dress code was relaxed. And it had been a *really* long time since Emilie had needed clothes for any kind of special occasion.

Throwing cash for the whole meal on the table, Kelly got up abruptly. "That's it. Come on. We're going shopping. Clothes. Lingerie. Shoes. Condoms."

Emilie burst out laughing and looked around to see if anyone had heard Kelly. Sure enough, they were getting some stares. "You don't have to pay," she said, rising.

"Oh, honey, I'd pick up the tabs of everyone in here if it meant you could be as happy as you deserve to be." Kelly slung an arm around Emilie's shoulders. "So let's go get you ready to get yourself some Hottie."

Chuckling, Emilie nodded. "Okay. I need to buy a Mother's Day present, anyway."

"Stuff for Hottie first. Gotta have your priorities straight," Kelly said. They left the restaurant and stepped into the parking lot. "Ain't getting no orgasm from Mama."

Emilie froze in her tracks. "That is . . . *so wrong* on so many levels," she said, unable to hold back her laughter.

Kelly shrugged. "Maybe. But it's true, too. Come on." She waved to her convertible. "Ride with me. I'll bring you back later."

"All right," Emilie said.

"You know, you should get these cherry-flavored condoms we used one time. They tasted pretty good, in case you wanna . . ." She gestured with her hand to her mouth.

"Oh my God, Kelly," she said, laughing as she settled into the passenger seat.

"What? Just being practical. Plus, why reinvent the wheel when I can share my bounty of knowledge with you?" She waggled her dark eyebrows.

Emilie shook her head, even as her thoughts flickered to the possibility of actually *needing* condoms. Her stomach fluttered. "Just drive, crazy woman. I can pick out my own damn condoms."

TWO HOURS LATER, Emilie dropped all her new belongings on the living room couch: one clingy red wrap dress that hugged her curves in all the right ways. One pair of hip-hugging jeans that did great things for her ass. Two new tops. A royal blue matching bra and panty set. And one box of Trojan Magnum extra-large condoms—because Kelly said it couldn't hurt to think positive.

Emilie chuckled as she dumped her purse and keys

on the coffee table and turned on some lights. Going out with Kelly was exactly what she'd needed. It had gotten her mind off of Manny, helped her unwind, and gave her a sense of reassurance that she wasn't making a big mistake. The affirmation was helpful because, in her own mind, judging Jack so incorrectly for so long had done a number on her confidence. But she was working on it.

And Derek was a step in the right direction.

She wandered into the kitchen. *Thump, thump.* Emilie tilted her ear and concentrated. Had she just—

Thump.

That sounded like—

Her basement door opened and someone stepped out. Emilie screamed and reared back against the counter.

"Em, it's just me," Manny said. The overhead kitchen light turned on.

"What in the ever-living fuck, Manny?" Emilie yelled, her body still on full alert, heart racing, skin prickling, tears pricking at the backs of her eyes. "You scared me to death. Wait. . . . Where is your Hummer?" She always knew when he'd come to visit because the big black monstrosity took up half her front yard, but it hadn't been out there tonight.

He thumbed over his shoulder. "Around back."

Emilie braced her hands on the counter on each side of her. "Uh, why? What are you doing here?"

"I just didn't want to leave it out front, that's all. And I had dinner with some friends in Arnold, so I thought I'd drop in while I was so close. Didn't expect you to be out at this hour." Manny crossed to the fridge, pulled the door open, and grabbed a soda. He was dressed all in black again, his hair pulled back in a knot at the base of his neck.

Uh-huh, Emilie thought. "Okay, but what were you doing in my basement?" Emilie *never* went down there because it was the world's biggest haven for the two things she feared the most—snakes and spiders. The fact that snakes had *no* legs and spiders had *so many* put them both at the top of her creeptastic list. So she liked to pretend that her basement, which was so small it was more of a crawl space, simply didn't exist.

"I heard something down there, so I went to look. I think it's a raccoon, which means there's probably a nest. I know you don't like to go down there, so I'll arrange a pest control guy if you want and then find the hole and get it patched." He took a long drink from his soda.

Emilie watched him, weighing and assessing his words. She was torn between thinking his story was a crock and wanting to hug him for offering to take care of the problem. Assuming there really was one. She'd never heard any noises down there before, but then again it was spring, so it made sense that a mama raccoon would be looking for a place to make a nest. Right? God knows she didn't want to check for herself.

"Sure, that would be, uh, great. Thanks, Manny."

He leaned against the kitchen counter and crossed his ankles. "Why were you out so late tonight?"

"I went out with Kelly after work," she said. No way was she offering up anything about Derek yet. That was all too new. It was entirely possible they'd just have a few nice dates and nothing more, so she wasn't tripping her brother's protective instincts until there was something to actually tell. Manny had been there through a lot of Emilie's hard times with Jack, so between that and being her big brother, he came by those instincts honestly. "Speaking of which, don't forget to buy Mama a present for Saturday. You're still coming, right?"

"Yeah, yeah, probably," he said, running a hand over his hair.

"No probably, Manny. She'll be crushed if you don't come." Emilie crossed her arms. And Mama would also drag her heels about the emergency psychiatric evaluation if she didn't get to see him.

"I've got some stuff going on, Em, but I'm planning on it. Okay?" he said.

She sighed. "Okay." She glanced at the clock on the microwave. 9:30 P.M. "So, what's your plan tonight? Are you sleeping over? Or . . ."

"I thought so, yeah. That okay?" he asked.

"Sure," she said, when what she really wanted to ask was why he wasn't staying at his own place. To which she'd never been. Heck, Emilie wasn't even sure their mother had been there. Not that she minded Manny spending the night. He'd done it many times before— after family get-togethers and right after Jack moved out when Emilie was still feeling shell-shocked, so it wasn't necessarily unusual. Still, something about it felt that way. Or maybe that was just their strange encounter from the other night talking. "I'll go make up the bed."

MARZ COULDN'T DECIDE which was worse: the hammer smashing his big toe or the nail driving into his heel. The torture would've sucked ass no matter what, but it was even worse for the fact that he no longer had the foot currently being smashed and nailed.

No bigger misnomer than "phantom" pain.

Sighing, Marz shifted and grimaced. The pain was always the worst at night. He could go all day without a twinge, but the moment his ass went horizontal, the fun started. Which often made spending time in bed a whole lotta pointless. And pain meds left him wired, which also did nothing for his chances at sleep.

Tonight was definitely one of those nights, so there wasn't any reason to keep lying there. Marz pushed the covers off and swung his legs toward the side of the bed. His left foot hit the cold concrete floor and the stump of his righty hung just over the edge of the mattress. Sitting in the dark, he gave his exhaustion a good shove into the background and blew out a long breath.

Swiping his hand along the side of the bed, Marz found his cell phone wedged between the mattress and box spring where he'd stuck it the night before. He thumbed on the flashlight application, throwing a dim glow over the mostly empty room. So much about what they were doing here was makeshift, including his temporary accommodations in the unfinished apartment on the top floor of Hard Ink.

But Marz didn't mind roughing it a bit. Hell, he had a mattress, a hot shower, and a roof over his head—it was damn near luxurious compared to some of the places he'd bunked down while in the Army. Besides, he'd sleep on the damn concrete if it meant being with these guys again. Even missing half his leg, he hadn't felt this whole, this together, this . . . *right* since the last time they'd all been in the same place. That was back in Afghanistan, before Merritt had discarded Marz and the rest of the team like so much trash and they'd been forced to shoulder the blame for the deaths of their friends.

And as long as he didn't have all the answers about how and why the shit had landed on him and his teammates—and who was behind it—Marz was going to bust his ass to find them.

He reached for his liner, socks, and prosthetic limb, and unplugged the latter from its charger. For the past two months, he'd most frequently worn an elevated vacuum limb that gave him a more complete seal between the socket of the limb and his skin, which was why Nick hadn't been able to pull it off. But the vacuum pump required nightly charging.

Half man, half machine. If he had to lose a limb, at least he got cool technology to replace it. Silver linings and all that.

Propping his phone up against the pillow cast light over his body and allowed Marz to see what he was doing as he rolled the urethane liner up his stump, over his knee, and upward yet to cover most of his thigh. Next went two thin stump socks that allowed him to slip his limb into the socket of the prosthesis. With those layers in place, he guided his leg into the socket and rose to his feet. He folded one of the socks down over the hard edges of the socket and then rolled the black rubber sleeve that allowed the vacuum up his thigh until it almost covered the liner. A button on the back of the artificial limb activated the vacuum, which he powered on with the tiny remote control he'd shown Nick. A *whirr* sounded as the vacuum sucked all the air from the space between the black exterior sleeve and the white urethane liner that sat against his skin, creating a seal that kept the prosthesis from moving against the skin at all. The fit was so tight, the limb nearly became a part of him.

Once, Marz had had to think through each step of this process, which was largely the same no matter which type of prosthesis he donned, save for the vacuum.

Now? Second nature. That was what you called adapt-ability, baby. Something you did when your only other choices were to crawl on your hands and knees or use a pair of crutches. Neither worked for him. You didn't emerge from eleven years of military service, eight of it in SpecOps, and lose the urge and the instinct to *always* be ready. For something. For anything.

So, he'd choose taking the time to put on the second foot, thank you very much. Even in the middle of the night. Even for a quick trip to the latrine or to get a drink of water. Every damn time. And, why not? Each of the four prosthetic legs he owned was as much a part of him now as his meat leg had been.

Marz slipped a pair of gym shorts and a T-shirt on, then stood up and stuffed his meat foot into the sneaker that matched the one on his limb. He dropped the little remote into his pocket and grabbed his cell, taking note that it was just coming up on four in the morning.

Ah, four o'clock, my old friend.

Hoping he didn't wake Beckett, Easy, or Jenna, with whom he was sharing this apartment, Marz tip-toed through the moonlit rooms, down the metal-and-concrete staircase to the second floor, and into the cavernous gym. The lights were on and Charlie was sitting at the computer. "Hey," he said.

"What are you doing up, dude?" Marz asked.

Charlie held up his bandaged hand. "Couldn't sleep," he said in a low voice. "It's bugging me."

Marz nodded as he crossed the wide room, feel-ing for the guy even though being around Charlie's brand-new amputation hit way too close to home. He remembered what those early days and weeks had been like—the pain, the loss, the grief—and it wasn't a place he liked to revisit. Given the catastrophic nature of his own injury, you might've expected his brain to do him a solid and block it all out. No such luck. From the glaringly bright sun hanging over that dusty road, to the fast, percussive blasts of gunfire all around him, to the indescribable agony of being blown to literal pieces, he remembered every last moment of what'd happened to him.

But Marz also remembered that Shane and Nick, despite Nick's own injuries, had been right there with him when it'd happened. The pair had staunched the worst of the bleeding and saved his life. And the whole team had been there in the days afterward before he'd been transported to Landstuhl Medical Center in Germany for surgery. When Marz had returned stateside, he'd had the other amputees he'd met at his physical therapist and prosthetist offices to commiserate with and get advice from. Given the way things had gone down for Charlie, he hadn't had any of that support. No doubt that made his hard situation a helluva lot worse.

Marz kicked himself for not speaking up about it all earlier. "Bugging you because of the pain? Or . . ."

Charlie peered up at Marz from underneath his hair. "The surgical site throbs, and sometimes I could swear that my fingers are cramped up." His gaze dropped for a split second to Marz's prosthesis, sticking out loud and proud beneath the hem of his shorts. "I mean, um, the ones that aren't there."

Marz settled into one of the folding chairs at the desk, and for the hundredth time his ass expressed its displeasure at the hard metal. "You know, every time I sit here, I hear Patrick Swayze saying, 'Nobody puts Baby in the corner.' "

Charlie gave a crooked grin. "Should we start calling you Baby now?"

Barking out a laugh, Marz scrubbed his hands over his face. "I've been called worse." He shook his head and released a sigh. "Could your hand be infected? Have Becca or Shane looked at it lately?"

"Becca changed the dressings before she went to bed. Said it looked good."

"Good. That's good," Marz said, turning in his chair to face Charlie. "I'm not going to lie to you. The phantom pain is a giant PITA. There are medicines that can make it better, but they made me feel foggy-headed. And there's always pain meds if you need them, but some of them hype you up so you can't sleep, anyway. It's all trial and error."

"So, you get it, too? The phantom pain?" he asked, his gaze not quite meeting Marz's.

"Yeah. I get it. Especially at night."

"Huh," Charlie said, picking at the edge of his bandage. "Think Eileen gets it?"

Marz smiled. He loved that the puppy got around like she had no idea she was missing a leg. "See, I knew I liked you. You like to know how things work, too." He shrugged. "I hope she doesn't experience it, but I bet she does even if she processes it differently. Where is the little runt, anyway?" The puppy had totally charmed every last hard ass in the place, but seemed to have taken a special liking to Becca, Charlie, and Jeremy.

"Oh, uh, I think she's sleeping with Jeremy," Charlie said. And was Marz imagining it or were the guy's cheeks turning a little red? Interesting. First Nick and Becca, then Shane and Sara, and then Easy and Jenna. And now Charlie was acting sketchy at the mere mention of Jeremy. Hard Ink was turning into the goddamned Love Boat.

Although, Marz was the one with the date tonight,

wasn't he? Guess that didn't give him a lotta room to talk.

Hoping to save the guy from whatever embarrass-ment he was feeling, Marz shifted closer to the desk and tapped a few keys, bringing up the main processing screen for the key search. It had been running most of the day and was only at twelve per cent. "It's moving, but it ain't fast."

"No. And I was just calculating an estimate of how long it'll take, given what it's finished so far," Charlie said, grabbing a piece of paper off the desk and pass-ing it to Marz. "At the current rate, it should take four-point-eight days to enter the entire sequence, and the point-eight of that has already passed. So, four more days."

Marz counted in his head. "So, we're looking at early Monday morning. Damn." He tossed the paper back to the desk. "That's a lifetime from now." Not just because Marz was impatient as all hell to learn what secrets that chip held, but because Church had to be hunting for the people who took out Confessions.

"Yeah, that's what I'm thinking, too. We're gonna need stronger hardware to do this any faster."

"Which means we might have to figure out a way for you to connect with your contacts without advertis-ing all over town that you're around." When Charlie nodded, Marz continued. "We'll talk to Nick. Let him know what's going on."

"Okay," the guy said.

"I'm glad you're here, Charlie. Apart from all the ob-vious reasons, your help has already been invaluable these past few days. We've got too damn many unan-swered questions and loose ends for me to handle by myself." And it was true. If it hadn't been for Charlie, and even Jeremy's help running some of these queries and analyzing the data being kicked back at them, Marz would be buried under a pile of printouts by now.

Charlie looked at Marz, his blue-eyed gaze intense and fervent. "After everything you all did for me and Becca, it's the least I could do. Especially since the Colonel was the one who ruined everything for your team in the first place."

Marz didn't like the note of guilt in Charlie's words, but he sure as hell understood the undertone of disappointment. One way or another, Merritt had let them all down. "Not your fault, Charlie."

"Not yours, either," Charlie said, brow furrowed over darkening eyes.

Marz glanced away. At least the Merritt kids hadn't inherited their father's lack of integrity. Both Becca and Charlie were damn good people, and the team was lucky to have them on their side in the midst of this clusterfuck. "Well, I thought I'd dig into Seneka and see what else I can find."

Charlie nodded. "I came up with a handful of other significant numbers to try. And something about these binary numbers is bothering me, too. I just cannot believe the bracelet is a coincidence."

"Seems like a stretch," Marz agreed. "Well, let's get to work, then, and catch us some bad guys. It'd be about fucking time."

Chapter 10

Marz leaned against the formstone covering the front of the Italian restaurant and waited for Emilie to arrive. A breeze made the warm, heavy air more tolerable, but summer seemed to have made an early appearance for the first week of May. He scanned the crowded little street in both directions.

All day, he'd been going back and forth about this date—vacillating between excitement at seeing Emilie again, to regret at continuing to see her under these circumstances, to suspicion about what she did or didn't know about her brother and just how involved she might be.

All of which was complicated by the team's mixed viewpoints on the matter. After Marz had told Nick about seeing Emilie again, Nick had informed the others. Which meant, of course, that it had become a topic of general conversation—whether it was a good idea, why he'd done it, and how to get the most out of it. Awesome for him.

But Marz had quickly convinced them it was a good idea. Emilie remained their most direct route to Garza, who was definitely involved with the Church Gang and very likely involved with Seneka. They needed to find him, and Emilie was their ticket to doing so.

That Marz actually *liked* Emilie? Well, he'd downplayed that part to the guys. In the grand scheme of things, his feelings didn't matter a bit compared to their mission. And her importance to the mission was rock solid. Didn't leave his conscience feeling any less battered, though. That was for damn sure.

As if his thoughts willed her appearance, Emilie came around the corner of the closest block-long wall of brick rowhouses.

And she looked like a fucking dream.

The dark blue top had swirls of yellow and green in it, but what most caught his eye was the depth of the V-neck. Her jeans appeared to be almost painted on, and hugged her curves beautifully, leading his gaze down to a pair of royal blue high heels that she was absolutely rocking.

Marz pushed off the wall and smiled as she approached, enjoying the show the entire way, especially since her smile was so big and open, too. For him.

"Hi," she said.

"Hi, there. You look fantastic," Marz said as she walked up to him. He tried not to stare at the narrow strip of sheer blue lace that ran down the center of her shirt, teasing him with hints of what was underneath.

"Thanks," she said. "You look very nice, too."

His jeans and black button-down held nothing on her. "Ready to head in?"

She nodded, and they made their way inside and were guided to a table, all of which gave Marz the opportunity to observe that Emilie looked every bit as good from behind. A strip of blue lace ran down her spine, wider than in the front, and those jeans fit her so sinfully good, he wouldn't have been surprised to learn they were illegal in six states.

"How was your day?" he asked after the hostess left them.

Something odd flashed behind her eyes. "It was . . . uh . . . okay," she said, her gaze sliding down to the table.

What had he said? Marz leaned down, trying to see her eyes, to get her to look at him again. "Hey, what's—"

When she looked up, she was trying to blink away tears. "I'm sorry," she whispered. She pushed up from her seat and nearly ran into their waiter. "Restroom, please?" she said.

The man pointed the way and turned to ask Marz if they wanted to order drinks.

"Give us a minute, please," he said, rising to follow her. He waited in the hallway outside the ladies' room, debating knocking on the door and confusion cluttering his thoughts. Confusion not just because he didn't know what had brought on her sadness, but because his gut was knotted and the center of his chest throbbed in a dull, sympathetic ache. He didn't like seeing her upset. An understatement, for sure.

Which just made that knot grow a whole lot bigger, because he knew he could hurt her, too. If she ever found out that their initial meeting hadn't been the accident he'd let her believe it was.

He lifted his hand to knock when the door finally opened and Emilie came out. She froze when she saw him and her mouth dropped open.

Marz stepped right up to her and gently rubbed her arms. "You okay?"

A fast nod. "I'm sorry," she said.

"Nothing to be sorry for. You just have me worried." He stroked his hands over her arms, the thin, soft blouse skimming over her skin.

She dropped her head, nearly resting her forehead against his chest. "I can't believe . . . I'm ruining this."

Marz couldn't hold back. He gathered her in his arms and pulled her against him. "Nothing's ruined," he said, his hand stroking over the silky waves of her hair.

For a minute, her muscles tensed, and he thought he'd offended her. And then the trembling of her shoulders and little hitching breaths revealed that she was crying. Or trying really hard not to.

"Aw, hey," he said, tightening his arms. The fact that her sadness hit him in the gut proved that this thing with Emilie was getting real. For him, at least.

She heaved a deep breath and looked up, then quickly rubbed at her face. "I am *so* sorry," she said. "Bet you haven't had a woman cry on a date before."

"That's only because I don't date much. If there was a larger sample, I'm sure I could make more of them cry." He smiled and winked.

Her lips tilted up, which only made him want to see her smile for real. "Why don't you date much?"

Derek hated to reveal this information in *this* moment—a moment when his feelings for her had risen to the surface and what was happening right now was real and true, not pretense. But the guys had agreed telling her he'd served might be the best way to get her to talk about her brother, and so it was a risk worth taking. "I was in the Army until a year ago and deployed for a lot of the last decade, none of which left a lot of time for trying to meet someone."

"Oh?" she said, her eyebrows rising in surprise. She released a breath.

Given how she was feeling, Derek felt like even more of an ass for using her to get to her brother. Guilt tormented him like nails on a chalkboard. Maybe he could find another way. "Look, we don't have to do this tonight if you'd rather—"

"No, I don't want to cancel." She met his gaze. "I just . . . I thought I'd pulled myself together, but when I went to tell you about my day, I realized that I hadn't."

"We could go sit down and you could tell me about it?" he suggested. When Emilie nodded, he guided them back to their table. As relieved as he was that she'd agreed to stay, a part of him wished—for her— that she'd chosen to go.

He needed to rein his shit in and stop letting his dick and his heart fuck with his head.

Emilie busied her hands with smoothing her napkin in her lap. "About two hours ago, I learned that one of my patients committed suicide. She was only twenty," she said. "I'd been working with her for over a year."

"Aw, hell, Emilie. I'm sorry. Twenty is so young. That's a damn shame." And, of course, his thoughts went immediately to Easy and stirred up the fear and concern he had for his friend.

"Thanks," she said. "I tried, but it's hard not to second-guess yourself."

"Well, don't. I'm sure you did everything you could."

She gave a little shrug. "I hope so. I didn't want to cancel tonight. But I'm sorry I let it ruin—"

"You didn't," he said, reaching across the table and capturing her hand in his. "I'm really glad you didn't cancel. And I'm glad you told me. You shouldn't be alone after something like that."

Emilie sipped her water. "Thanks. I really do appreciate the company."

"Me too." He gave her a small smile. "I just learned that one of my best friends is having suicidal thoughts, and it scares the shit out of me. That you're trying to help people who feel that way . . . well, I admire the hell out of it." So much for reining his heart in, huh?

Emilie's brow furrowed. "Is your friend getting help?"

Marz nodded. "Just started on some meds." Thanks to Shane's convincing an old, trusted family doctor that *he* was the one who needed the meds. Easy didn't have a regular doc who might've been willing to call in a prescription for such a thing sight unseen.

"I hope he'll consider therapy, too. The best results tend to come when a patient uses both."

Problem was, how to get that for him in the midst of all this bullshit. "I'll be sure to encourage him," he said.

The waiter took their drink order, prompting them to finally open their menus. After he brought their drinks and they ordered, Emilie said, "So, you were in the Army?"

"Yep. Eleven years. Been out for about a year." His gut squeezed and he found himself *hating* to use her for information.

"My, um, my brother was in the Army, too. He's been out for a little over two years now," she said. Was he imagining her reluctance to talk about her brother? And it was interesting that she hadn't mentioned Garza being SF, too. Marz was withholding that intel on purpose to protect his identity. But why wasn't she mentioning it? Most people were only too happy to emphasize a service member's participation in one of the elite units. It meant they were the best of the best.

Aw, hell. Maybe he was reading too much into it. He shoved the mental churn away. "Oh, yeah? Small world. What does he do now?" he asked, cutting a slice of bread off the warm loaf and offering it to her.

"I don't actually know," she said with a humorless chuckle. "He works for a defense contractor, but I'm not sure what he actually does. We haven't been as close since he got out."

Bingo. That was frickin' good enough confirmation about Seneka as far as Marz was concerned. If it looked like a zebra and sounded like a zebra, it was a damn zebra. So, SWS T-shirt plus sister's confirmation that Garza worked for a defense contractor added up to him. Also interesting was the insight into their relationship. Not as close anymore. So how did the stash end up in her basement? "Sounds like a decent place to land," he said, making sure to keep his voice casual. "But sorry to hear you're not as close. Maybe it'll change, though. Growing up like I did, I don't have family, but I do have close friends I consider like brothers. I drifted apart from them over the past year, but we're back in touch now and we're tight. Maybe that'll happen for you two."

"Maybe it will," she said, shrugging. "I'm just hoping he won't disappoint our mother by not showing on Saturday." She sighed. "Anyway. Did you do computer stuff in the Army, too?"

Marz nodded, not at all missing the abrupt change in topic nor the confirmation that Manny was at least invited to her party. "Yeah. Was in charge of communications and computers. Army's where I got most of my training. I did some community college after high school, but I couldn't afford college full-time. Part of the reason I went in the Army."

"Manny, too," she said. "My parents divorced when I was young and my father split, so we had to earn our own way after high school. I did it with scholarships. He did it with the Army."

"Nice," Marz said, finding more and more reasons to admire Emilie. Her devotion to family, that she'd made her own way through hard work and effort, and the work she did to help others, some of it unpaid.

Their food arrived, and they both dug in. Marz had ordered the chicken parm and Emilie, the cheese ravioli. Both smelled like heaven on a plate.

"I could never go in the Army," Emilie said as she speared part of a ravioli and took a bite.

Marz smiled. "Why's that?"

"Manny told me about the survivalist training he had to do. All the gross things he caught in the wilderness and ate. I couldn't do it." She shuddered.

Laughing, Marz nodded. "It's not so bad."

Eyebrow arched, head tilted, Emilie's expression was one of total disbelief. "I would starve before I could eat a . . . squirrel. Or, oh God, a snake."

"Snake tastes like chicken," Marz said. When Emilie's face squinched up, Derek laughed again. "It's true."

"No. Just no. Snakes violate my leg rule. Spiders, too. Don't even get me started on centipedes."

Oh, he had to hear this. "What's a leg rule?" he asked, grinning.

She pointed her fork at him. "Anything with more than four legs or less than two must die. No questions asked. Snakes and spiders squick me out so bad."

Marz burst out laughing. Emilie had just unknowingly issued him a death threat. Not that he believed for a moment she'd meant her words in any way other than as a joke about gross creepy-crawlies, but still. That was damn funny. "That so, huh?"

"Totally," she said, smiling. "I know, I'm such a girl, right?"

Marz chuckled. He wasn't touching that one with a ten-foot pole.

As they ate and talked and laughed, Emilie's sadness and hesitancy melted away. Marz was equal parts glad that he'd had a hand in lifting her spirits and remorseful that they'd shared some meaningful connections when he wasn't being fully honest with her.

Not to mention still not knowing just how much he could trust her.

Still, when the meal was over, Marz wasn't ready to part from her. Even though he knew he really shouldn't prolong their time together, either. Not when his heart was this engaged.

This was why soldiers didn't get involved with mission assets. Sometimes the means to the ends sucked ass even if you were one of the ones wearing a white hat. *Sonofabitch.*

Outside the restaurant, darkness had fallen over the crowded streets, and Emilie looked beautiful in the golden glow of the streetlights. "Thank you for being so kind. About my patient," she said.

Marz could only nod, because her compliment cut

like a blade through his guilty conscience. He caressed her cheek with his fingertips and wished they were two different people in a whole other time.

Emilie leaned into his touch. "It's a nice night. Wanna walk over to the water?"

No. No. Say no. "Yeah," he said, taking her hand into his.

They walked down to Eastern Avenue, and Emilie felt so damn right at his side that Marz could barely stand it. He wanted to push her away and tell her to run. He wanted to haul her into his arms and hold her tight. Instead, he just stroked the side of her finger with his thumb, needing to touch her, to feel her.

Following Eastern toward the water, they didn't talk, but it was a comfortable silence. The kind he rarely found, and then only with people he'd known for much longer. Ahead, the skyline shined with the harbor lights and the lit triangular glass of the National Aquarium.

Emilie tugged on his hand. "Is that a lighthouse?" she asked.

He looked toward the water, where some sort of building appeared to sit up on stilts. "I don't know. I've never explored here before," he said. "Let's go see."

Her smile was instant and made the yearning burn more brightly inside him. Maybe after all this, they could have something? They could *be* something?

Although the list of things standing in front of that possibility was so damn long.

At the far end of the pier was indeed a lighthouse. The red circular building stood atop black iron legs, with the light itself projecting out of the top of the roof. It had a charm about it that read old, and it had almost certainly come from somewhere else. A sign on a locked gate at the bottom of the stairs confirmed that and read, "Seven Foot Knoll Lighthouse, c. 1855, moved to this location 1988."

"Wow, this is gorgeous," Emilie said as they walked around the outside of the building, the sound of the water lapping against the pier providing a backdrop. "I love lighthouses. I collect little figurines of them."

"Do you have this one?" he asked. She shook her head. "Why do you love them?"

They came back around to the locked staircase again, and Emilie grabbed onto the railing and looked up. "I guess . . . they're romantic, I think. Places from another era. And so tied to the water. I think of the keepers who used to live in them, and wonder what it would've been like to ride out a storm or a fog so thick you could only hear the water all around you."

Drawn in by the passion and imagination of her words, Marz came up close behind her and braced his hands on the railing beside hers. The position brought his front up tight against her back. The contact sent an electric jolt through his body. Marz was playing with fire. He damn well knew he was. But that didn't make him want to pull away.

He just wanted more of the heat.

Marz nuzzled the side of her face with his nose, his lips. "Emilie," he whispered.

She turned her face toward him and offered her lips.

He couldn't refuse.

Capturing her mouth on a tortured groan, Marz poured every ounce of his longing and confusion and desire into the kiss. They grasped at each other and Emilie turned in his arms. He pinned her against the railing and planted his hands in her hair. She opened to him and accepted his tongue, sucking him in until Marz's blood ran hot and his hard-on ached. He ground himself against her and devoured every little moan and whimper and gasp she spilled.

Trailing kisses from her mouth to her jaw to her ear, Marz dragged a hand down her body and grasped her breast in his palm. She cried out and her head dropped back, drawing his mouth to her neck, where he licked and sucked and nipped as he kneaded her soft flesh. "You are so damn sexy."

Her hand flew to his hair and grasped the back of his head. "Touch me," she said. "Don't stop touching me."

Marz pulled away long enough to do a three-sixty scan. The lighthouse cast a dark shadow over them, and the pier was otherwise empty. His heart raced and his pulse hammered. He dove back in, trailing kisses down her neck to her collarbone, which he traced with his tongue. Her nails scratched deliciously at his scalp and her grip urged him down.

Through the thin material of her blouse and bra, he mouthed and flicked at her nipple. He shifted the deep vee of the neckline to reveal a lacy royal blue bra. He tongued her through the lace until she was panting and moaning and writhing against the railing.

"Oh, my God," she rasped as he shifted her shirt and moved to her other breast. This time, he tugged the lace down to bare the deep pink of her nipple. She tasted and smelled like something fruity and sweet, and it made Marz hunger for more. "Derek," she gasped. "Yes, yes, yes."

Her palm cupped and squeezed the bulge of his erection through his jeans. His hips jerked into the touch, craving more of her, all of her. He groaned and it seemed to egg her on, because she pressed and rubbed her hand against his trapped cock until he was panting and imagining taking her down to the ground.

"Jesus, Emilie, you're driving me fucking crazy," he said as he worked kisses back up her body to her mouth.

"I know just what you mean," she said. Her molten hot gaze met his. Eyes hooded, lips shiny and swollen, cheeks flushed, she was a freaking goddess standing under the moonlit sky. He felt the force of her beauty every bit as much in his chest as in his cock.

"You sure about that, babe?" he asked as he took her mouth in a deep, wet kiss. "Because my imagination has me stripping you of those fuck-hot jeans."

"Yeah?" She rubbed his cock in a long stroke with the heel of her hand. "Mine has us getting a room at the hotel back there. So I'm sure," she said with a smile.

Marz's heart hammered against his breastbone and his cock jerked, clearly liking her idea, too. Except, if he took her up on it, he was going to end up buried inside her for as long as she'd have him. And so long as this clusterfuck of a situation defined their relationship, he couldn't take things that far. Could he? No. Goddamnit, what was he doing? The haze of lust made it hard to think and easier to push the question away.

But maybe he could give her something.

Claiming her lips in another kiss, he ran a firm hand down the front of her body until he cupped the hot space between her thighs. She moaned and rocked into his touch, like she was as desperate for him as he was for her. He rubbed his fingers over the seam of the denim until she was moaning and pushing her hips forward into his hand. Their hands and arms bumped and rubbed in the tight space between them.

Boxing her body in tight against the railing, Marz leaned his forehead against hers and stared into her eyes. "Does this feel good?" he asked as he continued to tease and rub.

Her breath caught and she gave a fast nod. "Oh, yeah. So good."

He flicked his tongue over her lips, loving the way she attempted to capture it. "I bet you're really fucking hot here," he said, pressing a little harder between her legs to make sure she knew exactly what he was saying.

"Yeah," she said in a breathy little gasp that made him thrust against her palm.

"Bet I could make you feel even better," he said, sucking her bottom lips between his and giving it a little nip.

"Please," she said, one hand fisting around the side of his shirt.

The word speared through him, spiking his pulse and turning his cock to steel. "Right here, Em? Right now?" The very idea turned his blood molten and silenced every bit of argument against taking this even one step further.

Her body trembled everywhere they touched. She stared at him a long moment, and then she nodded. "Here," she breathed.

Marz had enough presence of mind to do another visual sweep of the end of the pier, and, finding it empty, he tugged the button free at the top of her jeans. Her eyes widened, like she was surprised, or excited. Watching her carefully for any sign of reluctance, he drew down the zipper slowly. One metal tooth at a time.

"Shit," she said. "Hurry. I need it. Need you."

Her urgency had every part of him achy with desire. "Yeah?" he asked as he skimmed his palm down the curve of her belly and into her panties. His fingertips encountered a soft patch of hair and then hot, slick feminine flesh. "Oh, you do need it, don't you? You're so wet for me." He circled his fingers over the top of her sex and devoured the string of little whimpers and moans and pleading words that spilled from her lips.

He could've lived on them.

She reached for his zipper, but Marz gently blocked her. "This is all for you, baby. I want to have all my wits about me when I watch you come."

"Derek, faster," she said, her hand reaching up to hold the railing above her. "Please."

"Anything you need, Em." Their lips so close they breathed each other's air, Marz swirled his fingers right where he knew she needed them.

Moments later, every one of her muscles went taut. "Derek, I'm . . . oh . . ." The word died in her throat as she held her breath through the orgasm.

"Aw, yes," he said. When her knees went weak, he wrapped an arm around her lower back to support her and slowly gentled his fingers.

She heaved a long, contented sigh. "Oh, my God. I'm lightheaded," she said with a chuckle.

Marz grinned and withdrew his hand. "Yeah? I'm glad," he said. And then he cupped her face and held her so she could watch as he sucked each of his three wet fingertips into his mouth. "Next time, you'll come on my tongue," he said. Somewhere, way far in the back of his mind, a very small part of him questioned the idea of a "next time."

"Oh, yeah?" she said, pushing off the railing and wrapping her arms around his neck. He arched an eyebrow and nodded, loving that she wasn't too shy to talk about this stuff. "Next time, you'll come on *my* tongue, too."

Which pretty much made "next time" a sure thing.

Chapter 11

At her taunting words, Derek licked his lips. "I'm gonna hold you to that," he said with mischief in his eyes.

"I hope you will," she whispered against his ear. She wasn't sure where this brave woman had come from, but Emilie liked her and hoped she stuck around. Jack had been conservative in the bedroom, so, over the six years they'd been together, Emilie had gotten used to censoring the way her mouth tended to run away when she was aroused. Apparently, that was done.

And thank God for that.

Derek gave her a hug and stepped back to right her clothing.

"I got it," she said, smiling up at him. God, he was so freaking gorgeous, especially with arousal sharpening the angles on his masculine face. Arousal for her.

Well, this day sure has been full of high highs and low lows, Emilie thought as she zipped and buttoned her jeans. Her heart panged for her patient, Cecelia. Derek was right. She'd been so damn young. The woman's death filled Emilie with the urge to live. To embrace life. To not waste a single second.

And right now? She was as high as she'd been in a long, long time. And hearing what *else* Derek wanted to do? She was pretty sure he could take her higher.

She was certainly willing to let him try. No more waiting, no more questioning herself, no more fear.

She'd just had an orgasm out in public. Where anyone might've seen them. Or heard them. And it had been freaking phenomenal.

Taking a deep breath, Emilie stared up at the sky and let herself bask in the moment. Derek came up behind her and wrapped his arms around her belly. It was just a hug, but it made her feel special and cherished and . . . *not alone* for the first time in a long time.

"There are a million stars tonight," Emilie said, gazing up at the star-brightened sky while he held her tight. Finally, she turned in his arms. They looked into one another's eyes and slowly but surely she realized that he was moving them, rocking them, slow dancing with her under the stars. She smiled. Sexy, gave good orgasms, *and* romantic. "We don't have music," she said.

He grinned, grasped her hand, and started to sing. He picked up the pace, and the dance turned playful.

Emilie was smiling so big her cheeks hurt, and chuckling, too. Because cute as he was—and he was freaking adorable, really—his singing was . . . atrocious.

"And yooooou, my brown-eyed girl . . ."

When they got to the *sha la la*'s, Emilie joined in. And then they were both singing and dancing and laughing through to the end.

When they'd finished butchering the song, Emilie hugged him and grinned. "Can I tell you something?"

"Of course," he said, returning her smile.

"You give excellent orgasms." His face totally lit up. She wrinkled her nose for this next part. "But, um, has anybody ever told you that—"

"I can't sing?" he asked with an almost proud smile.

"Uh, yeah?"

Marz nodded. "All the time." He shrugged. "I can't hear it, so it doesn't bother me."

Emilie burst out laughing.

"But I love how you softened the criticism with the compliment. Very nice."

She laughed so hard, tears sprung to her eyes. Happy tears, this time. "Derek, you're a good guy," she said when she finally calmed down.

He stuffed his hands in the pockets of his jeans and shuffled his feet like her compliment made him uncomfortable. "I'm just really glad you agreed to go out with me tonight, Emilie. I . . . I hope you know how much I mean that."

"I do. And me too."

He grasped her hand and they slowly walked back the way they'd come. Emilie didn't think she was imagining that his limp was a bit more pronounced than she'd ever noticed it before.

"Are you okay?" she finally asked. He looked at her with a question in his eyes, so she nodded to his leg.

"Oh. Yeah." He guided her over to the side of the pedestrian bridge and leaned against the thick cement railing. "So, uh, I have this." Derek grasped the leg of his jeans and tugged it up.

Shoe. Metal? Oh . . .

"Oh," she said, her brain processing the fact that Derek wore a prosthetic leg. Emilie glanced from the metal pole of his limb to his face, and she didn't think she imagined that his gaze was a shade more guarded than before. Which made her heart hurt a little. Had people rejected him in the past for having an amputation? *Oh, my God, my leg rule!* Emilie gasped and pressed a hand to her heart. "Derek, I'm so sorry about what I said."

"What do you mean?"

"My leg rule," she rushed out. "I didn't mean—"

He chuckled. "That was funny as hell. Don't give it a second thought."

Emilie breathed a sigh of relief, though she still felt bad. Open mouth, insert foot, much? "Is it bothering you tonight?"

"Not too bad," he said, dropping his pants leg and standing upright again.

Emilie fitted herself against the front of him, her legs in between his, and rested her forearms on his chest. "Did it happen while you were deployed?"

His gaze was still observing her. "Yeah, Afghanistan."

So, not just an amputation from an accident but from an injury received while in the service of his country. Another in a long and growing list of things to admire about this man. "I'm sorry," she said, finding it totally inadequate but unsure what to say to bring back his jovial mood from minutes before.

Derek shook his head and shrugged. "It's okay."

An idea came to mind, and it made Emilie's stomach

flip. But the longer she thought about it, the more she liked it. "So, I have an idea. But you totally don't have to do it."

His eyebrow arched and a bit of humor returned to his eyes. "Let's hear it."

Was she really ready for this? Emilie mentally brushed the question away. Inviting him didn't equate to a lifelong commitment, for God's sake. It was a summer barbecue. "If you're not doing anything on Saturday, would you like to come to my house for my get-together?"

His eyes went wide. "But . . . it's a family thing." She didn't know him well enough yet to know if what she heard in his voice was skepticism or wonder.

"It's not just family, though. Some people bring friends, too." When he didn't say anything, Emilie shook her head. "I didn't mean to make you uncomfortable. I just thought it might be fun—"

"No, it's not that," he said, rubbing his palms over her hands where they rested on his chest. "I don't really have any experience with big families is all. Don't wanna intrude."

Emilie smiled and took a deep breath against the ache in her chest. She could almost feel his solitude radiating off of him. "You can't intrude if you've been invited. Really." She pulled one hand free and cupped the hard angle of his jaw. "You don't have to answer now. Think about it and text me. I'd love to have you, but I'm being entirely honest when I say it's okay if you'd rather not. For whatever reason."

Derek looked into her eyes for a long moment and finally nodded. "I'd love to come. Count me in."

MARZ WALKED IN the back door of Hard Ink sure about three things. First, Garza worked for SWS. Second,

Emilie's party remained their best shot at locating Garza. And third, there was no fucking way he could attend that party without her knowing the truth.

The guilt was eating him alive.

Marz wasn't a dishonest person. He valued honesty and loyalty as much as any man could—and he'd seen firsthand what discarding those values could do. Hell, he'd experienced the fallout up close and personal. He was going to have to tell her what her brother was caught up in, and how that had led Marz to her.

As if his conscience wasn't kicking his ass hard enough, her saying he was a good guy had been like a punch to the gut. It had nearly stolen the air from his lungs. And then she'd followed it up with an invitation to spend the day with her and her family. To be welcomed in and introduced to those she cared about most in the world.

He refused to sully something so special—at least to him—by laying it on a foundation of lies. He *had* to come clean. Because he liked her in a way he hadn't felt in . . . maybe ever. And he wanted a shot.

Wasn't he due?

And who knew. Maybe Emilie wouldn't give him that shot. He couldn't say he'd blame her if that's how it shook out. But he wouldn't know until he'd laid himself bare and asked for her understanding. And her forgiveness.

Which meant he needed to hash this out with the team. They were bound to have an opinion—one he was going to have to win over if it didn't square with his own. But Marz couldn't keep doing this. He shouldn't have let himself develop feelings for Emilie. He knew that. He'd fucked up. But that horse had left the barn and there was no putting it back in.

He jogged up the metal-and-concrete steps to the second floor, punched in the key code, and entered the massive unfinished gym and found it unusually empty. Backtracking, he crossed the second-floor landing to the Rixeys' apartment door and keyed in another code.

Jeremy had beautifully remodeled the loft-style apartment, which was warm and masculine with its brick walls and exposed beams in the high ceiling. Everyone was hanging out in the big, combined kitchen and living room, piled onto the couches and chairs, relaxing and watching a movie on the flat screen. Chinese take-out containers covered the wide kitchen island. When the door closed behind him, a few gazes swung his way and a round of greetings rose.

Marz walked up behind one of the recliners and clapped Nick on the shoulder as he glanced to the TV in time to see Will Smith's character punch out an alien and welcome him to Earth. Ah, *Independence Day*. A classic.

"How was your night?" Nick said. Sitting on Nick's lap, Becca smiled up at Marz.

"It was good. Real good," he said.

"Learn anything useful?" Nick asked. At this, Beckett turned from his end seat on the closest of the two couches to listen in.

"I did. Kinda wanna chat about that, but it can wait til after the movie," Marz said.

Beckett's gaze narrowed. "We can pause it."

Nick pressed a button on the remote and the room went silent. All eyes turned to him. And then Nick's cell phone rang. "Ah, shit. Hold that thought," he said. "It's Miguel." He accepted the call and put the phone to his ear. "Hey, Miguel. What's up?"

Marz's stomach dropped, instinct telling him there

was no good reason for Nick's PI friend to be calling at almost eleven o'clock at night.

And, as the call went on, it became clear from this half of the conversation that the news wasn't great. When Nick hung up, his gaze scanned the room. "Well, boys and girls. We've got four more murders in lovely Baltimore City tonight. One more mid-level Churchman, which follows in the wake of the two from Tuesday. Two people that police think were innocent bystanders. Wrong time, wrong place kinda thing. And one off-duty cop—a guy that the department's internal affairs division has apparently been investigating for possible corruption."

"So that's three Churchmen down. Four, if you count Bruno. Five, if this cop was one of the guys in Church's pocket," Shane said from the corner of the far couch, Sara leaning against him. Bruno had been the high-level Churchman that had coerced Sara into a forced labor situation at the strip club. He'd also kidnapped Jenna in an attempt to make Sara give herself up after she'd run away—actions that had cost him his life.

"Who's doing it, though? Did Miguel say?" she asked. Her fingers played nervously with the long strands of the red ponytail draped over her shoulder.

Nick nodded. "That's part of why he called. They had a witness from one of Tuesday's murders who said she saw a Hispanic man fleeing the scene. And they have security-camera footage from the scene of the cop's murder. Another dark-haired man. Miguel said the ethnicity was unclear, but the guy's hair was in a ponytail again, which was part of Tuesday's description."

"So, same guy," Marz said, icy prickles running up his spine. "And he's Hispanic."

"Right," Nick said. "Miguel's contact at the department was going to send him a blowup of a still from the camera footage. He'll fax it over when he gets it."

A tense anticipation settled over the room, and then Beckett's cell buzzed.

The guy frowned as he fished the phone from his jeans pocket and answered. "Yeah?" Pause. "We just heard." Beckett put his hand over the mouthpiece and whispered, "Jackson." As in Louis Jackson, the guy in charge of the city's task force on gangs who Beckett and Nick had met nearly two weeks before when Charlie had still been missing. Turned out Jackson was Charlie's landlord's son, and he'd been helping them get up to speed on the lay of the gangland. "Was afraid you were gonna say that," Beckett said, and then he hung up.

"So, what's the RUMINT?" Marz asked, his stomach now reaching for the floor. *For fuck sake, what now?*

Becca frowned and whispered to Nick. "What's RUMINT?"

Nick smiled, but Marz beat him to the explanation. "Sorry. Acronyms are an affliction once you've spent any time in the military. Rumored intelligence."

"Right," Beckett said. "Word on the street is that Church has gone deep, deep to ground because it's an inside job. Someone's picking off his Apostles. Church has offered a million-dollar bounty to anyone who brings him those responsible for the murders. Or the explosion at Confessions."

Sitting on the floor between Jenna's legs, Easy ran a hand over his close-trimmed black hair. "Which is interesting, since, as we all know, it wasn't the same people." Easy had been their weapons-and-explosives guy on the team, and it was his handiwork that had destroyed Church's strip club last Friday night during their mission to rescue Jenna from the gang's clutches.

Marz nodded, his mind still stuck on the idea of the killings as an inside job. "I'm not the only one seeing the writing on the wall, am I?"

A ringing sounded from down the hall. "That's the fax. Hop up, sunshine," Nick said to Becca. She rose and he jogged down the hall toward his office. Becca, wearing a pair of flannel pajama bottoms and a tank top, busied herself collecting the dirty plates and cups from the dinner that sat on the coffee and end tables.

"I'll help," Sara said, rising to reveal that her outfit— from the boxers to the oversized tee—belonged to Shane. Marz's mind flashed to Emilie. The hints of skin beneath of the lace of her blouse and bra. What he wouldn't give to see her wearing nothing but clothing that smelled of him.

"You're thinking it's Garza," Beckett said, yanking Marz from his thoughts. "Right?"

"Makes sense to me," Shane said, looking to Marz.

That they were connecting the dots the same way he was filtered a little relief into his gut. "Question is, why the hell would Garza be picking off the Churchmen? And on whose order? Since we know he was working with Church at someone else's direction."

Beckett sat forward and braced his elbows on his knees. "Jackson said the gang's rep has taken a nose-dive. Maybe after the bombing and failed gun deal from Friday night, this secret partner decided Church was no longer reliable."

"So, if that's the case, then Garza's ending the partnership?"

"Real permanent, like," Shane said.

"Betcha didn't know it was Christmas?" Nick said

from down the hall. He returned to the room a moment later. "Or that Santa's name is really Miguel Olivero." He handed the printout to Beckett. Shane crossed the room to look over the guy's shoulder. Unlike Easy and Marz, Nick, Beckett, and Shane had met Garza when his team came through their base at one point a few years back.

"I think it's him," Shane said, staring at the page.

"Definitely him," Beckett said, his expression hardening.

"I think so, too," Nick said. "Hair's longer than when we knew him, but otherwise he looks like the guy I remember."

Marz released a long breath, his effort to understand what the hell Garza was up to leading him back to the scumbag's sister. "Emilie said Garza has worked for a defense contractor since he got out of the Army. About as solid a confirmation that the guy works for Seneka as we're likely to get."

Nick braced his hands on the back of the chair. "Speaking of her, what was it you wanted to talk about before the shit started hitting the fan?"

Bracing for a fight, Marz crossed his arms. "Right. Uh, well, besides the defense contractor work, Emilie also said she hasn't been close with her brother since he returned stateside. She wasn't real comfortable talking about that, either. Clammed up and changed the subject. I've gotta tell you, not a single thing makes me think she's in on any of this with Garza. Hell, I'm not even getting the vibe that she knows about any of it. She's just too . . . good, too genuine."

Beckett held up a hand. "Not a single thing besides the fact that she had a huge-ass stash of contraband in her basement, you mean."

Marz threw him a look. "Obvo, smart-ass. I'm talking pure gut-check instinct here."

Shane frowned. "So let's say she's totally innocent and unaware. The shit is hitting the fan for her brother, and now there's a bounty out on his head. What happens when he returns to her house to grab the stash and finds a bunch of baseball bats in the gun bags and flour instead of heroin?" he asked, referring to the fake items they'd put in place of the guns, heroin, and cash. They'd made sure the switcheroo wasn't obvious. Someone was going to have to open everything up to see it'd all been switched out and the real stuff was gone.

"Shit," Marz said, scrubbing his hands over his face. He'd been so focused on the fucking lies that he'd lost the forest for the trees. The forest being Emilie's safety. And *this* was why you didn't get involved with an asset in an investigation. "Nothing good, that's for damn sure." He planted his hands on his hips, his heart squeezing as fear slithered in. "Hell, maybe we should keep some protection on her. I could go—"

"Whoa. Hold on," Nick said. "Let's think about this, because we are short on personnel and high on problems that need solving right here. Do you have any reason to believe Garza spends time at her house?"

Marz thought about everything he and Emilie had talked about across their dates. "Truth be told, she hasn't mentioned him visiting. And we didn't see him while we were there. But he must've gone there at some point if he's responsible for putting the stash in her basement."

"No idea how long it's been down there, though," Beckett said. "And since we know he's responsible for these murders, that means he's in Baltimore tonight and was in town this past Tuesday. Circumstantials point to him being here."

Marz blew out a long breath. "Okay. At least until her family party on Saturday. Which brings me to the other thing I wanted to say. Emilie invited me to the party—"

"That's perfect," Nick said. "That's our chance to grab Garza."

Marz raised his hands. "Just hold up and let me say this. I get that going is good for the mission. But, I . . ." He shook his head.

Beckett shoved out of his chair and paced a few feet away. "Aw, for fuck's sake. Tell me you don't like this woman." He turned and stalked back up to Marz, the bulk of his shoulders straining the top of his gray Henley. "*Please* tell me that you kept your head on straight, your dick in your pants, and that you didn't get involved."

Anger slithered into Marz's chest. "Look—"

"Are you fucking kidding me?" Beckett said, a storm rolling in over his expression. "No offense to the ladies in the room, but this is a mission with real shit at stake, not the dating game. This fucking thing is heating up. We are being hunted. Hell, we have a goddamned bounty on our heads courtesy of one of the biggest gangs on the East Coast. So, please, Derek, tell me that you know what's important in all this."

That anger turned into a red-hot pressure that made Marz's chest feel like it just might burst. "Fuck you. I know what's at stake and what's important. I lost my leg over this situation. Or have you forgotten?" He felt like an asshole as the words spilled from his mouth, but he was maybe angrier than he'd been in . . . God, he wasn't sure how long. "Oh, *no*, you *never* forget about that, do you?" Annnd a little more of an asshole, now.

But he couldn't abide being questioned about his dedication, commitment, and seriousness. Not for a fucking minute. And not by the guy who was supposed to be his best friend.

Beckett's gaze went ice-cold and all emotion bled from his expression.

Marz turned away and faced the rest of the group, and he didn't miss the fact that the guys were looking at him like maybe he'd gotten a personality transplant in an alien abduction. Granted, anger wasn't something he showed a whole helluva lot. He shook his head. "I like her," he said in a low voice, refusing to feel ashamed of the first real feelings he'd maybe ever had for a woman. "I think I have to go to the party because it gives us our best opportunity of nabbing Garza. But I want to tell her what's going on. I feel like shit lying to her. I don't want to do it anymore and I don't think it's necessary. And now I think it's in the interest of her safety that she knows what's really going on around her."

Crickets. He met Nick's gaze, then Shane's, then Easy's. All the others were real busy not making eye contact.

Nick crossed his arms. "If you tell her, how do we know she isn't going to turn around and tell her brother?"

Beckett scoffed.

Marz squeezed his eyelids shut and mentally counted to five. It was the only chance he had at not taking a swing at the guy. Finally, he looked at Nick again. "I have no guarantee. Only thing I can offer is my instinct and my read of her. So it boils down to trusting me. Just like you did with Shane when he said he could trust Sara."

"He's got a point," Shane said, wearing a sympathetic

expression. It helped ease some of the pressure in his chest that Marz wasn't totally alone in this. "We had no guarantee Sara wouldn't turn around and tell Bruno what I'd told her. Or that she wouldn't set me up for an ambush when I thought I was meeting her." He put his arm around Sara's shoulders and caught her chin in his fingers. "Sorry, I never really thought any of that. Because my gut said you wouldn't." Shane looked at the other men. "Y'all did trust my read on that."

Nick rubbed his eyes and sighed. "Is anybody else as goddamned tired as I am?"

A low murmur of agreement rose up.

Marz sure knew he was.

"Look," Nick said, dropping his hands to his side. "I totally get where you're coming from. I sure as hell can't talk when it comes to having gotten involved mid-mission." He took Becca's hand. Marz could almost see the gears turning in his mind. Finally, Nick nodded. "I trust you. Always have. Go with your gut."

Relief flooded Marz's veins. "Thank you."

"We good?" Nick asked, scanning the rest of the group. Nods all around. Beckett gave a noncommittal grunt.

An awkward silence followed.

"Is that all?" Marz asked.

Nick shrugged. "As far as I'm concerned. Let's convene at oh-eight-hundred and figure out what's next."

"Good enough," Marz murmured, and then he turned and walked out. Up the steps. Across the unfinished apartment to his bedroom. He shut the door behind him.

All about the mechanics of moving now, he shut off his thoughts as he changed clothes and traded out his regular prosthesis for his running blade. He was a bundle of angst that needed to be worked out one way or the other. Because, the thing was, as much of an asshole as Beckett had been for saying what he'd said, he'd also given voice to some of Marz's own internal criticism of his conduct in this situation. And that shit burned.

He opened the door and nearly walked into Beckett.

Rearing back, Marz shook his head. "I don't want to do this," he said, nailing the guy with a hard stare. He pushed by him and didn't look back.

"Derek."

Just keep walking.

"Derek!" Beckett said louder.

Marz turned and looked over his shoulder. "Haven't you said enough tonight?" When Beckett didn't respond, Marz nodded. "I thought so."

And then Marz split. Despite the muscle fatigue that had made his thigh ache all day, he had a date with a treadmill. Way he was feeling right now, pounding the shit out of himself was the only way to keep his mouth shut and his fists from swinging.

Chapter 12

Emilie wasn't sure what woke her up. But the instant she was awake, she was sure that something wasn't right. The digital clock on her nightstand read 4:32.

As her eyes adjusted to the darkness, she realized it wasn't quite as dark as it should be. And then her vision adjusted further to realize that there was a low glow in the room. A low orange glow that moved over the ceiling. She glanced to the windows that faced toward the bay.

Her heart became a bass drum in her chest and her scalp prickled. Something was out there. What the hell?

She slipped out of bed and crossed the room to the window. She didn't have curtains or blinds up at either window facing the water, because she loved the view too much to block it.

For a moment, she couldn't make sense of what she

was seeing. Manny had built a fire in her backyard. Yeah, because, that's a normal thing to be doing at 4:30 in the frickin' morning.

Indecision gripped her right up until he tugged his T-shirt over his head and dropped it into the flames.

Gooseflesh broke out over her arms and neck. She couldn't think of a single good reason why someone would be burning their clothes in the middle of the night. But she could sure think of several bad reasons.

Not bothering to change out of her tank top and sleep shorts, Emilie took off across her room, down the steps, and back across the first floor to the back door. She yanked it open and flew out onto the porch, the chill of the night settling on her bare arms and legs. "Manny, what the hell are you doing?"

Holding his jeans in his hands, he whirled and jumped, his eyes filled with fear and his expression stricken. "Go back inside," he rasped, holding the denim to cover his hips even though he still wore boxers.

Ice crawled down her spine. "Not until you tell me what you're doing."

Manny shook his head. "Go in, Em. This doesn't involve you," he said, his voice almost tremulous.

It does now, she thought, but she bit back saying as much. Snark wasn't likely to help her in this situation. She stepped down to the grass and glanced to the jeans. "Why are you burning your clothes?" The grass was cool and damp under her feet.

He shook his head and retreated a step. This new fearful behavior set off all kinds of alarm bells in her head. She'd not seen him act like this before, and she wasn't sure how to read it. Another manifestation of his paranoia?

Manny tossed the jeans toward the fire, but his

throw went wide and only one leg fell squarely into the flames. He didn't seem to notice, because he crouched at a duffel bag by his feet and pulled out new clothes. Quickly, he jerked on a T-shirt and gym shorts. He toed off the boots he wore and stuffed his feet into a pair of sneakers, not bothering to tie them.

Emilie's belly knotted in suspicion and dread. Why would someone burn their clothes? She could only think of one reason, and it was one that required her to gather every ounce of courage she had. "Did you hurt somebody, Manny? Because if you did, we might be able to make it right. I can help you."

"Couldn't be helped," he said, voice like sandpaper. "It's kill or be killed now. Only way to keep us all safe."

Oh, God. He's killed someone. Not on a battlefield while serving his country, but here. Tonight. Tears immediately pricked the backs of her eyes. What had happened to her poor brother? To the man who had taken care of her, and she'd idolized, for most of her life?

Manny threw the gym-bag strap over his shoulder. "It'll all be over soon," he said. "You gotta trust me." He came to stand right in front of her, towering over her because of how much taller he was. "Do you understand, Emilie?"

She stared at him a long moment, then nodded. "Yes, Manny. I understand." And what she understood broke her heart.

He kicked his boots into the fire and swiped the jeans closer with his foot. "Good, now go inside and make sure everything's locked up. I'm gonna make this right," he said. And then he took off around the front of the house. A moment later, the loud rumble of the Hummer's engine sounded out.

Emilie stood there, absolutely frozen by an ice-cold

wave of grief and regret and sadness. If she'd submitted the psych eval petition two days ago, Manny would've been in a hospital by now. And whomever he'd hurt would probably be safe and snug in their bed right now. Her throat tightened and her gaze settled on the fire.

Her gaze settled on the jeans.

On instinct, she dashed toward the blaze, grabbed a denim belt loop, and tugged them out of the fire. All of one leg and part of the other had burned, but the seat and crotch of the pants remained intact. Flames still crawled up the material.

After a split second of indecision, she dashed into the house, grabbed the broom from the pantry, and flew back out. And then she beat the hell out of the clothing until she'd smothered every last cinder. Turning to the fire again, she thought to salvage the boots, too, but they'd been totally engulfed. And she couldn't see anything left of his shirt at all.

Setting the remains of his pants on her porch, Emilie turned on the outside faucet and unrolled the hose. And then she doused Manny's bonfire until it was nothing more than a smoking pile resting on a ring of blackened grass. Using the pole end of the broom, she knocked the pile apart, finding a few more red embers deep within, so she doused it again for good measure.

By the time she was done, Emilie was cold and shaky and just totally poleaxed by the realization that her once-loving brother had hurt someone. Had very probably killed someone, given his behavior and what he'd said.

With a last look at the remains of the fire, she dropped the hose to the ground, not bothering to rewind it, grabbed the jeans, and went back inside.

For a long moment, she stood in the dark kitchen,

everything inside her *not* wanting to see. Right now, the last thing she wanted was proof that what he'd said was true and not a delusion.

Taking a deep breath, she flicked on the light and spread the clothing out on the kitchen table.

A moan ripped out of her as her gaze landed on the dark red streaks and dots on the one hip and thigh. "No. No, no, no," she cried as she backed away from the sight. Her spine came up against the refrigerator.

Emilie slid down to the floor, curled her arms around her knees, and cried.

If she'd done something sooner . . .

If she'd fought harder with her mother . . .

If she'd been stronger and *faced* the reality in front of her. Just once.

But she hadn't, had she? And now Manny had hurt someone.

It was her worst fear come to life.

EMILIE WASN'T SURE how long she'd been sitting in a ball on the kitchen floor. But, by slow degrees, the sunrise filtered into the room.

Pain and regret sat like shards of glass inside her chest, but she couldn't fix what had happened. The only thing she could do was prevent the situation from getting any worse.

And, as far as she could see, that meant she couldn't delay submitting the emergency evaluation petition. She couldn't wait until after tomorrow. She couldn't give her mother the chance to see Manny first.

She just needed to act.

Emilie hauled herself off the floor and grimaced as her muscles and joints gave her the business for sitting in that position for so long. Keeping her eyes away from what lay on her kitchen table, she fixed her coffee and then made her way to the bathroom for a quick shower.

Fifteen minutes later, she was dressed and ready to go, not having bothered to dry her hair. She grabbed a hair band from her dresser and threw her hair up into a ponytail. Meeting her gaze in her bedroom mirror, she couldn't believe how bad she felt this morning after how wonderful she'd felt last night.

With Derek. Her date with him seemed like a lifetime ago.

She grabbed her cell phone from the charger and did a double take. The new-message icon was lit up. Who would've texted her over night?

The text was from Derek. *Good morning, brown-eyed girl. Need to talk to you about something when you have a minute. Call me?*

She stared at the message until she'd reread it at least five times, but whatever it was would have to wait. Emilie couldn't indulge in the fun that was Derek—

Derek. *Derek what?* How had she not learned his last name yet? Come to think of it, she didn't think she'd told him hers, either. Oh, well. Another time, assuming this thing with Manny didn't explode all over her life.

How can it not?

She really didn't know.

Downstairs, Emilie fished her laptop out of its case and clicked over to the still-open emergency evaluation form.

Her gaze scanned over the page until she reached the line asking for a description of the behavior that led her to conclude the evaluee had a mental disorder. Fingers shaking, she added a brief description of the events from last night, and then she hit print. From the direction of the tiny den that she'd turned into an office came the *chug-chug-chug* of the printer. She grabbed the form and folded it in three so it would fit in her purse, and then she carefully disassembled a frame with a picture of Manny in his dress uniform to take with her. When she was done, she returned to the kitchen, where she stood and stared for a long moment at the bloody jeans.

Whose blood is it?

The question turned the coffee sour in her stomach and made her glad she hadn't eaten anything for breakfast.

From a drawer, she grabbed the biggest Ziploc storage bag she had, and then she carefully folded what was left of the jeans in a way that kept the blood facing out. She stuffed them into the bag and pressed all the air out so she could zip it shut.

Blowing out a long breath, Emilie called the counseling center and canceled her day. She hated to do it, but this thing with Manny couldn't wait.

And then there was nothing left to stop her from leaving.

Almost mechanically, she gathered her things, walked out to her car, and pulled out of her driveway to make the trip to Baltimore. Since her brother didn't live in her county, the local police were useless where this situation was concerned, which meant she needed to visit the police station in downtown Baltimore, where the authorities would have jurisdiction to issue a Be On the Look Out bulletin and pick Manny up.

That forty minutes was the longest drive of her life.

THE CENTRAL BALTIMORE City Police Department inhabited a massive, foreboding building just a few blocks from where Emilie had dinner with Derek the night before. Once again, the juxtaposition of today's reality against the almost dreamlike perfection of last night's date struck her over the head like a two-by-four and left her with a dull ache she felt from the top of her scalp all the way down to her shoulders.

The inside of the station hummed with a frenetic energy. Phones ringing. People talking. Officers coming and going and escorting suspects and visitors here and there.

"May I help you?" a uniformed officer at the desk asked her.

Emilie hugged the Ziploc bag to her stomach, blood facing in, and nodded to the woman. "Yes, I need to talk to someone about filing a petition for emergency evaluation—"

"You need to go to the court—"

"I'm a clinical psychologist," Emilie said. Lay people had to go through a court procedure, but professionals with certain types of expertise could file the petition directly.

"All right, then. Have a seat and I'll get someone out to you shortly." The officer gestured to a long wooden bench at the side of the lobby.

Emilie didn't have to wait long. Within ten minutes, a uniformed officer leaned out a door on the side of the room and called her name. Her stomach flipped as she got one step closer to actually doing this. "That's me," she said as she rose and crossed to the handsome uniformed officer.

His eyes were so light they were almost yellow, a striking combination with his toffee brown skin. "I'm Officer Vaughn. Come on back," he said.

She followed him through the door and into a hallway with a row of gray cubicles. Portraits and plaques of past police commissioners and fallen officers decorated the scuffed white walls.

"In here," he said, gesturing to the last cubicle before the hallway opened up into a large and bustling room of desks.

Emilie sat in the hard plastic chair on the side of the desk and clutched at her purse and the baggy. Her insides felt shaky and unsettled, like she might throw up. What she was about to do couldn't be undone.

"So you're here to file a petition for emergency evaluation?" Officer Vaughn said as he settled into the chair and tapped his fingers against the mouse, waking the computer up and bringing the monitor to life. The BPD logo filled the screen.

"Yes, that's right." She fished the paperwork and Manny's picture from her purse. "It's for my brother," she said. "He hasn't been well for a while and in recent days he's deteriorated to the point where I'm concerned he's a threat to others. He refuses to seek treatment and is uncooperative toward any suggestions of help."

The officer scanned over the form, which detailed all his erratic behavior over the past days and weeks, his brow cranking down midway. "What's this about burning his clothes in your backyard?"

Emilie nodded and laid the bagged jeans on the desk, blood-side up. "I managed to pull these from the fire after he left. When I took them inside my house, I saw the blood so I bagged them up. His shirt and boots burned entirely."

Officer Vaughn typed his password into the computer and clicked through to what appeared to be a database search. His fingers clacked over the keyboard. "We've got two different things going on here. First, your petition appears to be in order, so we can issue the BOLO and search his known addresses and hangouts to pick him up. Second, your brother is a suspect in an ongoing case. Given this," he said, tapping his fingers on the plastic bag, "I'd like you to talk to the lead detective on that case."

Emilie's scalp prickled. Her brother was already on the authorities' radar. *God, what had he done?* "Of course," she said. "Can you tell me what he's suspected of doing?"

"I'll let the detective handle that. Just wait here a moment while I grab him," he said, rising from his chair.

"Sure," she whispered. When the man left the room, Emilie dropped her forehead into her hands. "Oh, God, Manny. What have you done?" she said to herself. At least she had proof she was doing the right thing by not waiting any longer.

"A moment" stretched into five minutes, then ten. Finally, Officer Vaughn returned. "Okay, Ms. Garza. I've issued the BOLO, which means however he's picked up, he'll be escorted to an emergency room, but he'll also be wanted for questioning. Detective Jeffers will be in shortly to talk to you more."

"Okay," she said, torn between relief and anxiety at the fact that she'd actually gone through with the process that could lead to Manny being involuntarily committed. Why was the right thing to do so often the hardest thing to do?

Officer Vaughn left her alone again, and every time someone passed in the hallway, Emilie sat up expecting it to be the detective.

Finally, a man wearing a brown sport coat with jeans came in, a badge clipped to his hip. "Emilie Garza?" he asked.

"Yes," she said.

"I'm Frank Jeffers." He slapped a file to the desk,

dropped into the chair Vaughn had used, and settled his gaze on the bloody jeans. "Officer Vaughn tells me you have information relating to one of my cases involving Manny Garza."

She swallowed hard. "Uh, I guess I might."

His gaze swung to her face and narrowed. He wasn't an unattractive man, but as she met his gaze, the word *beady* came immediately to mind. Distrust rolled off him, although she supposed that wasn't unusual given his line of work. "Why don't you start from the beginning?"

For a moment, Emilie struggled to determine what the relevant beginning actually was. Finally, she recounted his deteriorating condition, refusal to accept or seek help, his paranoia and belief that someone was after him, and the incidents at her house this week.

"Your brother is wanted for questioning in conjunction with a series of murders in the city. Can you verify his whereabouts on Tuesday afternoon and last night?" he asked.

Emilie gasped. "Murders?" As in, plural?

"That's right," Jeffers said, his face a practiced blank.

Thinking back over the week, Emilie shook her head. "I don't know where he was either of those times. I saw him on Monday afternoon and Wednesday night. He slept over my house on Wednesday and left Thursday morning when I did for work."

Jeffers pulled a small notebook from an inside jacket pocket. "Why did he stay at your house?"

"I don't know. It's not unusual. I divorced a few months ago and occasionally Manny would come stay with me." She shrugged. "It was hard being alone at first. But he's been acting odd lately, so I haven't been pushing because it agitates him."

After that, Jeffers asked her a series of questions to which she didn't have the answers: names and contact information of business associates and friends in Baltimore, known hangouts in the city, and whether he had a girlfriend. Apparently, the police had been to his house already and hadn't found him there. The more they talked, the more Emilie realized how superficially she knew her brother these days. Sadness created a weight on her chest. The only new information Emilie could provide the detective was Manny's cell phone number.

Jeffers fished in his sports coat and withdrew a business card. "Call me if you think of anything else or if you see him. He'll be transported to an ER first, of course, but we will need him for questioning, too."

Emilie nodded and accepted the card. "Of course."

Jeffers escorted her from the cubicle back out the hallway to the public lobby. He gave her a nod and then disappeared fast, like he was happy to be rid of her. Her emotions talking, no doubt.

Because the deed was done. She'd just taken steps to have her brother picked up and involuntarily committed. On one level, it didn't matter to the sadness and guilt clawing through her insides that the police had already been looking for him, because Manny would eventually learn what she'd done.

And Emilie didn't know if he would ever forgive her.

Chapter 13

*I*t had been another banner night of no sleep, so Marz was up well before he needed to be for the team's meeting at oh-eight-hundred. He checked on the key search and found it at forty percent. Progress, for sure. Didn't feel like it, though.

He made his way to the Rixcys' apartment and was happy to find Jeremy and Charlie up and fixing breakfast in the kitchen. "Oh, good. I'm not the only one rattling around already," Marz said.

"I don't rattle. I rock and roll," Jeremy said, turning so that Marz got a look at the writing on the guy's navy blue shirt. *HEAD Foundation. Please give generously.*

Marz laughed. Jeremy Rixey was good people. "Does that T-shirt work?"

Jeremy grinned and waggled his eyebrows, highlighting the piercing at the end of his right eyebrow. "Sometimes."

Charlie was shaking his head as he buttered some toast, but his quiet laughter proved that he enjoyed Jer's humor, too.

"And what's yours say today, Charlie?" Marz asked.

An unusually open smile on his face, he turned, butter knife still in hand. "I can actually live with this one," he said. "But I had to dig for it."

"I forgot I had that one," Jeremy said, pouring milk into his cereal. "Nick got it for me when he made it into the Special Forces."

The brown shirt had a picture of Mr. T from the old TV show *The A-Team*. Underneath it were the words, *Mr. T Shirt*.

Chuckling, Marz leaned on the granite island. "It's your fault if I spontaneously say, 'I pity the fool' "—he affected his best Mr. T voice—"for the rest of the day."

Charlie swallowed a bite of toast. "I think Jeremy's already said it three times this morning."

Marz grabbed a bowl and poured Frosted Flakes and milk for himself. The three of them ate standing up as they chatted.

"So I was thinking," Marz said to Jeremy around a bite of cereal. "I want you to do some ink for me."

The guy's face lit up like his T-shirt had just garnered him an offer. "Yeah? I'd be happy to. What did you have in mind?"

"I have some ideas on my laptop that I can show you. I want to start with one on the back of my calf. I want something where it looks like you're seeing inside my leg and it's metal and robotic inside. That sound like something you could do?" He'd been thinking about this one for a while, liking the idea of the human body as a well-oiled machine. It would be his first tat on skin beyond the parts of his body covered by shorts or a T-shirt. But he didn't have the same rationale for keeping himself unmarked where others could see as he used to. This cluster-fuck aside, there wouldn't be any more SpecOps for him, would there?

Jeremy looked at him a moment and nodded. "I can definitely do that. Likely be a big piece, though. Sure that's what you want to start out with?"

Marz smiled. "Not my first."

Jeremy lowered the spoon that had been almost to his mouth, his gaze going to Marz's bare, ink-free arms. . . . *Currently, anyway.* "Well, hell. Guess I shouldn't have assumed."

"No worries," Marz said, shrugging. "I've got twenty-four, actually."

Jeremy blinked. "*Dude,* you've been holding out on me," he said, pointing his spoon at Marz. "I am definitely getting my hands on you, then. Show me your ideas and I can draw something up. I'm booked all of today and I know you have a thing tomorrow," he said, making Marz's gut tighten in anticipation of coming clean to Emilie. "I can check my schedule for Sunday, though."

"That works," he said.

Just then, Nick and Becca joined them, Eileen right on their heels. Becca filled the puppy's dishes as Marz marveled at the size of Eileen's paws. They seemed to grow more every time he saw the mutt. A few minutes later, everyone else made their way into the kitchen, fixed their coffee or breakfast, and took up positions around the island.

"We're gonna need food again soon," Becca said,

emptying the box of Frosted Flakes into her bowl. "I can't believe how fast we went through everything."

"We're growing boys," Jeremy said, putting his arm around her shoulders.

"You're all garbage disposals, I swear," she said, chuckling and patting his stomach. Though, really, you couldn't have this many guys living under one roof and not go through the chow. "You're one of the worst and yet you're so lean. It's really not fair."

Hugging her in against his side, Jeremy winked. "It takes a lot of calories to be this awesome, Becca."

Nick gave Jeremy a playful shove as everyone chuckled. "Or to be such a big pain in the ass." Nick kissed Becca's cheek. "I'd like you to find a grocery delivery service. The way this situation is heating up, I want us out on the street as little as possible." He scanned his gaze over the group. "That goes for everyone."

The words settled a seriousness over the room that hadn't been there moments before, so Marz decided he might as well start talking shop. "I texted Emilie to let her know we need to talk. Will keep you posted." Marz could feel the disapproval rolling off of Beckett, sitting at the end of the breakfast bar on the island. Now that he'd had a chance to cool off, Marz felt like royal shit for the things he'd said to the guy, but part of him was still hurting, too. Because it seemed like Beckett's confidence in Marz had disappeared right along with Marz's leg. And that sucked some major ass.

Nick nodded. "Where are we on the key search for the chip?"

"I reached out to a few guys on new equipment," Charlie said. "Gonna take a day or two at best, which doesn't speed things up much."

"At about forty percent when I looked this morning,"

Marz said, feeling the weight of everyone's expectations on his shoulders. He didn't mind bearing it—he'd never mind bearing it for these guys—but it still left him anxious to show results. Not only did they need to know what information the chip held before they took on Seneka, but because it had been created by their colonel, it potentially promised to answer a whole host of questions. About why he'd thrown away his honor—and theirs. About what exactly he'd been involved with and with whom. And how it had landed on them, killing their friends and ruining their careers.

If the chip *didn't* shed light on some of those questions? *No. Not an option.* Marz would figure it out one way or the other. Just like he always did. "I gotta head downstairs and open up," Jeremy said, placing his bowl in the sink. "Grab me if you need me." He clapped Nick on the back.

"Yep," Nick said, giving his brother a nod.

When Jeremy left, Beckett clasped his hands on the granite and cleared his throat. The blue in his shirt made the blue of his eyes stark and bright. "Now that Jeremy's gone, I wanted to raise something," he said, surveying them all before staring at Nick. "Just thought I should bounce it off you before worrying him with it."

Nick's eyebrow arched. "Let's hear it." Marz eye-balled Beckett and braced for some bad news. Guy didn't talk a lot, in part because he was the type who thought through everything he said long before he said it. Which meant, when Beckett Murda had something to say, it was inevitably important and useful.

"I got to thinking. We're being hunted. Seneka may be involved, and they might've been involved with Merritt's dirty work in Afghanistan. Right?"

Everyone agreed, and Marz wondered where he was going with this.

Beckett met Marz's gaze. "Even if Seneka is behind Garza's killings, they *know* they're not the ones who blew up Confessions or ambushed the Churchmen's gun deal. Seneka has to be wondering who did. Which means both Church and Seneka would be looking for us."

Nick frowned, and ice slowly poured into Marz's chest. At some point, the people looking for them *would* find them, wouldn't they? The writing was on the wall for someone smart and informed enough to read it. His gaze scanned over Becca, Sara, and Jenna, standing near their guys and silently eating breakfast as they listened. He hated that things couldn't be more settled for the three women—they'd all been through enough.

"Yeah," Nick said.

Beckett turned his palms up. "I'm just playing this out here. Okay?" Nods all around. "We know Merritt was somehow involved with whoever or whatever WCE is."

A few months ago, Charlie had started receiving statements from a bank account in Singapore that had his father's name and Charlie's address. The bank had refused to provide Charlie access to the funds despite the death certificate he'd produced to prove his father had died. He could only see the account balance as well as the fact that there'd mostly been one depositor—something or someone with the initials WCE.

"So that makes me wonder if Seneka would've been involved with WCE, too." Beckett pointed at Charlie. "Charlie got nabbed after Church found out he was looking for WCE. And then Charlie got rescued—by someone who was also not Seneka."

Marz nodded, impressed as always with the way Beckett put things together. "Which would have to make Seneka wonder if it was the *same* person who rescued Charlie and kaboomed Confessions."

Beckett pointed at him, his eyes narrowed. "Exactly."

"Okay, granted," Nick said. "But where are you going with this?"

"Hang with me a second. *If*—and I realize this is a big if—Seneka asked themselves who is the one person, or one group, that potentially connected all those things together—"

"They'd come back to Merritt," Marz said.

"Yes. And if they were wearing their thinking caps, they'd come to us. The survivors of Merritt's ambush. *The* people who'd have the most to gain by saving Charlie—since he clearly found information proving Merritt wasn't on the up and up. Which backs the story we told."

"Or *tried* to tell," Easy said in a deadly quiet voice from his seat at the other end of the bar. They'd been roundly shut down by the army JAGs investigating the ambush and the team's conduct. The brass had finally given them a choice—freedom and keep their mouths shut or an all-expenses-paid vacation to picturesque Fort Leavenworth. The five of them had debated it, but decided to live to fight another day. They'd choked down the nondisclosure agreement, upon which their freedom hinged, and were sent home courtesy of an other-than-honorable discharge that sullied their previously stellar records and reputations.

"I follow all of that," Nick said. "But what does it have to do with Jeremy?"

Beckett tilted his head and gave the guy an expression that was almost sympathetic.

Oh, shit. Marz's brain got there a moment before the words left Beckett's mouth.

"Jeremy's a Rixey," Beckett said. "These assholes know our names. Hell, it was only the five of us who survived. If they put two and two and two together and get six, all they have to do is search for each of *us*."

Marz could see it the second Nick got it. If anyone involved in the conspiracy that had taken them down bothered to look, they'd find that Nick Rixey and his brother owned a business and lived in Baltimore.

"Searching for Rixey would reveal I live in Baltimore, and it would bring them here, to Hard Ink," Nick said, voice like sandpaper. "Which means Jeremy's in danger." Nick shook his head. "Which means we're *all* in danger."

"If they do the math," Shane said, holding up a hand. "I'm not trying to downplay this, because I think Beckett's onto something we need to keep in mind. But, clearly, they're in damage-control mode right now."

"Which for the moment is keeping them focused on Church," Easy said. "Or at least seems to be." Shane nodded.

Beckett looked at Nick again. "I wanted to talk to you about this before saying anything to Jeremy. I don't want to alarm him when there are a whole lot of *ifs* in the calculus I just ran. But I'm wondering what he'd think of closing up the shop 'til this is over. Minimize chances for noncoms to get involved or talk to the wrong person about who and what they've seen. And I'm also wondering what we might do to camouflage ourselves a bit here," he said.

Marz scrubbed his hands over his face. Beckett was

right both ways—both that it was a longshot that their enemies would work through all the steps that would lead to them, and that it was enough of a possibility to take precautions.

Nick braced his hands on the counter, his head hanging heavily on his neck. "That shop's his livelihood. As well as the livelihood of several other people. *Fuck*," he said.

"It was just a thought—"

"And a good one," Nick said with a troubled sigh. Finally, he looked at Beckett again. "I'll talk to him. I'd rather it not be a group thing at first." Marz didn't blame him. Let the guy have the privacy of his reaction, whatever it might be. "I can't guarantee what he's going to say, though."

Beckett nodded. "Fair enough."

A buzzing sounded from Nick's pocket, and he dug out his cell and placed it to his ear. "Hey, Miguel." Pause. Nick's eyebrows cranked down as he listened and nodded to whatever Miguel was saying.

What a godsend Miguel was. Retired BPD, a PI with lots of friends in all the right places around town, and a good man. He'd proved himself a friend to them all, time and again, over the past few weeks.

"This just gets more and more interesting, doesn't it?" Nick said, and then he signed off.

"What now?" Marz asked, wondering if the police had learned more about Garza and the shootings. On the one hand, it would be useful for the cops to get Garza off the streets before he killed anyone else or learned about the missing stash in his sister's basement. On the other, if he got captured, there went their chance to interrogate him themselves.

Nick scanned the group until his gaze landed on

Marz. "Not sure what to make of this, but Emilie Garza just left the central district police station. She filed an emergency psychiatric evaluation petition today. Against her brother."

EMILIE WAS GOING to have to tell her mother what she'd done. If she let that wait until tomorrow and her mother found out at the party, it would be so much worse. And—*Oh, God*—Emilie wasn't sure whether to hope the police did or didn't find Manny before her party. Either way could prove a disaster. If they did, her mother would be crushed by his absence—and at the reason for it. If they didn't and Manny showed . . . well, who knew what he might do.

Her cell phone rang from where it sat in the center console cup holder. *Derek.* Conflict fluttered through Emilie's belly. She wasn't sure she was in the right place to talk to him right now, but she also hated to ignore him. She thought about the text he'd sent this morning. What could he want to talk to her about?

Deciding to at least let him know she was in the middle of something, she picked up the call through her Bluetooth. "Hi, Derek," she said as she adjusted the hook of the earpiece. A siren wailed from somewhere behind her. She looked in her rearview mirror to find a police car pulling in right on her rear bumper.

"Hey, Emilie, I—"

"Crap. I'm sorry, Derek. I'm going to have to call you back. I'm getting pulled over by a cop. Not sure what I did."

"Oh," he said. "Are you okay?"

"Yeah," Emilie said as she glanced in her mirror. She was on a busy three-lane road heading out of Baltimore, and there was no curb lane to safely pull over. "Listen,

Derek," she said as she finally turned into the parking lot of a small industrial park. "I'm kinda in the middle of something today, aside from getting pulled over, I mean. I'll call you when I can, but I gotta go." She put the gearshift into park and glanced in the mirror again. The officer appeared to be looking at something on his dash. *One of those squad car computers? Probably.* He was likely running her license plate.

"Where are you, Emilie?"

"Um," she said, distracted by the search for her registration in the glove compartment. "Heading out of Baltimore. Shit," she said, fumbling the paper. It fluttered to the foot well in front of the passenger seat, forcing her to undo her seat belt. Leaning way over, she finally grabbed it. As she pushed herself back up, her elbow knocked her cell out of the cup holder and onto the floor below her feet. "Damnit."

"Emilie," Derek said, concern creeping into his tone. "What's going on?"

"I'm having a day here," she said, glancing behind her again to find the cop getting out of his car. *Damn.* If she fooled around reaching for her phone, would that seem suspicious to him? No sense taking the chance. She planted her hands at the ten and two on the steering wheel. "Um. The officer's coming, Derek, but I dropped my phone. Just hang on until I'm done, okay?" She unrolled her window and looked at the approaching man in her sideview—

Wait. That was Jeffers. Why would a detective pull her over for a traffic violation? Emilie's instincts sprang to life and made her scalp and neck prickle.

When he neared the window, she turned to look at him. "Detective Jeffers, did I—"

A gun appeared in her face, sending Emilie's heart beating into her throat. "Unlock the back door."

She made some sort of incoherent noise of fear and with shaking fingers hit the unlock button. "I—I don't understand," Emilie said, her voice breathy and tight.

"Emilie, who's there? What's happening?" Derek said in her earpiece, his tone lethally serious. Her mind raced, trying and failing to find an answer to that second question. The whole thing was so surreal, she was having a hard time processing it.

Jeffers got into the backseat right behind her and slammed the door. Emilie jumped. "Do exactly what I say and maybe you won't get hurt," he said.

"Emilie!" Derek said.

Shaking, she turned to look at Jeffers, but the gun's muzzle planted itself against her temple. "Did I tell you to turn around? Oh, and you won't be needing this." He ripped the earpiece from her ear and threw it out the window.

"Ow," she said, cringing and cupping her ear.

"Where's your phone?" he asked, his voice one step up from a growl.

"I knocked it on the floor when I got the registration out of the glove box. I think it went under the seat," she said, her voice shaky, her throat dry. If he took the phone, he'd find out she was mid-call. What would he do then? Cut off her lifeline to Derek for starters. *Oh, God, Derek, don't stop listening,* she thought, hoping he'd be able to realize she was in trouble.

"Good enough," Jeffers said. "Now drive."

"OH, FUCK," MARZ said, jumping to his feet and pressing his cell harder to his ear. The sound from their call had blinked out for a second, but then returned, more distant and tinny than before. What the hell was going on?

"What's the matter?" Charlie said, looking up from his computer.

Fear and anger skittered down Marz's spine and heated his blood. He muted his phone's mic. "Go get the guys, Charlie. I think Emilie just got carjacked by a cop."

"What?" Charlie said, rising.

"Go, Charlie. Hurry."

Charlie bolted across the room and wrenched open the door.

This couldn't be happening. If something happened to Emilie, Marz would wonder if he'd brought the danger to her door until his dying day.

Think, Derek, think. The tracking device! The one he'd planted on her car the night he and Beckett staked out her house. But he couldn't open the app connected to the device while he was on his cell phone. Goddamnit, he needed the guys here and he needed them here right this minute.

"Where are we going?" Emilie said, her voice brittle but her courage so obvious to Marz.

"When you need to know, I'll tell you. Now drive and shut the fuck up. And if you do anything erratic to attract attention, I'll put a bullet through your brain and then find your brother and mother next," the male voice said. Jeffers, he thought he'd heard her say?

The threat made Marz's breath catch in his throat. A long silence followed during which Marz nearly lost his mind.

Across the gym, the door burst open and the whole team streamed in, Beckett at the lead. Every man's face bore the same mix of emotions—concern, anger, and a readiness to fight. For him—and for what he cared about.

Marz lowered the phone, yanked a cord from underneath a pile on the desk, and used it to connect his cell to the computer's speakers. Then he put the call on speakerphone, sure to keep the microphone off.

"Was on the phone with Emilie when she got pulled over by a cop," he said as his friends, old and new, gathered around the desk. "She called him Detective Jeffers. From the sound of it, he demanded entrance to her car, threatened her, and is making her drive somewhere."

Making. The ways in which someone might compel such a thing were too infuriating to contemplate, but Marz's mind was filled with images of some monster holding a gun to Emilie's lovely brown waves.

"I'll call Miguel and see what he knows about this Jeffers," Nick said, whipping out his phone.

Marz looked at Beckett—and found total, lethal engagement and commitment hardening the angles of the man's face. "I need you," Marz said, his brain momentarily glitching on what to do next.

"Name it," Beckett said in an unwavering statement of solidarity that made Marz feel, for that instant, that they were their old selves again. Back before the ambush and Marz's amputation. Best friends and brothers who had one another's back no matter what.

"I put a tracking device on her car the night we watched her house. Can't get to the app because our call is still connected. Don't want to hang up in case they say anything else."

"I'm on it," Beckett said, finger flying over the screen of his cell. Beckett had the app, too, as he'd bought the devices.

Marz nodded, his heart was a freight train in his chest, and each fast chug seemed to rip at something inside him.

Please don't take her from me, too. Hadn't he lost enough? Hadn't he been alone enough? Marz blew out a long breath. Tension grew so thick in the air, he could've cut it with a knife.

"Shit, Miguel's not answering," Nick said. "Told him to call me."

"I got it," Beckett said, rounding the desk to stand beside Marz.

Without a second thought, Marz unhooked his phone again. "That's all we need. I'm going after her."

Beckett planted a hand on his chest and nailed him with a hard look. "Not alone, you're not. I'm going with you."

"Let's all go," Nick said. "You've got no idea where he might be taking her or what you might be walking into." He turned to Charlie. "Go down and tell Jeremy and Ike what's going on. Tell Ike to stay alert."

"On it," Charlie said, taking off across the room.

"Good," Marz said. "Then arm up and let's roll."

Chapter 14

Marz sat in the front passenger seat of Shane's pickup, wound tight as a fucking top. Shane whipped around a turn in the road, and Marz grabbed onto the hand strap, fully appreciating that his friend was hauling ass. The *only* reason Marz hadn't flipped his shit over the four minutes it'd taken them all to get their gear and pile into the truck was because the tracking app revealed that Emilie's car traveled in an easterly direction across Baltimore. In other words, in their general direction.

"People we care about being attacked is becoming a pattern I'd like to break," Easy said from the backseat, his voice like gravel.

"No fucking lie," Beckett said from right behind Marz's shoulder, one big hand gripping the leather of the seat.

Marz couldn't agree more, but he was concentrating too hard to make small talk. He held his cell against his ear so tightly the cartilage was starting to ache, and his eyes remained glued to the screen of Beckett's phone, where the app showed Emilie's car as a small blue dot moving across a map of Baltimore City. "Turn left at the next light," Marz said. "Let's try to intercept them before they get to their destination. Wherever that is."

"Roger that," Shane said.

From his cell phone, Marz heard a male voice bark, "Turn here."

"I can't get over," Emilie said.

"You will if you want to live," the man said. "Turn *here*."

Hang in there, Emilie. You got this. Just stay calm and do what he says. I'm on the way. Marz's chest throbbed against the noxious mix of sympathy, fear, and anger filling him.

Horns blared through his cell phone speaker. She'd obviously had to cut someone off. Marz wished he could see her to tell her how well she was handling this situation. Damn how he hoped he'd get the chance.

Watching the map, Marz saw Emilie's car turn north. Marz and the team pursued for a few more minutes, pushing hard to gain on them and adjust to further turns Emilie's car made.

Instinct pricked at something in his mind until Marz frowned and zoomed the map out a little. Ice sloshed into his gut. "Shit a fucking brick," he said. "What are the goddamned chances that they're headed toward the neighborhood where Church's storage facility is located and *not* going there?"

"None. Tell me what to do," Shane said. "Can we cut them off?"

Marz studied the map and tried not to think about that fucking storage facility. The one where Charlie had been held captive. The one where he'd seen several women locked up in the basement, too. Given that their badly outnumbered team had witnessed Church load the unconscious bodies of nine women onto boats belonging to drug dealers, it didn't seem a stretch to think that being sold or traded away was the likely fate for women the gang held as captives.

That couldn't happen to Emilie. That *wouldn't* happen to Emilie. Over Marz's dead body.

He bit out directions that Shane followed to a tee.

Marz had already sacrificed himself once for those he cared about. And he was more than willing to do it again.

EMILIE HAD NEVER been more terrified in her life. Of the gun muzzle planted against the base of her skull. Of the dirty bastard of a cop sitting in her backseat. Of the possibility that her phone had dropped Derek's call and she really was totally and completely alone in this situation.

A situation somehow related to her brother.

A situation his actions had somehow *caused*.

Anger and resentment rushed through her veins, and she reveled in their hardness and their heat. Those emotions strengthened her and sharpened her senses, and so were much more useful than the terror and powerlessness that she'd allowed to sneak in and take over. *No more.*

Even if Derek was still on the line, he wasn't here to help her. Which meant she'd have to help herself. But how? She could jump out of the car and take a chance at Jeffers shooting her or another car hitting her. That seemed fraught with danger. She could somehow work the name of the street they were on into a comment or question to Jeffers in the hopes Derek would hear, but that was likely to make the cop suspicious. He might be crooked, but he wasn't stupid, and he'd probably realize why she'd said it—namely, that she was trying to communicate with someone else.

What else?

Maybe she could ignore his directions and make a turn he hadn't commanded, buying her more time before they got wherever he was taking her. But if he shot her or busted that gun against the back of her head, she was going where he wanted whether she wanted to or not.

But would he *really* shoot her while she was driving and he was in the car? Emilie didn't know, but it was a choice between bad options and really, truly terrible options.

There *had* to be something, didn't there?

Heaving a shaky breath, Emilie glanced in the rearview mirror. "Does this have to do with my brother? Maybe I can help." A mix of old commercial establishments and run-down rowhouses lined the street, but she wasn't familiar enough with all of Baltimore to know exactly where they were.

The muzzle jabbed against the back of her head, making her suck in a breath. "You have a comprehension problem, Ms. Garza?"

"It's just," she said, hearing the shake in her voice even as she pushed on. "Maybe I can help without *all this.*"

He chuffed out a humorless laugh. "Oh, I'm counting on you helping, sweetheart." The malice in his tone unleashed goosebumps all over her body.

Emilie inhaled to try again, knowing she was treading on thinner and thinner ice.

Screeching wheels against pavement. Blaring horns. Emilie gasped and her gaze flew to the rearview again.

A big black pickup truck shot out of a cross-street and fishtailed onto the road behind her.

Jeffers lurched around in his seat and bit out a curse. The gun jabbed harder into her head. "Drive faster or die."

Emilie flattened her foot against the accelerator and the car jerked forward. Red glowing taillights formed a wall ahead at a stoplight. "There's traffic," Emilie said.

"Go around it," Jeffers growled.

"What?" she said. "How am I—"

"Just drive around the fucking cars!" he roared in her ear.

She flinched and gripped the steering wheel so hard her fingertips went numb. Turned out she didn't have to worry about how to stop or slow him down, because they were going to get broadsided running a red light. There was no way Emilie could do this. Unconsciously, her foot eased off the gas pedal.

Jeffers came up over the back of the seat, hovering over her as he shouted in her ear. *"Go. Just go. Do you fucking hear me? Drive!"* He punctuated his words by jamming the gun's muzzle against the side of her head.

Emilie pressed her foot down on the pedal, veered out into the wrong lane to go around the stopped cars, and barreled into the intersection.

"JESUS," MARZ SAID, his heart lodged in his throat as he helplessly watched Emily's Camry jerk out into the wrong lane and head for the intersection with no signs of stopping. Of course, she was just doing what

Jeffers had told her to do. No, what he'd *commanded* her to do.

"Fucking hell," Beckett said under his breath.

The Camry shot into the intersection. Into oncoming traffic. Amid a cacophony of angry horns and squealing brakes, one car skidded to a stop just in time, another spun out of control and slammed into the stopped car, sending it careening into the back quarter panel of Emily's car. The Camry's rear end swerved and she appeared perilously close to losing control, but then the car jerked straight again, rocking on its tires.

"If I stop, we lose our gain, so hang on," Shane said, abruptly shifting into the wrong lane to pass the stopped traffic, just as Emilie had been forced to do. Luck was on their side, because the combination of the accident and the changing lights cleared the way for them to cross the intersection without a problem.

Jeffers's continued shouting came through Marz's cell phone as the guy berated and badgered Emilie into doing what he wanted.

"Is there any way to cut him off from getting to the storage facility?" Shane asked, his focus and concentration like the sharp blade of a knife.

"No," Marz said. "It's about six blocks from here, but I don't want to lose sight of her. Not with the cop forcing her to take these risks. If she loses control of the car . . ." Marz shook his head, his gut souring. "Stay with her."

"Okay," Shane said.

Up ahead, the Camry flew through the tail end of a yellow light. Before they could get there, a tractor trailer started across the intersection.

"Sorry, Marz," Shane said as he nailed the brakes, sending them all jerking forward.

Gaze fixed on the map on Beckett's phone, Marz said. "They're straight ahead. Go when you can."

When the light finally turned green, Shane gave an impressive demonstration of aggressive driving, passing everywhere he could until they got around all the law-abiding drivers and were flying up the busy road.

"They're turning," Marz said, his gaze lifting from the map to scan the street ahead of them. Sure enough, about a block up, a white car was making a lefty across the road—and into one of Church's four front establishments called U-Ship-n-Store. "Just once it would be nice not to be right," he said. "It's the goddamned storage facility." Who the hell knew how many Churchmen they might face inside.

"I got 'em," Shane said. "Get ready."

A lethal, focused calm flooded through Marz, and the feeling was like an old friend. It was the feeling he'd always gotten before an op when they'd still been in the Army, his body's way of cutting through all the bullshit and paring things down to the essentials. He palmed his gun, itching to get off the busy strip, where an exchange of gunfire wouldn't be as risky to bystanders as being out on the open road.

They came to a rough stop across from the storage facility's parking lot, nonstop traffic coming the other way, preventing them from turning. "Come on," Marz said as he watched Emilie's car careen around the back of the main building. He put his hand on the door handle, one command to his muscles away from jumping out and making a run for it.

Fingers gripped his shoulder. Marz jerked his head around to find Beckett watching him and fully aware of what he'd been planning. He gave a single shake of his head. "Patience. We'll get her, but let's be smart so we don't lose any of us."

Marz heaved a breath and gave a sharp nod.

Shane turned hard left and screeched across the road and into the parking lot, the pickup jumping at the harsh hit to the uneven curb.

"Gonna pull up parallel to the back corner of the building. Stay low and get out on the driver's side so we have cover til we see what we're facing. Get ready."

Marz's muscles were braced to explode. The truck came to a stop and the inside erupted into fast, efficient activity as they poured out onto the far side. The Camry was already parked and what Marz saw sent red-hot rage flowing through his veins.

Emilie was resisting Jeffers's efforts to get her out of the car.

Scooting out of the truck, Marz couldn't tell what Emilie was doing. He whirled, aimed his gun across the hood, and assessed. It appeared Emilie was hanging on to something as Jeffers struck at her back, head, and arms repeatedly.

Finally, it must've been one blow too many as she sagged.

"Go, go, go," Nick said. In a series of coordinated actions they'd performed a hundred times before at as many different places, they bolted from behind the truck, using other cars and the corner of the building for protection. Beckett got off a few silenced rounds that took out the backseat window and glanced off the hood.

Jeffers fired back, his gun's retort echoing loudly off the storage buildings behind and to the side of their location. Marz crouched behind a black Lexus and aimed his gun, hoping for a shot of his own, but then Jeffers pulled Emilie's body up against him like a shield—her back to his front, his gun pointed at the side of her head. The only thing Marz liked about the sight was the fact that her eyes were open. She hadn't been knocked out by Jeffers's assault. Everything else turned his blood molten hot with rage.

"Who's got a shot?" Marz yelled, seeing his team-mates take up their own positions in his peripheral vision. If Jeffers got her inside the building, this situation would go from bad to worse in a heartbeat. Already, Marz worried that the sound of gunfire would draw more unfriendlies. Jeffers backpedaled faster, half dragging Emilie, who had a hard time moving her feet fast enough to keep up.

Problem was, Jeffers knew what the hell he was doing. Of course, he would. Which left Marz no choice but to take a chance.

He bolted from his hiding spot and raced low and fast across the lot toward the Camry.

"Goddamnit," he distantly heard Beckett curse.

"I'll kill her!" Jeffers yelled, keeping his gun trained on Emilie's head.

The words were like a sledgehammer to the knee-cap, but Marz shoved the pain away. He needed focus and discipline more than anything else right now. He shielded himself behind Emilie's Camry, which placed him maybe fifteen feet from the door—and from Emilie. Close enough to see the fear and pleading in her eyes.

Jeffers reached for the door handle. Marz looked for a shot but didn't have one, not without risking hitting her, too. The cop yanked the door open and ducked inside, but Emilie gripped onto the edge of the door as if to resist being taken in.

"Fuck," Marz said, admiring and fearing for her in equal measure.

She cried out, and then her fingers flew free and she disappeared behind the gray door. It slammed shut behind her.

The one thing working on their side was that they'd been inside this building before. The night they'd rescued Charlie from Confessions, they'd also raided this storage facility because they'd been told by a lower-ranking Churchmen that Charlie had spent some time at this location, too. So they weren't going in totally blind.

The team quickly convened at the door.

"On my count," Nick said, grabbing the door handle. "Three, two, one, go."

Nick opened the door, and Marz and Beckett cleared the opening and the hallway beyond, the team streaming in behind them. They cleared a utility room, a security room with several monitors depicting images of the business's service counter and parking lot, and a bathroom, making sure there weren't any enemies hidden behind them somewhere. From there, they entered a large room that appeared to be for shipment storage. The room was a maze of stacks of boxes of every shape and size. If anyone was there, they weren't going to be easy to find.

It was too damn quiet for a business in the middle of the workday.

The team got about five feet in when shots rang out.

Adrenaline flooded through Marz's body, honing his senses even as chaos erupted all around him. Two guns fired from across the room, and the team took cover and returned fire. Voices shouted commands, and Marz dove behind a stack of boxes, a whizzing sound letting him know he'd just gotten damn lucky.

Was one of the shooters Jeffers? Was Emilie in this holding room somewhere?

Marz peered around his boxes and made a dash toward the next set.

His movement attracted fire again, and the direction from which it came became more apparent as Marz watched where the rounds struck stacked boxes or the far wall. He had to take out that shooter and find the other one.

Marz looked to Shane and Beckett, who held positions to his right. Shane gave a series of hand signals indicating they'd flank the shooter and come up on him from both sides. Marz gave a tight nod and took off in a low, careful crouch.

Moving as quietly as he could, Marz used the boxes as cover and continued toward a long counter—the perfect hiding place for a shooter.

A muzzle came around the edge of the doorframe closest to the counter. Marz jerked back for cover just in time. Bullets tore into the boxes behind him, sending Marz all the way to the floor. Nick dove behind a trash can. Marz squeezed off a few shots and then released his spent clip and inserted a new one.

More gunfire from the doorway. Nick gave a signal that he and Easy would take out that shooter and secure the door. And then they were all in motion.

Marz, Beckett, and Shane converged on the counter. The African-American man—who Marz recognized from the photographs they'd taken at last week's drug deal—raised up to fire, not realizing how close his enemy had gotten. Without hesitation, Beckett put a bullet between the man's eyes.

Regret that it was all coming to this slinked through the back of Marz's mind, but now was not the time to contemplate their actions nor how their investigation had turned them into vigilantes. Even if these scum suckers deserved everything they got.

"Clear," Nick said from the doorway. As he protected that position, the others swept through the remainder of the room to ensure no baddies hid somewhere behind them. In the process, they found the stairs down to the basement behind a door in the corner.

So far, Emilie was nowhere to be found. Where the hell was she?

Moving forward in the building brought them to the public storefront, where customers paid for packing materials and shipping or rented storage units. Marz peered at the face of the man Nick had taken out, but this one wasn't familiar. The front was otherwise empty and a dead end, aside from the glass door that went out to the parking lot. Marz's gut said that Jeffers hadn't taken her back outside.

That left the basement. The team gathered near the door, and Nick met everyone's gaze. "On my count," he said, grasping the doorknob to the basement. "Three, two, one, go."

In a crouch, Beckett peered low around the door-jamb, earning some new gunfire. He returned fire and started down. "Clear," he called.

They rushed down, stepped over a body sprawled at the bottom, and spilled into the room below, a lounge from the tables and couches that filled the space. In one corner, there was a door to the outside, but it was heavily bolted from the inside, so no one appeared to have exited there. When they opened the interior door on the far side of the room, gunfire erupted again.

Easy grunted, drawing Marz's gaze. Blood soaked

into the torn shirt over his upper right arm. His gun arm. *Shit*.

"How bad is it?" Marz said.

Looking down, Easy shook his head. "I'm fine. Let's do this."

They cleared the doorway and then faced a long hallway with doors on both sides. Marz wanted to growl in frustration. This was taking too freaking long. Last thing they wanted was to give their adversaries enough time to call in reinforcements or for a passerby to hear the exchange of gunfire and call the police.

First room was empty. Second room held a huge cache of weapons and ammunition.

"Holy shit," Beckett said.

"A heroin empire requires a lot of firepower to protect, apparently," Marz said, but he moved on. There was only one thing he cared about finding. Emilie.

From down the hall, shots rang out again, pinging off the walls around them. A sharp intake of breath. Marz whirled to track the noise and saw Nick bleeding from the neck.

"Flesh wound," he said in a tight voice. "Let's end this fucking thing."

"Oh, shit," Shane said as he crouched and pushed open the third door. The hallway light illuminated the barred cells that filled the long, dark rectangular space.

"Fucking hell," Nick said.

Marz's skin crawled. Would Jeffers have stashed Emilie here? He felt for a light switch and then reared back in case someone took a shot. All stayed quiet. A few of them crept through the room while Beckett and Easy watched the door. Cell one was empty. So was cell two.

"We got two noncoms here," Shane said, staring into

the third cell. Marz joined him, hope flaring. But neither of the blond-haired women crouched on the floor beside a cot was Emilie. But goddamn if the gang wasn't into kidnapping as a regular thing.

"I'll take care of this," Shane said. "Go find Emilie."

As Marz retreated, he heard the women plead with Shane not to hurt them. He reassured them, his words filled with Southern charm.

Out in the hallway again, all hell broke loose.

"Incoming!" Beckett yelled.

They all rushed back into the cell room as an explosion rocked the hallway. Marz's head glanced off the cement floor, shooting a ringing ache through his skull. Debris rained down on them and the lights flickered.

Vision blurry from the hit to the head, Marz blinked, twisted his prosthesis free from a pile of rubble, and awkwardly pushed himself off the floor.

"Everyone all right?" Shane yelled as he ran toward them.

"Yeah," Marz said, accepting Shane's hand.

Three pissed-off affirmatives answered as the other guys dragged themselves off the floor.

Footsteps in the hallway. Coming their way.

Beckett stalked to the doorway, glanced around the jamb, and squeezed off three quick rounds as debris floating in the air around him. "Clear," he said.

"Stay with the women," Nick said to Shane, and then he turned to Easy. "See if you can find the keys." Both men nodded.

Stepping over pieces of drywall, chunks of cement, and two more bodies, Marz, Beckett, and Nick left the cell room and cleared two more rooms, then approached the last door on the hallway.

If Emilie wasn't here, where the hell was she?

Chapter 15

$\mathcal{B}$etween Jeffers's constant stream of threats and jabs with the gun at her head and the soft space under her chin, the throbbing of her skull and back from where he'd hit her earlier, and the way each fired shot ratcheted up the fear and adrenaline in her body, Emilie was holding on by a very thin thread.

But Derek had come for her. Somehow he'd found her and come for her. The GPS on her cell phone, maybe? Who knew. All that mattered was that, because of Derek, she was going to have a chance to come out of this alive.

Sitting in a chair in the corner of a dingy office, Emilie kept her eyes trained on Jeffers. If she got a chance to disable him, she would take it. Her brain raced as she considered what she might do to get his gun away from him or knock him out.

Three more shots echoed from the hallway. Closer now than before.

"Come on," Jeffers growled as he looked at his cell. The minute they'd holed up in this room, the guy had placed some calls. To whom, she didn't know, but it was clear that he expected help to arrive. And that Jeffers considered her someone that a church would want. Whatever that meant.

How did a police officer get away with being this fundamentally bad?

The doorknob turned, just the littlest bit. Unfortunately, Jeffers must've seen it, too, because he yanked Emilie from the chair by the arm and held her in front of him again. What a freaking coward this guy was.

The door exploded inward in a spray of wooden shards. Emilie barely bit back a scream as a huge dark-blond-haired man appeared in the doorway.

Jeffers fired a series of shots at the opening and the man jumped back and disappeared. A moment later, the man ran across the opening of the ruined doorway, firing as he moved. Emilie braced and flinched, waiting for her body to register the searing pain of a gunshot. But it didn't happen. Cement dust rained down from the wall above them.

And then another shot, and Jeffers hollered and jerked his gun hand. Where had that shot come from? But the answer hardly mattered because just then, Jeffers's weapon clattered to the floor as his hold loosened across her shoulders and throat.

Reacting on pure instinct, Emilie reached behind her, grabbed the man's crotch, and squeezed as hard as she could. He let her go altogether as he roared in outrage and pain. She scrambled to the floor for the gun, turned on her butt, and pointed it at her captor. She squeezed the trigger.

"Don't shoot!" came a voice from behind her.

But the bullet had already hit Jeffers in the chest, and the man went immediately pale as he grabbed his hands over his heart.

"Oh, my God," she said as the reality of what she'd just done sank in. Her world sucked down to the hole in the front of his shirt and the small stain of red spilling from it.

Derek crouched beside her and gently laid a palm on her forearm. He spoke words she couldn't hear as she watched Jeffers's body buckle and fall. "Emilie? Em? It's over," Derek said, the words finally penetrating the buzz between her ears. Two other men—the big guy who'd kicked down the door and a dark-haired man—rushed around them to Jeffers.

Slowly, she pulled her eyes away from the cop and looked at Derek. The relief on his face reached inside her chest. "Derek?"

"Yeah," he said with a small smile. "It's over now. You're safe." His hand slid up her arm to where her fingers still gripped the gun. He gently grasped the weapon and withdrew it from her hand.

Emotion surged through her—disbelief, guilt, relief, anger, fear, and an overwhelming gratitude toward Derek. Tears gathered in her eyes and lodged a knot in her throat as Derek gently took her by the arms and helped her up.

"I've got you now," he said.

Her knees felt like Jell-O. "Is he dead? I didn't mean to kill him," she said, staring at the growing circle of red on the dress shirt under Jeffers's coat.

Fingers gently forced her gaze away from the blood.

"I don't know, but it was self-defense, Emilie. You did nothing wrong here," Derek said, his voice filled with conviction. He pulled her into his arms.

Emilie melted against him, shaking so hard her teeth clattered and her back hurt. Part of her didn't want to see, didn't want to know, but she still found herself turning her head toward the group of men on the floor.

The men crouching over Jeffers fired a series of questions at him, but all Emilie could clearly hear was the sound of that single gunshot—the one with which she'd killed another human being—ringing in her ears.

"It's no use," the big guy said as he fished through the man's pockets, removing his wallet and cell phone.

"Then let's get the hell out of here before we get company," the dark-haired man said. He rose and turned toward her, and Emilie noticed he had an angry-looking cut across the side of his neck that had soaked the neckline of his T-shirt with blood.

But she didn't have time to ask about it, because they rushed her down the hall and joined four others—two men and two women—at the midway point. The women looked nearly as shaken and bewildered as she felt. One of the men appeared to have been shot in the arm. The dark red running down his brown skin immediately resurrected the image of the bloodstain on Jeffers's shirt. She couldn't get away from the blood.

Every time they passed a body on the floor, Derek's arm banded around her more tightly. Debris and destruction. Dead bodies. Bullet holes in the walls. It looked like a war zone. What in the world had she fallen into? And who—or what—was Derek really?

Upstairs, they made their way back the way she'd come in.

At a small room in the rear of the building, Derek

halted. "Wait a second." He turned to one of the other guys. "Let me grab the security footage." He darted into the room and Emilie gravitated just inside with him, not wanting to be separated from him. Not after he'd saved her. And not when his presence was the only thing keeping her from falling apart. "Damnit," Derek bit out. He turned toward her, but his gaze looked over her shoulder. "The footage from today is gone. All of it."

"Shit," the dark-haired man said as he dragged a hand over his head. "So we missed someone."

"Or someone came in after us. Either way, we're on the grid now," the big man said, stark blue eyes flashing. "Nothing we can do about that. Let's go."

The men hustled Emilie and the other two women out the back door. When Derek directed Emilie toward a truck, she looked up at him. "My car. My things."

"What do you need?" he said, guiding her toward her damaged Camry. "Can't take the car. The damage will attract the attention of the police."

Emilie thought of Jeffers's obvious corruption and an icy certainty tossed her belly. "We can't call the police on this, can we?" Silent tears slipped down her cheeks. "That man . . . the one I k-killed . . . he was a detective. I saw him at the station this morning." *Oh, God. I haven't just killed someone. I killed a cop.*

"I know," Derek said.

For some reason, his answer wasn't as surprising as she felt it should be. But her mind was spinning from how crazy and surreal she found this whole situation. If she couldn't trust the police, who could she trust? Who were the good guys? It was like her world was a snow globe and someone had just given it a strong shake. She no longer knew which way was up. "Um, m-my purse and laptop, please," she said. "Oh, and my cell phone is on the floor."

Derek retrieved the items and walked her across the parking lot to a black pickup. The same one that had followed her earlier.

"We've got too many for the truck," the big guy said, "so I hot-wired the Lexus. I'll bring the women. And Easy's gonna ride with me. We'll follow you back."

Words were exchanged that Emilie didn't hear as Marz helped her up into the tall backseat. Marz climbed in beside her. Her hands shook so bad that it took her three tries to secure her seat belt. Then two men jumped into the front seat and they pealed out of the lot.

"Hey," came Derek's soft voice from beside her. "Are you okay?"

Emilie braced her hands against the seat as the truck took a turn too fast. "Uh, yeah. I think. I don't even know." She wasn't really sure what exactly had happened yet. Or maybe it was that her brain didn't believe it. Either way, her body trembled and her thoughts were a jumbled mess.

Derek gently cupped her jaw as his gaze ran over her face. "We'll get you checked out when we get back to our place. Our driver's name is Shane," he said, nodding toward the handsome man with blond-tipped hair. "He's a medic. And Nick's girlfriend is a nurse."

Emilie could hardly believe that it had just been last night that she and Derek had their wonderful date. What would she have done if Derek hadn't come? What would've happened to her? She stared into his brown eyes and found comfort and affection there. A warm pressure filled her chest—something that was entirely for and about him. "Okay," was all she could say as she reached out and brushed some white dust from his brown hair and the shoulder of his gray shirt.

The dark-haired man, Nick, turned in his seat. "I hope you're all right." When Nick's gaze went from her face to the window behind her, Emilie looked over her shoulder.

A dark Lexus followed them with the big man at the wheel.

Turning back, she looked where Nick was holding the edge of his t-shirt against the wound on his neck. "You're bleeding," she said. "And so was the guy in the other car. I think you all got the worst of it." All Emilie had were some bruises from Jeffers striking at her and a lifetime's supply of bad dreams.

"That was Easy," Marz said. "He took a hit to the arm."

"I'll call Becca and let her know what's headed her way," Nick said, facing front again and placing a phone to his ear.

"I know there's a lot coming at you right now, Em," Derek said, taking her hand. "But I'll explain everything when we get back."

"To your place? Where's that?" Emilie asked, giving voice to just one of the probably million questions bouncing around between her ears.

Derek's smile was small and almost apologetic. "Not far."

Part of Emilie wanted to lose herself against the warm strength of Derek's chest and block everything else out. But another part—the part Jack's infidelity had damaged inside her—yelled that Derek was keeping all kinds of things from her. She knew he was ex-army, but he'd come after her, guns blazing, with a whole *team* of guys. Who did that? What kind of person had the ability to do that? Could he *really* be just a computer guy? Her head throbbed as she tried to come up with answers that made any damn sense. So she denied herself his comfort, even though she could almost feel his desire to take her into his arms.

That yelling voice got louder and louder inside her head until she had to know more. "How did you find me, Derek?"

He sighed and looked down at their joined hands where they rested on her denim-clad knee. Little cuts covered the back of his hand and forearm. Cuts that hadn't been there last night. He'd gotten hurt saving her. "Did you get my message from this morning?" he asked.

"Yes," she said, staring at those cuts.

"I've wanted to talk to you since last night. I'm done keeping things from you, and while I think it'd make more sense if I could tell the story from the beginning, I'll answer your questions now if you really want," he said, his thumb stroking over the back of her hand.

Oh, God, I was right. He is *keeping things from me.* Her stomach squeezed and nausea threatened. She hadn't thought she could feel any worse than she did when they'd left that building, but she'd been wrong. "Tell me," she whispered.

His eyes held none of the humor or playfulness she'd associated with him since that first time they'd met. "I put a tracking device on your car. My team and I have been looking for your brother. That's what led me to you."

For a moment, the words just floated there. And then they began to sink in.

Tracking device.

Manny.

Led me to you.

The pain in her head suddenly had nothing to do with Jeffers hitting her. "So, what? Like, an investigation?"

"Yeah," Derek said with a sympathetic gaze.

"I thought you did computer work," she said, her mind reeling.

"I do."

She scoffed and swallowed hard against the knot suddenly lodged in her throat. "Just not the typical nine-to-five in a cubicle kind."

He was such a handsome man that part of her hated to see the pain and sadness on his face, but the last thing she wanted right now was to find him attractive. Not after he'd lied to her. Not after he'd used her. Not after he'd broken her trust.

It all came back to Manny once more. After everything she'd been through—because of him—she was as angry at him as she was worried about him.

God, she suddenly just felt angry at *everyone*.

"You were just using me to get to Manny," she said, the words gritty and bitter on her tongue. She pulled her hand away from his and crossed her arms. Hurt flashed through his eyes, and Emilie looked away so she didn't give into the still-present desire to receive his comfort, and give hers in return. She glared out the window. "That's why I don't know your last name, isn't it? You didn't really want me to know who you are."

"God, I hate this," Derek said. The regret in his voice drew her gaze back to him. "I hate that you got caught up in this. And I'm sorry." He met her gaze, and she couldn't deny the sincerity there even as her heart wanted to protect itself and harden toward it. Derek glanced downward, shoulders hunched, and seemed to gather himself, and then he looked her straight in the eye. "It did start out that way, Emilie, but when I showed up at your work that afternoon and said I hadn't been able to stop thinking about you, that was true. That was real." He heaved a breath. "And my last name's DiMarzio. Derek DiMarzio. I never offered it because I feared your brother would recognize the name if you mentioned it."

She turned her face toward the empty seat beside her, not wanting to get sucked in by his handsome face and pleading eyes. "It was all based on lies, Derek," she said in a thin voice. "How do you expect me to believe it was real? Any of it?" Her mind resurrected the images of them laughing together, talking, kissing. She remembered the feeling of his lips on her breasts and his hand between her legs. *Oh, God.* It'd all been a show.

"I don't," he said.

Surprise rocked through her. She hadn't expected him to validate her opinion, only to justify and turn things around to blame her. Like Jack had done. Slowly, she turned to look at him. Derek always seemed to wear his emotions on his expression and in his eyes, and right now both appeared absolutely gutted.

His smile was so sad. "That's my greatest fear, that you won't be able to forgive this. And I'd understand, because I know lying to you was unforgiveable. I wouldn't blame you," he said, kneading at his thigh and making her wonder despite herself if his leg was hurt, too. "But I hope you'll at least give me the chance to explain."

But Emilie wasn't sure there was anything he could say to make all of this okay.

Chapter 16

$\mathcal{T}$hings with Emilie were going about how Marz feared they would. Piss poor. Not that he blamed her in the least.

She'd been carjacked, used as a human shield, and had taken a life in self-defense. Right now, she was entitled to feel any way she wanted. But, damn, if that wasn't a horrible backdrop against which to come clean to her.

All he wanted to do was take her in his arms and hold her there for the rest of the day. Proof that she was alive and safe and there with him. Proof that he hadn't lost her in that goddamned storage facility. But even though he'd rescued her and she sat right next to him, the heat of her thigh warming his, he was pretty sure he'd lost her anyway.

She looked at him, her eyes filled with distrust and

accusation, and he felt the physical distance she was keeping from him like a punch to the gut. And every bit of it was of his own making.

Another casualty of this whole catastrofuck of a situation that'd started over a year ago on a dirt road in another country. *Sonofabitch.*

Shane eased the truck to a stop at the chain-link gate to Hard Ink's parking lot. He pressed a button on a remote control and the gate swung open, and then the truck crunched over the gravel and parked.

Emilie's expression was ten kinds of skeptical as she took in her surroundings. Filled with abandoned industrial buildings, this neighborhood wasn't much to look at.

"We're here," he said, ignoring the throbbing in his forehead. He opened the door and hopped out, and then offered her a hand down. She ignored it and used the armrest on the door instead. Derek swallowed back the hurt and shut the door.

Damn. He'd been so close to something great with her that he felt the loss like a . . . well, almost like an amputation. Empty as his chest felt, he was pretty sure his heart had been ripped out. But it didn't stop it from hurting like a motherfucker.

The whole group crossed the lot and made their way inside and up the stairs to the Rixeys' apartment. The two women who they'd rescued from the cell looked as shell-shocked as Emilie.

The team was barely through the door when Becca came running to Nick and gave him a onceover. His shirt was a bloody mess. "Oh, God, what happened?" she asked. Nick gathered her in his arms and hugged her in tight against his uninjured side. Charlie stood right behind her, his face a mask of concern.

From the corner of Marz's eyes, he saw Shane and Sara, and Easy and Jenna, repeat the same relieved reunion. And a hot, sour wave of jealousy flashed through Marz's blood so hard and fast that he nearly doubled over. At the back of the group, Beckett was gesturing to the women they'd found to sit on one of the couches.

"Just grazed," Nick said to Becca. "Take a look at Easy first, 'kay?"

Becca dashed a tear away from the corner of her eyes and nodded. "Come have a seat, Easy?" She guided him to one of the tall stools at the breakfast bar, where she'd laid out an array of medical supplies. Shane's big first-aid kit sat on the floor beside her.

On the trip home, Easy had stripped off his black t-shirt and wrapped it around his biceps. Together, he and Becca unwound the ruined clothing and she went to work on him.

Marz turned to Emilie. "Can I get you anything? A glass of water?" God, her face was so pale.

Emilie put her hand to her head. "I don't feel so good."

Marz cupped her cheek in his palm, and his heart lurched at getting to touch her again. And at the fact she didn't pull away. But her skin was cold and clammy. "Come sit down," he said, guiding her to one of the couches. She sat shakily, and Marz crouched in front of her. "You might be going into shock."

"Can I help with anything?" Beckett asked from over Marz's shoulder.

"Orange juice," he said. "Thanks."

With a nod, Beckett crossed the crowded room. Marz's gaze caught sight of Shane patching up Nick's neck before returning to Emilie. Too many close calls today. He braced his hand on the cushion next to her and watched as Emilie looked from one person to the next around the room. "Hey," he said, pulling her gaze back to him. "Try to slow your breathing and take nice, deep breaths."

She blew out a shaky breath but did as he asked.

Beckett returned with the juice. With a thanks, Marz took the glass and put it in Emilie's hand. "Drink some of this. Let's try to get your blood pressure back up." She took a long drink. "This is Beckett, by the way."

"Uh, hi. And thank you," she said.

"Welcome," he said with a nod, and then his blue eyes turned to Marz. "So, uh, any thoughts on what we do with these women?"

Marz turned to see the two blonds huddled on the couch together, watching everyone and looking very wary. "Just find out who they are and what their story is." Beckett looked like Marz had just told him to don a pink tutu and do a dance. Marz almost chuckled. "Never mind. Just sit with Emilie." He turned to her and pretended he didn't see the wariness on her face, too. "I'll be right back."

Crossing to the other couch, Marz debated what to say to put the women at ease. He sat on the coffee table in front of them. "Hi," he said. "I'm Derek. You're safe here. No one's gonna hurt you."

"Who are you?" the one with the long blond hair asked. "Why did you help us?"

"We're just some guys who are trying to do the right thing," he said. "No way we were leaving you there. What are your names? How did you get in there?"

"I'm Haven, and this is Cora. Our car broke down and we trusted the wrong people to help us," she said, looking down at her lap and picking at a thread hanging off the hem of her jean shorts.

Cora's bright green eyes flashed. "It wasn't our fault, Haven. The guy had a freaking tow truck. It looked legit."

Marz leaned forward and braced his elbows on his knees. "Of course it wasn't your fault. Trust me, we've had a lot of interaction with the Church Gang and they're bad news any way you define it. They prey on women and they sell them." A gasp sounded out from behind him. He looked over his shoulder to find Emilie staring at him, clearly listening. *Good. She needed to hear these things, to realize what was at stake.* Marz turned back to the girls. "So it definitely wasn't your fault, Haven. Okay?" The girl nodded, but it was the nod of someone being polite, not believing. "How long were you there?"

Haven shook her head. "It was hard to tell because there weren't any windows. But judging by the meals they brought us, four days."

"Jesus," Marz said, scrubbing a hand over his face. "Are you from Baltimore? Is there someone we can call for you?"

The girls looked at each other and Marz saw it the moment they decided not to answer that question. Or, at least, not to answer it honestly. "We were passing through," Cora said with an expression that dared him to push. "And there's no one."

Sooo, clearly there was a story there. Interesting that they hadn't asked to call the police, either.

"Do either of you want something to eat or drink? Can I get you anything?" Marz asked.

Hope flared in Haven's blue eyes. "Would it, um, be possible to take a shower? I understand if not, it's just—"

"We can definitely make that happen. Don't worry.

And relax. You're safe here. Promise. As soon as we get my friends patched up we'll figure out how to best help you."

"Thank you," Haven whispered, her voice cracking. Cora took her by the hand and pulled her in for a hug.

Feeling like he was intruding, Marz looked across the room to where Sara and Charlie watched as Becca worked on Easy's gunshot wound. Though he wasn't making a sound, E's expression was pinched with discomfort. Jenna stood at his side and held his other hand.

"I'll be right back," he said to the women. Was he imagining it or was Emilie's gaze following him as he crossed to the island? Wishful thinking, no doubt. More of that punched-gut feeling rocked through him. He joined Shane and Nick as Shane finished bandaging the neck wound. "Okay, boss man?"

Nick arched an eyebrow. "I'm not the boss. But I'm fine. Just a scratch."

Shane gave him a hard stare. "A scratch that would've been catastrophic if it'd hit an inch to the left."

The thought impacted Marz like a bucket of ice over his head. They'd all lost enough, and Marz refused to lose any more of these men. They were his family of choice. His brothers in every way that mattered.

"Yeah, but it didn't." Nick clapped Shane on the shoulder. "Thanks for the repair job."

Shane nodded and turned toward Becca and Easy. "You need a hand, Becca?"

"No," she said without looking away from her work. "We're doing good."

As Shane nodded and cleaned up, Marz and Nick walked over to Easy. "Shit, E," Marz said. The bullet had torn clean through his deltoid.

"Yeah," he said, voice tight. "It's all right." Like hell it was. And, really, this was the last thing the guy needed to deal with. Wasn't he already feeling bad enough?

"Ain't nothing about any of this all right, Easy," Nick said, and then he looked at Becca. "How bad is it?"

"Honestly? It was messy, but he was lucky. If the bullet had hit the bone or lodged inside the arm, we would've had a much trickier situation," she said, tugging off her bloody gloves and donning a clean pair. "Jenna, would you like to help?"

"Yes," she said, eagerness plain in her tone and expression. "Of course."

Becca grabbed a long roll of gauze. "Put on a pair of gloves and come apply pressure." The women went to work.

Since those two were busy, that left Sara to ask about helping Haven and Cora. Marz pulled her aside and explained what was going on.

"I'd be happy to help them," she said. "I'm just really glad you rescued them, too."

Marz nodded. "Come on, I'll introduce you." This time he didn't have to wonder if Emilie was watching him, because her brown-eyed gaze bounced between him and the women, concern clear in her expression. A few minutes later, Sara grabbed some drinks for herself, Haven, and Cora, and guided them down the hall to the room she shared with Shane.

Scrubbing his hands over his face and pressing his fingers into his aching temples, Marz heaved a deep breath. Shit, he was tired. And, damn, if adrenaline letdowns weren't a bitch.

Shaking it off, he crouched beside Emilie again, needing to check in with her even if he was the last person she might want to talk to. Her face was still too pale. "Feeling any better?"

A quick nod and she lifted her glass. "Yeah. This is helping. I feel like I'm decompressing."

"I know what you mean. Just take your time. When you're ready, we'll talk." His gut clenched at the thought of where that conversation might lead.

"Okay," she said. "Are Nick and Easy all right?"

Marz glanced toward the island. "Yeah, they will be. Would you give me a second?" he asked. When Emilie nodded, he rose and crossed to Nick. "Hey, man," he said.

"What's up?" Nick asked in a voice that sounded as tired as Marz felt.

"You should go tell Jeremy what's going on. He's gonna wanna know. And he should hear about that"— Marz pointed at the bandage on Nick's neck—"from you. "

Since Marz had spent a fair amount of time teaching Jeremy the ropes on running their comms and computer research, he was well aware that Jer often felt bad about not being able to help more. Jeremy wanted to be kept in the loop, and Marz didn't blame him one bit. Nick was Jer's older brother, and Jeremy had nearly lost him once when two bullets had cracked Nick's pelvis and perforated his intestines in an ambush. Jeremy deserved to know the four-one-one.

"Roger that," Nick said. "I'll grab a clean shirt and do it now." He disappeared down the back hallway. "Marz, why don't you let me clean up your arm?" Shane asked.

Twisting his forearm this way and that, Marz examined himself. *Just scratches, except . . .* He twisted his arm again and something glinted in the overhead light. *Shit.* "Yeah, I think you'd better. I've either got some glass in there or I'm so awesome I sparkle." He wasn't really feeling the humor, but he felt like they could all use it.

Shane gestured to the chair and rolled his eyes. "Ass. Chair. Now."

"Dude. Why have you gone monosyllabic on me?" Marz asked, his gaze going from Shane to Emilie. She frowned as she watched them.

Nick returned wearing a gray button-up. Rolling his sleeves, he made for the door.

"Mind if I come?" Charlie asked. "I feel bad for not giving him a head's up earlier, but he was with a client."

"Not at all," Nick said. They left together.

Shane sighed. "Sorry. It's not you. I'm just fucking pissed off." Shane's sister had been nabbed off the street near their house at the age of eight, so Shane had always felt protective of and responsible for women in trouble. No doubt today's discovery of the two women at Church's storage facility was picking at that particular scab. Hard.

"You got 'em out," Marz said as he took his seat.

A single nod. "I know," he said. "Are you limping worse than normal or is it just me?"

Aw, hell. He really didn't want this attention. "Just you," Marz said. They had two gunshot and three kidnapping victims to help. Last thing anyone needed to worry about was the fact that he'd twisted his right knee when the explosive blast had knocked him to the ground.

"Bullshit," Beckett said from across the room.

Marz nailed Beckett with a stare. "*Ohhh,* so *now* you're feeling talkative." Emilie's glass was empty, and she spun it in her hand. "Could you make yourself useful over there and please get Emilie some more to drink?"

She held up a hand. "I'm okay. I feel better." She carried the glass into the kitchen and settled it in the sink, then turned and braced against the far side of the island.

Beckett came and joined her, his arms crossed over his chest. Both of them watching Shane pick glass out of Marz's arm was about as comfortable as having an armful of glass in the first place. Marz actually hadn't registered how much it stung until Shane started working.

Tweezers. *Plink.* Tweezers. *Plink.* Tweezers. *Plink.*

The more Shane picked at the debris in his arm, the harder Marz's head pounded. He absolutely loathed the idea of doing this, but everyone else was busy. "B, will you find me some ibuprofen, please?" He rubbed at his forehead above his left eyebrow.

Beckett's eyes went wide. He was the one person Marz made a point of not asking for help unless the guy offered or Marz had no choice. Not because he thought Beckett wouldn't do it—he would. But because Marz didn't want his best friend to see him as any weaker than he already did.

"Careful," Shane said, eyeballing Marz. "You're gonna have a shiner."

"Oh," he said, dropping his hand. A moment later, he accepted four little red pills and a glass of water from Beckett. "Thanks."

His friend gave a tight nod. And then it got quiet and awkward again. Marz felt like whistling. Or telling knock-knock jokes. Or sticking a fork in his eye. Literally, anything would've been better than having the woman he wanted and the friend who couldn't *not* worry about him watch him get doctored up.

Bracing his hands on the counter, Beckett dropped

his head and rolled his neck. Marz frowned as the guy eyeballed Emilie, because Marz could almost see the wheels turning in his friend's head. "Did you know Derek saved my life?"

"Beckett," Marz said, as surprised to hear those words come out of his friend's mouth as he was embarrassed that Beckett was telling Emilie.

Her mouth dropped open and she shook her head.

"Our Special Forces team got ambushed at a roadblock," he said, completely ignoring Marz. "Seven didn't make it. I'm only here—"

"B."

"—because Derek knocked me out of the way of a grenade. Instead of being blown to bits, I only had a busted-up leg and this," he said, gesturing to the scars around his eye. "Lost a little vision, too. But Derek"— Beckett met his gaze, and Marz's chest got tight at the emotion in the other man's eyes—"well, he lost a leg. And while he lay there bleeding to death, he told jokes. Worst injury of any of us, and he told jokes to keep everyone's spirits up."

Marz felt Shane looking at him, but he couldn't meet the guy's gaze, because hell if Beckett's words weren't lodging a freaking giant knot in his throat.

Beckett twisted his lips and his Adam's apple bobbed on a hard swallow. "He is the most loyal and self-sacrificing person I've ever known—"

"Jesus, Beckett," Marz said, dropping his face into his hand. Why the hell was the guy doing this right now?

"—and he didn't have a choice but to lie to you. To protect us and to protect you. And since he was protecting us, he couldn't immediately trust you. Not when you were the sister of a man who, I'm sorry, we know is involved in criminal activity and we have more than a passing suspicion was involved in the corruption in Afghanistan that led to the ambush, our friends' deaths, and our discharge from the Army."

Emilie blinked at him, mouth and eyes wide.

"So, I hope you'll give my man here a chance, because he deserves it. And because there's a lot you don't yet know."

Holy shit. Did . . . was it possible that . . . Had Beckett just pleaded Marz's case to the woman he liked, not eighteen hours after chewing his ass out for liking her? Why? It was possibly the most words Marz had heard Beckett utter at one time since they'd been reunited almost two weeks before. And Beckett had uttered them trying to help mend fences.

Realization dawned on Marz. Mend fences. Not just between Marz and Emilie, but between Marz and Beckett, too.

It was like a piece of himself had been lost, and Beckett's words had clicked it back into place.

Marz raked his hand through his hair, emotion making it so he didn't quite trust his voice.

"Okay," Emilie said. "So what else don't I know?"

EMILIE WAS BEING torn in two. Knowing that Derek had used and lied to her made her want to shut him out. More than that, it made her *need* to shut him out to protect her heart and mind from re-experiencing the kind of pain that Jack had caused. She couldn't go through something like that again. *Ever.* But between Beckett's impassioned words and watching Derek put those poor women at ease, a big part of her wanted to believe Derek was a good man caught between a rock and a hard place, and, therefore, she wanted to give him a chance. Not to mention, she wouldn't be sitting here if it weren't for his risking himself to rescue her.

We're just some guys who are trying to do the right thing. That's what he'd told the women. If Manny really had done all the bad things Beckett said—which seemed more and more likely given the way he'd behaved at her house, his blood-stained clothing, and the fact that everyone in the world seemed to be after him—Emilie supposed she could understand why Derek might have kept some things from her. Intellectually, she could understand, anyway. Emotionally, though, it was a little harder. Okay, a lot harder. Because when she'd first heard the words that confirmed he'd lied to her, it had put her right back in the moment when Jack's mistress had shown up at her front door.

Emilie took a deep breath. "What else don't I know? It's clear my brother's in a lot of trouble. So, tell me. Tell me everything." She glanced from Beckett to Derek, and damn if the naked emotion in Derek's expression didn't reach inside her chest and chip at the walls she'd thrown up around her heart.

"Fair enough," Derek said to her, his gaze scanning over her face. Was that longing she saw in his eyes? "We done here?" Derek asked Shane.

"Almost," he said, bandaging a few of the deeper cuts.

"Would you please check Emilie out when you're done with me?" Marz asked him. Shane nodded.

"I'm feeling better," Emilie said in a low voice. Here she was pushing him away and he was still trying to take care of her.

"That's good," Shane said. "But you just experienced a pretty traumatic experience and you were struck multiple times. I'll be quick, but an exam is a good idea," he said, his gray eyes asking for permission.

"Okay," she said. She *had* been feeling bad, and with each passing minute since the crisis ended, her body seemed to register a new bruise or aching joint, as if she'd been under anesthesia and now it was wearing off.

"You're good to go, Marz. And keep up with the damn ibuprofen for your leg," Shane said.

Emilie took Derek's seat and, true to his word, Shane was quick. All her vitals came back normal, and there was nothing to do for the bruises and tender spots she had other than to ice them and let them heal. Derek handed her some pain reliever and, when Shane was done looking her over, introduced her around. Taking care of her, again.

Finally, Derek held out a hand. "Let's go talk," he said.

Don't take his hand. Don't take his hand. Don't take it. Emilie slipped her hand in his, no less conflicted than she'd been since their truck ride here, yet was pulled to Derek by something deep inside her.

He led her out of the apartment and across the landing to a huge room that once must've been a warehouse or a factory. Now it was a gym. Why had he brought her here?

"To the extent that I have one, this is my office," he said, pointing to an L-shaped plywood desk in the back corner of the room. He pulled two metal folding chairs together and gestured for her to sit.

For some reason her belly did a flip-flop. As she sat, she wasn't sure whether or not she wanted to be persuaded by whatever he wanted to tell her. Actually, that wasn't really true, was it? Emilie wanted to be persuaded, because she wanted Derek. His smile, his humor, his loyalty toward his friends. His kisses. But she was *afraid* of being persuaded. Afraid to go one more step forward with him. Because where Derek was concerned, Emile felt the same longing she thought she'd seen in his eyes. And if she gave into Derek's words and her desire, then her heart was going to be all the way in this. Which meant he could break it again, just like Jack had.

"I never said 'thank you,'" Emilie said as Derek sat next to her. "The words are entirely inadequate, but no matter what, I mean them."

"When I heard you get carjacked, there was no choice. I had to rescue you. I had to protect you. I had to get you back."

Heat skittered down Emilie's spine. One of the things she missed about having a relationship was having a partner who had your back in all things, so the conviction of Derek's words spoke to a fundamental need inside her.

She nodded. "Tell me."

He laced his fingers together in his lap. "It's a long story, so bear with me. Like Beckett said, over a year ago my team was ambushed and a lot of us died or were injured. Turned out our colonel was involved in smuggling heroin out of Afghanistan, and that blew back on us. About two weeks ago, the five of us who survived reunited to rescue Becca's brother, Charlie—the blond-haired guy who was at Nick's apartment when we arrived—from the Church Gang—"

"That's what Church is? A drug-dealing gang?" she asked, her memory vaguely recalling the newspaper article she'd read mentioning them. So *that's* what Jeffers meant. She shuddered. And felt slightly less sick about having shot him, killed him. Though just thinking that thought made her heart skip a beat.

"Yes," Derek said. "*The* drug-dealing gang. Most powerful one in Baltimore, with sway up and down the East Coast. They have lots of important friends in their pockets, which means we haven't been able to go to the police or to an ER if someone is hurt. We don't know everything about why the gang took Charlie— our deceased commander's son—but we do know it has something to do with the ambush and whatever our commander was into. In trying to learn more about the connection between the gang and Afghanistan, we came across Manny, who some of my teammates met over there."

The mention of her brother made her belly tighten with a dark anticipation. Part of her didn't want to know all the vivid details of what Manny had done, but a part of her *needed* to know, needed proof that her belief that he was troubled had been correct.

"Emilie, your brother was part of a deal that exchanged money and women for drugs. He's been working with the Church Gang, although he's doing it on behalf of someone else. We think it's Seneka, the security contractor he works for. And we believe Seneka— and therefore Manny—may have been involved in what happened to us during and after that ambush."

She pressed a hand over her lips and shook her head, her mind reeling at the thought of Manny involved in selling human beings. The brother she'd idolized her whole life! The one who'd stood up to high school bullies on behalf of the weaker kids. The one who'd stood up for *her* time and time again. "O-Okay," Emilie whispered, although there wasn't a thing okay about it.

Derek nodded. "We needed a way to confirm Seneka's role because, after we got Charlie back, we decided to try to clear our names. You see, the five of us were blamed for the ambush. Our previously clean performance records were suddenly marred with behavior problems and low marks. We only kept our freedom because we agreed to keep our mouths shut about corruption or conspiracy. The other choice was Fort Leavenworth. So we looked for Manny, but the guy is not easy to find. No mentions on the internet. Unlisted phone numbers. No address." Derek cleared his throat. "And then we found you."

"Oh," she said, her stomach sinking.

"Yeah." He heaved a long breath. "We staked out your house on Monday night. That was when I placed the tracking device on your car. We were only hoping Manny would show up so we could question him. When he didn't, we decided I should try to meet you to see if I could learn about your brother through you. I know that was wrong, but we were desperate and out of time. It's not a good enough excuse, I know, and I certainly didn't feel good about it—then or now . . ."

Emilie studied Derek's handsome face, and found nothing but sincerity and regret there. "Okay," she whispered, her brain scrambling to compartmentalize everything that had happened. Her kidnapping. Shooting Jeffers. Learning Derek had lied, but also finding her way to viewing the situation from his perspective. What would she have done different?

"Tuesday afternoon while you were at work," Derek said, dropping his gaze, "Beckett broke into your house to see if he could find a number or address for Manny."

Emilie's mouth dropped open on a gasp and prickles ran down her spine. "Oh, my God, he *what*?"

Derek pulled out his phone and worked his thumb

over the screen. "It was wrong, I know, but we were desperate to find proof that could clear our names. Truth be told, we still are." He turned the phone toward her and asked, "Emilie, does this look familiar to you?"

Heart racing in her chest and outrage swirling in her belly, Emilie grasped the cell phone and stared at the picture. A pile of suitcases and long canvas bags. "Not at all," she bit out and pushed the cell back into his hand.

"I didn't think so. Right from the beginning, I didn't believe you had anything to do with it. This picture is of a stash of heroin, cash, and semiautomatic guns Beckett found in your basement."

"What?" She rose and paced, each step intensifying the pounding in her head. Emilie really didn't think she could get anymore gobsmacked than she was at the revelation that a stranger had broken into her house. But, nope, she was wrong there. "Can I see the picture again?" she asked, her gaze going immediately to the screen when Derek handed it to her. It was definitely the old coal bin in her basement. "I didn't put it there. I didn't have anything to do with it. I don't even go down there because I'm scared of snakes and spiders." *God* Manny had brought guns and drugs into her house? *That's* what he'd been doing in her basement?

"I believe you," Derek said, trust plain in his gaze. "But given my teammates' safety was on the line in all of this, I couldn't fully trust you with my story right away. But every time we met, my gut said you weren't involved in Manny's illegal activities, which was why I told the guys last night after I got home that I was coming clean with you."

"That's why you texted me this morning?" she asked, feeling even more torn than before.

"All of this," Derek said, gesturing with his hand, "was why I didn't take you up on the offer of getting a hotel room. I couldn't let myself be with you when I'd lied. Though I sure as hell wanted to," he said, heated eyes running over her body. "And I didn't want to come to your party with it unsaid, either. I know how important your family is to you. And, never having had one, I know how important it would be to me, too. I didn't want to disrespect that."

She wasn't sure whether her heart or her body reacted more. Her heart so appreciated what he'd said about her family, and the reminder that he didn't have one opened up an ache in her chest. The mention of her fantasy of taking him to the hotel right near where they'd made out passed a tingle through her lower body. Was it really possible that their date had just been the night before? It felt like whole days had passed since then. Days during which she'd been kidnapped, shot someone in self-defense, and learned her brother was a criminal. It nearly made her head spin. "Derek—"

"Wait. There are a few more things you need to know." He tilted his head as if to assess her. She nodded, certainty filling her that whatever else he had to say wasn't going to be good. "That string of murders in Baltimore this week?"

Emilie's stomach dropped to the floor as her brain resurrected the image of Manny's blood-spattered jeans. "Manny," she said softly. Not a question. Not after what the cops had said this morning.

Derek pressed his lips together and nodded. "Yeah."

Her mind whirling, Emilie released a shaky sigh. Derek had once again confirmed her worst fear where Manny was concerned. He truly had returned from war a changed person. Maybe no one returned from something as brutal as war unchanged, but either way, the end result for Manny was something dark and twisted. "I filed an emergency psychiatric evaluation petition this morning. Last night, Manny showed up at my house in bloody clothes, and then he built a bonfire in my backyard to burn them. It was only the worst and most recent in a long line of abnormal behavior."

Something fierce and protective shot through Derek's gaze. "Shit. We switched out the stash in your basement with flour and basement bats. Did he notice?"

She shook her head, kinda relieved to learn her basement wasn't full of contraband anymore. "He never came in the house."

"Good. That's good," Derek said. "How was he otherwise?"

Emilie hugged herself. "Honestly, he seemed scared. I'd never seen him like that before."

"The head of the Church Gang put a million-dollar bounty on his head, so *all kinds* of people are currently looking for him. That might be why." Derek kneaded at his thigh, and Emilie wondered how badly his limb was bothering him.

She sat heavily back into her chair. "That must be what Jeffers meant," Emilie said. "He told someone on the phone that I'd be valuable to Church. Why, I don't know."

"Probably because you represent a way to your brother, who they want."

"Oh, God," Emilie said, feeling lost and confused and like she didn't know whose life this was. She braced her elbows on her knees and dropped her face into her hands. "This is a nightmare."

"Yeah," Derek said. "That's for sure."

Emilie peered at Derek, and he suddenly looked utterly exhausted to her. Dark circles marred the skin around bloodshot eyes. She was completely over- whelmed by this situation and she'd been in the middle of it for a matter of hours. It sounded like Derek had been caught up in it for a year. Concern and sympathy poured through her. "I'm sorry for what happened to you and your friends," she said. "And for whatever part my brother played in it."

Derek gave her a small smile and a nod. "I'm sorry for lying to you."

"Thank you," Emilie whispered, looking down at her lap. Thing was, she didn't know what to say after that. What she wanted and what she thought were best for her—*safest* for her—were two different things, and she didn't know where that left her. Or them. She pushed to her feet and paced again. When she turned back to him, he was right behind her. Her heart thundered a quick beat against her breastbone.

He took her face in his hands, and while her mind said to pull away, her body insisted on staying right where it was. "I wanted a chance with you Emilie. I *still* want a chance with you, if you'll let me."

The intensity of his gaze and closeness of his hard body sent a rush of heat through her blood. She released a shaky breath as her gaze fell on his lips. "Derek," she whispered.

Slowly, he leaned in. Closer. And closer. Until his lips hovered just shy of hers. A small whimper of need escaped from her throat, and then he was on her. The kiss was demanding and urgent and needful. His arms wrapped around her back and head and tugged her in tight against him. She felt him harden against her belly, and desire jolted through her, landing most intensely between her legs. The kiss turned frenzied. Harsh breaths. Whimpers and grunts and moans. Rough, grasping hands.

God, she just wanted to lose herself in him, in these feelings, and forget all the rest of this was happening.

The ferocity of her desire for him sent her heart into a gallop. It scared her. The power of these feelings and this need was unlike anything she'd ever had with Jack.

It took every ounce of her willpower, but Emilie pulled away.

Derek's face was a mask of sexual need and promise. One she knew she wouldn't be able to resist, no matter how messed up her head was. She needed time, space, some clarity. And she wasn't going to get it if all she could think about was inviting Derek between her thighs. Her belly clenched at the thought.

Emilie shook her head and met his expectant, wary eyes. "Derek, I want to go home. Right now."

Chapter 17

Emilie watched as the heat cooled from Derek's expression and he frowned. "I don't think that's a good idea, Emilie."

Somehow, she knew he was going to say that, but she wasn't staying here. She needed the comfort and normalcy of her own place. She needed to find a way to turn her world right-side-up again. And she needed not to be tempted by Derek in the midst of this chaos—no matter how much her body demanded that she give in, lose herself in him, and forget everything else.

"Derek, I *need* to go home," she said, crossing her arms.

He stepped closer, and Emilie instinctively stepped away. If he kissed and touched her again, she wasn't sure that she'd have the willpower to pull away a second time. But she didn't miss the twinge of hurt that flashed through his eyes.

Derek jammed his hands in the pockets of his jeans. "Your house isn't safe. The gang knows who you are. Any other dirty cops working with Jeffers will know who you are. If we could find you, anyone else looking for your brother eventually could, too."

Frustration swamped her. "Okay, I'll grant you that. But what am I supposed to do? I can't stay away from my home forever. I have a job in Annapolis, a life there. And, oh God, I have thirty people coming over for a party in less than twenty-four hours." *Shit, shit, shit.* How could she have forgotten? She still had so much left to do before she'd be ready— Her thoughts froze. If the house really wasn't safe for her, then it wasn't safe for anyone. But, God, canceling less than twenty-four hours before was going to be a nightmare.

Just then, someone knocked on the door on the other side of the gym and it eased open. Beckett leaned his head in. "Nick called everyone together for a meeting in here in five minutes. Wanted to give you a head's up."

"Thanks," Derek called. "You can come in."

As if things hadn't gotten weird enough between her and Derek, they got even more awkward when Beckett joined them, his gaze glancing back and forth between them. To be honest, Beckett was pretty intimidating— huge, serious-faced, scarred—but the things he'd said about Derek had nearly melted her heart. And that was part of the problem in a nutshell.

Within a few minutes, the space around Derek's desk was packed with people. Some she'd met over in the apartment and some she hadn't.

"Should I leave?" Emilie said, unsure of her place with Derek, let alone with the whole group.

"No," Derek said. "Stay. You're in this now," he said. His gaze cut to Nick. "She's up to speed."

"All right," Nick said, nodding. "Let's get started." For the benefit of the non-team members, he recounted what had happened—a lot of which had to do with her brother. The murders he'd committed, the bounty the gangbanger had placed on Manny's head, her filing of an emergency psychiatric evaluation petition, and everything that had led to—including the fact that Derek and his friends had been caught on camera rescuing her at the storage facility, which meant their enemies now had a better-than-average chance at identifying who they were.

Emilie's stomach squeezed with guilt. She wanted to apologize, but she didn't feel like it was her place to interrupt.

Leaning against the wall next to Derek's desk, Beckett cleared his throat. "Well, what I laid out yesterday as a possibility of being identified, I think we now have to count as an eventuality. The only question is how fast they'll put names with the faces on the security footage. Nick, did you have a chance to, uh . . ." Beckett's glance bounced toward another brown-haired man standing at the back of the group. He had piercings in his lip and eyebrow and tattoos . . . pretty much everywhere.

"Just now," Nick said, his expression sympathetic.

"And?" Beckett asked as all the men's gazes swung toward the tattooed man.

"Jess is downstairs rescheduling the weekend's appointments. I'll close up until Monday and then reassess from there," the tattooed man said, crossing his inked arms. "And I wanted to clear it with you first, Nick. But I have to tell Jess what's going on."

"Of course," Nick said. "At this point, it's a matter of safety."

"I'm sorry this is spilling over on you, Jeremy," Derek said, his hip perched on the edge of his desk.

Jeremy nodded. "Rather be safe than sorry. Plus, it'll give me time to address the idea of camouflaging Hard Ink," he said.

Beckett pushed off the wall and strode closer. "Meaning?"

"Off the top of my head . . . what if we moved all the signage for the tattoo shop over to the other side of the building? There's no way to keep someone from looking for Nick or me, or from finding this address, but we might be able to confuse which side of the building the shop and residences are on." Emilie vaguely recalled the L-shape of the building from when they'd parked in the lot out back.

"What would you need?" Beckett asked.

Jeremy ran tattooed fingers through his longish dark hair. "I'd need to move the shop's door and signage to the other side and add some exterior lighting over there. And then I'd need to chain or board up the real door's location. Make it look unused. We'd also need to do something to block out these windows"—Jeremy pointed across the room to the tall windows that ran up the front of the building—"and the ones in our apartment. Or we institute a blackout, which would be a pain in the ass. And then maybe install some interior lighting on the second and third floors on the other side to make it look lived in."

Nick turned to Beckett. "Think that'll help?"

The big guy shrugged his huge shoulders. "It's a good start, and I think it's a precaution worth taking. We should get at it right away."

Emilie's stomach dropped farther. The fact that they'd been caught on that security footage had created so much of a threat that they had to do all this? And it was all her fault. *No, it wasn't. It was Jeffers's.* Which chipped away a little more of the guilt she felt over shooting him. How many other people like her had he hurt? Or worse . . .

"I'll help," a bald-headed man with a cutoff denim jacket said. "And I can get some of the guys over here to help, too."

"Thanks, Ike," Jeremy said, clasping hands and bumping shoulders with the other man.

"Appreciate that, Ike," Nick said. "It's bad enough Jeremy has to close down. I would hate for anything to happen to the building given all the hard work he's put in here over the past few years. And there are just too many of us living here now to take any chances." Murmurs of agreement went around the group.

Ike nodded. "Maybe you should consider hiring some of my guys for the duration of this. Extra security."

Nick exchanged looks with the other men and got lots of nods of approval. "I like the sound of that. Think we can arrange to get some guys over here this weekend?"

"For the right price, I don't see why not," Ike said.

"You know," Derek said. "If we had more bodies, we could set up lookouts or even a defensive perimeter within the neighborhood. There's one main way to Hard Ink—from the north. Going south of here dead ends into the water. Going east of here hits the rail yards. Anyone coming at us is going to be coming from Eastern Avenue. We've already got cameras up down the block, but bodies would provide a deterrence factor."

Emilie followed the conversation like she was watching a tennis match. She didn't know these people well, but as she listened she couldn't help but be fearful for them. It was like they were planning a war. She recalled the scene at the storage facility. That's exactly what this seemed to be.

"That's smart," Beckett said, crossing his arms. "And maybe we invite ourselves into the abandoned warehouse across the street and set up a sniper's roost over this whole corner." He looked at Ike. "Think your guys would be open to anything like that?"

"I don't see why not," Ike said. "We got quite a few ex-military among us, so there are definitely guys with exactly this kind of expertise."

"Good," Nick said. "After this, you and I can work on getting that set up, if that's okay." Ike nodded. "All right, next. We rescued two women today from a cell in the basement of Church's storage facility." Ike's face went from thoughtful to livid, the scowl downright scary. And Emilie had thought Beckett was intimidating. "Question is, what's our plan where they're concerned?"

"I talked to them and, honestly, they're acting a little squirrelly about where they're from and what their situation is. Didn't want me to call anyone. Wouldn't really volunteer much. So there's a story there," Derek said.

"Can't turn them over to the police," Beckett said. "What happened this morning with Emilie proves our fears that the cops are in Church's pockets."

"Agreed," Nick said. "But we can't just hold them here, and I don't want to put them out on the street to fend for themselves."

"I talked to them a little," Sara said from where she stood behind Shane's chair. "I think they're running from something. But I couldn't get any specifics, either."

Ike crossed his arms and nailed Nick with a hard stare. "We can take them. If they want."

Emilie frowned. Take them? What did that mean?

Nick's gaze narrowed. "I don't—"

"That's actually a good idea," Jeremy said. Was Emilie imagining some resemblance between Nick and Jeremy? They both had the most striking pale green eyes. "The Ravens help out people like this all the time."

"Explain," Nick said.

"We protect people that need protecting," Ike said. "Child abuse victims, domestic abuse victims. The criminal justice system is a freaking drawn-out process, and it's a long time between charges and jail time. We make sure people feel safe in their homes, don't get intimidated by assholes trying to get them not to testify. That kind of thing. These women have a past they're trying to outrun, they're welcome with us. We can give them a way station and help them figure out what's next." He shrugged one big shoulder. "If you want."

Emilie's eyes went wide as she listened to Ike. And here she'd thought him scary. Although, if she was in need of protection, he was *exactly* the kind of person who'd make her feel safe. Because who in their right mind would challenge that guy? "Having been kidnapped and imprisoned, they've been through a pretty big mental and emotion trauma. Forgive my question, but is that something you're prepared to handle?"

Ike gave her a nod. "Doing what we do for as long as we've done it, we have resources in place."

"Well, it's pretty amazing," she said. Ike gave her another nod. An offer to talk to the women nearly spilled from her lips, but she was hoping to go home. Wasn't she? Not stay here and work.

Nick tilted his head and finally nodded. "Okay, let's

talk to them about that. Appreciate your willingness to help them, Ike."

All day, Emilie had been swamped with the feeling that she'd stepped into someone else's life, or fallen down the rabbit hole into some alternate version of reality. But these guys . . . even with her confusion over Derek's lies, she couldn't help but admire this group of ex-soldiers and their friends. From how they'd administered medical care to two of their own, to their willingness to help complete strangers—including her—she found them sympathetic, honorable, and likable. People she wouldn't mind getting to know better.

She sighed and rubbed her forehead as the achiness from Jeffers's blows flared. From the corner of her eye, she spied Derek watching her, a concerned expression on his handsome face.

"We have another thing to consider," Derek said, pushing off the desk and tucking his hands in his front pockets again. "Emilie has asked to go home."

Emilie cut her gaze to Derek and suddenly became aware that everyone else was looking at her.

"That's not such a good idea," Nick said, frowning.

"So, what? I need to cancel my party, abandon my house, and remain in hiding until this blows over? What if it never blows over?" Emilie asked, frustration and just a little panic getting the best of her. Maybe if she started placing phone calls right now, she could prevent at least a few of her more distant family from making wasted trips.

"I'm gonna ask something, and I apologize in advance if it offends you," Beckett said. "But is your brother supposed to come to this thing tomorrow?"

A wariness crept through Emilie's belly. What would these guys do with Manny if they found him? She'd stepped over quite a few dead bodies on the way out of that storage facility, so she knew they were lethal when they needed to be. But then again, they'd risked themselves to rescue three women they had no connection to. She glanced at Derek, and he gave her a small nod. "He's supposed to, but he's not exactly reliable right now," she finally said. "And the police might pick him up before then."

"Possibly, but they gotta find him first. In our experience, that isn't easy." Beckett scrubbed his hands over his face. "I think we should let Emilie go, she should host the party, and some of us should go with her in case he shows. Both for protection and to detain him," Beckett said, crossing his big arms. "This party remains our only solid lead on finding him."

The *let Emilie go* part of what Beckett had said bugged the crap out of her, and she couldn't bite her tongue. "You don't get to decide whether to 'let me go'," she said, meeting Beckett's icy blue gaze. "Unless you've freed me from that basement only to hold me prisoner yourselves."

Derek stepped closer and looked her in the eyes—there was an emptiness in his that unleashed an ache in her chest. "Of course not. He only means it in terms of your safety, Em. We would never force you to stay here, but we don't want you to go home only to end up in some other lowlife's basement."

Right. That was fair. *Way to overreact, Em.* "Okay," she said, feeling chagrined. "I'm sorry. I'm just a little off-kilter after this morning." She sighed. "What do you plan to do with my brother if he does show up?"

The men traded glances in some sort of silent conversation. "We need to question him about his role with Church and with Seneka," Derek said. "Beyond that . . ."

Nick turned toward her. "Look, your brother can't remain free no matter what. He's killed six people this week, and he's being hunted down by all kinds of people who'd like a million-dollar payday. For his safety and the safety of others, he needs to be taken off the streets."

For his safety and the safety of others. Wasn't that exactly what she'd been thinking about all these days she'd debated filing the petition? She couldn't disagree with Nick's assessment, much as it pained her. "Okay, but what exactly does that mean?"

Nick shook his head. "Honestly, I'm not sure yet. I think the first step is to find him and figure out what's going on with him, and then go from there. Maybe we drop him at the hospital when we're done questioning him and he goes into the evaluation process you initiated."

That could work, couldn't it? And, no doubt, it'd be better for these guys to find him than someone like Jeffers, right? Or this Church guy? Right. Didn't keep her stomach from squeezing, though. "Okay. So, then, I'm going?"

"Yeah," Derek said. "But you're not going alone. Because this party is now part of our mission."

THIRTY MINUTES LATER, they'd divided into teams and Marz had packed a bag for the stakeout. He was coming down from the third-floor apartment when he heard the sound of arguing voices echoing through the stairwell. Beckett? But who was the other one?

He passed the Rixeys' apartment, where Emilie was waiting for him, and continued down to the first floor.

When he reached the last set of steps, he froze at the scene down below. "What the hell are you doing, B?"

Beckett had his gun trained on a petite woman standing against the cinder block wall outside Hard Ink's door. "I found her sneaking around. She won't tell me who she is or what she's doing here."

The woman's green eyes absolutely blazed as she planted her hands on her hips. "I wasn't sneaking around, you idiot. I was going upstairs. And who the hell are you, anyway?"

"I'll ask the questions," he said, voice harsh. "Who are you and what are you doing here?"

Marz made his way down to their level, his gaze on the woman's face. Something about her was familiar, but he couldn't place it. She wore a pair of snug dark-blue jeans and a sheer white blouse with a white tank beneath it.

"I'm not answering your questions," she said, smirking and crossing her arms. Almost like she was baiting Beckett.

Jesus.

"First, because I belong here. Second, because you're an asshole. And third . . . never mind, those two are enough. Now please lower your weapon before I lose my shit on you."

Beckett's head tilted like he was trying to figure her out. She belonged here?

Just then, the door to Hard Ink swung open and Jeremy, Ike, and Shane came out, brainstorming plans for camouflaging Hard Ink.

"Oh, shit. What are you doing here?" Jeremy asked when he saw Beckett and the woman. "Easy big guy." Jer stepped in front of her and held up his hands. "So, uh, perhaps some introductions are in order."

"Jeremy, move out of my way," the woman said, pushing him to the side. "This is such bullshit. What the hell is going on around here? Who are all these guys?" She leveled her glare at Jeremy.

"Everyone, this is my sister, Katherine," Jeremy said, rocking on his feet. "Who has apparently stopped by for a *surprise* visit."

Beckett lowered his weapon on a heartbeat, the severity bleeding out of his expression. *Was that . . .* Were his cheeks turning red?

Marz burst out laughing, and both Beckett and Katherine turned scowls on him. "I'm sorry," he said, laughing so hard his eyes were tearing. "It's just . . . I have known this man for a decade and never once seen him blush."

Jeremy was trying not to laugh. And failing. Chuckling, he gestured to the group. "You know Ike, of course, and these are some of Nick's friends from the Army, here for a visit." Jer went through a quick round of introductions, leaving Beckett for last. "And this is Beckett Murda."

Katherine flung her long brown hair over her shoulder and eyeballed him. Marz tried to swallow his laughter. But this moment would go down in the history books. Beckett Murda pulled a gun on Nick's little sister. And blushed when he realized it. *Priceless, really.*

"A little head's up would've been nice, Jeremy," Beckett said. "You know, with the way things are right now."

Jeremy held up his hands, inadvertently framing the words on his T-shirt which read, "There's a party in my pants. You're invited." "Sorry. I didn't know we were expecting company. Besides, shorty here doesn't really strike me as a threat."

She punched Jeremy in the arm. "I may be small but I'm feisty."

"Ow," Jeremy said. "Why do the two of you always hit me?" Grinning, he put an arm around her neck and pulled her in for a hug. "And I know you're feisty. I now have a bruise to prove it."

"Shut up," she said, smiling. "I didn't hit you that hard."

Footsteps sounded out above them, and Marz turned to see who was coming. Nick and Easy were making their way down, packs over their shoulders.

When Nick hit the landing above them, he did a double take and froze. "Kat? What are you doing here?" He hustled down to the ground level.

"It's nice to see you, too, Nick," she said with a sigh. "What is with you guys today?"

"What?" he said, surveying the group. "What am I missing?"

Marz put his hand over his mouth to hide the grin that grew there, a grin that turned into chuckles as Beckett glared at him.

Katherine pointed at Beckett. "Rambo over here pinned me to the wall with his gun."

Marz lost it again as Nick turned to look at Beckett with a *what the fuck?* expression on his face.

"Didn't know who she was," he said to Nick in a gruff voice. "Sorry."

"Why are you apologizing to him?" she asked. "I was the one you threatened to shoot. And I'd love to know why you couldn't have just *asked* who I was rather than pulling a gun. This isn't the freaking Wild West," she said, gesturing with her hands.

Nick stepped in front of her. "Okay, you're right. It was just a misunderstanding, right Beckett?"

"Yeah, sure," Beckett said, his tone not at all agreeable.

Katherine rolled her eyes. Marz was back to trying not to chuckle again. He'd never seen someone *less* intimidated by Beckett Murda than Katherine Rixey.

"But, seriously, what are you doing here?" Nick asked as he hugged her.

"Just needed a weekend away, so I thought I'd come hang with you guys. Is that a problem?" she asked, an emotion Marz couldn't identify flashing through her eyes.

Nick ran a hand through his hair. "Uh, no. No. Course not. We just, uh, have a lot going on right now."

Katherine looked over the group. "Clearly."

"We're doing some construction on the building, so it's not going to be very relaxing around here," Nick said.

She crossed her arms and tilted her head. "Why do I get the feeling you're trying to get rid of me?"

"No, I'm not. I mean, it's good that you're here." Turning to Marz, Nick made an *oh shit* face. Having his sister here was surely not on his top-ten list for this weekend. Not given the threats hanging over their heads. "So, change of plans. I think I should stay here instead."

"I'll go," Shane said. "You can help with things around here."

"Roger that," Nick said with a nod.

"Then let's get this show on the road," Marz said. "I'll go get Emilie."

Chapter 18

$\mathcal{I}$ need to go to the grocery store," Emilie said as they neared Annapolis. She was sure they weren't going to be thrilled with the news, but it couldn't be helped.

"Um, do you have to?" Derek asked, sitting next to her in the backseat of Shane's truck. "It'd be better to get things scoped out and set up at your house before it gets late."

"The thirty people coming tomorrow expect, you know, food and stuff. So, yeah, I'm sure," she said.

"All right," Derek said, his lips twitching like he was trying not to smile. "Just make it as quick as you can."

"Between the five of us, it shouldn't take too long." And wouldn't this be fun.

"Uh, come again?" Beckett said, twisting around to look at her from the front seat.

"You all can help," she said, smiling just a little at

Beckett's obvious displeasure. He grunted. "It's just a little grocery shopping."

Next to her, Derek chuckled under his breath. Without turning around, Beckett reached his hand over the seat and flipped Derek the finger.

Emilie didn't know what to make of the exchange, but figured it must be okay, given Derek's amusement.

"You love me, B," Derek said.

"No, I don't," Beckett said, totally deadpan.

Emilie couldn't help smiling at that one, especially since what Beckett had said about Derek earlier in the day totally belied his gruff words now. Seeing Derek interact with his friends had done nothing to help the confusion Emilie felt where he was concerned. By turns, Derek had been kind, funny, humble, considerate, and protective. And that wasn't even taking into consideration the bravery he'd shown in coming to rescue her this morning. Her gaze fell to the bandages on his arm. He'd sacrificed himself. To save her.

But he'd also used her and lied to her. Which was more important, more informative? Which was the one her heart should listen to most?

Damnit. If her history with Jack wasn't what it was, maybe she wouldn't feel so conflicted now. But she did. And she wasn't sure how to tip the scales one way or the other.

Within fifteen minutes, Emilie had guided them to an upscale store known for its fresh meats and produce. She felt a little ridiculous as she walked into the store, a team of muscled badasses following her. She grabbed a cart for herself and pulled out another, which she gently rolled toward Beckett.

His gaze narrowed and he released a long-suffering breath. "This place makes me feel like I'm underdressed." Emilie's gaze quickly scanned down over his jeans and black T-shirt, the sleeves straining around his biceps. She couldn't imagine a single woman in this store complaining about what this man was wearing.

"Excuse me," a woman called from behind them. As the shopper removed a cart from the long row of them, she eyeballed the guys warily, and then she rolled over the hardwood floors into the huge, lush produce section.

"See?" Beckett said, arching an eyebrow.

"You're fine," Emilie said, smiling. She thumbed through her phone until she found the shopping list she'd compiled yesterday over lunch. *God, that seemed like a million years ago.*

"Here," Derek said, looking over her shoulder. "I can forward that to everyone's cell phones and you can tell us what parts to get."

"Okay," Emilie said, handing over her phone. A moment later, the guys all pulled out their phones to receive the text. "So, I'll get the produce and dry goods. And, um, Shane, could you get the bread and desserts?" He nodded. "Let's see . . . Easy, could you get the paper products and drinks?" Another nod. "Beckett, could you get the salads? That'll be over at the prepared food counter." He sighed and nodded. Emilie looked at Derek. "And maybe you could get the meat?"

"He gets the meat," Shane said, elbowing Beckett. "I get desserts and you get salads. She clearly likes him better."

Heat crawled up Emilie's cheeks and she looked down at her list again. "You all can switch. I don't care."

"No way," Derek said. "The meat is mine."

"Don't take that out of context," Easy said.

"Oh, my God," Emilie said, biting back a smile.

How she could find humor in the midst of this day, she wasn't sure. But she had to admit it provided a needed release. "Let's go. I thought you all were in a hurry."

Emilie headed into the produce section, and Derek followed. She pointed toward the back wall. "The meat is all along the back," she said.

"We'll get there," he said. "But I'm staying with you."

She came to a stop next to the twelve varieties of lettuce. "So you're my shadow now, huh?"

He stepped closer, close enough that she no longer felt the chill of the refrigeration on her arms. His eyes were heated and intense. "You're not safe right now. And I'm not taking any chances."

The words and the closeness and the intensity made Emilie catch her breath. "O-Okay," she said, her gaze dropping to his lips. She shuddered and turned away.

As she worked her way down her list, Derek remained a solid presence behind her, beside her, watching over her. It was weird and kinda nice at the same time. And then it was gone.

Emilie turned, but Derek was nowhere to be found.

"Psst."

She turned toward the sound.

Derek slowly rose from behind the table of bananas, balancing a pineapple and bunch of bananas on his head. He wiggled his hips like he was dancing, and everything fell off. He caught the fruit in his arms before they hit the floor and gave her a sheepish smile.

Emilie tried not to smile as she turned back to the case of berries.

A few minutes passed. "Psst," she heard again.

A smile already tugging at her lips, she looked over her shoulder and found Derek holding two huge melons of some sort under his T-shirt.

"Derek! Put those back," she said, looking to see who had noticed him. His playfulness eased some of the tension from her shoulders. There was no denying or forgetting the horrible stuff that'd happened today. The circle of blood spreading on Jeffers's shirt after she'd shot him would no doubt provide fodder for nightmares for a long time to come. But it was just as true that she'd survived a near miss this morning. She'd *survived*. And a part of her wanted to say *screw you, bad stuff* and grab life with both hands. A little laughter, a little joy, didn't seem like too much to ask, did it?

Her last stop in the produce section was at the asparagus, which she planned to marinate and grill. She felt eyes on her, and did a double take at Derek holding possibly the world's largest zucchini in his hands with a totally amused grin on his face. He waggled his eyebrows.

Emilie couldn't help but give in to the urge to laugh. "Okay," she said. "I'm all done here."

"Oh, good," Derek said. "Let's go see what fun we can have with the meat."

Fifteen minutes later, the five of them met at the front of the store, carts laden with everything from her list. "Awesome job," she said.

Beckett leaned on the handle to his cart and eyeballed her. "We're prior Special Forces. The best of the best. A prissy supermarket is hardly going to throw us a curve."

All the men nodded.

"Okay, well, next time you're getting the part of the list with the feminine products on it," she said, trying to keep her face straight. Would there be a next time? Not to make the guys grocery shop, but just to hang with them, to get to know them better?

Beckett grimaced and wrinkled his nose like something smelled bad.

Emilie burst out laughing—and she wasn't the only one. "Never taunt a woman into figuring out how to torture you," she said. She patted him on the shoulder to the general amusement of the other guys.

Beside her, Derek laughed. "You're batting oh-for-two with the ladies, my friend." A lesser man might've withered under Beckett's glare, but Derek just laughed again.

Outside, the guys took care of loading the groceries into the back of Shane's pickup. Emilie watched as four very attractive men stretched over the lowered tailgate to place the bags in the truck bed. A girl could get used to that, for sure.

She sighed and tried to remember that these guys were with her because she was in danger. And they planned to defend her and her house. Not to mention capture Manny.

Right. Guilt crept into her belly like curdled milk. Knowing it was the right thing to do didn't make it feel any better.

It didn't take long to get home, where Beckett and Shane did a sweep of the house before they'd let her go in. Finding the house empty, they carted all the bags in for her. Her kitchen felt inordinately crowded with all these big men filling it.

"So, what's the plan?" Emilie said when they'd brought everything inside. "How do you all do what you need to do?"

Leaning against the kitchen counter, Derek looked . . . pretty freaking hot in her space. "We'll set up a defensive perimeter on the land side," he said. "What kind of vehicle does your brother drive? In case he shows up."

"A black Hummer."

Derek nodded. "You won't see us or hear us, but we'll be out there watching and listening. Don't worry about a thing," he said. "If anyone shows up or anything happens, we'll be here."

If only not worrying was that easy. "If Manny comes, I don't think he'd try to hurt anyone. He loves our family too much, and he's always been very protective of me and my mother."

"Maybe so," Derek said with a nod. "But you never know how a cornered man will react."

An awkward silence hung in the middle of the room, and all Emilie wanted to do was cross the kitchen, snuggle into Derek's chest, and tell him to be careful.

"Okay, let's do it, then," Derek said, pushing off the counter.

"Um, wait. What about dinner for you guys? Should I"—she shrugged, kinda at a loss but not really wanting them to leave—"make something for you all?"

"No," Derek said. "But thank you. You shouldn't do anything to indicate that we're out there at all. It's just a regular night at home for you." He started to turn, like he might come toward her, and then dragged a hand through his hair and stopped. He nodded, as if to himself. "Uh, in case it needs to be said, I won't attend the party tomorrow. Not just because I'll be with the guys keeping watch, but because I know things aren't settled between us, and I know you're not sure about me. But I really appreciated the invitation, Emilie. Just wanted you to know that."

Without looking back, Derek followed the rest of the guys through her house and out her front door.

Emilie pressed her hand to her chest, trying to soothe the ache suddenly lodged there. It took every bit of strength she had to keep her feet planted right where they were and not chase after him. Between his expressive eyes and his handsome face, his sincerity and his humor, and the million other things she liked about him, she couldn't be around him and think straight.

So then why did letting him leave feel so wrong?

THE PARTY WAS just getting under way. And Marz was sitting out in the woods watching it from the outside. Which was pretty much a metaphor for his life where anything related to family was concerned.

A few cars had arrived and parked along the side of Emilie's long driveway, but otherwise everything was normal as pie.

Marz sighed and shifted positions. He was going to need a whole bottle of ibuprofen and an appointment with a massage therapist by the time this day was done. He and his three teammates were split up—two in the woods on each side of the driveway, so the solitude combined with the lack of activity had made it one long night. Which had given Marz way too much time to sit and think of how he'd bungled this thing with Emilie. First, in developing an interest to begin with. Second, by lying to her and having to come clean in the aftermath of being freaking kidnapped. Of course, the lying couldn't be helped. The lives of his teammates and their collective chance at redemption had depended on it.

But no matter how he tossed and turned it, Marz couldn't find any real reason why that should matter to Emilie. After all, they'd just met. Hadn't even known one another for a full week yet. What could possibly convince her to overlook all his many faults and give him a chance?

And, given the fubar of their situation, should he really want her to give him that chance? Because he and his team had no shortage of danger, enemies, and problems to deal with in the immediate future.

A better man would leave her to her once-peaceful life and walk away.

So, then, why did the thought of that create a hollow ache right in the center of him?

Because he was a greedy bastard. And he wanted a place to belong, someone to claim him—for once— and someone to claim in return.

Sonofabitch.

Marz had never realized exactly how lonely he was until that very moment.

Shaking the bullshit out of his head, he did a one-eighty scan of the yard. Emilie had set up folding tables and chairs on the water side of her house. She'd decorated by stringing colorful paper lanterns between the corners of her house and the trees, making him long to go help her every time she got up on the ladder. She'd brought out a row of coolers and filled them with ice and drinks, and soft music Marz couldn't quite make out floated on the perpetual breeze that came in off the water. Between the sun and bright blue sky, and the waves lapping gently at the beach, it was a perfect fucking day.

Norman Rockwell would've been inspired.

More cars arrived and the party really got under way then. Fifteen people. Twenty. Twenty-five. Marz couldn't imagine being related to that many people and having them all come to visit. It was like observing strange customs in a foreign country.

Children ran around the yard playing. A couple of men set up a game of horseshoes down by the beach.

The smells of grilled food and the sounds of laughter carried on the air toward him.

And in the middle of it was Emilie, who looked fucking sexy in a turquoise outfit with a loose V-neck top over a snug miniskirt that hugged her thighs. She wore her wavy hair in a thick braid over one shoulder, which accentuated the long lines of her neck. And if all that wasn't enough to drive him insane, she had on a pair of high red sandals that made her legs look like they went on forever.

And Marz could've been at her side. He sighed. Coulda, woulda, shoulda.

But the one thing that didn't happen was her brother showing up. Which was par for the damn course.

Sunlight shifted across the yard as afternoon turned into early evening. Some of the partygoers settled in for another round of grub, the paper lanterns shedding a soft, colored glow over the tables now cast in the shadow. As darkness threatened, Emilie's family departed in dribs and drabs until there were only a few cars left. On the far side of the house, two guys folded up the tables and chairs and removed them at Emilie's direction. Marz was glad she had the help, but he sure would've liked to have been the one doing the helping.

"Looks like we're gonna have a no-show," came Beckett's voice through the earpiece Marz wore.

"Roger that," Marz said, frustration filling him with impatience and restlessness. Where the hell was Garza? For all they knew, he could've already fallen into enemy hands. And then where would they be? He withdrew his cell and texted Nick. *Check in with Miguel to see if BPD has picked up Garza yet. No show, here.*

Marz sighed. Without Garza, they'd still have the chip. And, with less than forty hours until the key search should be complete, they'd just have to hope it gave them enough answers and leads that they could keep moving this mission forward.

But forty hours seemed like a lifetime right now. Knowing they were being hunted filled Marz with an anxious dread.

A little while later, her male relatives emerged from the front door with Emilie and an older lady right behind them. The women stayed on the porch and called good-bye to the guys, which left only one car remaining. Emilie's gaze scanned over the yard, and Marz got the distinct impression she was looking for them. And then, abruptly, as if she'd caught herself, she turned and went back inside.

Had she been thinking about him? Or was that wishful thinking?

Through the trees, Marz slowly became aware of a loud engine, the sound of it deep and growling the closer it came.

"You all hearing that?" Marz asked into his comms. Three affirmatives came through his earpiece.

The sound reached the driveway. And turned in.

"Sit tight," came Beckett's voice.

A black Suburban rolled into view and promptly performed a three-point turn so that it parked close to the porch but facing back down the driveway. Marz's shoulders fell. Not Garza's Hummer after all. The engine quieted. And then boots dropped to the ground and ran toward the house.

"Someone have a visual?" Marz asked, the beast of a truck in his line of sight.

"Not his vehicle, but that's Garza," Shane said.

But the guy was on the porch and through the front door before Marz had a chance to react. *Fuck*.

Chapter 19

Emilie kicked off her sandals and glanced at the mountain of dishes covering her counters. The party had been a huge success. Everyone ate a lot and had a great time. And, bonus, no family drama.

Her mother stepped up to the sink and turned on the water, and some of the dish stacks were quite possibly taller than she. With shoulder-length salt-and-pepper waves, she'd always been something of a force of nature. Taking charge of their family when Emilie's father left. Working two jobs to make ends meet. Mediating family disputes to everyone's satisfaction.

"You don't have to do that, Mama," Emilie said as her mother loaded silverware into the dishwasher. "I can take care of it. This was your special day and you have a long drive." Plus, now that they had a quiet house and it was just the two of them, Emilie needed to tell her what was going on with Manny. All day, her mother had looked over her shoulder every time someone new arrived, her shoulders falling when it wasn't Manny. Emilie had never dreaded a conversation more in her life because she knew it was going to break her mother's heart.

"I don't mind, and I don't want to leave you with all this mess," she said.

Emilie joined her at the sink. "I don't mind, either. Really. You know I enjoy entertaining. I'll put some music on and all this will be gone before I know it."

Her mother gave her an appraising look and nodded. "All right. I do like to be home before it's all the way dark." She turned off the water and dried her hands on a towel with a sigh. "And I guess Manny isn't coming . . ."

"I know, and I'm sorry." Bolstering her resolve, Emilie took a deep breath. "Speaking of which, I need to share some things I learned about him," she said in a rush.

Crossing her arms, her mother dropped her gaze to the ground. "If you must."

Frowning, Emilie studied her mother, trying to figure out the meaning of her demeanor. "A lot has happened," Emilie said, starting out slowly. Problem was, no part of this story worked for easing her mother into the train wreck that had become Manny's life. Better to just rip off the Band-Aid and get it over with. "And it all boils down to the fact that he's in a lot of trouble, Mama. He showed up here night before last wearing bloody clothes, which I only saw because he woke me up in the middle of the night making a fire out back to burn them. He all but admitted to me that he'd hurt someone.

So I filed the psychiatric evaluation petition with the police, only to learn that Manny is wanted for questioning in a string of murders in Baltimore this week."

There, she said it. She'd told her mother everything except what'd happened to her the day before. Which was a whole other can of worms. One crisis at a time.

Shoulders trembling, her mother nodded and finally raised her head. Watery brown eyes stared up at Emilie as she twisted at the towel in her hands. "I know, *mija*."

She . . . knew? "Know how?" Emilie asked, confusion swamping her.

Her mother switched into a fast Spanish as she often did when she was upset, her voice colored by the strain of tears. "The police called this morning to question me. To see if I knew Manny's whereabouts. They told me why. I just can't believe it."

"So . . . you knew everything before you even got here today?" Emilie asked, weariness seeping into her bones. She'd worried all day about this conversation and it turned out her mother already knew. Which hopefully meant she'd had time to accept it.

"Yes," her mother said, her brown eyes filled with pain.

She took her mother's hands. "It's all true. You have to believe it. For Manny's sake—"

The front door whipped open and banged against the wall behind it. Manny stalked through Emilie's living room, eyes wide and bloodshot, hair a ragged mess, like he'd been digging his hands through it.

Emilie's heart was immediately a runaway train, taking off fast and picking up speed. A rush of conflicting emotions followed. Happiness and relief that he was still alive. Fear at what he was doing here. Worry that he'd behave erratically in front of their mother, up-setting her further. Knowing Derek and his guys were probably already closing in helped her stay calm.

"You made it," she said, forcing normalcy into her tone.

Manny walked straight up to Emilie, grabbed her by the throat, and bent her backward over the counter. "You disloyal little bitch. You turned me into the pigs. You told them I'm crazy. You have *half* the city search-ing for me now!" he shouted.

Struggling for breath and for a way to brace her back from the sharp pressure of the awkward position, Emilie said, "I'm sorry, Manny. I love you, but you need help." Her stomach knotted with fear as tightly as his hand held her throat.

"Emanuel! Stop it this instant!" their mother yelled, pulling at his arm but making absolutely no dent against his greater strength. Emilie coughed and sputtered.

"I'm sorry, Mama," he said, eyes boring into Emi-lie's, "but some betrayals cannot be forgiven or ig-nored." Meaning what? The possibilities made her scalp prickle and her stomach plummet.

"Which is the bigger betrayal?" Mama asked, beat-ing at his arm. "Emilie trying to get you help or you killing people? Let her go, *mijo*!"

With a curse and a shove, Manny released Emilie's neck and paced away. Suddenly, he punched a stack of dishes that went whirling across the kitchen, exploding into a million pieces as they hit the counter, cabinets, and floor, and stalked to the basement door.

Oh, shit. The fake stuff. He's going to find the fake stuff.

As soon as Manny disappeared from sight, Emilie grabbed her mother by the shoulders, snagged the older woman's purse and bag of gifts, and hustled her toward the front door. "We have to go. Now. He's not stable. I don't want you to get hurt." Emilie's voice was scratchy from how tightly Manny had held her.

"I'm not the one he hurt," Mama said, brow furrowed over wide, panicked eyes.

"I'm okay. Come on, Mama. There's no time to talk." She guided her out onto the front porch and rushed her down the steps. Was this Manny's Suburban?

Movement in her peripheral vision had Emilie turning to see Beckett in a low run from the far side of her yard. *Oh, thank God.* She scanned her gaze over the other side of the yard and found Easy running toward her, waving her away. Emilie opened the car door and tossing her mother's bags inside.

"Come with me, *mija*," her mother said.

Emilie was tempted. She really was. But she didn't want to bring this mess to her mother's doorstep, which made her remember Jeffers's threat to find Mama. "Listen to me. I don't want you to go home. Go to Rosa's for the night. Okay? Just to be on the safe side. I'll call you later. Promise me."

"Okay, okay." Her mother got into the car and shut the door.

"Emilie!" came Manny's roar from inside the house. *Oh, shit!*

"Go. Drive safe." Emilie rushed backward out of the way.

Just as Mama pulled a fast U-ey over the grass and sped down the driveway, Manny exploded so hard out of the front door that the Plexiglas in the storm door shattered into a spiderweb design. And three big, male bodies came rushing across the yard toward them.

Emilie was right in the middle of it all.

Her gaze zeroed in on Manny stalking toward her with a baseball bat and a wad of newspaper scraps he threw into the air. The paper fluttered on the breeze. "What did you do with it?" he growled, marching toward her. Emilie rushed backward.

"*Freeze!*" came Derek's shout. "Hands on your head and freeze."

Manny pulled a gun and waved it in a wide circle, firing off two rounds that sent the guys ducking for cover. A return shot caught Manny in the shoulder but he didn't react to it at all. It was like he didn't even feel it.

Emilie's foot caught in a divot in the grass and she tumbled backward onto her butt. Hard. "Manny, no!" Emilie said. "Put your gun away. Nobody shoot! Please, nobody shoot!"

Was he really going to beat her with a bat? Was he really this far gone?

Sadness ripped through her because the answer was staring her in the face. He lifted the bat.

Another shot hit his arm, blood spraying on the grass, but it didn't deter Manny nor stop the bat from its downward arc.

A body landed atop hers, knocking the air from her lungs.

And then a loud, metallic *clang* rang out.

Derek had raised his leg to take the hit with his prosthetic limb.

In a quick series of moves, Manny spun to a position behind Emilie's back, and pointed his gun down at the two of them. "Drop the weapons or he gets a bullet to the brain. You might get me, but I'll get him, too."

Oh, God, no! "Manny, just go," Emilie cried.

"Not going anywhere 'til I have my money, my

guns, and my drugs. So it looks like we're at a fucking stalemate," he said, voice twisted with anger and hate. He placed the gun's muzzle against the back of Derek's head. The sight made her nauseous. "Where is it, Emilie?"

"I don't have it, Manny. I didn't even know you had anything down there," she said, thinking on her feet . . . or back. "I was kidnapped by a city cop yesterday. He took me to a storage facility in Baltimore. Knew all about both of us. I barely got away with my life," she said. "Maybe he'd already been here before that all happened," she said, desperate for him to believe the lie.

"Fuck! *Fuck!*" Manny yelled, punctuating his outbursts with jerks of the gun against Derek's skull. Between her anticipation of the shot and her inability to draw deep breaths due to Derek's weight atop her, Emilie was starting to see spots floating around the edges of her vision. He swung the gun in an arc toward the other men. "Wait a minute," he said, eyes toward where she thought Beckett stood. "I fucking know you," he said, waving the weapon.

"Shit," Derek bit out.

"You know me, too, motherfucker," came a voice from behind them.

Manny whirled, fired three times in the direction of the voice, and raced for the Suburban, firing wild shots behind him as he fled. Emilie braced for the searing impact each time, or for Derek to cry out in pain, but neither happened.

The Suburban rumbled to life and pealed out of her driveway, engine racing. Derek rolled off her onto his stomach, weapon drawn and firing after the vehicle. Gunfire rang out all around. Emilie curled into a ball on the grass and covered her ears with her hands. Eyes closed, she could almost convince herself she was listening to a fireworks display, there were so many *pop, pop, pops*.

And then it stopped, and only the sound of the roaring engine in the distance cut the evening air.

Head ringing, Emilie rolled to her hands and knees and scrabbled toward Derek. "Are you okay? Oh, my God, are you okay?" she asked as she reached him.

Kneeling on the ground, he caught her in his arms and cradled her to his chest.

And Emilie clutched on to him like he was the air she breathed.

"I'm sorry," she cried, her body running on pure adrenaline. Her thoughts totally boiled down to their most important essence. And that was Derek. And the fact that she wanted him. All night, she'd regretted not having understood and forgiven right away. By morning, she knew she couldn't live the rest of her life punishing every other man who crossed her path for Jack's mistakes. And as she'd stood on her front porch looking out into the woods, wondering where Derek was, all she wanted was him by her side. "I'm sorry. I understand what you did. And I'm sorry."

"Ssh," he whispered in her ear, gently pulling her the rest of the way into his lap and rocking her. "Don't worry about that now." He pulled away, but Emilie held on tighter.

"Don't leave," she said, an uncontrollable shaking settling into her bones. Yet he was steady, unwavering, rock solid. She pressed her face against his throat and breathed him in. "Please don't leave me."

"I'm not going anywhere. Hey," he said, stroking her

hair. "Look at me." His deep brown eyes were warm, reassuring.

Her breathing ragged, Emilie eased away enough to meet his eyes. "Is your leg okay?" she asked, the *clang* of the bat still ringing in her ears.

"Sore, but okay. I'm made of fucking titanium. In a fight with a bat, I win." He smiled. *He smiled.* They'd just survived hell and Derek unleashed that warm, adorable, sexy smile she so associated with him.

And her heart welled up inside her chest.

"Are you okay?" he asked, gently stroking the side of her face.

A fast nod. "Yeah, yeah. Well, mostly." It was a little hard to count herself as okay when she couldn't hold herself still.

The smile slipped off Derek's face as his gaze moved downward. "What's this?" he asked, fingers tracing her throat.

"Nothing that matters," she said, wondering just how bad it looked.

"Like hell it doesn't." He leaned down and brushed a kiss over her neck. And another. "Fuck, I'm sorry we let him get away. We were trying to take him alive. God, I think we hit him at least three times."

"Four," Beckett nearly growled from where he stood over them.

Derek nodded. "It was like the bullets were bouncing off of him for how much he seemed to feel it. And I just couldn't take him out standing five feet in front of you."

"I know," she said. "I saw that. God, maybe he's on drugs. Can't heroin turn off your pain receptors?" All she knew was that she no longer recognized her brother. Manny was completely and totally gone.

"Jesus, maybe so," Derek said, stroking her hair behind her ear.

"Here," came a quiet voice from over her shoulder. "Let me help you up." A dark brown hand extended toward her.

She grasped it and needed every bit of Easy's assistance to rise to her feet. Her knees were like jelly. "Thank you."

"Welcome," he said.

Still clutching onto Easy's arm, she turned and watched as Beckett and Derek clutched one another's forearms, and Beckett hoisted his friend to his feet.

When Derek was upright, he listed to the side like his leg wasn't quite strong enough to support him, but Beckett caught him. "Just give it a minute," the big guy said, voice like sandpaper. "You got clocked in the leg pretty good."

"I'm okay," Derek said. "Really."

"Just give it a minute," Beckett said. "You don't always have to be too strong to accept help. No one here thinks you're weak."

Derek's eyes went wide as he gazed at his friend. How could anyone think Derek weak? The guy had saved her twice in two days and used his own body as a human shield for hers. He'd been hit with a bat and still had enough presence of mind to try to take out her brother's fleeing truck.

Not one thing about any of that read as weak.

God, it was quite possible that Derek was the strongest man she'd ever known. Her gaze ran over the T-shirt that did nothing to hide the muscles of his shoulders and arms, then downward to how those blue jeans hung on his lean hips. He was definitely the sexiest man she'd ever known.

And she wanted him.

Thunder rumbled in the distance. Then a little closer. When had it gotten cloudy? It was quite possible that hours had passed since she'd ushered her mother to her car and sent her away.

"Shit, Shane. You're bleeding," Easy said.

Emilie twisted her head. Sure enough, the dark green shirt over Shane's shoulder was reddish black, the stain getting a little bigger, and then a little more, as she watched.

"Let's go inside," Emilie said as fat raindrops began to fall. "Clean Shane up."

Derek wasn't able to hide the marked limp he had as they crossed the yard, and she hated to see him hurting. And hated even worse the knowledge that her own brother was to blame.

"Lean on me, wouldya?" Beckett said. "Don't want you hurt any further." Derek accepted Beckett's help up the porch steps, their arms clasped around each other's shoulders.

Emilie looked at her broken door, but she simply couldn't worry about it right now. Inside, they made their way to the kitchen, and she flipped on the lights. *God, what a mess.* "Have a seat," she said. "I'll get the first aid kit and some supplies." She dashed to the bathroom, grabbed the kit from under the sink, wet some washcloths, and collected a few towels.

She returned to the kitchen and settled everything on the table. Thunder boomed directly above them, making her jump. The *pitter-patter* of rain sounded out against the windows.

A hand fell on hers. Derek. "I'm sorry I didn't get to you in time to stop all this. By the time we realized Manny was the driver of the Suburban, he'd booked it inside."

"Don't worry about it, Derek. Really." She opened the first aid kit for Easy.

"Shirt off, McCallan," Easy said against a boom of thunder. The rain came down harder, gusts of wind off the water buffeting the back of the house.

"Don't get that offer every day," Shane said, wincing as he worked the cotton up and over his head. "Just grazed. Again." Emilie looked to see the extent of his wound. He had a bloody streak where his arm met his shoulder. Not too deep, but it was ragged and messy.

"You know, you two are dating sisters. You really didn't need to get matching GSWs, too," Derek said. The guys chuckled. And there went Derek, lightening the mood again.

Soon, Shane was all patched up, and he pulled out his phone. "I'm gonna brief Nick." Emilie lowered herself into the chair next to Derek. "Hey," Shane said after a moment. "Got a minute?" Shane recounted everything from the time Manny arrived—his assault on her, his discovery of the fake stuff in her basement, attacking her and Derek, and the gunfight. "He got away," Shane said, regret and exhaustion plain in his voice. "He's totally off the deep end."

Beckett leaned his hands on the back of Derek's chair. "Hey, ask him how the changes to Hard Ink went. And how many Ravens he got on board to help us."

Shane passed on the questions and nodded after a minute or two. "Okay, man. Catch ya later." He dropped the phone to the table.

"What's the word?" Beckett asked.

Emilie looked at Shane, eager to hear how the things the team had brainstormed yesterday were turning out. The more time she spent with them—and especially with Derek—the more she rooted for them, worried for them, and felt like their problems were also her own.

"Nick said the changes to the building look totally convincing. They moved the shop's door and all its signage around to the other side of the L, installed two exterior lights on that side, and Jeremy even spray painted a big piece of graffiti over the boarded-up opening to the real door. They also got the lighting set up on the interior of the decoy side and covered the windows of the residences with sheets of black plastic."

"That must've been a pain in the ass," Derek said, kneading at his thigh.

"No doubt," Shane said.

The lengths to which they were going to implement these precautions really drove home just how much danger they were all in.

"What about the Ravens?" Beckett asked again.

Thunder cracked so loud, the windows vibrated, and then lightning flashed bright enough to further illuminate the kitchen. Shane leaned forward and rested his elbows on the table. "Ike apparently brought three guys with him this morning and seven more are supposed to come tonight."

"It's a shit night for a bike ride," Easy said, leaning against the counter.

Derek nodded. "No lie. If they're coming from their main club, that's like forty-five minutes outside the city."

"What happened to those two women?" Emilie asked. "Did they end up going with Ike?"

"Yeah," Shane said. "One of Ike's guys took them out to the club this afternoon."

"That's good, I guess. Right?" Emilie asked. "I hope they'll be okay."

"Me too," Shane said. He blew out a long, troubled breath. "After Sara and Jenna—and then you yesterday morning—I've had my lifetime fill of that fucking gang abusing and abducting women."

"A-fucking-men," Easy said.

What had happened to Sara and Jenna? Emilie had met the two red-headed sisters at Hard Ink, but she hadn't had much time to talk to them. Or any of the women, really. Emilie looked at Derek and frowned.

Derek mouthed that he'd tell her later.

She nodded, rested her head on her hand, and surveyed the kitchen. "I'm just going to throw all that stuff away," she said, her exhausted gaze scanning over the mountains of dishes. A little while ago, cleaning up from the party hadn't seemed like a big deal at all. Now, tackling all that seemed insurmountable.

"Well, with five of us, it wouldn't take so long," Beckett said in a quiet voice, echoing her teasing words from the night before, when she'd asked to go shopping.

Underneath all that scary gruffness, there was one helluva nice guy. Not that Beckett seemed to want anyone to know. "Yeah?" she asked.

He nodded.

And he was right. Emilie rinsed the dirties and directed them where to put the clean things away. Shane loaded the dishwasher, using his uninjured arm. Derek sat in a chair at her side and dried platters, pots, and pans that wouldn't fit in the dishwasher, and Beckett and Easy put all of those things away in between sweeping the broken dishes from the floor. It took about fifteen minutes to clean it all up. Lifesavers, once again.

The storm whipped up while they worked, turning the world outside the kitchen window pitch-black. The thunder was loud enough to shake her house.

Fingers stroked the bare skin of her leg, and she looked down to find Derek gazing up at her, his expression regretful and sympathetic. "We can't stay here. And you can't, either."

Emilie sagged against the counter, fatigue making her limbs heavy. "I figured. So, then, where do I go?"

"Come home," Derek said, taking her hand. "With me."

Chapter 20

$\mathcal{M}$arz's next breath hung on what Emilie would say. He'd heard loud and clear what she'd said outside, but that was also in the heat of the moment. Just minutes after bullets had literally been whizzing over their heads.

He ran his gaze over her. Long wavy strands had come free from her braid. She had small smears of mascara under the corners of her eyes. And red marks that looked like they might bruise marred the smooth skin of her neck—Marz's blood boiled about that. Manny Garza wouldn't get a second chance to hurt his sister. Ever.

And despite how the crisis had disheveled her appearance, she was still the most beautiful woman he'd ever known. But it wasn't just the physical that drew Marz to Emilie.

She had an inner strength he admired. The way she'd gotten her mother to safety, despite having just been assaulted. The way she'd come up with a plausible story about the basement stash on the fly, unknowingly giving Shane time to come up behind Garza. The way she'd worried over Marz when the crisis was all over.

Lightning flashed outside the window, and a long, rumbling thunder followed. Emilie's house groaned against the onslaught of the wind.

Finally, she squeezed his hand and nodded. "I don't want to be anywhere else but with you."

The words were like a salve to his soul, binding up wounds he'd carried since he'd been a child. He knew what she'd said didn't mean forever, nor did she offer him a long-term commitment. But she wanted him. The way he wanted her. And right now, that was efuckingnough.

He rose to his feet and folded her in his arms. "I'm sorry for lying to you," he whispered in her ear.

She nodded against his throat. "I'm sorry for not understanding sooner."

He shook his head. "Don't you even worry about that, Em," he said hugging her tighter.

Someone cleared their throat.

Right. They had an audience.

Pulling back, Marz gently rested his hands on her shoulders. "We should go. Pack a bag. Whatever you think you might need for at least a week. More if you want."

"We're going back where we were yesterday? To the Hard Ink building?" she asked.

Marz nodded. "That okay?"

"Yes, of course. But I was thinking. If I'm going to

be gone that long, all this food I have will go bad. Why don't we take it?"

"A soldier will never say no to free food," Shane said. "We'll handle that. You two go get Emilie packed."

"There are grocery bags in the pantry," she said, pointing to the closet in the corner behind Shane.

"I'll go retrieve the truck while you're working on that," Beckett said. They'd hidden it on the same abandoned farm road as the other day, so Manny wouldn't see it and wonder who was at his sister's house.

"In this?" Emilie asked. As if emphasizing her point, thunder cracked and the lights flickered. "You'll get soaked."

Beckett shrugged. "I'll dry. No biggie."

"What about an umbrella?"

His friend's eyebrow arched. "I don't do umbrellas. But, uh, thanks. Be back in a bit," he said, heading out.

Emilie watched after him, then turned to Marz. "Coming?"

"Lead the way," he said, satisfaction rolling through his blood.

Keeping ahold of her hand, he followed her through the house and upstairs to her bedroom. Lightning flashed across the space just before Emilie hit the light switch. The room managed to be both cozy and airy, with big windows opening up the walls on three sides. The view must've been spectacular during the day. The white wooden furniture was all clean lines and simple touches, and stood out against the honey-colored hardwoods and pale blue walls. "Okay," she said, gesturing to the neatly made dark blue bedding. "Feel free to have a seat. I'll be quick."

Derek eased his hip onto the mattress, fucking reveling in the fact that she'd invited him into her most pri-

vate space. The room smelled of her, fruity and sweet.
And as he ran his hand over the blanket, he couldn't
believe the way the past twenty-four hours had turned
around for them—from untold lies to broken trust to
reconciliation. They'd lived a week in the past two
days. At least, that's the way it felt.

From the closet, Emilie grabbed a small suitcase and
loaded it with jeans, shorts, shirts, and other necessi-
ties. He didn't miss her hesitation as she gathered her
things from her lingerie drawer, nor the fact that she
didn't try to hide the silky panties and lacy bras as she
tucked them into her case. Seeing her handle her un-
derthings shouldn't turn him on as much as it did, but
maybe his growing need for her was more about reaf-
firming that they'd both survived this day than about
the tiny pair of black silk panties folded so innocently
atop the pile of clothing.

A need that was intensified by the fact that he was sitting on her bed, the linens still tinged with her scent, as
if they'd just rolled out from under the covers. Marz's
heart beat faster at the imagining. He fisted his hands
in his lap to keep from reaching out for her.

Thunder blasted the nighttime world, sending Emilie
jumping.

Marz hated to see her so on edge, but he could hardly
blame her. "Okay?"

"Yeah. Just think I've had enough of things going
boom for today," she said with a small, brave smile. *So
damn pretty.*

"Amen to that." Especially since the tally had been
too damn high. Three of his teammates had been shot,
several of them had nicks and cuts from falling debris
after the explosion at the storage center, and Marz had
encountered the business end of a bat. That was more

than enough. Hell, that was more than enough from now 'til the end of time. For fuck's sake.

"Be right back," Emilie said, slipping into an adjoining room and turning on the light. The sounds of drawers opening and closing, and items being gathered, made their way out to him. And then it got silent for a little while. Except . . . was she talking to herself? It was hard to tell over the relentless rain. The sound of cardboard ripping, then a crinkling, and then she was shutting out the light and returning to him, a flowery bag and some brushes in her hands. She dropped those on top of everything else. "Okay, I think that about does it." She looked around the room as if she wasn't really convinced.

"Come here," he said, holding out a hand. Her feet bare, she rounded the bed, that snug, little skirt no less sexy than it had been the first time he'd laid eyes on it. He grasped her hand and pulled her to stand between his thighs. His groin tightened at the proximity, but really, he just wanted to offer her comfort. Resting his hands on her hips, he tugged her in a step so he could look into her eyes. "You okay?"

"Yeah," she said, tracing her fingers over his face. Down his cheek. Over his brow. Across his bottom lip. She might as well have rubbed the bulge in his jeans for how much the light, dragging touch set him off. "I want you to know something."

"Okay." His thumbs rubbed softly over her hipbones, the thin stretchy cotton of the skirt all that separated his skin from hers.

She took a deep breath, like she was bolstering her courage, and then she met his gaze. "I was married. It ended a couple years ago, although the divorce wasn't finalized until just after last Thanksgiving. He cheated on me." She shook her head, and Marz's gut started a slow descent to the floor. "No, it was worse than that. He had a whole other family. He lied and schemed and chose them over me in the end. Not that I would've taken him back at that point, but even though I didn't want him anymore, it was a blow to realize he didn't want me, either. Hadn't for a long time. And here I'd spent years fretting over why he didn't want to start a family with me. He didn't need to. Already had one."

"Oh, hell, Emilie. I'm so sorry," Marz said, immediately understanding how what he'd done probably hadn't looked so much different in her eyes. Hell, he was lucky she was giving him a shot at all. "And what I did brought all that back up for you, didn't it?" *Damnit.*

"It did, but that's not why I wanted you to know." Her hands smoothed down his neck to his shoulders, and she leaned in closer. "I'm a work in progress where trust is concerned, so I'd always rather you be brutally honest than lie to me. Even a little white lie. Okay?"

Marz ran his hands up her back, drawing her closer yet. "I don't want to keep anything from you, Em. Not ever again."

"That's all I ask," she said with a nod, her face so close to his that the fallen tendrils of hair from her braid created a thin curtain around them.

And inside that bubble, the air suddenly sparked red hot.

Marz held back, not wanting to take anything she wasn't ready to give.

But then she whispered, "Kiss me."

He didn't need to be told twice.

The kiss was blistering in its intensity. They clutched at one another tightly, lips crashing and sucking and pulling, swallowing each other's gasps and moans.

Marz was rock hard in an instant, and nearly out of his mind with desire. Every masculine urge within him demanded that he bury himself deep inside her and never let go.

"God, Emilie," he rasped, pulling away from her lips to taste her neck, her collarbone, the skin along the vee of her shirt. His hands dragged down her back, landing on her ass. "Do you know how fucking crazy this skirt has made me all day?"

She shook her head and pressed herself closer. "No," she said, rubbing her thighs together.

His fingers bunched the soft material higher and higher, until his hands landed on totally bare skin. "Oh, fuck. Tell me you're wearing panties."

Her nails lightly scratched down his back, and even over the T-shirt, it set every one of his nerve endings alive. "Thong."

"Yeah," he said, his fingers finding and tracing the thin silky line downward, to where her cheeks met.

Emilie moaned. "Derek," she said, her hips jerking toward him.

"What, baby?" He massaged and lifted the round globes of her ass, allowing his fingers to inch closer and closer to her heat with each teasing squeeze. He licked up her neck. "What?"

"I know we don't have time," she whispered as she pressed herself backward toward his exploring fingers.

"Time for what?" he asked, kissing up over her jaw and claiming her mouth again. The pads of his fingertips caressed her opening.

"Oh," she moaned, her face a mask of pleasured torment. "Time for you to get inside me."

Fuck. That.

In a few quick moves, he pushed her from between his

legs, crossed to shut the door, and plastered her front against the window looking out over a vast black nothingness.

"Oh, God, oh, God. Hurry," she whined, helping him tug up her skirt and push down her thong.

Marz tore open the front of his jeans and shoved down his boxers, and his cock spilled out in his hand, long, hard, and inked with the heavy black lines of two Chinese characters. "Fuck." He pulled back and his muscles ached at the retreat. "Do you have a condom?"

Emilie pointed behind them. "In the floral bag in the suitcase."

He tore open the zipper, and a whole lot of condoms spilled out. He'd have to ask about that later. Right now, he was all about tearing the wrapper open and rolling the rubber up his length. And then he was back against her heat again, his weight pushing her up against the glass. "Are you sure, Emilie?"

"Never been more sure in my life," she said, peering over her shoulder.

On a groan, Marz penetrated her opening, gliding all the way home on one long, slow thrust. She was so wet it was a fucking dream, and the tight heat of her made him tune out everything else. He didn't hear the rain battering the window. He didn't feel the weight of the ticking clock. He didn't know anything except his cock inside the tight welcome of her body.

"Oh, Derek. Yes, yes, yes."

His balls already ached with heaviness, and he bit down on the tendon that sloped upward to her neck. Her cry made him harder, and he reached around to the front of her dress and tugged at the neckline until he freed her breasts to the glass. "I'm not going to be able to go slow, Emilie. I'm strung too tight for wanting you."

"Do it," she rasped. "Take me however you want."

"Oh, baby. Hands on the fucking glass."

The speed with which she moved to comply untied the last string of his sanity. He gripped her tightly, one arm around her shoulder, the other around her belly, and let himself loose.

He took her in a series of hard and fast strokes, just bottoming out inside her before he withdrew to the tip. His hips slammed against her ass, creating a delicious sound like a well-placed spank. Over and over and over.

"Aw, God, Emilie. Take my cock. Take all of me."

In time with his frenzied thrusts, a constant stream of moans ripped from her throat. Half-formed whispers spilled from her lips. "Yes, yes. God, yes."

Need clawed down Marz's spine. "I." Thrust. "Can't." Thrust. "Get." Thrust. "Deep." Thrust. "Enough." He yanked her hips out from the glass.

Emilie's fingers raked at the smooth surface, and her breath fogged the window. She chanted his name like it was the air she breathed, and it shoved him closer and closer to the edge.

"Tell me you want me," he rasped, biting down on her neck again. And God did he love the way she writhed and whimpered at the bite. "Tell me you need me. Tell me you love having me buried inside you."

A fast nod, and pleading eyes peered over her shoulder. "Want you," she said on a rough exhale. "Need you. Love your cock inside me."

The words sent a rush of pressure to his balls. God, he wasn't going to last much longer.

"Right hand. Rub yourself. Make yourself come while I fuck you." His hips flew against her, the hard, fast rhythm starting to tire his right thigh, but it was so fucking worth it.

She moved immediately, her right hand dropping between her legs. "I'll do anything for you," she said. "God, I'm so wet."

"Jesus, Emilie. Stroke yourself. Just the way you like it. And know you're gonna make me come so fucking hard." His orgasm barreled down on him like a semi and nailed him in the back, sharpening his thrusts and burying him deeper inside her. "Ah, fuck, coming."

"Don't stop. Don't stop. Just like that. Hard," she said, her words almost a babble. And then they cut off, she held her breath, and her core fisted around his cock.

"Yeah, baby, yeah," Marz cried, his release erupting in a series of almost painful spasms. He shook and shuddered against her, fucking her through both their orgasms until her white-hot channel stopped milking him.

His knees almost gave out.

Hers definitely did.

Marz pulled her into his arms, nearly carrying her to the bed, where he sat on the edge and lifted her into his lap. She curled into his chest and neck, her breasts still heaving in exertion, and it was the sweetest fucking thing. God, she felt so freaking right there. In his arms. Against his heart.

And they were both nearly fully dressed. Her outfit was askew and her thong hung around her ankles, and his jeans hung around his thighs, only baring his hips and ass. And yet it had been the most mind-blowing sex he'd ever had. Because she knew who he was—his weaknesses, his losses, the kinds of bad things he was doing for what he believed, to the bottom of his soul, were pure, good reasons—and she still wanted him, still needed him, still accepted him.

"Talk to me, baby," he said, pressing a kiss to her forehead.

"That assumes I've regained the ability to perform that particular function," she said, soft laughter in her voice. "Jesus, Derek, that was so, so good. I don't think I have any bones anymore."

"I know just what you mean." But the clock was striking midnight for them, and their stolen moment was about to turn into a pumpkin and some mice on the side of the road. "I hate to rush—"

"We have to go. I know." She reared back and met his gaze. "Oh, my God. Do you think your friends will know?"

Marz tried to hold back his reaction. He really fucking did. But a grin that big wasn't staying under wraps. "Probably. And now they're all a bunch of jealous bastards."

She slapped his chest and buried her face. "Oh, my God."

He was having none of it. Tipping up her chin, he arched an eyebrow. "No shame, Emilie. Not for this."

"No," she said. "Never for this."

They made quick if somewhat wobbly work of putting themselves back together, and then Emilie zipped up her suitcase.

"So, uh, big plans?" he asked, pointing at the spilled condoms before she'd finished closing the bag.

Emilie rolled her eyes and smiled. "My best friend Kelly told me to be bold and be prepared."

Marz laughed. "I like her already." And then he pulled Emilie in for one, last, searing kiss. The kind that had his body stirring already again despite his utter exhaustion.

Then he grabbed her suitcase for her and they made their way downstairs. Where there was a whole lotta staring off at the ceiling, faking napping, and whistling going on. *Fuckers.*

Marz cleared his throat. "We ready or what?"

The harassment was immediate. "Oh, like *we're* the ones holding up the show," Easy said.

"Y'all need a couple more minutes?" Shane asked. "Round two?" Emilie buried her face against Marz's arm, but her shoulders shook hard.

Wet from head to toe, Beckett folded a towel over the back of a chair, flicked out the last few lights, and stalked toward the door, passing Marz and Emilie at the bottom of the steps. "Fly's open," he said, not even making eye contact.

No, it wasn't. Marz wasn't falling for that shit. Still, he walked out the door with a big-ass grin on his face, because he had his best friends around him and his girl on his arm. And for this minute in time, that was enough. To him, that was fucking everything.

Chapter 21

A horn blared, jarring Emilie awake. She hadn't meant to fall asleep. But they'd been sitting still in nearly stopped traffic so long that the steady drumming of the rain on the roof of Shane's truck had lulled her into unconsciousness.

"Have we moved much?" Emilie asked Derek, lifting her head from his shoulder. They were sitting in the backseat, with Easy on her other side.

"No," Derek said, kissing her forehead. "Road's closed ahead. There's a huge accident. Like, ten cars."

She looked out the windshield to the watery sea of red taillights ahead of them. It was the worst storm Emilie had seen in a long time. When they'd come across the Severn River Bridge on Route 50, the wind gusted so hard that it had shoved Shane's truck into the next lane more than once.

Shane turned in the driver's seat and held up his smartphone, an image of a map on the screen. Almost every road was depicted in red. "Traffic's like this everywhere. At this rate, we won't get home til the middle of the night." He lowered his phone and rubbed his eyes. "I should call Nick and let him know where we are." He put the cell to his ear and waited. "Hey, man." Pause. "We're all fine, but traffic's at a stop with this weather. We're gonna be a while." Pause. "Aw, hell. Really? Well, after driving in it, I guess I can't blame them."

"Bad news?" Beckett asked when Shane hung up.

"The other Ravens couldn't make it with this weather. They'll be down tomorrow," Shane said.

"That's a bummer, but it's only a matter of hours," Derek said. Murmurs of agreement went around.

Speaking of phone calls, Emilie should call her mother. But a part of her just wanted to get where they were going and have a few minutes to collect her thoughts before placing the call. She also didn't really want to have it in front of all the guys. Not that they didn't know what she'd have to say, but because she thought it was more respectful to her mother. No doubt the others would be able to tell how upset Mama was from her side of the conversation, and Emilie didn't feel like that should be up for general consumption. Instead, she shot off a text for now: *I'm fine but am stuck in traffic with this storm. Will call you in an hour or two. xo.*

Message sent, Emilie snuggled closer into Derek's side, and he released her hand and put his arm around her shoulders. Just what she needed. And after what they'd shared in her bedroom, she really wanted this closeness with him. God, Derek could be funny, he could be sweet, he could be sexy—and holy freaking crap, he could fuck. The rough, rasping, dirty talk streaming from his mouth might've gotten her to orgasm all on its own. She pressed her lips together tight to keep from grinning.

A half hour later, traffic started to move. After crawling for nearly forty minutes, they were diverted off the highway altogether onto a much smaller four-lane commercial strip.

"Oh, God. This road's busy under normal circumstances. This is going to take forever," Emilie said. Traffic moved so slowly that it took them eight changes of the stoplight at the end of the exit ramp before they got through.

"Anyone else hungry?" Derek asked.

The guys all chuckled. "Leave it to you to bring up food," Beckett said.

"Every time," Easy said. The car crept forward a few feet at a time.

"What?" Derek asked. "Tell me your asses aren't hungry."

"Of course, we are. But you're always the first one to bring it up." Beckett looked out his window and then tapped his finger against the glass. "We could run for the Border."

"Aw, yeah," Derek said, peering out the window.

Smiling at Derek's reaction, Emilie leaned closer to Easy to see what Beckett was talking about. All she saw was—hell to the no. "Please tell me you're not talking about Taco Bell."

"What's wrong with the Bell?" Derek asked.

"Generations of my ancestors are rolling in their graves at that question," Emilie said, unable to keep from smiling at his mock-outrage expression. "Besides, I have some great leftovers if you're in the mood for Mexican."

"Yeah, but they're in the back of the truck," Derek said, rubbing his stomach. Thankfully, Shane had a cover for the truck bed or all her belongings would be floating back there by now.

Emilie chuckled. "All right, I've registered my protest. Do what you have to."

It took Shane almost fifteen minutes to get over into the right-hand lane and reach the entrance to the restaurant.

Emilie scanned the shopping center on the far side of the parking lot behind the Taco Bell for other places to eat, but almost all the businesses were dark. And then her eyes settled on the green-and-red neon sign of the Courtyard Marriott. "I have a crazy idea," she said as Shane pulled around the restaurant. "How long have we been sitting in traffic?"

"Over two hours," Shane said.

"Before you pull up to the drive-through, hang on a minute," she said. The truck rolled to a stop and Shane looked over the seat. "How much longer do you think it'll take to get back to Baltimore?" Emilie asked. "Another two hours? More?"

Shane nodded. "I wouldn't be surprised."

Emilie pointed out Easy's window and smiled at each of the guys. "Why don't we just stay at a hotel tonight? Courtyard Marriotts always have those restaurant areas where they serve breakfast in the morning. There'll be a microwave. We could have our very own feast and get out of this traffic and weather. I mean, get food here if you really want to, but we could take it to the hotel."

"Homemade trumps fast-food every time," Derek says. "So it sounds pretty damn good to me. And, honestly, I wouldn't mind stretching my leg."

Emilie wondered exactly how badly he was really hurting.

The other men exchanged looks and finally nodded.

"Anyone want food from here?" Shane asked. Negatives all around. He backed the truck out of the drive-through lane and headed in the direction of the hotel.

The good news was that there was a huge canopy over the driveway in front of the Marriott's lobby doors, so they wouldn't get soaked going in. The bad news was that they were not the first people to have this idea. Shane just managed to fit his truck into the carport behind two other cars. "Might as well make sure they have rooms before we unload," he said.

"I need to use the restroom, so I'll come too," Emilie said.

They all hopped out, and Derek helped her down from the truck and took her hand. She adored that he didn't mind showing affection for her in front of his friends. What she didn't like so much was his marked limp. She'd seen him when he wasn't hurt and knew it wasn't usually this noticeable. Hell, she wouldn't have even guessed he was wearing a prosthesis before he'd showed her.

Luckily, they still had rooms available. Shane, Beckett, and Easy decided to share one room, and she and Derek got another. Which was awesome. Except for the repeat round of razzing that it unleashed. Emilie couldn't help but laugh, though.

Annnd she couldn't help but wish they could go to their room . . . Right. This. Very. Minute.

Guilt stalked at the back of her mind and paraded

all the reasons why she shouldn't be finding any joy right now. Manny's breakdown, her shooting Jeffers, and the threats that hung over all their heads topped the list. Honestly, though, those were the exact reasons she *needed* a little joy. Something to even out the cosmic scales. Something to help her cope and let her forget, even if for just a little while.

"I'll go get your suitcase while you find the bathroom," Derek said.

"Take a load off," Beckett said, arching an eyebrow at his friend. "I'll get it."

Emilie nodded. "I should call my mother, too. She's probably freaking out by now."

"I gotta park the truck," Shane said, "so I'll go with you, B."

Easy pulled his phone out of his pocket. "I'm gonna call Jenna. Meet you over there?" he asked, pointing to a big open room with lots of tables and chairs.

"Yeah," Derek said as they all went their separate ways.

Emilie used the restroom, then found a little unoccupied nook off the lobby with a pair of couches. She sat and sagged back against the cushions as her mother answered with, "Are you okay?"

"Hi, Mama. Yeah, I'm okay. Did you get to Rosa's all right?"

"Yes, but I hated to leave you. What happened after I left? I saw him come running out of the house."

"He totally freaked out. Just like I thought he would," Emilie said, telling her the truth without overwhelming her with the specifics.

"Meaning what, *mija*? I can handle it, you know." Sighing, Emilie debated—apparently a few seconds too long because her mother said, "I want to know, Emilie."

"Okay," Emilie said in a low voice. She hated to recount it—both because she wanted to spare her mother and because she really didn't want to relive it herself. "He threatened to hit me with a bat." A gasp came down the line. "A friend I had there in case this very thing happened protected me and then Manny drew a gun. They tried to get him to turn himself in and he wouldn't. And then he started shooting at everyone and took off."

"Oh, dear God," her mother said. "Was anyone hurt?"

"Yes, but not badly." At least, she hoped Derek wasn't hurt worse than he was letting on. That limp was really worrying her. They spoke a few more minutes—mostly Emilie trying to reassure her mother she was fine, and then Emilie said, "I'll call again when I can. I'm not going to stay at my house until this is over. If you see Manny, call the police, Mama." Jeffers's image popped into her mind's eye and she shook her head. "Better yet, call me. My friends will know what to do. Just remember, he's not *our* Manny anymore."

The sadness in her mother's agreement broke Emilie's heart.

When the call was over, Emilie returned to the dining room to find all the guys gathered and the bags of food unpacked on the counter by the microwave. Emilie took a deep breath and pasted on a happy face. "Okay, let's get cooking."

While a dish of beef enchiladas was reheating, she took the lids off the pasta salad, corn-and-black-beans salad, and ceviche with shrimp. And then she reheated the chicken tortilla soup, the rice and beans, and the corn bread she'd baked.

Derek offered to help, but she wanted him off his feet. And, honestly, keeping busy helped her bottle up the sadness she'd felt after the call with her mother.

Soon, everything was done, and she found some heavy paper plates in one of the cabinets under the counter.

"Dig in everyone," she said.

They didn't need to be told twice.

Emilie smiled at their enthusiasm and at their compliments. She'd always loved watching other people enjoy what she'd made. The conversation flowed around the table, ranging from discussions about the food to joking around to telling old stories. What they didn't talk about was the situation they were all in the middle of. So she guessed she wasn't the only one who needed a distraction from reality.

She didn't eat much—her stomach was too tied up in knots. She mostly sat back and watched and listened. From their easy familiarity, to their ability to call one another out, to the stories they told, it was clear the four men shared a tight bond.

"So, was it better than Taco Bell?" Emilie asked when the meal wound down. Mischief filled Derek's eyes. "Answer carefully," she said, smiling.

"Hell, yes," Shane said, rubbing his stomach. "I'm happier than an old dog with a new bone."

"Your inner redneck is showing, McCallan," Easy said.

"I fly that flag loud and proud," Shane said, grinning.

"Definitely better," Beckett said, wiping his mouth with a napkin. "Thanks."

"Yeah," Easy said. "Appreciate you sharing all this food with us."

"I'm just so glad it didn't go to waste." She pushed out of her chair, but Derek rose and leaned over her.

He planted a quick kiss on her lips. "Fantastic, Em. Thank you. Now, you sit. We'll clean up."

"You sit with me," she said in a low voice.

A question flashed through his eyes, but he acquiesced without asking. From behind Derek, Beckett gave her a nod. Guess her effort to make him stay off his feet wasn't all that subtle.

"You two should go settle in," Beckett said. "We got this."

Both Emilie and Derek protested, but the guys all insisted. Before long the two of them made their way to the elevators. As soon as the doors closed, Derek boxed her in against the wall and kissed her like it had been months since they'd last touched one another. The kiss was slow and deep and arousing, especially as his erection grew against her belly.

He pulled away and leaned his forehead against hers. "Love in an elevator," he sang softly and shifted his hips against hers. "Lovin' it up when I'm going down."

Emilie chuckled. God, he was absolutely, ear-bleedingly tone deaf, but she adored that he couldn't care less. He was fun and spontaneous and playful. There wasn't an ounce of pretense about him. Derek just was who he was.

And his genuineness was so compelling, so attractive, that Emilie gave into the urge to throw her arms around him and hug him tight.

Ding, ding.

"Come on, pretty girl," Derek said, grabbing her hand in one of his and the handle to her suitcase in the other. He carried a backpack of his own on his shoulder.

The room was decorated in dark greens and otherwise lacked much personality, but it did have a very comfortable-looking king-sized bed that filled the center of the space.

"How are you?" Derek asked, placing her suitcase and his backpack by the side of the dresser. "I know you were upset after your phone call but I didn't want to ask in front of everyone." He turned toward her.

"Better now," she said, falling into his open arms. "I just hate upsetting her. And there's not even any resolution I can give her yet."

"Yeah, but you should be proud of yourself, Emilie. You got her out of that house and away from the danger. You took great care of her in the midst of that moment. I know I was proud of you," he said, rubbing her back.

"Thanks," she whispered.

Derek hugged her tight. "I'm really sorry for whatever role I played in pulling you into all this."

She eased back and met his gaze. "Derek, you have nothing to apologize for. None of this is your fault. Manny's messed-up life would've exploded with or without you. The only difference is you wouldn't have been there to rescue me if you hadn't been in my life."

"Okay," he said, kissing her forehead.

"So now it's my turn to ask," Emilie said. "How are *you*? *Really*. I didn't want to ask in front of the guys."

He gave her a small smile. "Mostly okay, but my leg hurts."

Emilie's heart squeezed—both at his pain and at his honesty. She imagined it wasn't easy for a guy like him to admit any sort of weakness. The thought made her recall Beckett's words from earlier. *You don't always have to be too strong to accept help. No one here thinks you're weak.* That Beckett felt the need to say that only solidified her suspicion.

"What will help?" she asked, looping her arms around his neck.

"I have pain meds, but they give me insomnia sometimes."

"Well, I'll stay up with you if that happens. But you should take them, don't you think?"

"Yeah," he said. He patted her hip and crossed to where he'd dropped his pack on the floor.

Emilie sagged onto the edge of the bed. "You know, they probably have a Jacuzzi. Would that help?"

"I wish," he said, digging in his bag. "I used to love them. But the heat causes the blood vessels in my stump to dilate, which causes my limb to swell up so much it becomes a struggle to get my prosthesis on. So I avoid them now."

"Oh," she said, shoulders falling.

Derek rose with an orange prescription bottle in his hands, and then he disappeared into the bathroom. Emilie collapsed backward onto the mattress and luxuriated in the soft bedding against her back. She definitely felt where Manny had bent her over the counter, not to mention the tender spots from Jeffers hitting her. She stroked her fingers over her sore throat and hoped it wouldn't bruise. She really didn't want to explain how she'd gotten the marks.

Derek emerged a few minutes later. He smiled, walked up to the bed, and leaned over her, his hands on each side of her head.

"Mmm, I like this view," she said, his proximity and the position stirring her blood.

"Me, above you?" he asked, heat slipping into his dark gaze.

Emilie nodded, and Derek's gaze narrowed. "What else do you like?"

Her stomach went on a loop-the-loop. "The way you talked to me. Against the window."

Derek pushed his hips between her thighs and slowly

rocked against her core. "You're very inspiring," he said, humor sliding in behind the heat in his eyes.

She didn't want to ruin the mood, but she needed to check. "Does your leg hurt too much for this?"

A quick kiss. "No, but if it does, we'll find a position that puts less stress on it." He waggled his eyebrows.

"Yeah? Well, in that case, am I inspiring you right now?" she asked, arching a brow. She loved how free she felt with him to say whatever came to mind.

One at a time, his hands manacled her wrists against the bed. "Definitely." He circled the bulge in his jeans against her clit, although the tightness of her skirt kept him from getting as close as she needed him.

Her heartbeat took off at the promise of his touch. "Derek," she whispered, wriggling her fingers. God, she wanted to pull her skirt out of the way.

"What, Em? What do you need?" His gaze bore into hers and scorched the blood running through her veins.

"You." She lifted her feet up onto the edge of the bed and spread her thighs wide—and almost cheered when the movement drew up her skirt and increased his access to her.

"My touch?" he asked, rocking into her.

"Yeah," she said, lifting her hips to meet his thrust.

"My mouth?"

Given how amazingly he kissed, she could only imagine the skill with which he could apply his lips and tongue elsewhere. "Yes."

"My cock?"

"Please," she whispered.

Derek released her, slid back off the bed, and pulled her to her feet. Her clothes were off before she'd realized what was happening. His eyes absolutely blazed as they looked over her body, drinking in the lacy black push-up bra and thong she still wore. "Take them off," he said, rubbing his lips. "Slowly."

Emilie dragged her hands up her stomach and squeezed her breasts, her gaze connected to his, and then reached around and undid the back clasp. She pushed her arms together, plumping her cleavage as the straps tumbled down her arms, and then she dropped the bra to the floor. Enjoying the expression of abject need he wore—hooded eyes, open mouth, shiny bottom lip from how he kept running his tongue over it—she drew out the removal of her thong. Hooking her thumbs beneath the thin straps on her hips, she moved them over her skin, then turned, bent at the waist, and slowly, very slowly, dragged them down her legs.

"Jesus, look how wet you are already." She rose— only to feel the press of his big hand on her back. "Not yet. Slip a finger inside yourself." The mattress creaked, and Emilie realized he'd sat to watch her.

The thrill of knowing his eyes were on her every move nearly made her tremble. She reached between her legs, circled her fingertips in her wetness, and slowly slid her middle finger deep inside.

"Fuck yourself, Emilie," he rasped. A metallic *zip* and the rustle of denim told her he was partially naked behind her.

She ached to see him, touch him, go to him, but she did as he asked, finger-fucking herself and adding a second finger when her need for him made her ache. A tingling pressure built up where the heel of her palm pressed against her clit. "Derek," she said, hearing the pleading in her tone.

"God, that's sexy," he said. "I'm stroking myself watching you."

Emilie looked behind her. Oh, damn. Legs spread, Derek sat on the corner of the mattress, one hand fondling his balls, the other moving over his length, his wrist twisting at the head. She wanted that. She wanted to make good on the promise she'd made the night they'd made out in the shadows of the lighthouse.

Turning, she lowered herself to her knees and crawled toward him, her hands settling on his thighs. She gently squeezed, her left hand feeling a thickness under the denim covering his right leg that must've been part of his prosthetic limb. She scooted as close as she could, her hands slowly closing in on his cock.

His skin was hot to the touch. She fisted her hand around him, and he groaned. Leaning in, she opened her mouth, wanting to feel the weight of his cock on her tongue. Her eyes landed on a series of black lines, and Emilie tilted his erection toward her.

Tattoos. He had tattoos on his cock.

"Holy shit, Derek," she said looking up at him wideeyed and awed. She'd never seen anything hotter in her entire life. "Didn't this hurt?"

He stroked her hair, tucking a lock of it behind her ear. "Not too bad. I was still on a lot more pain meds when I had it done. I sorta went through a period where I decided if my body had to be modified, I wanted to be the one to decide how, when, and where."

She really admired that attitude. "What does it say?" she said, tracing her fingertip over the Chinese characters.

He petted the top of her head. "One stands for life, the other for saving life." He stroked her hair again. "Take me in your mouth, Emilie."

Her core contracted at the command. She swirled her tongue all around him, making his skin slick and wet, and then she sucked him in deep.

Both of his hands flew to her hair and pressed lightly against the back of her head. "How deep can you go, baby?"

Emilie took a big breath and impaled her mouth on him until his head filled her throat.

"Oh, fuck." His hands pressed harder. "Hold it, hold it, hold it," he rasped, and then he let her go.

She drew up and sucked in another deep breath. And did it again, and again.

Emilie had always loved the way a blow job could make a strong man lose control, and it was more true with Derek than it'd ever been with anyone else. He was a warrior, a protector, a trained killer if she wanted to be brutally honest about it, and he was shaking in her hands.

"I don't want to come like this," he said, voice gritty and deep.

Sucking hard, Emilie withdrew.

"Jesus." He kissed her, hard, and then he lay back. "Get up here. Straddle me. My fucking turn."

Heart racing, Emilie crawled up over him, her legs straddling his stomach. She rubbed herself against his cock.

"Not yet, Em. I want you over my face."

Butterflies tore through her insides. She'd never done this in that position before, but just imagining it was making her wetter.

Derek helped guide her knees over his shoulders, and then he grabbed her ass. "Ride my mouth, Emilie. I want your orgasm down the back of my throat."

"God, Derek," she said as she slowly lowered her lips to his. He grabbed her ass cheeks harder and sucked her clit into his mouth, flicking it mercilessly with his tongue. She cried out and grabbed her own thighs for support. And then she let her hips move exactly how her body demanded.

"That's right," he rasped against her. "Ride me. Use me." He plunged his tongue inside her.

The orgasm came out of nowhere. One moment she'd been hanging in a pleasured stasis, the next, she was shattered. He banded his arms around her thighs, holding her tight against his sucking lips and flicking tongue as the inside of her pulsed over and over again. When it was over, she fell forward onto her hands, her head hanging. *Good. God.*

"That was fucking beautiful," he said, pulling out from under her and coming up behind. He hugged her, his front against her back, his arms around her belly. "Beautiful, Emilie."

"That was amazing, Derek, but I want you inside me."

"Aw, you're aching for me, aren't you?" he whispered against her ear, his cock twitching against her sensitive opening. She nodded, and he kissed her cheek. And then he was gone.

Emilie turned to see him shed his T-shirt, kick off a shoe, and lower his jeans and boxers to his ankles. He stepped out of the clothing with his good leg, but left it hanging around the ankle of his prosthesis.

All she could do was stare. Because Derek was all lean, cut muscle covered in ink. Beautiful, bold colors sat side by side with stark black abstract lines and patterns. Some sort of large bird—a phoenix?—covered his entire right shoulder. A flock of blackbirds flew over his heart. A strand of upright bullets circled his left biceps, initials underneath each one. All the way down his left side, there was a thorny vine twisted with barbed wired, which wrapped around his thigh where it appeared to draw blood. And there was lots and lots of writing in all different sizes and styles.

"Turn around," she said.

His back was every bit as impressive. The phoenix reached over his right shoulder and down to his shoulder blade. The rest of the top half of his back was a series of interconnected tattoos—a large abstract design punctuated by dark red roses, big stars filled with the American flag, and a symbol made up of a pair of crossed arrows and a dagger. And more words. Who would've thought all of this was under those clothes? God, she wanted to lay him out and explore him until the morning.

"You're beautiful, Derek," she said. His cock stood straight out as he turned, and it drew her gaze lower, to the black sleeve that hugged most of his right thigh. Below that, a metal cylinder attached to a thick rod that extended down into a low, brown boot. Was it weird that she found his prosthetic limb so sexy? It meant that he'd survived, adapted, and thrived. It revealed a man who could bounce back from life's hardest knocks, which in turn was evidence of a man with a whole lot of inner strength. Plus, damn, it just looked hot.

He stroked his cock, his trademark grin forming on his face. "You like what you see, Emilie?"

"Very much," she said, her gaze focusing on the way his hand worked himself.

Holding the base of his erection with one hand, he jerked faster with the other. "Maybe I should just let you look, then."

"No!" she said, desire spearing through her. "Need you."

He grabbed a condom from her suitcase, then stalked to the bed and sat on the edge. Working his pants leg off over his prosthetic shoe took a little work, but as soon as he was free of his jeans, he hoisted her further up the mattress and settled himself between her spread thighs. "I'm all yours, baby. Whatever you need, whatever you want, I will give it to you freely. All you have to do is ask."

Chapter 22

$\mathcal{M}$arz hadn't meant to lay himself out there like that. The words had spilled unthinkingly from his lips—and they hadn't just been about the sex.

All the time he'd spent with Emilie this week, they'd just seemed to click on every level . . . A man could get used to all of that, especially a man who'd never had it before.

And he didn't want it to end.

But right now, she needed him. And he had no intentions of making her wait.

Kneeling tight up against the backs of her thighs, Marz took himself in hand and guided his head to her opening. He didn't want to be fast about it again. He wanted to savor, to memorize all her little tells and re-actions, to indulge in every wicked fantasy they both had. But something about Emilie always took him from aroused to nuclear in mere seconds.

Slowly, he sank into her core until she'd taken him all. "Look at your body suck me in, Em." Nothing had ever felt more right.

She lifted her head and looked down her body to where they were joined. "So good together," she whispered, and then her eyes met his.

Something about the way she'd said those words reached inside his chest and drew him down on top of her. He wrapped his arms around her shoulders and hunched himself around her as he withdrew and thrust. "I want to wear you over every inch of my skin," he said against her ear.

As fatigued as his right thigh was, Marz wouldn't last long in this position, but he didn't want to give up the closeness, the intimacy, the depth of his body within hers just yet. He came at her hard and grinding, but kept the pace slow so she felt the impact of every thrust.

Emilie uttered a stream of pleas and moans, her hands grasping his shoulders, his back, his ass. She locked her ankles around his lower back, and the sensation of being claimed had him groaning into her neck.

He wanted more of it.

"I want you on top of me, Emilie. I want you to get off on me and use me and take me however you want." He kissed her then withdrew. Lying on his back, he guided Emilie on top of him.

"I'm going to take all of you, Derek. Are you ready?" She used two fingers to separate her lower lips.

"Do it. I want it." And, aw, fuck, the sight of her sinking down on him, her body swallowing his, speared a jolt of electricity down his spine and into his balls.

Bracing her hands on his chest, Emilie raised and lowered her hips in a series of fast, shallow thrusts. He jerked his hips upward on each one, trying to bury himself deeper. He wanted it. He wanted it all.

Then she started taking him deep. Instead of lifting and lowering, she ground her clit against his lower belly, shifting her hips forward and back. And between her heat and her wetness and her tight little channel, Marz was going fucking insane. "It's so good," she said, her hands going to her breasts, massaging and plucking and pinching her nipples.

Marz grabbed her hips and moved her faster. "You want to come all over me again, don't you?" He ground her hard against his pelvic bone.

She nodded and gasped. "Yes."

"Make me wet with it, Em. Close your eyes and picture something that especially arouses you," he said. Her eyelids fell shut. "Now, what are you looking at?" he asked, nearly gritting his teeth as her core sucked and tugged at him.

Small whimpers spilled from her throat. "You, fucking me from behind, like in my bedroom. But not there this time."

A thrill shot through him. "Where?" He rocked her harder, faster.

She licked her lips, her breaths coming in pants. "Somewhere . . . public. You come up behind me in a library and pull up my skirt like you did before."

Aw, hell, yes. "And then I take you right there against the stacks, where anyone could walk by, where you have to swallow every single noise you yearn to make."

"Yes," she said. "Or at a crowded concert where you have to stand tight up against my back. The crush of all the people hides what we're doing as you pull up my skirt and sink in deep."

Jesus, he liked the way his girl thought. "But some

of them know, don't they, Em? They know you opened yourself up to me right there in the middle of everyone, some of them pressing up against you, their heat warming your body. The other men are *hard* knowing what we're doing. But they don't get to have you."

"Oh, yes," she said, her voice going tight. "Only you."

A fierce male satisfaction roared through him. "Goddamned right. Now, where else? Tell me everything."

Her hands fisted against his chest, her nails scraping over his skin. "Oh, God, Derek."

"Keep talking," he bit out, the effort to hold back from chasing his own orgasm turning into a burn low in his belly.

"On a crowded subway. You wear a long coat that hides us as you press me to the window, pull up my skirt, and drive into me. And I'm already so wet from you teasing and fingering me that my thighs are slick."

"We are making every fucking one of those come true," he growled.

Emilie's face crumpled and she cried out, her core squeezing him over and over like a white-hot fist. Her arousal poured over his cock.

"Come here, baby," he said, urging her down flat onto his chest. He banded his arms around her back, grabbing the remains of the thick braid for good measure, and then lifted his knees so he could use his heels for leverage to fuck her hard and fast.

He let himself off the leash and slammed upward into her, his hips pistoning, his cock gliding easily in and out of her because of how wet they both were. Emilie's moans got louder, more desperate. "Take me. Just take me," he gritted out.

"Yes, yes, yes, Derek. Don't stop," she cried.

Not a fucking chance. Keeping the hand pulling her

hair tight around her back, he reached down with his other and grabbed her ass. He kneaded her cheek, used his strength to push her down harder on his cock, and let his fingers roam closer and closer to the tight pucker of her rear. Dipping his fingers lower, he wet the tips with her slick arousal, and then swirled circles against her hole.

Emilie's back arched and she moaned.

"Has anybody ever played with you here?" he asked, pressing a little harder against her.

"No," she whispered. "But it's so sensitive."

Marz nodded. "Would you like me to play with you here?"

She wriggled against his hold and pressed herself backward toward his touch. "Yes, just . . . slowly."

"Aw, baby," he said, lifting his head to kiss her forehead. "I'd never do anything to hurt you."

He swiped his pointer finger through her wetness again, and then he pressed the tip against her opening. "Bear down, Emilie, and you'll take me easier."

A string of babbled whimpers fell out of her mouth.

Marz felt it the moment she complied, because her muscles squeezed his cock inside her pussy. His fingertip slipped inside her ass.

"Oh, God," she said, rearing up so hard that he released her hair and back. "That is insane."

He swirled his finger against the tight ring of muscle inside her, familiarizing her body with his invasion. And Emilie started pushing back on his cock and his finger, taking him in to the knuckle, then more.

Marz's orgasm barreled through his blood, grabbed him by the balls, and had him shouting as it erupted out of him. He had enough presence of mind to remove his finger gently before grabbing her hips and slamming her down on his cock as his body flinched and shook.

"Aw, Jesus," he said, the spasms turning almost painful from the force of his release.

He gently withdrew, removed the condom, and pulled her down to the bed beside him. They lay facing one another, their knees and legs intertwined. And she was totally relaxed, her eyes soft and unguarded. The fact that her shin and foot rested against his prosthesis didn't seem to bother her at all. His heart was already opening to her, and that just wedged it apart a little more. She really did accept every part of him.

And he'd never felt more like he'd found a person he could belong to in his entire life. He stroked strands of hair off her face. "You're so fucking special to me," he said, kissing her softly. In that moment, he didn't care one bit that he was laying himself bare to her. Because with each passing moment, she was owning him more and more.

THE WAY DEREK was looking at Emilie made her heart feel too big for her chest. God, he'd cracked her wide open—all her darkest fantasies and forbidden needs on display—and accepted everything he found inside her. It was like she fit inside her skin for the very first time.

"You're special to me, too," she said, so, so surprised to be experiencing feelings like this again.

They lay there for a long time, looking into each other's eyes, exchanging soft, affectionate kisses, and just touching.

"We're falling asleep," Derek said after a while. "Let's get ready for bed?"

Emilie's body felt almost sluggish as she dragged herself out of bed and to her feet. She grabbed some things from her suitcase and carried them into the bathroom.

You just had sex, she thought at her reflection in the mirror.

Emilie shook her head. *I just had the* best *sex ever.*

Yeah, that was more like it. All this time, she'd been a caged bird and hadn't even realized it. One night with Derek and she felt freer than ever before. Despite the horrors of the past two days, it lifted a weight from her shoulders.

Minutes later, she emerged in a pale pink nightgown that ended just higher than mid-thigh. Derek smiled, pushed off the bed, and kissed her before he took his turn getting ready.

When he rejoined her, he sat on the edge of the bed, his back mostly toward where she leaned against the headboard, and he appeared decidedly less relaxed— shoulders bunched, jaw tight, eyes no longer at ease. With his lean muscles and miles of ink, he was still the most gorgeous man she'd ever seen, but she wanted the sweet, playful light back in his eyes. Emilie frowned. What could account for the change?

Her eyes scanned over his back and side. Tucked under his right arm, inked script on his ribs read, "For those I love I will sacrifice." He'd certainly proven that. Her gaze scanned down, and found the words *Carry On* in block letters running sideways down his right hip to the top of his thigh. Derek was a living embodiment of the idea of wearing your emotions on your sleeve— except he wore his on his skin.

"What's wrong?" she finally asked, her belly threatening to take a nosedive. Please don't let her have misread him. Please don't let her be the only one getting sucked into this.

Because they might've been a crazy, too-fast whirl-wind, but Emilie definitely felt herself taking a step off a cliff. It wouldn't take much at all for her to actually be *falling*.

Derek shook his head and shrugged. "Gotta take my prosthesis off."

Emilie waited for more, but that was all he said. "Okay."

He rubbed the back of his neck, drawing her gaze to the intricate collision of tattoos across his back.

"Derek, talk to me."

He shifted toward her, drawing his right leg up on the bed so he could face her. "It's not attractive, Em. The amputation site, I mean. And sometimes, the whole prosthetic limb thing feels downright emasculating. If I get up in the middle of the night—which I almost always do, because of phantom pain or nightmares or just plain old insomnia—I either have to use a cane, crawl on the floor, or go through the steps to put the limb back on." His words spilled out faster and faster as he spoke, and his eyes were almost bleak. "I've ad-justed to that to the point it's almost second nature. But I . . ." He dropped his gaze like he was suddenly fascinated with the architecture of his prosthesis. "In all the months since I've had to wear this, I've never gone through a night with another person. You've been through so much today, and I don't want to ruin this moment of . . . fucking perfection we managed to carve out of the chaos—"

"Hey, no, don't worry about any of that, Derek," Emilie said, grabbing his big hand in both of hers. As if his fears didn't melt her heart enough, the fact that he also thought what they'd shared was perfect absolutely lit her up inside. "I want to know all of you. And I don't want you to hide your challenges and struggles from me. I want to help, where I can. Or just be there for you, where I can't. To me," she said, laying her hands over the metal shaft of his limb, "there's absolutely nothing emasculating about the fact that you wear this. I look at this and what I see is a badge of honor. You saved Beckett's life, Derek. He lives because of what you lost. That is the opposite of emasculating." She scooted closer to him on the mattress. "That is strength, courage, selflessness, friendship. I'll echo what Beckett said this afternoon—when I look at you, I don't see a single ounce of weakness. And there's nothing you could do to ruin what we shared."

His eyes were ablaze with emotion, and the glassiness she thought she saw there reached inside her chest and squeezed her heart. "I just don't want you to think I can't protect you," he said in a voice so low it was just above a whisper.

Emilie's heart raced in sympathy and understanding. She hadn't worked with many amputees, but she'd read enough to know that they often struggled with issues of body image and negative self-esteem. They had to relearn skills of daily living like bathing and dressing, and retrain their bodies in the basics of balance and agility. She imagined that process might be especially frustrating for someone who'd served as an elite warrior in some of the most dangerous conflicts around the world. But not one bit of it changed how she felt—or was starting to feel. "How could I ever think that when you've saved me again and again?"

"Shit," he said, raking a hand through his hair. "Just getting all caught up in my head. Happens sometimes."

She took his face in her hands. "Hey, give yourself a break. That would be understandable under normal circumstances. But today was nowhere near normal, Derek."

"You're easy to talk to, you know that?" He leaned his face into her touch.

Emilie grinned. "I've been told that a time or two."

His eyes went wide. "I don't know why I didn't think of this sooner. But will you . . . do you think you could talk to Easy?"

"About?"

"He's the friend I told you about at dinner the other night. The one struggling with thoughts of, uh—"

"Suicide?" she asked, a knot lodging in her throat. "*Easy's* suicidal?" she asked again. Derek nodded. In two days of interacting with him, she hadn't seen anything in his behavior that tripped a red flag. But, then again, he did always sorta hold himself out from the others in the group. And social withdrawal was one of the most common signs of depression. "Damn, I'm so sorry, Derek. If he agrees, I'd be happy to talk to him."

"Come here," Derek said, pulling her into his arms. He held her for a long moment, and then sighed. "Okay, let me take this off so we can get some sleep," he said.

Emilie was fascinated watching him, and was so damn appreciative that he explained what everything was and why he did what he did. Perhaps the coolest part was when the little remote control in his pocket released the vacuum seal inside the sleeve, allowing him to roll it down. He set the whole limb aside.

"Why do you wear those?" she said, surprised to see layers of socks underneath.

"The stump socks protect the skin and help perfect the fit," he said rolling down both socks. Underneath those was yet another layer, a whitish rubbery sleeve that hugged his skin. Derek slowly rolled that piece off, too, finally baring his skin to her eyes.

And, of course, there was nothing ugly about the amputation site. It was jarring to see his leg abruptly end in nothingness just a few inches below his kneecap, and the scar from the wound's closure was raised and pronounced, but otherwise what she noticed was that the skin all around his knee joined seemed puffy and swollen.

"Does that feel better?" she asked.

Derek gave her a small smile. "Yeah. Kind of a relief."

"Good," Emilie said, laying her hand on his right thigh. It was smaller than the other one, as if he'd lost muscle mass, and his skin was almost hot to the touch from being underneath all those layers, but what she most noticed was the way Derek's gaze latched onto her touching him. She smoothed her hand upward, then down again, this time going below his knee.

Suddenly, he grabbed her hand and brought it to her mouth, and then he pressed a long kiss to the center of his palm. His Adam's apple bobbed as he swallowed hard, and then he pressed her hand over the bare inked skin of his chest. It was the sweetest gesture, especially paired with the affection so plain in his gaze.

"Ready to go to sleep?" he asked.

"Yeah," she said, scooting back and helping him pull down the covers. They both slid under the cool, white bedding. When Derek tugged her in tight to lie with her head on his shoulder, he reached over to turn out the light. "You know, this is the first time I've spent a night with someone in years, too."

He kissed her forehead and urged her knee to slide up across his hips. "Well, it won't be the last."

SOMETHING CRAWLED OVER his leg. Again and again. Until the sensation dragged Marz out of the best sleep he'd had in as long as he could remember.

Awake now, the tickling annoyance flared until it turned painful and sharp—and he could no longer stay still. Regretting disturbing Emilie, he slowly twisted his upper body out from under hers. The red glow of the digital clock on the nightstand read 4:35.

"You okay?" came her sleepy voice in the dark.

"Need to get up for a while," he said.

"Leg bothering you?" she asked, yawning.

He really respected the way Emilie just addressed his issues head on—and in so doing, totally disarmed them as issues. "Yeah."

"Turn the light on," she whispered.

Marz found the switch in the darkness. The golden glow made him flinch and squint until his eyes adjusted. He looked at Emilie and almost pinched himself. Long, dark brown waves framed her face and sprawled across her pillow, and he didn't think he imagined that her eyes were soft and filled with affection. For him.

Which made it suck all the more that his body wouldn't just let him lie back and enjoy the feel of her. But this particular sensation unleashed a restlessness through his muscles that demanded his attention. He sat up and swung his legs over the edge of the bed.

Emilie sat up, too, and surprised him by hugging him from behind, her thighs spread along the outside of his own. "Hi," she whispered into his ear.

He smiled, which in and of itself was remarkable, given the achiness and resentment toward getting up that he felt. "Hi."

She kissed the side of his neck, and then her upper body drew back, leaving her hands on his shoulders.

She kneaded and worked at the muscles until Marz was groaning. As it continued, the massage totally distracted his body from the phantom pain until it actually disappeared altogether.

Slowly but surely, she worked her way all the way down to his lower back. When she was done, Marz peered over his shoulder. "That felt so good I might actually be able to go back to sleep," he said, more than a little awed at what she'd done for him.

"Good," she said, making room for him as she slipped beneath the covers again.

Marz turned her way, gathering her into his arms and molding her tight against his chest, his head on her shoulder.

"Have you ever tried mirror therapy?" she asked him.

He'd heard of it but never pursued learning how to do it. It was supposed to essentially trick the brain into believing the amputated limb still existed by substituting the reflection of the whole limb for the damaged one, and thus combat phantom pain. "No," he said, somewhat surprised that she knew about it.

"If you want, I could show you some time. A physical therapist would really be best to work on it with you—"

"But I'm not gonna have the freedom to do any PT any time soon. That would be great, Em."

"No problem," she whispered, her voice sounding leaden with sleepiness. She turned in his arms and pressed her back to his front, wriggling in close.

His cock had already stirred during the massage, and now the pressure of her rear against his hips made him hard. He grabbed her hips and gently thrust himself against her, but gradually his movements became harder, more needful. Emilie's small moans and the way she pressed herself back into his thrusts said that she was right there with him. Derek's arm surrounded her upper body and he hunched himself against her, reveling in the friction against his cock.

But for as much as he wanted her, none of the frenzied need settled into his blood this time. Which meant he could spend his good old time driving her wild.

Buzz, buzz.

The sound invaded the haze of lust that had settled over his brain. Why would someone be texting him at this hour? Given the guy seemed to share Marz's insomnia, maybe it was Charlie with something about the key search?

Buzz, buzz.

Another incoming message. Except, why didn't his gut buy that as a possibility?

Torn, he kissed Emilie's shoulder. "Gimme a second."

Her gaze followed him as he rolled over to reach for his cell. His hand no more landed on the device when three heavy-fisted pounds landed against their hotel room door.

Emilie gasped.

"What the fuck?" Marz said, an icy cold fear trickling down his spine and raising the hair on his head. "Em, see who that is. You can get there faster than me. Just use the spyhole first. Something's wrong."

She flew from the bed as Marz thumbed open his messages.

He had two of them, both from Nick. Marz's stomach crashed to the floor in a way that hadn't happened since the moment that roadblock in Afghanistan went ass over tits.

SOS, read the first message. Why the hell was Nick sending out an urgent appeal for help? Marz flicked to the next message, and the two words he read there froze the blood in his veins.

Under attack.

The air sucked in on Marz as Shane barreled into the room, Emilie right behind him. Wearing nothing but a pair of boxers, Shane had his phone pressed to his ear and his face was as white as the sheets.

No, no, no, this can't be happening.

"Jesus, Marz," Shane rasped. "Hard Ink's being attacked. Right now."

Chapter 23

The minute Marz had his prosthesis back on and his jeans hiked up, he picked up his phone and dialed Miguel Olivero, Nick's PI friend who had been helping them since the beginning. The phone rang and rang and finally went to voice mail. So Marz hung up and dialed again. This time, someone picked up.

"Hello?" came a rasping, half-asleep voice.

"Miguel, it's Derek DiMarzio." Marz dressed while he talked. Emilie flew through the room collecting and packing their things.

"What's happened?" Miguel said, all the sleepiness instantly gone from his words as his instincts kicked in.

"I don't have the details, but Hard Ink is under attack. Most of the team got waylaid south of the city last night by the storms, so Nick is seriously short-handed. It's gonna take us a half an hour to get there."

"I'm on it," Miguel said.

"You don't know what you're going to be walking into," Marz said. "Is there anyone you trust implicitly who can back you up?"

A moment's pause, and then Miguel said, "A hundred percent, yes."

"Then do it, Miguel. Just get to them as quick as you can."

They were all loaded into Shane's truck less than five minutes later, but it had felt like a lifetime. Beckett at the wheel, they pulled out of the hotel's parking lot into the predawn darkness like the devil himself was chasing them.

Easy and Shane were still on their cells with Jenna and Sara, who'd called when the shit had first gone down. But since the women were hiding in the basement underneath Hard Ink, they didn't have any additional information beyond the fact that there had been some sort of explosion, they'd heard the steady percussion of semiautomatic gunshots, and all the men had gone to find out what had happened.

All the men. Which meant that Jeremy and Charlie, neither of whom had combat experience nor much familiarity with weapons, were out there dealing with whatever had come at them in the dead of the night. *All the men* probably also included Ike and the handful of Ravens that had arrived before the storm. Which meant, best-case scenario, Nick had five or six men backing him up.

Guilt sat like burning motor oil in Marz's gut. They should be there. *They should be there.* And instead of being there, Marz had spent the night getting laid. He roughly raked at his hair.

His brain raced. Attacked how? Attacked by who? And what was happening now?

But they didn't know the answers to those questions, and they wouldn't know until they arrived on the scene. Which would take about twenty-five minutes of driving time on the mostly empty highways to achieve.

It was a fucking eternity.

He blew out a long breath.

Emilie quietly laced her fingers between his and squeezed.

Her expression wore the anxiety and fear that Marz felt but couldn't let surface. And, aw hell, he shouldn't have thought that way about their time together. He cherished it beyond words. It wasn't her fault that they got delayed. Truth be told, it wasn't any of their faults. Not like they controlled the damn weather. He leaned over and kissed her in silent apology.

But none of that was going to matter one goddamned bit if anything happened to their friends.

"Fuck!" Beckett roar, pounding his fist against the steering wheel as he raced at ninety miles an hour around a sedan.

The fact that Marz could count on one hand precisely how many times he'd ever seen his best friend lose control of his emotions like that highlighted just how dire things truly were.

Tension hung so heavy inside the cab, you could've cut it with a knife.

"Anything new?" Marz asked, his gaze ping-ponging between Shane and Easy. Both men looked at him with the same lethal anger in their eyes that he felt and shook their heads. "We need a plan for when we get there. We can't just drive into the middle of it."

"We don't even know what 'it' is yet," Beckett said.

"Or that we'll get there in time to be of any goddamned use. Whether this attack is Church or Garza or Seneka or the fucking Easter Bunny, this has got to be a hit-and-run. No way any of them would risk getting caught or identified by sticking around long enough for the authorities and the media to get on site."

Probably true. Which meant, goddamnit, Beckett was right.

Beckett took the big, curved flyover ramp to Interstate 695 faster than was strictly safe. Marz put an arm around Emilie and grabbed the hand strap above his head.

"Hey," Marz said, a thought coming to mind. "Ask Sara and Jenna if Becca's with them."

"She is," Easy said.

"Tell her to call her EMT friends and see if they'll come over with their rig. Just a precaution. If we can't be there in time to help, we can sure as shit be ready to deal with the aftermath."

Easy relayed the message. "Calling them now," Easy said.

"What else can we do?" Marz murmured to himself. *Jesus. There has to be something.*

Both Shane and Easy suddenly jolted, like they'd received a shock.

"What?" Marz asked, dread a crushing presence inside his chest. "What the hell was that?" Another sharp turn as Beckett veered off on the first exit they came to, which put them on the parkway that would dump them into downtown Baltimore. The gray light of dawn filtered into the cloudy sky.

"Just stay there," Easy said. "I'm no more than fifteen minutes out from you, Jen. Don't move from where you are." In the front seat, Shane was rushing out similar sentiments. Marz was about ready to lose his shit when Easy turned to him, his expression stricken. "There was a big explosion."

"Another one?" Marz said, incredulous. "Just what the hell are they fighting?'

Easy held up his hands, and then he turned his body toward the window. His words were hushed, like he really didn't want to share them. "I'm so fucking sorry I'm not there with you. And I'm sorry to say this for the first time now, but I need you to know. I love you, Jenna. Do you hear me? You keep yourself safe until I get there."

Marz felt like they were trapped in a slow trudge to the gallows. And it was clear the other guys felt the same way. They sat in a tense silence as they came into the city past the two huge stadiums and headed east. With all the lights, their progress slowed significantly.

"Five minutes," Easy said into his phone when they hit Eastern Avenue.

Two minutes later, Shane leaned forward in the passenger seat and craned his head like he was looking at something in the sky. "Fuck me running."

"Jesus," Beckett said, glancing in the direction of Shane's gaze.

"What?" Marz said, sitting forward so he could see what they were looking at. *Oh fuck.*

A plume of black smoke rose into the early morning air. In roughly the direction they needed to head. No way the explosions at Hard Ink weren't related to that. *Sonofabitch.*

Emilie put a hand on his back. "What is it?"

Marz turned to her, so fucking sorry that he couldn't give her just one moment of peace and safety. "It looks like Hard Ink is on fire."

BECKETT FLOORED THE accelerator, jerking them all back against their seats. Marz's gut burned, the remains of last night's dinner in his system threatening an all-out revolt.

"It's over!" Shane nearly yelled. "Nick's sister just came to let the other women know they could come out."

Thank fuck!

"What?" Beckett said, his gaze jerking toward Shane. "Why wasn't she down there with them?"

"I don't know, man," Shane said, dragging his hand through his hair until Marz worried it might start coming out in clumps. "Just get there."

Beckett took the turn onto Hard Ink's street so hard, the pickup came up on two wheels. They barreled down the road, blowing through the stop signs in the generally quiet industrial neighborhood. From two blocks away, they could see people standing in the street with smoke billowing around them. There didn't seem to be any emergency vehicles on the scene.

"Aw, shit," Marz said. All their friends filled the street and seemed to be congregated around something. Becca and Charlie's blond and the Dean sisters' red hair stood out in the group. Becca was crying against Charlie's chest. The entirety of Marz's innards went on a freefall, leaving him hollow and achy and unable to take a deep breath. Who was Becca crying for? Who lay in the center of that group?

The truck passed a car that looked like it had been broadsided by a tank, and then Beckett hit the brakes so hard in front of the gate to the parking lot that the truck skidded on the gravel.

Marz drew his weapon, threw the door open, and hopped out. "Be right back, Em. Let me check this out first." He took off for the group, the other men right behind him. Blood on Becca's hands and shirt jumped out at him, sending ice through his veins. "What's happened?" Marz yelled.

His first thought was *Not Nick, not Nick, not Nick.*

But then a wave of guilt swamped him, because there wasn't a single person at Hard Ink that Marz would be okay losing.

He pushed passed two men he didn't recognize who stood at the edge of the group. Nick and Jeremy appeared to be kneeling over someone, and the instant Marz saw their matching dark chocolate hair he got a little dizzy with relief. "Nick!"

Nick's gaze whipped toward him and the guy rose to his feet. "Jesus, Marz," he said, his face and arms smudged black here and there. Blood seeped through the bandage on his neck.

Marz clasped Nick's hand. "I'm so fucking sorry we weren't here. What hap—" At that instant, Marz's gaze landed on the person lying on the ground in the center of the group.

Miguel. The circular, dark red wound on the man's forehead told Marz everything he needed to know. Miguel was dead.

Putting a hand to his own forehead, Marz struggled to breathe. "I . . . I . . What . . ." He shook his head and grappled for clarity. "I asked him to come help you."

"He came," Nick started, his voice cracking, "just as the attackers were leaving. Tried to block them with his car, but they were in fucking armored Suburbans. They rammed the car and shot him when he dove out of the way."

Aw, damn, Miguel. So fucking sorry. Marz had pulled him out of his bed, and the guy hadn't given a second thought to helping. And he'd lost his life for it. For them. Another among too many good men taken out because of Frank Merritt's treachery and greed. *Goddamnit.*

"How many more have to fucking die?" Easy said, his tone like ice.

Nick looked over his shoulder toward the intersection, where the side of the building they'd camouflaged fronted the crossing street. "Maybe two more," he said.

Marz took a mental headcount. All their guys were here. "Who?"

"Ravens," Nick said as the rest of the team gathered around. "The sonofabitches had a rocket launcher. Launched some sort of high-penetration projectile against the building. A whole section of it collapsed. We were on the roof engaged in a firefight. I couldn't get to the guys before their part of roof caved."

"Christ," Beckett said. "How long do you think until the authorities get here?"

"None of us called 911," Nick said. "For obvious reasons. And I'm sure our attackers didn't. Otherwise, this neighborhood is pretty sparsely populated and generally loathe to get involved. So, hard to say."

"At some point, the plume of smoke will draw attention either way," Derek said.

Jeremy's face was paler than usual and his eyes were a little wild. He had nicks and cuts on his arms. "Ike and Meat are over there going through the rubble, hoping to find them alive."

Nick shook his head. "There's no fucking way," he said in a low rasp.

"Let's go be sure," Marz said. "We'll help. If there's even a chance, how can we not?"

Nick gave a tight nod. "Let's do it." But instead of

walking in the direction of the building, Nick turned back to Miguel's body. He crouched at the older man's side and laid a hand over the older man's heart. "I'm so sorry, Miguel."

They'd all lost a friend, an ally, a brother, and Nick most of all. Marz's throat went tight and he mentally apologized again as Nick rose to his feet.

Marz turned toward Shane's truck, and found Emilie standing by the front of it, shoulders hunched, arms crossed, expression on the verge of cracking. He jogged over to her and gathered her tight in his arms.

She shuddered against him. "I can't believe this. I didn't know that man, but I can't believe we just came to your home and found *this*." Emilie pushed free from his grip enough to look him in the eyes. "I know you hate that you weren't here, but all I can think is what if you *had* been here. What if that had been you?" She covered her mouth with her hand. "I'm sorry."

"I understand, Emilie. Trust me. We are way, way off the reservation here." He blew out a long breath.

"Did you know him?" she asked. "The man that died."

Marz nodded, remembering back to their first op within this clusterfuck of a mission—rescuing Charlie. They'd had conflicting intel that he could've been at one of two locations. Marz, Beckett, and Miguel had made up one of the rescue teams, and Miguel had fit with them like he'd been with them for years. "Not well, but I liked him a lot. Had the opportunity to work together a few times over the past weeks. He was a good man. True. One of the few friends we had." He closed his eyes and shook his head. "God, he'd just become a grandfather again."

"Oh," Emilie said, her voice wavering. Tears spilled from the corners of her eyes. "I'm so sorry."

"I want you to stay right by my side, okay? There are a couple of Ike's guys trapped in some rubble on the other side of the building. We're gonna go look for them, but this remains a hot zone as long as things are this unsecured." He took her hand in his.

"Okay," she said. "Wait. Rubble?"

"Yeah," he said, exhaustion stalking at the back of his mind. But he couldn't give into it—he *wouldn't* give into it. His leg, his head, his insomnia—none of it mattered in the face of what had happened.

They caught up with everyone, and Nick introduced Marz to the two bystanders he hadn't recognized— Miguel's friends. The ones the man hadn't hesitated to trust.

"This is Detective Kyler Vance, BPD," Nick said, gesturing to the younger of the two men. Marz shook his hand. Dark hair, blue eyes, plain clothes. Guy probably wasn't much older than Marz. And he was current BPD. Maybe that shouldn't have unsettled Marz, but after everything they'd learned, it did.

"I see the questions in your eyes," Kyler said. "Miguel was my godfather. He and my dad were partners on the force for years. He got us up to speed on the way over here. I'm aware you all have very good reasons for distrusting BPD." He swallowed, hard. "But you can trust me. I want justice for Miguel. You can count on me for anything." His unflinching gaze met each of Marz's teammates' eyes.

Marz nodded, appreciating the man's words and feeling Miguel's loss anew. As hard as it had hit him, he truly felt for the long-term relationship Kyler had surely had with Miguel.

"And this is Hugh Vance, Kyler's father and Miguel's partner," Nick said.

Jesus. It didn't get much tighter than partners, did it? Marz shook Hugh's hand. "So sorry for your loss." He looked at Kyler, and the family resemblance struck him over the head. "For both of your losses."

"I'll second Ky's sentiments. We are with you in this as much as you want us," Hugh said with grit in his voice.

"We really appreciate that," Nick said. "I respected the hell out of Miguel. Can't believe he's gone." He glanced down the length of the building. "Let's go see if we can help Ike."

"We'd like to stick around and help if that's all right," Hugh said.

"Absolutely," Nick said.

"I hope you don't mind," Kyler said, "but the authorities are coming down on this one way or the other. So I called for some PD and FD guys I *know* we can trust. They'll be here shortly."

Nick gave a sharp nod. "Appreciate it."

As a group, they walked to the corner of the block.

And Marz's breath caught at the destruction. "Jesus Christ," he rasped, walking out into the street to get a fuller view of it. The whole center of the rectangular building had caved in, from the roof to the ground, creating a cascading mountain of rubble that spilled into the street. Small fires burned here and there, but luckily the interior's emptiness and the cinderblock-and-brick construction kept them from spreading. And the guys had all been on the top of that when it happened? They were lucky any of them survived.

"Oh, my God," Emilie said, hugging herself against

Marz's arm. "What if they hadn't made this side of the building look like the real side? That could be Hard Ink right now."

She was right. Marz's gaze went directly to Beckett, whose anger had brought out the hard angles in his face. He got the credit for this idea. Him and Jeremy, for going along with it.

"Any luck?" Nick called to Ike and another Raven that Marz recognized from another mission but didn't know well. *Meat, Jeremy had called him?*

Ike braced his hands on his hips. "No. Not heard anything, either. No way we can move all this by hand. I called in a favor with a guy I know who runs a construction company. He'll be in-bound within the hour with some equipment. Dead or alive, I'm not leaving my brothers here."

Marz totally understood that.

"We'll help however we can, Ike," Nick said, climbing the pile toward him. "Really fucking sorry I couldn't get to them in time."

Ike gave him a nod. "I know," he said. "Wasn't your fault. But I can sure as shit tell you that this is no longer just your fight. Dare's already called a meeting and a vote. I suspect the Ravens will be in on this of their own accord by day's end." Dare Kenyon was the Ravens' club president, and he'd been a part of last Friday's mission against the Church Gang.

Marz was glad to hear of the Ravens' plans to fully join forces with them, because he and his teammates needed the help. Obviously. But he hated the reason they'd come to this decision—that they'd very likely lost two of their own.

As he watched, Meat climbed the still-smoking

rubble pile toward the open second floor and held out his hand. An orange tabby cat stared at him a long minute and scurried away. Marz could hardly believe his eyes. The stray must've been in the building when the blast occurred—and survived. Go fucking figure.

Emilie rested her forehead against Marz's shoulder and shuddered out a breath.

"Hey," Marz said. "We're okay." Or as okay as they could be given what had come at them out of the darkness.

"I know," she said, her voice tight as a cord. She looked to the left, away from all the death and destruction. "I know," she said again.

And then she went stock-still.

"Derek?" She tugged on his arm.

Marz followed her gaze across the intersection. His eyes went wide when he finally realized what she was looking at. "That's a pair of boots."

"Could that be one of their guys? Maybe he crawled out of the way," she said, her gaze filling with hope.

"Nick! Ike! We've got a body over here," Marz said, taking off across the intersection. "Shane, might need you."

Footsteps ran up behind him as Marz reached the far corner. The man lay on his stomach in the trash-filled gutter that edged the street.

"Oh, shit," Marz said, his gaze landing on the back of the man's shaved head. Or, where the back of the man's head used to be. But a point-blank shot had taken care of that.

"Christ," Shane bit out.

Emilie gasped and covered her mouth. "Oh, God," she said, anguish pouring back into her eyes.

"Don't look," Derek said, pulling her against his chest. He was quite sure she'd seen more than enough dead people the past few days. He hated that, for her.

"How the hell does this fit in?" Nick asked, coming to stand by Shane.

"I don't know, man. Lemme roll him." Shane took ahold of the man's arm and eased him onto his back.

The man's forehead was gone, but the rest of the face—

Oh, God. Oh, no.

Emilie turned her head to watch Shane.

Derek wrenched himself in front of her, his head shaking. "Come with me," he said, taking her by the shoulders and bodily moving her away.

Away from the executed body of her brother.

"What? What are you doing? Derek, stop," she finally said, pushing against his chest.

And Marz had thought the space around his heart couldn't hurt anymore. This was going to devastate her. "Just come with me. Okay?" No way did she need to see his ruined face. She should not have to live with those images in her head, haunting her waking hours and her dreams.

She looked toward the boots, and scanned the others. Those who knew Manny Garza—or knew what he looked like—dropped their gazes to the ground. Emilie frowned. "I don't . . ." She shook her head. "Why?" she asked, nailing him with a stare.

"Emilie—"

She pulled out of his arms and ran toward the man. Marz took off after her and caught her around the waist.

The gasp that ripped out of her throat was so loud it must've hurt. "No! No!" She twisted out of his arms, falling to her knees at her brother's feet.

And then she screamed and screamed.

Chapter 24

Nononono, this can't be! Manny!

The scream came from someplace inside Emilie she never even knew existed. A place where agony and fear and hopelessness lay in wait to suck you in and drag you down. She thought she'd been in pain at the loss of Jack from her life. This moment taught her she hadn't had the first clue what pain actually was.

God, she couldn't breathe. Emilie couldn't focus on anything except the terrible, bloody facsimile of the handsome face she'd known her whole life. She couldn't hear anything except the pounding rush of her pulse in her ears.

Warmth surrounded her back, and words came to her as if through a long tunnel, warbled and indistinct.

Without consciously deciding to do it, her hands reached out and settled on Manny's boots, then upward, to the hem of his jeans. These were the same clothes that he'd worn to her house the night before, but sometime in the last twelve hours he'd shaved away all those beautiful waves.

She forced herself to look at his face, to confront the reality that someone had put a gun to the back of his head, shot him at point-blank range, and dumped his body in a gutter.

It brought the second of the fears she'd had for him to life. That he'd get hurt. Just as he'd already hurt others.

Still, despite everything he'd done, he didn't deserve this. *No one* deserved this.

My fault. This is my fault. I waited to get him help, and now he's gone. Disposed of like so much trash.

In the back of her mind, she became aware of a sound. She couldn't place it until it was so loud it hurt her ears. *Sirens.*

The minute she reconnected to the world around her, her stomach violently heaved.

Emilie twisted to the side and planted her hands on the rough, crumbling blacktop as her body expelled the first wave of vomit. She wretched again and again, but she hadn't eaten anything this morning, and not much last night, so it was just hard, clenching dry heaves that bowed her whole body until she thought she'd break. Gravel dug into her bare hands and her knees through her jeans.

When the heaving finally slowed, she realized that heat was still against her back.

"Oh, God, baby, I'm so sorry. I've got you, Em. I've got you. Sshh."

Derek, embracing her and holding the hair back from her face as she sat on her hands and knees in the middle of a war zone.

When her body finally relented, Emilie's muscles went loose and she sagged. But Derek was right there to catch her. She twisted in his arms and curled into his chest.

One of his hands held her tight across the back and the other cradled her head. "I've got you. I'm so sorry, but I've got you. I'm here for you."

A fast nod was all she could manage.

"Let's get you inside, Em," Derek said against her ear.

She lifted her head and looked him in the eyes. "I know he did horrible things," she said, her voice thick with tears. "I know he did. I know he killed. But he was my brother. And he wasn't always like this."

Derek caught her tears with his thumb and wiped them away. "I know."

"I can't leave him lying here, Derek. I'm all he has." And, oh, God, he died thinking she'd betrayed him.

Derek's dark eyes were so soft with compassion and affection. "He won't be left. The authorities are here. They're going to want to take some pictures of the scene. The coroner will take Manny's body, and we'll make sure he has your contact information."

The authorities were here? Emilie pulled herself from the little bubble her mind had constructed around them and scanned the street. The Hard Ink guys formed a circle around her and Derek, and right behind them stood Becca, Sara, Jenna, and Katherine. But between all of them Emilie could just make out several large red fire engines, an ambulance, and at least one white BPD squad car.

Head swimming, Emilie looked at Derek again. "Do you think he felt it?"

Shane crouched down next to her and took her hand.

"He didn't feel it, Emilie. He was gone before he could know it happened. In situations like these, it's a mercy that our brains can't process information faster."

It was a mercy. Because she couldn't bear the thought of Manny suffering—at least not any more than his obvious mental illness had already caused. "Thank you," she said.

"Let's get you up," Derek said.

"I can do it." Though, in truth, her body was weak and shaky from the violence of her heaves. Derek and Shane both helped her up. "What's happening?" she asked, her gaze settling on a group of men—Nick, Beckett, Miguel's friends, and men in various uniforms—having an animated conversation over by one of the two fire engines.

"Not sure," Derek said, his arm around her shoulders. "But Nick will fill us in." He turned to Shane and Easy. "I think everyone who doesn't need to be out here should come inside. There's too damn much we don't know right now."

"Roger that," Shane said, and he and Easy gathered everyone not part of the conversation and urged them in.

"Hold up. We need to do a walk-through of the building first," a fireman said, hand in the air.

Derek groaned and pressed a kiss to her ear. "I'm sorry."

"For what it's worth, that whole side is totally intact," Jeremy said, stepping up next to the firefighter. "I own the place and have been rebuilding it. The explosion didn't impact that arm of the L."

The fireman nodded. "Then it shouldn't take long to clear it. Just sit tight." He gathered a few guys to join him while the others doused the small fires burning here and there in the rubble pile.

"Why don't I come with you?" Jeremy asked. "The interior is controlled by keypads. You won't know the codes."

The man he'd spoken to before looked at him a long moment, then finally nodded. "Come on." Emilie watched all this as if she were watching a television show—like it was distant and unreal.

"Let's go over here." Derek guided Emilie to the back of the open ambulance. "You got a blanket she could use? She's in shock."

"I can examine her," the paramedic said, handing Derck a blue blanket.

"No," Emilie said, the question jarring her from the fog. "I don't want that."

"Ssh, it's okay. I've got you," Derek said, wrapping the blanket around her shoulders and hugging her to his chest.

By slow, slow degrees, Derek's touch and warmth made her feel more present in this situation. It was a mixed blessing.

Fifteen minutes later, they had the all clear to go inside. Emilie returned the blanket and walked toward the others with Marz by her side, his arm around her waist.

"I don't want to leave Nick," Becca said, the blood stains on her hands and shirt darkening as they dried.

Identifying with the desperate need in the other woman's voice, Emilie held out her hand. "He'll probably worry about you out here. He's got Beckett, and Ike's here. And the police. He'll be fine. Come in and get cleaned up. I'm sure he'll be in soon." It made it easier to deal with her own pain if she focused on someone else's.

Katherine stepped up beside Becca and gave her a

small smile. Emilie had met her briefly before they'd gone to her house on Friday night. With her dark brown waves and bright green eyes, Kat was really quite stunning, even with her face smudged by ash and arms and hands nicked up.

From the explosion?

"Emilie's right," Katherine said.

Becca looked back and forth between them for a moment and finally nodded. She slipped her hand into Emilie's and held her arm out to Katherine, and the three of them made their way toward a chain-link fence on the far side of Hard Ink, Marz right behind them.

"I'm so sorry about your brother," Becca said.

"Thank you." The words came out mechanically, Emilie's brain still not quite processing the reality of what she'd seen, of what had happened, of the fact she'd never hold or see or touch her brother again. And, *oh God*, she was going to have to tell her mother—and break the woman's heart for real this time. Heaving a shaky breath, Emilie peered up toward Becca through blowing tendrils of her hair. "I know he probably did bad things to all these guys. No one here owes him anything, but I do. I can't forget the other thirty years of his life just because he made a lot of very bad decisions during the past few." Images flashed through her mind's eye—of the sheer wildness in his gaze as he choked her in her kitchen, of the unmistakable determination on his face to beat her with that bat. It all made her so tired, and so very sad. "I don't know, maybe that doesn't make any sense."

"It does, Emilie," Becca said. "Everyone will understand where you're coming from. And you tried to get him help. But you can only help someone who wants it."

"Yeah," she said.

"You know," Becca said, looking at Katherine. "You were pretty freaking amazing going out there with the guys." She turned to Emilie. "Katherine fought with the men. She was up on the roof with them when it collapsed."

Emilie had to agree with Becca's assessment. Would she have had that kind of courage in that situation? *You killed that cop.* True. But he hadn't given her much of a choice.

Katherine shrugged. "I know how to shoot and I figured they needed all the bodies they could get," she said matter-of-factly.

Becca chuckled. "I know how to shoot, too, but Nick wouldn't hear the first word about me helping."

"Well, I've never been much of a listener," Katherine said, bumping Becca's shoulder. "And he's not in love with me."

"Yeah," Becca said, smiling. Her expression made it totally clear that Becca felt the same way about him.

A yearning opened up inside Emilie's chest, but it quickly crashed into the big ball of grief she felt over Manny, and that swamped her with guilt for even thinking about anything else. His loss was an ache that blotted out almost everything—her kidnapping, her injuries, the fact that she'd shot and killed another person. All of that felt distant and inconsequential in comparison to the hole in her heart.

Shane jogged ahead to his truck, parked at an angle with the back end almost in the middle of the road. He reached into the driver's side and apparently pushed a release on the gate, which swung inward.

Soon, they made their way to Nick and Jeremy's apartment. They filled up the couches and chairs, a sort of collective shock and exhaustion hanging over them. No one talked much. Jenna and Sara mirrored

Emilie's position, tucked in under the arms of their men.

She was glad for the sisters, that their brains weren't filled with the images of a dead sibling the way hers was. She couldn't stop seeing the destruction the bullet had wrecked on Manny's skull.

Jeremy and Charlie sat huddled together on one of the couches—Jeremy with his elbows braced on his knees and his head in his hands, and Charlie with his arm around the other man's back.

Abruptly, Charlie grabbed one of Jeremy's hands and pulled him to his feet, and then without a word led him around the room and down a hall. As much as Jeremy had tried to duck his head, Emilie had seen that his expression was probably a short moment away from crumpling.

Katherine stared after Jeremy like she wanted to follow but also didn't want to interfere. She traded a worried look with Becca, who sat beside her.

Poor Jeremy. From what she understood, the tattoo shop and the building were primarily his. And now at least part of it had been demolished.

Emilie's throat clogged with tears again, and she closed her eyes and let them flow against Derek's chest until she felt his shirt dampen. And then, miraculously, her eyelids got too heavy to lift, and she didn't remember anything else.

SLEEP WAS EXACTLY what Emilie needed, so Marz was only too glad to hold her against his chest and let her find some comfort and solace in him as long as she could. Nick had come in about an hour after the rest of them and laid out the big pressing question they all faced—whether or not to remain at Hard Ink. And, if they fled, where they might go.

But they couldn't go anywhere before the key search was completed. Disconnecting the computers at this point risked needing to start the process over from the beginning. In the craziness that had been the past two days, Marz had totally lost track of Charlie's idea to try to acquire more powerful hardware to run the search, but it was probably just as well. Between Emilie's abduction on Friday and the attack on Hard Ink this morning, the fates were making it pretty damn clear that they all needed to keep their heads down and not pull anybody new into this clusterfuck. So that meant they still had between twelve and eighteen hours before the search found the key to unlock the encrypted microchip they'd found in Becca's bear.

Given the forced cooling of their heels, Nick had told everyone to think about those two questions and plan to reconvene for a debrief and discussion in the gym at five o'clock—by which time he hoped to hear from Ike how the Ravens had voted on the question of taking on the team's mission as their own.

Emilie hadn't budged once while Nick spoke, so Marz hadn't wanted to wake her to go up to his room. Instead, he settled into the corner of the couch with Emilie tight against him and let himself pass the fuck out.

It didn't happen right away.

For a long while, a horror movie played against the insides of his eyelids. The GSW to Miguel's head. Manny's gruesome execution. Emilie's mourning for her brother, which had nearly ripped his heart from his own chest.

"Marz. Hey, Marz." Something was shaking him. Or someone. His eyes felt like they'd been glued together, and they opened blearily to find Easy standing over him.

"We're supposed to meet in the gym in fifteen, but I thought you two might want to grab some food first." He pointed toward the kitchen. "Becca made a big pot of homemade chicken noodle and a bunch of rolls. They're still warm."

"Thanks, E," he said. Had he really slept for six hours straight? Almost unheard of. "Be right over."

Easy clapped him on the shoulder and left.

Looking down, Marz found Emilie still asleep against him, though at some point, she'd turned over and scooted down so her head lay in his lap. The fact that he hadn't felt her move like that spoke to just how damn tired he'd been, too.

His gaze ran down her body—over the mint green shirt she wore, over her jeans to her bare feet. And then back up again to where her dark brown hair sprawled across his lap. And all he could think was, *This is right where she belongs. With me. By my side. The two of us facing the world—good and bad—together.*

And that was the moment his heart cracked all the way open and overwhelmed him with the realization that he hadn't just gotten involved with Emilie Garza. And he hadn't just had mind-blowing sex with her. He'd fallen in love with her.

He'd fallen in love for the first time in his life.

The admission—and his acceptance of the truth of his feelings—made it temporarily harder to breathe. But then he studied her face—so beautiful and peaceful in sleep—and everything inside him calmed as if, even on a physiological level, he recognized the rightness of the two of them together.

And that was damn hard to come by. He would know, because he'd never had it before.

Truth be told, he never thought he would.

"Hey, Em," Derek said, stroking the hair off her face. "Wake up."

"Hi," she said, her voice a dry scrape.

"Hi." Now that he'd admitted his feelings to himself, his chest filled with a warm pressure that yearned to be set free.

"What time is it?" she asked, pushing up on one hand.

"Almost five. That's why I woke you. We're going to have a meeting to figure out what we know and where to go from here. You don't have to go—"

"No, I'd really like to," she said.

Derek nodded. "Well, then, I thought we should get some food before we do. Becca made chicken noodle soup. Think you could handle some of that?"

Emilie peered over her shoulder into the kitchen, where a huge pot sat on the stove. "Aw, that was sweet of her. Sounds fine."

They crossed to the kitchen and Derek pointed Emilie to the bathroom. While she was gone, he ladled soup into bowls and grabbed them rolls and butter. He'd just gotten drinks and set everything up at the breakfast bar when Emilie returned. She stood at the edge of the room hugging herself, her hair sleek again as if she'd brushed it.

"Come on over," he said, watching her face.

She was fighting back tears.

He went to her in an instant, his leg grumbling at the fast movement, and folded her in his arms.

"One second I was washing my hands, the next I was looking at Manny's head again. And then I felt horrible because he was shot and killed this morning, and I spent the afternoon immediately afterward taking a nap."

"That nap was total self-preservation, Emilie. Your body needed to shut down. This morning was beyond traumatic for you. So, to quote one of my favorite people ever, give yourself a break."

That almost eked a smile out of her. "I'll try."

"Come on. A little food will help." He guided her to a bar stool and then hopped up himself. He dug in more enthusiastically than she did, but at least she got a little something into her stomach.

When they were just about done, Charlie and Jeremy emerged from Jer's room. In the few weeks that Marz had known Jeremy Rixey, he'd never seen the guy so emotionally trashed. Eyes bleak, shoulders fallen, his mouth in the shape of a frown.

Marz couldn't find any humor in the guy's Easy Lay Carpeting Co. shirt, not when he was so visibly upset. He pushed off his stool and stopped the pair of them before they crossed to the door. "Hey, how're you doing?" Marz asked Jer.

He shrugged one shoulder and barely made eye contact. Damn, if the guy's eyes weren't red, too. "Okay."

Marz clasped his hand around the side of Jeremy's neck. "We will make all this right by you, Jeremy. Your business, the building, all of it. I'm really sorry."

"It's not the building," he said, finally meeting Marz's gaze head on. "I mean, the building sucks. I just . . . can't help but think maybe we wouldn't have lost so many people if Nick had had better backup than me." He shook his head. "If I'd have reacted quicker, I wouldn't have slid down the broken roof, and Nick wouldn't have had to waste the time helping me that he could've used to save Ike's guys."

Marz glanced to Charlie, and he could see how Jeremy's self-torment was tearing the other guy up.

"Jeremy, that was simple physics. Any of us, in that same situation, would've needed the same help. It's not your fault those men died. The fault rests in one place and one place only—the men in those armored Suburbans. You fucking rose to the occasion. Despite your lack of training in this stuff, you did what needed to be done. There's no shame in that. Only honor. And you have as much of that as any one of us. Tell me you won't forget it."

Jeremy looked at him a long moment. "Okay."

He patted Jeremy's cheek. "Okay. Look, go ahead over. Tell Nick we'll be there in a minute."

"Yeah," Jer said, heading toward the door again.

Charlie looked over his shoulder and mouthed, "Thank you."

Marz gave him a nod. Damnit, if they all didn't hold PhDs in beating the shit out of themselves.

Emilie turned toward him. "You really have a way with people, do you know that?"

"I just call 'em like I see 'em," he said, warming under her praise.

She gave him a small smile. "Should we go over?"

"Sure you're done?" he asked, eyeing the remaining soup in her bowl.

"Yeah."

They made quick work of cleaning up their mess, and then Marz gently captured her against the counter. "You don't have to come to this, Emilie. I could give you the highlight reel later."

She shook her head. "I want to stay with you. And I want to know what's going on. If that's okay," she said, ducking her chin.

"Of course it's okay," he said, tilting her chin up with his fingers. "You belong here now. You're one of us."

And I want you to be mine, he wanted to add, but he held back—for now. She had enough to deal with at the moment. "But I, uh, just want to warn you. We've got security cameras trained all over this building. I suspect Nick may want us to look over the footage . . ." He let the words hang there.

"They might show Manny," she said, hugging herself.

Given the locations of the cameras, he could say with near certainty that they *would.* "They probably will," he said.

She seemed to think about it for a moment, and when her lip trembled, Marz's heart broke a little for her. But then she nodded. "I can handle it."

"Then let's go join the others and figure out what the hell we're going to do."

It was the most subdued all-hands meeting they'd ever had, so it didn't take much for Nick to call them to order.

Marz studied Nick's gait, the dark hollows beneath his eyes, the stiffness in the way he turned his head, and immediately knew his friend was hurting.

"All right, everyone," Nick said, his jaw ticking as he surveyed the group. "We've got a lot to talk about, so let's dig in. And let me start off with an apology."

What the hell for? Marz frowned and looked to his other teammates, who seemed equally confused.

"I invited you here. And I offered you safe haven," he said, looking particularly at the women. He braced his hands on his hips and shook his head. "And I know I let you all down today—"

"How do you figure?" Jeremy asked, jumping to his feet among a low murmur of similar sentiments. Eileen paced around him and whimpered.

Nick tilted his head and held out his hands like he thought the answer was obvious. "I probably failed you most of all—"

"Jesus, Nick," Jeremy bit out as he clawed his fingers through his hair. "You haven't failed me. You have *never* failed me." He waved a hand around at the rest of the group, leaning against the wall, sprawled on the floor, and sitting on folding chairs. "And you haven't failed anyone else here, either."

Nick pressed his mouth into a thin line and shook his head. "I brought my war to your fucking doorstep, Jeremy. That's pretty easy to see. And now your livelihood's been impacted. Your life is in danger." He pointed to his sister. "Kat's life is in danger. And not a single person in this room signed on for *this*."

"That's fucking bullshit," Beckett said, arms crossed, feet spread wide, expression set in a hard scowl. "This is *exactly* what the five of us signed on for. The minute you told us you thought Charlie's kidnapping somehow connected to what went down in Afghanistan, each of us came here knowing that, if it was true, things were likely to get worse before they got better."

"I totally agree," Marz said, sitting next to Emilie in a folding chair. He hated to see Nick beat himself up this way, but it was clear that the events of the day had played a number on all of their heads.

"Absolutely," Shane said, giving his best friend a hard stare around Sara, who sat on his lap. Arm around Jenna, Easy nodded.

"I wouldn't be alive if it wasn't for you," Jenna said. "For all of you."

"Neither would I," said Charlie, his voice gruff.

"Me neither," Emilie said in a low voice. "You saved me, too."

Her chin trembling, Becca stared at her hands folded in her lap. "We are a whole lot like the Island of Misfit Toys," she said, sending a low chuckle around the room. "But we are here and we are safe because of you. Because you opened your home to us." She stood next to Jeremy and grabbed his hand. "Because you fought for each of us. Because you listened to a stranger's plea for help, and as a result of that saved a whole lot of people who might never have gotten the help they needed." She walked up to Nick and took his hands in hers. "No one here expected a guarantee of complete safety. Not given the circumstances that brought us together. And no one here is any less committed to seeing this through because today happened. So be pissed about it or punch something or scream or rant, but don't feel guilty, Nick. What happened was not your fault."

Marz hugged Emilie in against his side. Damn, if he wasn't feeling a tickle at the corners of his eyes.

"You know I love any chance to call you on your bullshit," Katherine said, rubbing her palms over her thighs. "So I'm going to have to side with Rambo over there on this one. I've obviously been playing ten kinds of catch-up on what's going on around here, but I didn't see a single thing today that you did to fail anyone. They had a rocket launcher, Nick. I mean, seriously. Is there even any way to defend against such a thing? As far as I can see, there's nothing you could've done to prepare for that. So, pull it together, bro, and help us figure out where we go from here." The expression on her face was much softer than the words, especially when she winked at him.

Yeah, she was a Rixey, all right. Marz smiled and nodded.

"Shit, okay," Nick said, blowing out a long breath. Becca pushed onto tiptoes and kissed him on the cheek, then turned toward where she'd been sitting. But Nick grabbed her and hugged her back in against his front. "Stay here with me, sunshine?" She nodded.

Before, the couple's closeness would've set off an ache inside Marz's chest. Sure, he would've grinned through it or razzed them or made a joke, but it would've eaten at him all the same. He looked at Emilie, and found her looking up at him. "I've got you," he whispered.

"I know," she said back.

"Okay," Nick said. "I have a few things that might actually count as good news."

"Well, thank fuck for that," Shane said, smirking.

Nick flipped him the bird. "First, Ike called. The Ravens are on board. And since they're doing this of their own accord, we don't have to pay to hire them anymore. They're in this because they want to be."

A round of cheers and applause went around the room.

"Ike and Meat did recover their men's bodies from the rubble this morning. Once the coroner releases the bodies, the Ravens will take them out to the clubhouse to be laid to rest." Nick shook his head. "We'll figure out in the next day or two how our relationship with them is going to work. Second piece of good news. Kyler Vance."

"Miguel's partner," Marz offered, guilt once again threatening to overwhelm him.

"Yeah," Nick said, his brow furrowing for a moment. Nick and Miguel had been close, close enough that the older man was willing to risk his life for Nick. "This guy is with us and he's already proving it. The media will receive an official police report saying that a gas line break caused today's explosion here, and that until public works can fully assess the situation, the neighborhood has been evacuated and the roads blocked off."

Holy shit. Marz's gaze cut around the room. "Are the roads *actually* being blocked off?"

"That's the plan," Nick said. "They're going to be putting in Jersey barriers. And Kyler's going to sell this to whoever he needs to for as long as necessary."

"Miguel told me he trusted Kyler and his father implicitly," Marz said. "And Miguel's word was always gold."

"Amen to that," Nick said. "So we now have a couple things going for us that should be part of the decision of whether we stay or go." He counted off on his fingers in front of Becca's body. "First, we finally have someone inside the police department who we can trust. Second, we have a media story saying we've evaced this neighborhood. Third, we will have a city-mandated, three-hundred-and-sixty degree perimeter installed around this building. And, finally, we'll have a large contingent of Ravens here to provide additional defense."

Silence all around for a long moment, as if everyone waited for someone else to start the conversation.

"I don't want to run," Sara said. "I contemplated that life, and to some extent I lived it with all the lying and the faking around Bruno." He was the higher up in the Church Gang who had forced her into a sort of debt peonage relationship at the gang's now-destroyed strip club. "We might be safe for a while if we fled, but if they want us, will they really stop coming at us?"

"The answer to that is easy—*no*," Beckett said. "What Nick just enumerated gives me the confidence to think we should stay here. And I could work on some additional defenses of my own, too."

"Not to cut off the conversation if someone has an opposite view," Becca said, "but is there anyone who wants to leave Hard Ink and never look back?"

Complete and utter crickets.

Nick's eyes went wide. "Then I guess that's settled."

Smiling, Becca turned her head and kissed him.

"Well, okay. So, the next thing I thought we should discuss—" Nick reached into his pocket and retrieved his phone. "Sorry. Oh, it's Kyler. Speak of the devil."

Marz took a deep breath. *Good news or bad?*

"Yeah?" Nick answered. Vance apparently had a lot to share because Nick's side of the conversation was filled with a lot of one-word encouragements and responses. *"What?"* he asked, his tone suddenly urgent. "Are you sure?" Pause. "What are they thinking?"

Shit. What is it now?

"Thank you, Kyler. We are going to owe you. Bigtime." Nick hung up, shaking his head in disbelief. "Miguel had told Kyler about the huge cache of weapons at the storage facility. Kyler managed to get a search warrant for the facility this afternoon, and about an hour ago they raided the place."

"And?" Marz asked. No doubt just having the storage facility neutralized was good news, but it didn't seem big enough to have caused Nick's reaction.

"Jimmy Church was there. He resisted arrest and opened fire on the SWAT team. They took him down. He's dead."

Sara gasped the loudest, and then whoops and cheers went up around the room. Marz rubbed his hand over his lips, so surprised and relieved that the major focus of their energies the past few weeks had now been taken out. He turned to Emilie and found her eyes glassy and her body trembling.

Her eyes flashed to his. "Do you think Church had Manny killed? Do you think he died because of that bounty?"

"It's possible," Marz said, tucking a strand of hair behind her ears. He hated to see her so torn apart. Given how badly Manny had been compromised—both his stability and his anonymity—it was also possible that Seneka had decided he'd outlived his usefulness and become a liability.

"Then is it horrible that I'm glad this Church guy is dead? Is it horrible that I'm feeling less and less guilty about what I did to Jeffers?" Her lip quivered.

"Aw, no, baby. It's not horrible at all. I've been a soldier my whole adult life, but I don't love violence. Still, sometimes it's kill or be killed. Church and Jeffers both reaped what they sewed." He kissed her softly on the lips.

She closed her eyes and rested her forehead against his for a long moment. "Okay," she finally whispered.

Nick leaned toward the desk and knocked his fingers against the mouse, drawing Marz's attention and waking up the computer tied to the various security-camera feeds. "I spent the afternoon watching what happened here this morning from various angles," he said. "Marz, I'd like you to go through and try to screen capture and enhance any faces, the license plates, and any other clues you see."

Marz nodded.

"But from my cursory scans, I think we can safely say the following. The attackers were skilled, coordinated, well-equipped, and well-funded. Watching them, I get a serious military vibe. Definitely not just Churchmen. Couple that with the armored vehicles, rocket launcher, unending supply of ammunition, and we've got military with deep pockets."

"Seneka," Beckett bit out.

Marz couldn't agree more.

"That's where my gut's going," Nick said. "Which is why I'm hoping Marz can spot something that might nail it down for sure. The other thing the footage reveals . . ."—pale green eyes focused on Emilie and Marz in turn—" . . . is, uh . . . about Emilie's brother."

Emilie didn't bat an eyelash. "I need to hear it, whatever it is."

"He was one of the attackers. He came in the second of the three Suburbans. After the rocket launcher fired, he was forced out of the vehicle and shot. The SUVs left immediately afterward," Nick said.

Marz rubbed Emilie's back, which trembled from the effort to restrain the emotion inside her. He felt so damn bad. "So he was shot by his own team?" he asked.

"It appears that way," Nick agreed.

Marz squeezed Emilie's hand. "So it was either the Church Gang, which was actively hunting Manny but now is largely decimated throughout its top ranks, or Seneka, who no doubt would not appreciate the attention that Garza's arrest might bring to them. Both had motivation."

"And access to beaucoup weapons," Shane said. "Though I don't recall seeing any rocket launchers in that weapons' cache."

"I'd like to propose waiting until after the key search completes overnight or tomorrow morning before I dig in to that footage. The more computing power stays focused on that task, the faster we gain access to the microchip. Can that work for everyone?" Marz got agreement all around.

"I'd urge you men," Nick said, his gaze indicating the rest of his teammates, "to all watch some of the footage. Your eyes may pick up something I missed. Otherwise, a shift of Ravens will arrive within the hour to set up security for the night, and Kyler said the Jersey barriers will be installed first thing tomorrow morning. So, everyone, take some well-earned downtime tonight, because tomorrow we'll get the information we need to determine where to focus next."

A chorus of amens and about-damn-times rang out.

And, *fuckin' A.* It *was* about damn time something went their way. And their new allies gave Marz a spark of hope that they actually had a fighting chance to beat whatever the hell it was that they were up against.

As everyone rose and talked, Marz leaned toward Emilie. "What would you like to do?" he asked.

Raucous laughter rang out from where Shane, Katherine, and Jeremy stood.

"I don't know," she said. "But I'm not sure I'm feeling super social right now."

"Well, we could grab some drinks and snacks and head up to my room. I'm sharing an apartment upstairs. It's nothing special to look at by any means, but it's quiet and private."

A small smile played around her lips. "That sounds more my speed."

Marz kissed Emilie's cheek. "Then let's blow this popsicle stand and not look back," he said.

An actual grin. It didn't last long at all, but it felt like a huge victory all the same. Because when you loved somebody, it turned out that their pain was your own, and that nothing mattered more than putting that person at ease. Derek didn't mind any of this at all.

In fact, he wouldn't have it any other way.

Chapter 25

So, welcome to my humble abode," Derek said, pushing open the door to his bedroom and flicking on the overhead light. He settled bottles of water and a bag of pretzels on the floor near the bed.

"Thanks," Emilie said. It really was every bit as utilitarian as he'd warned her it was. Cement floors, unpainted drywall, and minimal on furnishings. But right now, Emilie didn't need five-star luxury. She just needed a place to collect her thoughts. A comfortable bed on which to rest her strung-out body. And Derek.

She definitely needed Derek.

He'd been an absolute rock through the whole nightmare of this day. He always seemed to anticipate what she needed and say just the right thing. Those were rare gifts, especially when things hit rock bottom as they had today.

And it made her realize that Jack hadn't only denied

her his honesty, he'd also never really been there for her in the unconditional, accept-you-at-your-ugliest, always-have-your-back way that Derek had taught her she could have.

If Jack hadn't cheated, I'd have never met this amazing man.

The thought nearly made her gasp as the realization set in. Maybe it had all worked out exactly as it was supposed to. The idea that fate might want her and Derek to be together was fun to contemplate, but what Emilie really wanted to know was what *Derek* wanted.

Could he want her in his life the way she wanted him?

Because she wanted to go all in.

"The bathroom's just down the hall," Derek said. "Make yourself at home. If you forget the codes to the doors downstairs, just ask me or anyone."

"Okay," she said, his voice jarring her from her thoughts. Which was a good thing, because she had something she had to do before she could think about anything else. She settled her bags in the corner next to her suitcase, and her gaze tripped over three more prosthetic limbs Derek had lined up against the wall. She wanted to ask him all about them, but first things first. "I have to call my mother," she said, facing Derek.

He heaved a breath and crossed the room to her. "Aw, hell," he said. "I'm sorry, Em. I know that's not going to be easy."

"No," she said, her throat tightening as she anticipated actually saying the words *Manny's dead* to her mother. "No parent should ever have to outlive their child. Anyway." She shook her head. "I hate to do this over the phone, but it's not like I can see her in person right now. The last thing I'd want to do is bring any kind of danger to her doorstep."

Derek nodded. "Take your time. I'll give you some privacy."

"Stay?" she blurted, out of instinct more than intention.

"Of course," he said, and he drew them to sit on the edge of the bed.

Before she could put it off another second, Emilie pressed Dial.

"Emilie?" her mother said by way of answering.

"Hi, Mama," she said, hating that her grief colored her voice.

"What's wrong?" Sure enough, her mother had picked up on it, too.

Emilie inhaled a shuddering breath. "I have some bad news."

"What, *mija*?" she asked, her voice wavering.

"Manny, uh . . ." She shook away the fear and grief that threatened to wash over her. "Manny's dead, Mama," she said, her voice barely above a whisper.

"No. Oh, no, Emilie. That can't be true," she rasped.

"I so wish it wasn't," Emilie said, unable to hold back her own tears. "But I saw him with my own eyes. The criminals he was involved with shot him."

The only response was a soul-breaking, gut-wrenching wail.

Derek moved on the bed behind her, and placed his legs on either side of hers. And then he wrapped his body around her back and just held her.

And Emilie was pretty damn sure that he was single-handedly responsible for holding her together.

A lot of time passed with Emilie standing vigil to her mother's grief. And sharing some of her own.

"Where are you, Emilie?" her mother finally said through her tears. "Come home to me."

Emilie's stomach squeezed. "I can't. The bad guys know who I am. It's not safe for now," she said. "I'm sorry. I promise I will come as soon as I can, I just don't know how long that might be."

"My poor Emanuel really lost his way, didn't he?" Mama shuddered a shaky breath.

"Yeah, Mama. He did."

It took them a long time to hang up, and Emilie felt horrible and worried and drained when the line disconnected. She really wished she could be there in person to help her mother through.

She tossed her phone beside her on the bed. As shattered as she felt on the inside, a numbness was settling over her. Right now, she didn't have more tears to cry.

Derek hugged her and pressed a kiss against her shoulder. "I know that was hard."

"Yeah," she said. Even her voice sounded emotionless. She turned in his arms and met his gaze. "I know it's early, but I would like nothing more than to get out of these clothes and hide under the covers for as long as the world will let me. And I'd really like it if you'd hide with me."

He smiled that trademark playful grin. "I will never turn down an invitation to hide under the covers with you. That's a guarantee."

Too tired to worry about modesty, Emilie stripped down to her purple panties, then fished a pale blue camisole out of her suitcase. With no ceremony at all, she flopped down on Derek's bed and tugged the covers up to her shoulders.

Wearing only his boxers, Marz sat on the edge of the bed and removed his limb. And then he shifted under the covers with her. "Now," he said. "Does hiding under the covers involve covering the head, too? Or just the body?"

Such a sweet, cute man. "Just the body. Covering the head makes it a fort."

His eyes went wide. "Is that so? Duly noted."

She pushed herself across the pillow, pressed her lips to his, and then turned over and burrowed her back into his front. "Would you hold me?"

"Baby, I will always hold you," he whispered as his arm slipped around her ribs. His big palm cupped under her breast.

She took solace at the feeling of them wrapped so tightly together. His warm touch was proof of life— that she'd survived, that she had the choice to live where Manny didn't. For a long time, she lay awake, her eyelids refusing to close and her mind refusing to shut down.

And then she tuned into the soft, even breaths that marked Derek's unconsciousness. Focusing on him calmed the storm in her own head. And she appreciated that so much. Right now, it meant everything.

EMILIE AWOKE INTO near-blackness, and the only thing that didn't send her into a terror was Derek's scent on the sheet, his heat all around her, and the hard press of his erect cock wedged against her ass.

Experimentally, she pressed back into his hips, and they surged forward against her. The small moan she unleashed was entirely involuntary.

The jolt of pleasure in that one small exchange pierced through her numbness and made her want—no, *need*—more. She didn't just want the sex for the sex. She wanted to lose herself for a long while

and forget the horrors of the past day. She wanted to
experience life so boldly that she couldn't help but believe that she'd survived. And she wanted to connect
with Derek so hard and so deep that she'd never again
feel alone.

Heart already kicking up inside her chest, she ground
back against him again.

He met her thrust with one of his own and his hand
massaged her breast.

Reaching down her body, her thumb hooked her panties and she pushed them downward. His hand joined
hers in a flash, and together they pushed the scrap of
lace far enough that she could kick them off. Derek
worked his boxers off next.

"I wasn't expecting this, Emilie," he whispered in her
ear, setting off chills all over her skin.

"I wasn't, either," she said. "But I need it, Derek. I
need you to help me lose myself. Just for a while. I
don't want to think at all."

"You want me to do all the thinking for you?" he
asked, rocking his bare cock against her ass, his hands
roaming her front.

"God, yes," she said, arousal already coating her
opening and making the tops of her thighs slick.

"Let me get a condom." He pulled away.

She reached back a hand and grabbed his arm.
"Would you feel comfortable doing it without one? I
never went off my birth control, silly as that probably
was. And I'm clean, I swear. Before you, I hadn't had
sex in over two years." She was desperate to feel him as
much as she possibly could.

"I'm clean, too, Emilie, and you are going to feel
every inch of me." He pressed wet, open-mouthed
kisses against her shoulder, her spine, her neck. "Roll

over on your stomach," he said, shoving the pillows out of the way.

"Oh, yeah," she said as she removed her tank and he settled over her ass.

"You're gonna listen to my voice and nothing else. Do you understand?"

"Yes."

"You can't have my cock if you don't listen." He stroked light, teasing fingertips down her back, and then he softly fucked the cleft of her ass cheeks.

"Derek," she whined.

"Stop thinking, Emilie. Just feel my cock. That's all you worry about." He settled on his knees again, his thighs straddling hers, and pushed his cock between her legs. She cried out when he grazed her opening, and then penetrated her inch by maddening inch. He withdrew halfway and stopped. "Use your body to fuck me. Work yourself on my dick."

She moaned as she rotated her hips. Bracing her hands by her shoulders, she used the leverage to rock herself back onto him, impaling herself on his length.

"That's it. Fuck my cock, Em. Get me nice and wet."

God, his words were like a blowtorch, licking flames over every nerve ending. But as good as it felt, it was making her crazy to not have him driving into her. She wanted to feel his hips slam into her ass so bad she could hardly breathe. "Please move," she finally cried.

He smacked her ass and pulled out. "Who's doing the thinking here, Emilie?"

"No!" The emptiness hurt. "You. You are. Please." She rocked her ass cheeks against his balls, begging with her body for him to return to her.

He slid back into her core. "You need it bad, don't you, baby?"

"So bad," she said, groaning in victory when his weight fell heavily over her back.

He wedged an arm under her chest, one hand taking tight hold of a breast, and then he wrapped the other around her head, forcing her face to the side and using his hand to cover her mouth. Just the feel of that alone made her pussy twitch around him.

His hold tightened everywhere, immobilizing every part of her except her calves and feet. And then his hips flew.

It was a frenzied madness. She'd never had a man move so fast inside her in her life.

"You're going to take me, aren't you?"

She tried to nod.

"You're going to feel me own you, control you, cover you."

A smothered moan ripped from her throat.

His hand tightened against her mouth and around her breast. His hips impacted her ass so hard and fast, she wouldn't be surprised to find bruises from his hip bones. And she'd fucking love it.

How did he know just what she needed? Because she was so overwhelmed by him she couldn't do or see or think about anything else but him.

She could think about body parts. Getting enough air to breathe. The way the head of his cock stroked her G-spot. Those were things she could handle.

"Stop thinking, Emilie," he growled in her ear. "All you need to know is my cock."

Yesyesyesyes.

Deep. Hard. Fast. Thick. Filling her over and over until it was her entire world.

Her orgasm crashed over her and she screamed against Derek's hand as her body bucked under his weight.

"Fuck. You just gushed on me. And you're going to do it again." He shifted his hips and legs, changing his angle inside her, and then he removed his hand from her mouth and replaced it with a devouring, claiming kiss. Using a fist in her hair to guide her head, his tongue invaded her mouth so aggressively that all she could do was suck on it as he fucked her.

"Aw, you like your hair pulled, don't you, Em." She gulped for air and moaned, his words hitting their mark in her brain and between her legs. Intense pressure built behind her clit. Derek tugged her hair tighter, setting off a low burn in her scalp. "I bet that pull travels right down your spine and makes your pussy clench."

"Derek, Derek, Derek," she said in time with his thrusts. When he wrenched his weight off her back, she almost cried.

A big hand landed in the middle of her back, holding her down. His other dragged down her back and his thumb slipped between the cheeks of her ass. He pressed against her anus.

"Oh, God," she said, jerking under him.

"You want to be filled everywhere, don't you? You want to feel me in every part of your body?"

"Yes, Derek," she rasped.

Slowing his hips, he pushed his thumb lower until it slipped into her pussy right alongside his cock. He gently moved it back and forth, and then he slowly fucked her with his thumb wedged inside, making her feel fuller than she'd ever felt.

"Look how good you take two. So fucking sexy."

She would've agreed, except just then, he withdrew his thumb from her pussy and pushed it against the ring of her ass. It took less than a minute before he'd penetrated her all the way up to the second knuckle, and she wasn't sure she'd breathed once the entire time. She was on sensation overload.

He settled into a rhythm of withdrawing his thumb from her ass when his cock sank into her pussy, and then fucking her ass deep with his thumb when his cock withdrew.

It took about twenty seconds of that before her body tightened like a corkscrew and then blew apart into a million floating pieces. She buried her face against the sheets and wailed at the freeing force of the release.

"Shit, Emilie. That was too fucking perfect. You're gonna make me come." Derek's hips flew against her, his thumb buried deep. "Oh, God, here I come." He unleashed a pleasured groan that sounded so damn sexy it made her stomach flutter, and she felt the fast jerking wetness of his come inside her. "Holy fuck," he rasped as he gently withdrew his thumb and laid his weight atop her again, his cock still deep inside her core.

In that moment, Emilie was so perfectly relaxed, so perfectly sated, so perfectly at peace that all she knew was the intense gratitude and awe and emotion she felt for this man. "I love you, Derek."

She gasped, the reality that those words had just left her mouth dispelling the haze of lust from her brain. *Oh, my God! Oh, my God!* What the hell had she just done?

And why wasn't he saying anything?

Oh, God.

Derek withdrew his cock and lifted off of her. And then he flipped her onto her back, straddled her belly and braced his hands by her ears, his handsome face just visible right above hers. "Say it again."

Her stomach flipped as she met his gaze. And it was absolutely blazing. "I love you, Derek."

"Again," he rasped, lowering himself until his forehead rested on hers. "Please."

Her arms surrounded his shoulders. "I love you, Derek."

He shuddered out a breath. "I have waited thirty-two years to hear another human being say those words to me."

Her head spun at the admission. How could anyone *not* love this man? She would make sure he heard it every day from here on out.

He stroked her hair. "And I'm so fucking glad it was you, Emilie. Because I love you, too."

"You do?" she said, the impossible goodness of this moment making her sure she must still be asleep. "Say it again."

His grin was immediate and huge. "I love you, too, Emilie." He kissed her, a soft, soulful meeting of lips and tongue that made her chest feel too tight to contain her heart. After a few moments, he slid down on his side beside her, and hugged her into his chest.

She'd returned to her senses enough to recall all the things she'd wanted to forget. And the pain of her loss was as ever-present as it had been all day. But the amazing, powerful, transformative thing about love was that it gave you the strength to persevere, the will to fight, and a soft place to fall when the world became too much.

He'd given her everything she needed to walk through this grief and make it out on the other side. Eventually, at least.

"I love you," she whispered against his chest.

He hugged her tighter, and then drew in a deep breath. "And Iiiiiiiiiii-ee-iiii will always love yooooooooou," he sang, or rather butchered, the old Whitney Houston song.

Impossibly, Emilie burst out laughing. "Oh, God, that's horrible, Derek." She pushed out of his arms, grasped one of the pillows from the edge of the bed, and planted it over his head. He continued to warble from under the cotton, and Emilie couldn't stop laughing.

Their playfulness quickly escalated into a pillow fight, and then a wrestling match, and of course she ended up underneath him.

Win-win in her book.

"I'd been trying to figure out all day how to make you smile, because it's the most beautiful fucking thing to see." He stroked her face. "I know things aren't okay right now, Emilie. And I know things might yet get worse. But I will be there for you and protect you and love you every step of the way."

"I know you will. And I will, too," she said, amazed at the adoration in his eyes.

"Thank you for loving me," he said, and there was a note of pain in the words that nearly broke her heart.

"Oh, baby," she said, pulling his head down to her shoulder and wrapping her arms around him tight. "It's the easiest thing I've ever done."

Chapter 26

Wasn't it funny how life could give you your best day ever the dawn after you'd had one of your worst?

That was exactly what it felt like to Marz.

That Emilie loved him was a miracle beyond any he'd ever expected to experience. And it filled him with a sense of hope, a sense of invincibility, and a sense of strength he'd never really felt before.

Because, no matter what, he wasn't alone.

He hugged his arms around Emilie's waist, where she sat perched on his left leg. After what they'd shared, he hadn't wanted to be apart from her even a little.

They were all gathered at Marz's desk in the gym, a little before six in the morning, watching the key search count down its last several minutes. He was strung so tight with anticipation, that he literally couldn't watch the clock anymore. And thus Emilie had landed in his lap.

Would this chip provide them with any of the answers they needed? Would it give them a way to regain their stolen honor? Would it allow them to find redemption for their fallen friends who could no longer find it for themselves?

"Three minutes, Marz," Charlie said from a chair at the desk beside him.

"I can't look," he said, his voice muffled against Emilie's back.

Someone smacked the back of his head.

"Ow, motherfucker," he said, wrenching around to find Beckett grinning behind him. Well, as close as Beckett got to grinning.

"You did all this hard work. Watch it."

Emilie kissed him and got up. "Do what you need to do. I'll be right here." She stepped back next to Becca and Katherine.

Ding, ding, ding.

At the sound of the computer notification, Marz's gaze cut to the screen. "Holy shit," he said. The running numbers had turned into just one number. One *long-ass* number framed by a box. "Nobody move," he said.

Charlie chuckled, but Marz could feel the tension and anticipation rolling off of him, too.

Marz grabbed his phone and took a picture of the screen, then grabbed a piece of paper and hand wrote the key, with Charlie double-checking him as he went.

"We're all dying here, Marz," Nick said from over his shoulder. "Translate for those of us who don't speak geek."

Minimizing the key search, Marz clicked over to the external drive containing the chip. "If we've all been good boys and girls this year, Santa Marz is going to bring you presents in juuust a minute."

A login box popped up for the external drive.

Moment-of-truth time.

"Check me, Charlie," Marz said as he typed in the key. Finally, he'd keyed in the entire string.

And then Marz pressed Enter.

A spinning icon appeared in the center of the screen and then it transformed to a directory listing. At the top it said,

USER NUMBER: _

PASSWORD: _

Blinking cursors appeared after each one.

"Does that mean what I think it means?" Beckett asked.

Marz wanted to smash something with his fists. Five days invested only to hit another brick wall.

Charlie stood and rifled through the papers on Marz's desk. "Where are the binary numbers from Becca's bracelet?"

"Stop!" Marz said. Charlie's hands flew off. "There's a system." He reached across the desk. Second pile over, all the way at the bottom, because it was a smaller sheet of paper he didn't want to lose. "Ta-da!" he said.

"Do it, Marz," Nick said.

They had two numbers because Becca's line-and-circles charm bracelet could be read from left to right and right to left. There was no indication if one way was the right way. But if these *were* the keys to this username and password, the lack of guidance on the bracelet made sense. This required two numbers, and the bracelet gave them two.

USER NUMBER: 631780

PASSWORD: ******

All Marz could hear was the low hum of the processors and fans on the machines, as if everyone was holding their collective breaths. He hit Enter, and his stomach dropped. Incorrect login. Please try again.

Fine. He'd reverse them this time.

USER NUMBER: 162905
PASSWORD: ******

Blowing out a long breath, he hit Enter again. Long pause, and then a directory of file folders and file names popped up in a huge and scrolling line.

"We're in!" Marz said, shooting from his seat with his fists in the air. He and Charlie hugged. Cheers and whoops and shouts of *good work* filled their corner of the room. And Marz felt like he was fucking ten feet tall.

"Proud of you," Emilie mouthed to him.

He put a hand to his heart and let those words sink in.

And then he was back in his seat, his head one of about six all crowding in.

"Is it just me or are there a shit-ton of documents here?" Nick asked.

"Shit ton and a half," Marz said, his mind already organizing the huge job that lay ahead of him. "It's gonna take some time to go through it all, but let's play a little *What's behind Door Number One*, shall we?"

"How 'bout the one called Investigation?" Beckett suggested, pointing to the line on the screen.

"Why not?" Marz clicked the folder icon, and a series of files named by dates appeared. He clicked on the earliest date, almost three years before the ambush that had ended their careers, and it launched in Microsoft Word.

Mission Needs
Required Afghan Contacts:
  Farmers
  Warlords
  National Police
  Border Police
  Special Narcotics Force
  Ministry of Counter Narcotics
  Minister of Defense
  Port Authorities

  Buyers

Mission Needs? What mission?

"Anybody else following this?" Nick asked. A rumble of no's. "Open another one."

Marz clicked on a file from about three months later. It seemed to be a log from a regional counternarcotics task force responsible for destroying captured opium and heroin, and it listed amounts captured and amounts destroyed by date.

"They don't match up," Marz said, drawing his finger across the screen. "There's always more captured than destroyed."

"Two guesses what was happening to the difference," Shane said.

"Merritt kept records for the smuggling business?" Beckett asked. "What kind of sense does that make? And why would he send them to Becca?"

Nick shook his head. "Keep going, Marz."

Scrolling down, he chose at random. One file seemed to be an inventory of farmers in one particular region, with notations next to each. They didn't have the key to it to know what those notations meant, though. At least, not yet. Another file was a list of Afghan warlords, not by real name but by nickname. Marz recognized a few from the counternarcotics work their SF team had done. Notes next to each warlord's name included things like: "French, 18-" or "American, 24-" or "Japanese, 18-". One read, "American, 18-, blond."

"Are those notes the warlords' fucking preferences for girls?" Shane asked, disgust plain in his voice.

"It's like a goddamned menu," Easy said.

That was when it struck Marz—those dashes after the numbers weren't dashes at all. They were minus signs. *Eighteen minus. Twenty-four minus.* Meaning, that age or younger. His stomach soured.

Marz switched back to the directory and chose a document with a date exactly six months after the initial file. It was a heavily redacted letter with all names, places, or other identifying information blacked out, but Marz's eyes tripped on one word: *deniable.*

In the special operations world, *deniable* usually referred to covert operations in which operators often worked out of uniform to perform certain tasks so their government could deny any involvement if the whole thing went south.

"What is this meaning to you?" Marz asked, pointing at the word.

"Paired with the phrase 'assignment evaluation' at the top there," Beckett asked. "Sounds to me it's talking about a deniable covert operation."

"Look at the last line of the third paragraph," Easy said, nodding. The unredacted part read, "reaches into the command structure."

Marz's instincts were starting to set off alarms. Something was just feeling off here. He opened another document, which seemed to be a list of code words relevant for interactions with farmers. But what did the code word indicate to the farmers to do?

Sighing, Marz went way far down the list, to the next-to-last file, dated about six months before the ambush that ended their careers.

It was a Request for Reassignment. Frank Merritt appeared to be asking to be removed as commander of their Special Forces team and reassigned to SAD as a solo operative.

"What the hell is SAD?" Marz asked.

"I'm putting my money on the Special Activities Division—the CIA's covert paramilitary operations unit," Nick said.

"Merritt wasn't involved in an illegal black op," Shane said. "He was involved in a clandestine assignment on behalf of . . . somebody. Go back out to the file listing and scroll to the bottom." Marz did. "He requested this transfer and then almost immediately sent these files in a hidden, heavily encrypted chip to his daughter a half a world away."

The Earth's plates were potentially moving under Marz's feet here. If Shane was right, that meant— "He was working undercover?" he rasped.

Nick stood bolt straight, his fist pressed to his mouth. "Yeah. And this was his insurance policy. In case something went wrong or his cover was blown. That first document was about thirty months before the transfer request. This is looking like he'd gone undercover, knew he was being made, and tried to"—Nick swallowed, hard—"tried to get away from us before it blew up in his face."

Merritt . . . wasn't dirty.

The room went deathly quiet, and then Nick turned around and made his way to Becca. "I was wrong, sunshine. He wasn't dirty. He was exactly who you always believed him to be. I'm so fucking sorry. All this time . . ." He shook his head.

She sucked in a halting breath and threw her arms around Nick's neck.

Marz pushed up from his chair and laced his hands on top of his head. Merritt had tried to protect them. Their commander hadn't betrayed them as they'd believed all these long months. The only man Marz had ever respected as one might a father had, in fact, cared. About him. About all of them. Looking at each of his teammates' faces, Marz saw that they appeared as shell-shocked as he himself felt.

Charlie stood with his arms crossed and his eyes to the floor. He'd been as convinced as the five of them of Merritt's corruption. It was like they'd had a 1000-piece jigsaw puzzle nearly fully assembled and it had gotten knocked to the floor. They had to put the pieces together again from the beginning.

From a beginning that started with Merritt as innocent as the rest of them.

"Jesus," Marz said. "This changes everything."

Nick turned from Becca to face them again, and he didn't try to hide the wetness around his eyes. "We rethink everything we know, starting now. And we go through these files with a fine-tooth comb, because Merritt was a master strategist, and he wouldn't have included what he did here unless he thought it important to revealing the other players and their activities."

Marz dropped back into his chair and went out to the directory again. He started at the top and slowly scanned downward. He clicked one labeled Accounts, which took him to a subdirectory with more files—as he opened some of them he realized they represented different parts of the exchanges Merritt must've tracked.

At the bottom of the Accounts files was one listed WCE. "Guys," Marz said, "a file on WCE." God, they'd been looking for information about who or what that acronym represented from the beginning. In fact, it was Charlie's search for that acronym on the Web that had apparently brought him to the attention of the Church Gang, and his interest in WCE was part of the reason he'd been abducted, interrogated, and tortured.

A lot of the documents in the WCE file recounted the Singapore bank account information they already had from Charlie. But one document gave them something new.

It identified Merritt's WCE contact as GW.

It listed a phone number in the 703 area code—Northern Virginia.

And it recorded a seven-digit code.

Holy shit. Marz's heart raced in his chest. Now they were cooking with gas.

"Charlie?" Marz said, pointing to the code. "Didn't you say the bank account required a seven-digit code to access the funds?"

"Yeah," he said, stepping closer.

"Check it," Marz said, "while I look up this phone number." Fingers flying over the keyboard, Marz brought up a number lookup, but it said it was unlisted. No big surprise there. So Marz followed a hunch and opened up the webpage for Seneka Worldwide Security.

And . . . bingo.

"This number in the WCE file almost definitely goes to a SWS extension. The specific number is unlisted, but the public number shares the same first seven digits: 703-555-4000 for the main operator, and 703-555-4264 for the direct line," Marz said, turning to Beckett. "Grab me a burn phone?"

Beckett went to where their supplies were stored along the wall in front of the desk and retrieved one of the disposable—and more importantly, untraceable—phones. "Here you go," he said, "but I bet it doesn't work."

"Let's see." Marz dialed the direct number, feeling like they were so much farther along than they'd ever been before.

It picked up on the very first ring. "This extension is no longer in service. Please hang up and try again or press zero for the operator." He pressed zero. Two rings later, a woman's voice came on the line. "Seneka Worldwide Security. How may I direct your call?" Marz disconnected. "Definitely Seneka. They're the key to all of this."

"Shit," Shane said. "So Seneka was involved in what happened to us *and* connected to WCE, who deposited millions into a secret bank account for Merritt. Money which he appears never to have touched, it's worth noting."

Murmurs of agreement all around. More proof that Merritt hadn't been corrupt. Bad guys didn't just leave twelve million in an account for several years without ever making a withdrawal.

"Now that we have the code, should we access the money and move it somewhere this WCE doesn't know?" Beckett asked, his eyes still wide from the revelation about Merritt.

Charlie gave a hard shake of his head. "I wouldn't. Not unless you want to attract their attention. I'm pretty sure one of the ways they narrowed down on me was through my efforts to get into that account."

"Well, it's been sitting there untouched for over a year, so it's secure there until we're ready to move it," Marz said.

"And when we're ready, that twelve mil will go a long way toward leveling the playing field against Seneka," Beckett said.

Marz nodded and met his best friend's gaze. "Amen to that."

"So, how do we make amends to a dead man?" Easy asked, his arms crossed tight over his chest.

"By telling the story he wanted told," Nick said, pointing to the computer.

"I'll get on it," Marz said. "It's just going to take a while to wade through." And he was going to have to push hard to gather as much data from these records as he could before their next threat emerged.

"I'll help," Charlie said.

"So will I," Becca said.

"Hell, we can all take parts of it to read, but you should set up some sort of organizational system so we can keep track of where any leads we find are coming from," Nick said. "Besides, having been so wrong about the man, I'd like to read for myself what he was really doing."

"Roger that on both accounts," Marz said. "I feel like we're finally getting somewhere. You know?" And he was pleased to the bottom of his soul to know Merritt hadn't betrayed and abandoned him the way he'd believed all these long months. The realization snapped a broken piece of himself back into place.

A lot of nods and cautious enthusiasm, except from Beckett, whose face was set in a frown.

"I do agree," he said. "But if Seneka is our next target, it's like going from the minors to the majors. Yesterday morning proved that. And we got lucky we didn't lose more people. It would be damn nice if we could find who Merritt was working for, because I bet they'd put us on a far more even playing field to take this on."

Beckett was right. Otherwise, they were going to have to David-and-Goliath it and hope that worked out in their favor. But they'd faced uneven odds before.

Marz turned and found Emilie, and he made his way to her.

"Good news, then?" she asked, wrapping her arms around his neck.

"More good than bad, I think."

"Sounds like a good day to me." She gave him the prettiest smile and pushed up onto tiptoes to whisper in his ear. "And, who knows, it could still get even better." She lifted her eyebrows in invitation.

And Marz threw his head back and laughed.

Who the hell knew what the next step of this clusterfuck was going to bring them. Not him. Not any of them.

But what Marz did know was that this clusterfuck had a silver lining of pretty major proportions, at least for him. Because in a few weeks' time, he'd reunited with his brothers, made at least some amends with his best friend, learned his mentor didn't betray him after all, *and* found a woman to love—who loved him back. That was a good day by his books.

Marz hooked his arm around Emilie's shoulders, turned to the group, and rubbed his stomach. "Anyone else hungry?"

Chuckles went around the room.

These fuckers had all eaten some chow in their day. Why'd they always give him such shit?

"The world is shaking under your feet and you're thinking about pancakes," Beckett said, rolling his eyes.

"Actually, I was thinking about bacon. But pancakes on the side would be completely satisfactory," Marz said, making Emilie chuckle. And, damn, did that feel good.

"I'd be happy to make breakfast, Derek," Becca said, leaning against Nick's chest. And was Marz imagining it or had this news about her father put a sparkle in her blue eyes that hadn't been there before? He hoped so, because she deserved it.

Shane elbowed Beckett as they started to cross toward the door. "It's not a prosthetic limb, it's a hollow leg."

"You know," Marz said, "that would actually be freaking cool. It could be refrigerated, and you could keep drinks and snacks in it."

Beckett just stared at him.

"When I'm a kabillionaire, off my refrigerated prosthetic hollow leg, don't ask to borrow a drink. That's all I'm saying." Marz held open the door to the hallway and everyone streamed through.

"It's hard to believe he's the brains of the operation sometimes," Beckett said as he went into the Rixeys' apartment.

"The brains and the beauty, Murda. And don't you forget it," he called.

Jeremy and Charlie were the last ones out, and Marz brought up the rear—only to find his girl waiting for him in the hallway.

A mischievous look on her face, she waited until the apartment door closed behind the guys, and then she slowly pushed Marz backward against the brick wall and kissed him like she was starving and he was a feast.

"What's this for?" he asked when they came up for air.

"Just because I love you," she said.

Love. Brotherhood. Loyalty to the end. What more could a guy ask for?

Yep. Best day ever, for sure.

Acknowledgments

$\mathcal{M}$arz, Marz, Marz. He's one of my favorite characters I've ever written, but his book was like a hard, slow labor that just might require a C-section to deliver. And I love Marz, Emilie, and the whole Hard Ink gang all the more for the challenge.

I owe a *lot* of people for helping me along the way with this book. First, as ever, my editor, Amanda Bergeron, who went to extraordinary lengths to help me keep this book on track. It's a wonderful experience having an editor who's not only a creative partner, but a cheerleader, a staunch defender of your time and health, and a strong advocate, too. Thank you so much, Amanda! I'm so glad you loved Hard Ink!

Next, I need to thank you tireless and diligent critique partner, Christi Barth, who once again immersed herself in the Hard Ink world with a careful read, comments, and questions that never let me get away with a *thing*. If someone is described wearing clothing in this book, it's entirely due to her! *winks* In all seriousness, the Hard Ink series would not be what it is without her, and I so cherish her insights and friendship!

I also want to thank my agent, Kevan Lyon, for all the scheduling assistance, support, and cheerleading she provided along the way. Behind every successful author is an amazing team of hard-working, book-loving people, and I'm lucky to have someone like Kevan on my side. My best friend and fellow author Lea Nolan also deserves major thanks for helping me plot out the whole second half of this book on brown Panera Bread napkins, which now reside for posterity in the bottom of my laptop case.

These acknowledgements would not be complete without a huge shout-out to my wonderfully supportive husband and daughters, who went on vacation sans Mom because I was behind on my deadline. I literally couldn't do what I do without their support and love, and I appreciate it to the bottom of my heart.

I also want to give a nod of acknowledgement to reader Bethany Croyle who shared a story with me about a date she once had with an amputee veteran where she shared her "leg rule," where anything with less than two or more than four legs must die! It was such a perfect funny for Emilie that I asked to incorporate it into Emilie and Marz's date, and Bethany kindly agreed! Let me also say a huge thank you to AmputeeOT, the social media screen name of a woman who posts educational videos on YouTube about what life is like with an amputation. Watching *lots* of her videos gave me the confidence to feel I could do Marz's story justice.

Finally, I give thanks to my Heroes for being such wonderful fans and supporters, and to my readers, for being the bestest readers an author could have. Thank you for allowing my characters into your heart so they can tell their stories over and over again.

LK

Loving the men of Hard Ink?
They're back and they're hotter than ever in

HARD TO BE GOOD

Hard Ink Tattoo owner Jeremy Rixey has taken on his brother's stateside fight against the forces that nearly killed Nick and his Special Forces team a year before. Now, Jeremy's whole world has been turned upside down—not the least of which by a brilliant, quiet blond man who tempts Jeremy to settle down for the first time ever.

Recent kidnapping victim Charlie Merritt has always been better with computers than people, so when he's drawn into the SF team's investigation of his army colonel father's corruption, he's surprised to find acceptance and friendship—especially since his father *never* accepted who Charlie was. Even more surprising is the heated tension Charlie feels with sexy, tattooed Jeremy, Charlie's opposite in almost every way.

With tragedy and chaos all around them, temptation flashes hot, and Jeremy and Charlie can't help but wonder why they're trying so hard to be good …

Coming Spring 2015
From Avon Impulse